THE STARDUST GRAIL

ALSO BY YUME KITASEI

THE DEEP SKY

THE
STARDUST
GRAIL

YUME KITASEI

FLATIRON
BOOKS
NEW YORK

THE STARDUST GRAIL. Copyright © 2024 by Yume Kitasei. All rights reserved. Printed in the United States of America. For information, address Flatiron Books, 120 Broadway, New York, NY 10271.

www.flatironbooks.com

Map and interior design by Jonathan Bennett

Library of Congress Cataloging-in-Publication Data

Names: Kitasei, Yume, author.
Title: The stardust grail / Yume Kitasei.
Description: First edition. | New York : Flatiron Books, 2024.
Identifiers: LCCN 2023056374 | ISBN 9781250875372 (hardcover) |
    ISBN 9781250875389 (ebook)
Subjects: LCGFT: Science fiction. | Thrillers (Fiction) | Novels.
Classification: LCC PS3611.I8777 S73 2024 | DDC 813/.6—dc23/eng/20231208
LC record available at https://lccn.loc.gov/2023056374

Our books may be purchased in bulk for promotional, educational, or business use. Please contact your local bookseller or the Macmillan Corporate and Premium Sales Department at 1-800-221-7945, extension 5442, or by email at MacmillanSpecialMarkets@macmillan.com.

First Edition: 2024

10 9 8 7 6 5 4 3 2 1

For my father, who loves books
and who introduced me to *Star Wars* when I was ten.
A New Hope is the best one, by the way.

THE INTERSTELLAR WEB

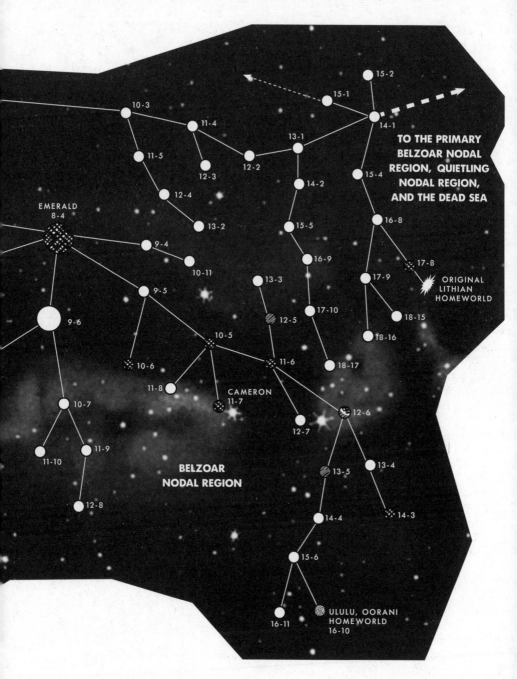

KEY

	COALITION OF THE NATIONS OF EARTH		LITHIS (BELZOAR)
	SETTLER UNION		QUIETLING
	BELZOAR		OORANI
			NODAL COLLAPSE

PART I

THE STUDENT

The largest private collection of rare artifacts from other worlds could be found in central New Jersey at Princeton University, and if anyone knew Maya Hoshimoto was a thief, they wouldn't have let her anywhere near there.

Fortunately, no one did.

And anyway, she wasn't a thief anymore, just a thirty-one-year-old graduate student entering her second year toward a PhD in comparative cultures—who happened to know a lot about foreign artifacts.

It was an excessively pretty end of summer, the kind where the birds were chirping and a few flowers hung drunk from their stems, but the air had just an edge of premonition to it. For Maya, who had grown up off-world under a dome, weather of any kind still felt like a gift.

Maya wandered into the subbasement room of the Dr. Frank R. Humbert Alien Artifact Collection and Rare Books Archives, where staff were unboxing recent acquisitions. Her friend Pickle, one of the assistant archivists, looked up and grinned at her. "How do you always know when we've got a delivery? I didn't even know you were capable of waking up before ten."

"Obituaries," Maya said, then realized that maybe this wasn't the kind of thing a graduate student paid attention to: that the grandson of a famous explorer, Dr. Nkosi, had died in his bathtub a month ago. She added: "I saw the van outside."

Most material ended up sitting in storage for a couple of decades, but the Nkosi Foundation had dropped a hefty monetary donation to ensure that these items were given priority treatment.

Maya watched them remove artifacts from the boxes onto two long tables lined with black velvet. Her studies included an internship with the archives, which had a special relationship with the Department of Comparative Cultures. And while the pay was ridiculously low, she enjoyed hanging out here. She was friends with most of the staff, and every once in a while, they came across something truly special, something that might, just maybe, unlock a constellation of discovery.

"Quite a personal collection," said one of the other grad students.

Maya raised an eyebrow. What she saw so far was disappointing: counterfeits and other common items. She reached for a round stone object etched with wavy lines.

"According to the inventory notes, those are worth more than your yearly paycheck," said Pickle.

"Really? I know I don't get paid much, but these are just personal hygiene products from the current era," said Maya. She lifted it closer to her nose and inhaled a complicated scent, almost like chocolate with a burnt undertone. Fashionable right now on certain Belzoar worlds. "Even accounting for the cost of interstellar shipping."

The others stared at her.

"What else we get?"

"This one's a thousand-year-old Frenro sculpture." The other grad student offered a peek.

"Mmmm." Maya reached for the snarl of metal and stone. It reminded her of an old friend and a ship and all the ever-changing stars she'd left behind to be here.

"Careful!" said Pickle.

"This one's fake too. And I'm always careful." She lifted it higher, so its polished facets caught the light, and examined the smooth surface.

"Bullshit," sputtered Brian, a conservator for the Artifacts Division. "It's been authenticated. It's one of the most valuable pieces of his collection."

Maya probed one of the metal bits, ignoring his protests. "These types of Frenro sculptures are like a memory box of places a Frenro has lived, hence the mixed media."

"Yeah, and?"

"This piece here is"—she scanned it again with her ocular lenses— "quartz."

"So?"

"Quartz that appears to contain a significant amount of nitrogen," Maya said. "Nitrogen in high concentration is poisonous to Frenro."

"Oh my god. So true," said Pickle with a laugh.

"And this fragment here"—Maya pointed out a black shard—"is a settler-manufactured data chip, the kind we used to make." During the war, she meant, but didn't say. She remembered her parents assembling the tiny parts that went into them every night at the kitchen table. Best to avoid mentioning it in mixed company.

Brian came to examine it.

Maya would have liked to linger over the rest of the items, but there was a blinking in her lenses indicating an incoming call from her lead academic adviser, and it unfortunately could not be ignored.

CHAPTER TWO

Her old silver Planet 9 bomber jacket barely kept out the chill of the stacks she'd retreated to for privacy. No need for anyone else to witness her humiliation.

The subbasement was a solid 18 degrees Celsius, dry, and dimly lit, to keep mold and deterioration at bay. The south side of the floor held metal shelves full of as yet untouched artifacts and the long tables where they'd been unpacking the Nkosi shipment. The north side boasted rare volumes and correspondence—Pickle's domain. There were never many people around.

Maya slipped into the expandable-meter gap between the shelves and slouched against the cold metal frame. The gloom was bearable, except it reminded her too much of the banged-up, dusty orange world she called home.

She removed a chunky camera ring from her pinky and balanced it on the lip of a shelf, then touched her earlobe.

Dr. Liam Waterson's head materialized above a row of mint condition crimson-bound minutes from some conference on interstellar relations.

His face was puffy and pale under a shock of red hair, except for a flush that blotched his cheeks and neck. Scowling, as usual. For as long as Maya had known him, he was irritated or anxious or both, and there was something comforting about his consistency.

"What is this?" he asked, without preamble.

So he had read the paper.

He'd called a week ago and asked her to send over what she'd been working on this summer for *Xenology*, a premier scientific journal. Liam wanted her to get a head start on accruing publication credits—important if she wanted a future in academia. Extra important if she planned on focusing entirely on museum studies rather than fieldwork.

Except she hadn't been working on the paper. She had spent the last two months hiking and attempting to catalog every flavor of ice cream in New Jersey. Which left the only acceptable option of somehow condensing what should have been several months of research into seventy-two hours and appending a description of a concert she'd once attended while high on otherworldly psychedelics. Still, considering it was closer than Liam had ever been to another world, she thought it a fine enough contribution to the field. Fine enough-ish.

Maybe the detail about people vomiting acid on the carved stone floor and getting stuck when her soles began to melt was a little too much.

"It's just a rough draft. To give you the general idea."

"This isn't a research paper. It's a personal essay." Maya may have grown up speaking Settlement Japanese, but her English was fine, and still Liam enunciated every consonant like he wasn't certain she understood. "You can't submit this. I gave you an *extremely* detailed outline, and you've driven over it backwards and forwards with a truck. How have you not made more progress? The deadline for submission is in *three days.*"

She decided to try for flattery first. "I figured as the foremost human expert on Belzoar culture you'd appreciate the unique set of firsthand observations."

"Thank you for reminding me at every opportunity of all your 'field' experience," snapped Liam. It was a sore subject. He might be an expert, but he had never left Earth due to a serious fear of flight, rooted in some wealthy childhood trauma involving a private plane. Despite this, his research techniques were excellent, and he was (Maya hated to admit) brilliant, which was how he had managed to develop cutting-edge theories without leaving New Jersey.

"No, sorry, I didn't mean that. Look, all we have to do is sprinkle in a little data and, like, charts, and this will be another award-winning—"

"What data? What charts?" Liam's voice jumped an octave. "And I told you to stop referencing your precious mystical grail in any papers. This was supposed to be a paper about Belzoar music. Which your grail has nothing to do with, even theoretically. And if it did—I'm telling you, no serious scholars write about it."

"That's why it's fresh!" Maya attempted a smile.

"It's a *myth*," he growled.

Maya crossed her arms. "It's real. Frenro have seen it with their own eyes. Er, visual receptors."

"Like when? A thousand years ago? Everyone knows Frenro don't have the best memory," said Liam.

At this point, Maya could have pointed out that only one of them had *met* a Frenro, let alone operated an LLC with one, but she decided accepting the lecture was the quickest route to ending the conversation. Her committee of three advisers was already down to two after a disagreement over an interpretation of Belzoar courtship practices that she maintained was problematic—the interpretation, not the practices. Her advisers were now just Liam and Dr. Barnes, a professor who had been "on the verge of retirement" for fifteen years and was happy for Maya to do whatever she wanted. If Liam dropped her too, the Department would likely ask her to leave.

Liam scrubbed a hand through his beard. "This is a fucking nightmare. Like actually, this is the manifestation of a recurring nightmare I have." At least he was transitioning from anger to anxiety, so that was good. "I just—I don't know what to say. I've been trying to give you a chance, but you don't make it easy. It's like you don't care. Why did you even come back?"

Because passion can be dangerous, she could have said, *and I'm too old to keep chasing ghosts*. But she said nothing, because when she said nothing, Liam tended to keep going until he tired himself out. Maya ran a finger over a neat row of books. She inhaled the scent of paper and dust and that sweet-acrid chemical glue they used for reassembling ceramics.

She had first come to Princeton for graduate school ten years ago. She and Liam had started in the same cohort. But Maya had taken a leave of absence in her first year to explore an existential crisis, and Liam had gone on to graduate and publish a book that was not only suitable for a mainstream audience but a bestseller. Now Maya was starting over, and Liam was a prodigiously young, tenured professor at their alma mater.

His husband, Quintin, was an old friend of Maya's. Small galaxy, academia. That was, in fact, how Maya and Liam had reconnected when Maya decided to come back to Earth and give academia a second try.

Maya had been good at school once. She'd graduated with high honors from undergrad back in the day. And she did have impressive field experience. Last October, newly returned to Earth, she'd helped Liam publish a journal article that got stellar reviews. She even enjoyed life at the university when she wasn't drowning: the way a conversation at two in the morning could crack open your mind, the discoveries you might find combing through archive materials no one else had bothered to unbox, the possibility that you might be able to contribute something to the universe without anyone getting hurt.

But lately, every time she sat down to work, she seemed to get distracted. She'd survived her first year with a brutal slog that had been helpful for pushing away all other thoughts. But then summer had come, and since she'd eschewed the fieldwork route that most of the other students took, she'd been left knocking about campus.

"... There are only so many ways I can dodge the Chair asking about your performance metrics." The Chair of the Department already held it against Maya that she hadn't done fieldwork the past summer. Maya wrinkled her nose. She liked to fantasize about a time when academia wasn't about raw numbers—articles published, conferences attended, colleagues "supported," awards won, and grants pulled in. But she supposed if there was one thing people were good at, ivory tower or no, it was cramming themselves into some sort of grind.

She'd been so proud when she was admitted ten years ago, the first settler from PeaceLove to attend an Earth university, and one of the famous old ones at that. Her mother had cried, and her father had been insufferable. But then it was miserable. She'd come back, because she thought it would be different now that she was older, more mature, wiser, and smarter, with nothing to prove. But also, she didn't know what else to do.

"Send me a new draft by noon tomorrow," Liam was saying. "We need to get you back on track or ..." He leaned ominously into the conjunction.

"That bad?" Maya asked. She was joking, but not really. She didn't want to know the answer, because deep down (not that deep), she was as vain as the next person. She adjusted the books before her so they formed a precise red line.

Liam shook his head. "We want you to reconsider fieldwork."

Maya's finger jerked one of the soft leather volumes out of formation. She didn't mean to leave Earth anytime soon if she could help it, even if missing space sometimes felt like having the refrain of a favorite song rattling around in her head without being able to hear it for real. "You never did any fieldwork."

"Well, you're not me!" snapped Liam. "And you don't exactly love the museum stuff."

Fair. She struggled with the quietude. It left too much space for guilt and grief to sneak in the window in the early morning so she couldn't bring herself to get out of bed. She'd come here for a fresh start, and yet some days she could barely drag herself to lectures.

"What about that fieldwork proposal you put together a while back? I talked to Professor Muhammad, and he'd still take you."

"That was under duress. I'm *not* spending a semester in the Belzoar Nodal Region," said Maya.

"The Chair wants to put you on probation. You haven't just been struggling, your work has been *bad*, and it's offensive, because I know you know this, and you're capable of doing better, so really you're just wasting my time. I don't have the bandwidth to save you from yourself. I can't spend all my time propping you up. I have other responsibilities. My own problems. So, this afternoon, five p.m. Come by, and we'll go through it. And follow the outline this time."

He cut the connection before Maya was able to retort: *I don't like your new mustache, so I guess we both have issues with how the other one spent the summer.* For the best.

She put her head down on a cart of unshelved materials. The sudden silence pressed inward. She tried to imagine she was out there in the black, enfolded by a blanket of starlight. No, even with her eyes closed, she could feel everything around her; she was drowning in the excess of matter.

Liam was always direct and often rude, but rarely this *harsh*. And what made the lecture worse was that he wasn't wrong. Therapy had helped, but she just didn't fit here, never had. Lone settler woman among all the rich and privileged Earth-born students. But she wasn't one to give up.

She needed to find Pickle.

CHAPTER THREE

Her friend was in their uncomfortably bright, tiny basement office, carefully removing paper books from an old, dusty box. One of the many reasons Pickle was hoping for a promotion was that they'd finally get an office upstairs with windows.

They hooted when they saw Maya. "Brian is so pissed. He thinks you're right about the fakes. You always gotta ruin everything."

Pickle was five years younger than Maya, with a newly minted PhD in library science and a specific expertise in space exploration of the twenty-first and twenty-second centuries. Having never left Earth, Pickle reveled in Maya's swashbuckling stories of space. Pickle, incidentally, wasn't their real name, and they didn't particularly like pickles.

"What's wrong, my puppy?" Pickle asked, registering the expression on Maya's face. Pickle had star-shaped blue glitter tattoos smattering their neck, a violet mohawk, and home-printed retro wire-rimmed glasses that magnified their eyes. They also had all the sense of humor and mischief that Liam lacked, which is why Maya and Pickle got along so well. They flipped over the book and examined the spine with an expert eye.

It was black, with flaking white-gold-embossed lettering and yellowing artificial pages that suggested late twenty-second-century production. It looked like small-batch printing, possibly even a single-batch. The Chinese characters on the spine were faint but legible. Maya's ocular lenses superimposed a translation: *Dr. Wei Huang*. And more faintly: *Expedition of the* Traveler, *A Memoir—Vol. 5.*

Maya's next words died on her lips. "What's that?" she asked, seized by a sudden, total lust.

Her friend admired the volume with a gleam of desire that matched Maya's own. "This is the *actual* most valuable item from today's delivery. So. Fucking. Cool. Right? The boss said I was in charge of it until she gets back." They kept going but Maya no longer processed what they said.

She imagined she could smell the book from across the desk. Her fingertips itched to touch its paper pages, feel the faintest silty layer of dust from its decay.

One of the most famous space explorers of all time, Dr. Huang, had led an expedition 120 years ago deep into foreign regions of space, all the way into the Dead Sea itself. Six crew members had embarked. Only two returned—Huang and Nkosi. And the records of what happened were patchy, intentionally redacted by the crew, or so people said, as if they'd wanted to ensure no one could ever trace their path. Some believed they'd found something they didn't want anyone else to know about.

They'd been hunting for a device that could create the nodes that led to new worlds—a "stardust machine," once common, now lost. Rumor was they finally found it at the end of a seventeen-year search—but if that were true, then where was it?

More than a century since that journey, and the voyage of the ship, the *Traveler*, was shrouded in mystery. Many of the reports of its crew had been destroyed or lost, including this volume, the fifth of six, of an unpublished memoir. Until today.

Maya thought she might faint with excitement. Despite being Earth-born, Dr. Huang was something of a folk hero to settlers. She was a polyglot who spoke eight languages, including Mandarin, English, and Japanese, and at least one Belzoar language. She'd discovered most of the settlement planets in her first expedition. Maya couldn't believe this long-lost volume had been stuck in some person's private storage with no one to appreciate what it really was. She could only imagine its contents.

"Hey, are you listening to me?"

"Hmm, what?" Maya asked.

"I was asking if you could give a tour of the Collection to some potential donors. It's a big deal. They just messaged today that they're *here* on campus, and sorry they didn't give us a heads-up, but they'd love to just 'stop by' in an hour, and I'm freaking out, okay? You know I don't do public speaking. If you do this, it'll get me—and you—major points with the boss. I bet you could get out of inventory duties for a month. Please say you'll help me."

Normally, the archives should've had someone more important than Maya give the tour, but Pickle's boss, the Executive Director, was away on vacation, and Brian was painfully awkward and in a funk over the fakes in the delivery they'd just received. Whereas everyone knew Maya gave fantastic tours, on account of knowing dozens of interesting, obscure facts about the artifacts that even some of the archivists didn't, thanks to her previous career.

"I can't," Maya said, wrenching her eyes from the book. "I have to pull off an academic miracle in the next few days, and—listen." Maya leaned close and abandoned all attempt at nonchalance. "Can I read that?"

"Oh," said Pickle. "I'm sorry. We haven't digitized it yet, and access is by Executive Director authorization only. And anyway, someone's already requested and been approved for it. That's why I pulled it."

"Who?"

"A visiting professor. Some guy who came down from Yale especially for it."

Maya frowned. "How did he even know we had it? You just unpacked it. We haven't added it to the catalog yet." Generally, he shouldn't have had access until the whole collection had been processed, and even then only to the digital copy.

"Maybe he reads the obituaries too," Pickle deadpanned. "I heard he talked to the Foundation about private acquisition but couldn't get them to sell. When he heard we won the auction, he worked out some special deal with the Executive Director." Maya wondered what kind of pull this guy had.

"But I'm your *friend*." She collapsed into the narrow space between Pickle's desk and the wall. Pickle didn't have room for a second chair for guests. "And I'm going to be expelled." She wasn't above guilt-tripping when rare materials were involved. So she told Pickle about the call with Liam. "The missing two volumes are supposed to extensively cover their time in the Belzoar regions. I bet everything I need for my research is in that book."

"Your paper on Belzoar music?" Pickle said. "Didn't Liam give you an outline with suggested sources? I'm holding one of the greatest finds of my life, and you want to use it for an itty-bitty paper?"

"Come *on*," begged Maya. "Just let me *smell it*."

Pickle cackled and relented. It was something the two of them had bonded over, this insatiable curiosity: Maya's for other worlds and Pickle's for the past, both realms unknowable in their own way.

They cracked the case with a pop and a hiss.

"I'll hold it," said Pickle. "You can look over my shoulder. But no drooling. And don't even *think* about recording."

The volume creaked beneath Pickle's fingers. Maya clutched their arm. Her whole body trembled with excitement. They turned the pages slowly together, Maya's lenses translating the Chinese into Settlement Japanese as they went. Descriptions of months spent aboard the ship, the day-to-day antics, the fixing of things. Forget the paper, Maya wanted to hole up in the reading room with this book and devour it.

"Wait," she said, reaching for the page to stop Pickle from turning it. Pickle swatted her finger away before it touched the paper.

"What?"

Maya was busy reading the description of the crew's past rendez-vous with a Frenro traveler:

> *Calendar's account of the stardust machine was the first tangible evidence we've had in over fourteen years that what we seek still exists. Calendar even described it: less than a meter tall, brown cylindrical trunk, not metal but more organic. At the top and bottom, something like tentacles or roots—though it is unclear if this is just because Frenro tend to describe many things as tentacles.*

"Stardust machine," said Pickle. "Isn't that the thing they were search-ing for?"

"It—it can't be," said Maya.

"Why not?"

"No, I mean yes, I mean—" Maya stared at the description. Words fluttered in her chest. She wanted to tell Pickle she *knew* this machine that supposedly could construct gateways between solar systems. She'd dreamed of it.

"Are you all right?" Pickle asked, shutting the book and turning around. "You look like you need to sit down." They offered their chair.

Maya shook her head. Her brain was whirling. Because she was filled with a sudden certainty that Dr. Huang's machine was the very same object she had sought fruitlessly for nine years before returning to Princeton. "I need this book," she told Pickle. "Just a few hours."

"Okay . . . no, sorry," said Pickle. "The professor is coming by to use it this afternoon. But I can ask the boss if you can help me digitize it, and you can look at it then. Maya? What's going on?"

Maya couldn't meet their gaze. *Why did you even come back?* "Like you said, this is an incredible find." Could she steal it just for a few hours? Well, yes, she could. But she wouldn't. She was reformed.

"I'm your *friend*," said Pickle, flicking her words back at her like an accusation. "And now I feel like you're lying to me."

That stung, but only because it was true. She wanted to tell Pickle everything. But that required answering questions Maya wasn't sure she was ready for.

Maya shut her eyes and listened to the building sigh. It was in quiet moments like these when time felt like a membrane surrounding her, as if she just stuck out a finger and poked, she might find herself tumbling into a different time and place. It didn't work like that, of course. Not on Earth anyway. "I need to make something right."

"And a book will help you do that?"

"It might. I hope so."

Pickle pursed their lips. "Does this have something to do with what-ever you were doing before you got here?"

"Contractor for a small independent shipping company."

"Sure. Accounting and tracking shipments, blah blah blah." But Pickle was trying to meet her wherever she was in the fog, and they both knew it. Pickle slipped the volume back in the vacuum case. They waited with the same patience that made them so good at their work.

"I have this friend who has been looking for something for almost a hundred years," said Maya, and then she winced, because she'd been avoiding thinking about how she'd left things with Auncle, and now she was again.

"I take it this friend isn't human. . . . Wait, does this have to do with your obsession with the so-called grail?"

"It's not so-called," said Maya.

"Well, it's called that by you, so . . ."

"Fine," said Maya. "I gave it that nickname, but it's a real object. You know a couple of hundred years ago, Frenro stopped being able to have children? Around the same time the last of these things was seen. Which is not a coincidence. My friend Auncle believes it's a critical part of the Frenro ecosystem, without which they can't conceive—like flowers without honeybees. Auncle wants children more than anything."

Already, she could feel the path calling her back, the sugar-sweet high of obsession still within reach. She had given up the quest because she had learned the hard way it would eat the years of her life and spit her out old with nothing to show for it but a trail of mistakes. Auncle hadn't understood why she'd left, hadn't been able to. No, she couldn't do that again—but if she figured out where it was, she could at least tell Auncle.

Pickle was considering what she'd said. "The Frenro can't have children anymore? Why don't more people know this? That's heavy."

"There aren't a lot of them left to talk about it. I've only met six in my lifetime."

"Wow." Pickle's eyes filled with tears. "That's horrible."

"This stardust machine—I think it's my grail. Their grail. And this book could be the key to finally finding one. That's why you have to let me borrow it."

She thought she had Pickle close to yes. But then Pickle pivoted away, flicking at an invisible message. "Damn. Those important visitors I told you about are here. So listen. How about a deal . . ."

Which was generally how all Maya's wild and terrible adventures started.

She said yes.

CHAPTER FOUR

Maya congratulated herself on how far she'd come in terms of personal growth. It was 11:00 a.m., and she wasn't even thinking about stealing the Huang book. Though it would have been easy. The building was desolate during August, and the volume was just sitting in a hold cabinet with a lock so simple Maya could have hacked it eyes closed with one hand while sipping tea. But she'd given up that life when she'd sucked in her first lungful of natural air in over a decade.

She still couldn't wrap her mind around the fact that she and Dr. Huang had pursued the same object, a century apart.

She'd been obsessed with the legend of Dr. Huang's expedition when she was a child: the journey to other worlds beyond human space, the camaraderie of the crew of the *Traveler*, and the discoveries of long-lost civilizations.

She leaned back against the welcome desk of the archives, appreciating the mild yellow sunlight streaming in through the front windows.

Her eyes lifted to a quote by Dr. Wei Huang inscribed over the front entrance: *You can't live in the universe without leaving footprints.*

Perhaps it should have said: *You can't live without damaging things.* Maya grimaced.

A message from Liam appeared in her feed. She opened it with a double wink. There was a pitted slab of building block displayed in the middle of the lobby, the remnants of an ancient civilization. The words in her ocular lens hovered over it like a caption.

Just wanted to say sorry. Have some personal stuff going on right now, and I may have unfairly transferred some of that. However, substance of what I said was all accurate. See you this afternoon.

What personal stuff could have him so off-kilter? He had everything: a perfect marriage, a sterling professional reputation, two bestselling books, a house that was fully paid for, a trust fund, and three parents who doted on him. She envied him.

Notable, though, that he'd said nothing about the Huang book. She'd sent him a message, hoping he might intervene and prevent it from being handed over to the Yale professor. It was a sign of his distraction that he wasn't already down here demanding to see it.

Sighing, she went back to skimming research materials with one eye and watching for Pickle's wealthy couple from Minnesota with the other.

The deal that Pickle had offered was this: Maya would give Judy and Emon Bond a tour that would convince them to cut a big fat check to support the archives, and in return, Pickle would temporarily "process" the Huang book for a few hours while Maya looked through it.

So here Maya was, plotting how to convince this couple to make a sizable donation. She could tell them the swashbuckling story about how the Humbert Archives ended up with the American flag upstairs. Midwesterners loved that one.

The heavy doors opened, allowing the entry of a blue-and-yellow clamshell delivery drone. It made a beeline for her.

She held out a hand automatically, and it handed her an obsidian box, one of those cheap projectors you could order if you didn't have a projection ring—or you didn't want to be tracked.

She scanned it for a name and nearly dropped it in confusion: *Auncle*. But Auncle wasn't in system, Auncle couldn't be—

The doors opened a second time and her visitors entered. She shoved the box into her pocket and replastered on a smile.

Both wore short sleeves and matching baggy blue trousers upcycled from former NASA jumpsuits. From their attire, the zealous gleam in their eyes, and Pickle's description of them, Maya already knew their type. Which was to say, well-meaning space enthusiasts.

"Hello! I'm Emon, and this is Judy," said Mr. Bond. "We heard you're a student. Three cheers for Old Nassau, eh?" According to Pickle, these folks had recently inherited a highly profitable plastic decomposition company and were in the market for worthy causes.

She felt their eyes scroll past her patched bomber jacket and low-quality cloth pants that should have been recycled several years ago. One of the things she'd sworn to herself this time around was that she wouldn't try to blend in. But conformity could be a comfort, and there were times when she regretted her choices; everything about her screamed settler.

"Nice to meet you," she said, and then remembered to offer a hand to shake, Earth-Western-style.

He started to take it before his gaze settled on the tattoo pattern outlining her left eye like a ring of ancient keys. She'd gotten it in college as a way of embracing what she was, to the extreme consternation of her parents, who didn't approve of tattoos of any kind. There were only two reasons people got this one: either because they were from Earth and young and foolish and thought it was "like, just kind of quantum," or because they had grown up on one of the outer system settlements and were Infected as children. As Maya had been.

Most Earth folks might mistake it for the former, but the Bonds knew space. Out there, it was a mark of pride that you had survived, that you were something more than normal human. But on Earth? Well.

Emon dropped his hand and coughed, pretending he hadn't.

The book, Maya told herself. *You're doing this so Auncle can find the grail.*

"Welcome to Humbutt!" That was the student nickname for the building. Maya clapped her hands with more cheer than she felt. "We are going to have a *fun* time!" She was overdoing it. Sweat trickled down the inside of her shirt, and her voice sounded too loud in her ears.

"Bless you! We sure are!"

She led them to the elevator. The museum was on Humbutt's fifth floor. The base of the building was encased in stone, with excessive faithfulness to the Gothic architecture that still dominated campus. Above the second story, the building transitioned to glass and steel and mycelial concrete, and the effect was jarring and hideous. Naturally, it had won several architectural awards.

"I just *love* your accent," said Judy, as a segue to asking what she really wanted to: "Where are you from?"

"PeaceLove," said Maya.

"The Japanese one," Judy explained to Emon.

"Ah, I've been to Tokyo a couple of times," said Emon. "Amazing place. They've got a seawall almost as big as the Great Wall. And I just love the people."

"I've never been," admitted Maya. Her father's parents were climate refugees from some of the smaller cities swallowed by the rising sea. "My mother is from New Jersey, though. I still have family here." It was one of the reasons she'd wanted to come to Princeton: to get to know the family she'd only exchanged video messages with over the years.

"Wonderful," said Emon.

She leaned in to let the retina scanner at the elevator bank capture her eye. "As you can see, security is tight," Maya said, knowing they'd be impressed. "Unless you're authorized, you can't see the collection without a guided tour." Some of Maya's ex-associates would have given several appendages for just five minutes unattended inside the collection, but to date, no one had ever successfully broken in. The words had their intended effect; both of the Bonds straightened in anticipation.

They filed into the elevator. The box in Maya's pocket vibrated. She squeezed it, and it stopped.

"How'd you get into xenology?" asked Judy as the lift rose.

"Oh, ah, it's always been a passion of mine." Not quite a lie.

"Same here! Have you ever been to the California Museum of Other Peoples?"

Just once, a few years ago for a job, but she wasn't about to say that. Fortunately, the question had only been asked as an excuse for Judy to add, "We were just there a month ago and saw some really incredible stuff—honey, remember that Oorani skin we saw? It was *studded* with diamonds."

"Here we are!" said Maya, ignoring the comment.

The elevator doors opened, and they disembarked into a cold foyer. Before them stood a vault-like door with an automated security station in front of it.

"Will we get to see the Belzoar mineral composition?" Emon wanted to know.

"Absolutely."

"Can we . . . can we touch it?" There was a superstition that if you touched a Belzoar mineral composition, you would have good luck for a year. It was also a rare and priceless artifact, and there was no way anyone would be getting their oily human fingers on it on Maya's watch, trillionaires or no.

"There's a model that imitates the texture well," Maya promised instead. She hated to disappoint before the tour had even started.

Maya worked through the usual security measures—a physical lock and key, a coded entry point, more thumb and retinal scans—before the vault swung open. They were authorized to be here, and yet Maya felt all her nerve endings tingle in anticipation, as if she were here for a job.

Which she was. Just not that kind.

The Bonds pushed greedily into the first room.

The artifact collection was organized across four rooms. The first three were roughly in chronological order, one room for each era of human interstellar exploration: the First Contact era; Early Exploration led by Frank Humbert, for whom the collection was named; and the Early Settlement period, of which Dr. Huang was the leading pioneer.

The couple oohed and aahed over the quaintness of everything in the First Contact room: mobile phones, commemorative food and drink containers from the welcome ceremony, notebooks, and stuffed eight-legged Belzoar dolls that resembled spiders more than the actual people.

The curators had done a good job. Stirring orchestral music swelled as they moved through the room. Hope lingered in the air like perfume: of a cleaner, more peaceful Earth, science and advancement, traveling to new worlds, and being part of something bigger than one single rock going round a sun.

Maya pointed out the framed photo of the James Webb telescope next to shifting, grainy first images of a black patch in a field of stars: the anomaly that had appeared a tenth of the way between Mars and Jupiter only a decade after the first successful crewed mission to Mars. At the time, the only permanent presence outside Earth was the ISS II orbiting the planet and two occupied bases on the moon.

All people knew was they'd never seen anything like it: a dark thing the size of two cargo ships that lacked the expected mass or gravitational distortion of a black hole and expanded a few millimeters each year.

The Bonds admired the pitted and battered piece of metal that covered a third of the ceiling. They read the mosaic of faded corporate logos: sponsors of one of the first probes.

A year into scientists' study of the anomaly, they'd been surprised by Belzoar probes popping out of it. "That's when we realized what we had been looking at was a node that led to other worlds and people." Belzoar explorers showed up shortly after to assess their new neighbors, and if they hadn't been impressed, they at least hadn't crushed humans with their superior technology.

She could tell she was doing a good job by the number of their questions. She ushered them through the exhibit fast enough to keep their excitement stoked, but not so fast that they felt cheated.

The adjacent chamber was a large, dimly lit room with long rows of cases featuring tools of the first exploration teams of other worlds: a laptop that had belonged to Dr. Frank Humbert himself, a camera, and plastic replicas of ration bars. Maya pointed out a few more objects, offering tidbits like: "That set of cutlery is worth more than a five-bedroom house in Princeton," and "There's a museum in Germany that blew a third of their annual budget on a counterfeit bag that was supposed to have belonged to Frank Humbert."

They drooled over the original spacesuit with *HUMBERT* embroidered over the chest. Maya politely stopped Emon from running a hand over several space rocks.

The box in her pocket buzzed again. She squeezed it and fired off a message. *Need a few! Sorry!*

"I can't wait to show you this next room!" she chirped, as if she didn't hate it. It was filled with long rows of cases featuring various tools and clothing from humanity's first off-world settlements. The main feature was an alternate-reality projection of a domed city, which stretched out beyond the walls.

And she was hit by that complicated wave of homesickness and alienation. The feeling of seeing yourself in a display case: your food, your dress, your whole way of life, pinned and neatly labeled—like being boiled and reduced on an electric stove to be eaten.

She gave a cursory wave at a few gems of the collection: a scrap of tenting from the first Chinese Settlement, the American flag—when she told the story, it landed as well as she'd anticipated.

"Everything finds its way home again, eh?" said Emon.

If only that were true.

Maya liked to imagine how it must have felt the first time people went through a node and found themselves in a solar system halfway across the galaxy. To really see with their own eyes that other life was out there, that there were yellow suns just like Earth's, and other people who were as curious and yearning as they were.

"It must have been exciting," said Judy, taking Emon's hand.

The box in Maya's pocket vibrated again. "I'm sorry, if you can just give me a moment," Maya said to the Bonds, not wanting to break the flow but worried that something was wrong.

A life-size, towering squid-like figure filled the room.

Judy and Emon gasped.

Auncle was already speaking.

"Mayyyaaaa." The voice seemed to reverberate. Her friend's shape nearly scraped the ceiling.

Auncle was not, in fact, Maya's auncle.

"My friend," Maya explained.

"I have been trying to reach you and—"

"Are you all right?" Maya asked.

"Yes and no," said Auncle. "I am doing very well, but the future may tell a different story, and—"

Not an emergency then. "I will call you in thirty minutes, okay?" Maya told xyr. "It's great to see you again." And it was, like stepping outside and realizing the sun was shining, and it was going to be a perfect day. But what the hell was Auncle even doing in call range of Earth?

Maya stuffed the cube back into her pocket and looked back at the Bonds, who had recovered from their shock and were grinning like they'd just won a trip to Venus.

"Amazing. Was that a real, honest-to-god Gatekeeper?" They advanced on her, eyes gleaming.

"That was Auncle, who is definitely *not* on Earth, since that would be illegal, and yes, xe is real, and by the way, they prefer 'Frenro.' Shall we keep going? We've only got twenty minutes left before we have to get out of here, and I know you wanted to see the composition, right? You'll love it!"

They made no move to follow.

"How do you even know one?" Judy wanted to know. "Did you meet it, her, xyr, sorry, out there?"

"We were business partners," said Maya, swallowing past a sudden ache in her throat. There were multiple reasons she didn't want to talk about this.

"But not anymore?" asked Judy.

"I thought there were almost none left," said Emon.

Maya fled into the next room.

It had an unrecognizable metallic smell that was sharp and funky. The lighting was dim as dusk, overlaid with a projection of the night sky. Tacky, but pretty too. Arranged clockwise around the room were dramatically spotlighted objects that gave the Humbert Collection its fame: artifacts from distant worlds.

Half of them scholars hadn't yet identified. Maya had caused a stir last year when she'd figured out that one of the more beloved objects was just a pile of extraterrestrial excrement.

There, in the case by the door, was a flat piece of volcanic rock, intricately carved with a depiction of a city long gone. Civilization: unknown. The world was devoid of sentient life by the time other explorers arrived. A plaque next to it identified the donor as *Anonymous*.

A relatively small thing, and yet it had covered Maya's application fee and up to ten more years of tuition, stipend, room, and board. She didn't mention this to the visitors.

She paused by the set of sculptural figures next to it. The label speculated these were Frenro toys, *though no human has ever encountered a juvenile Gatekeeper*. Her fingers curled against the glass without her being conscious of it.

"Mother of Jesus," whispered Judy Bond, all questions about Auncle thankfully eclipsed as Maya'd hoped. They were staring at the object in the center of the room.

They were meant to stare. This was the star of the show, after all, the grand prize of the entire collection. It was the size of a chair, suspended just above the ground: a jewel with ninety-nine sides, each face shimmering with a liquid quality. In front of it was the model Maya had promised them, beautiful despite the dullness of the film of fingerprints smeared all over it. But it was the original version that emanated a wave of sound: musical, cacophonous, in and out of human range of hearing, a never-ending waterfall.

"Wo-ow," Emon Bond added for good measure.

As always, underneath a swell of joy and hope and love, Maya felt disgust—because this shouldn't be here. It was one of ten compositions that had been carted home from an abandoned Belzoar space station by an excited scientific team.

"What is it really?" Judy asked Emon, voice wavering a little.

Maya answered for him: "Art."

CHAPTER FIVE

Pickle was waiting for them down by the welcome desk, chatting with a virtual projection from a box that was much better quality than the cheap recyclable one in Maya's pocket. It was the Executive Director, piping in from a freshly reconstructed beach in Puerto Rico.

"Hello," she said. "I'm so sorry to have missed you—"

"Oh no," said Judy. "It was a wonderful tour—and with a colonist too!"

"Settler," Pickle corrected, but Judy didn't seem to hear them.

Maya prayed for the muscles in her face not to betray her. The settlers of the Outer Worlds had left Earth for a multitude of reasons—escaping drowned countries and conflict, searching for adventure. The War of Independence had broken out twenty-eight years ago after rising disagreement over trade and foreign policy. When the settlers won, they vigorously ditched all uses of "colony." The people of Earth, of course, continued to use the word.

"We even got to meet a special friend," said Emon.

Pickle gave Maya a questioning look.

Judy was talking now about how spectacular the Belzoar composition was, and how freaked out she had been by that Gatekeeper—"Frenro," said Pickle and Maya at the same time—"Hm? Oh yes, and the extraterrestrial gemstone collection was stunning, simply stunning."

Thankfully, the Executive Director signaled to Pickle that they should retreat to the office for a more private chat. Pickle called over their shoulder—"I'll be right back!"

Which left Maya drumming her fingers at the front desk and wondering whether she could go and help herself now to the book downstairs. But first she needed to call Auncle. She hoped xe hadn't gotten xyrself into trouble without her.

She went out into the sunshine, blinking against the brightness. She never wore the prescription sun-goggles that were supposed to protect her spacer eyes. She found a comfortable spot on a bench and set the projector on the ground in front of her.

The archives were located in the southwest part of campus near the newly rebuilt historic two-car light-rail, affectionately known as the "Dinky," that connected the campus to the main train line. Directly to the north was the art center, theater, and dormitories, and beyond that, the town itself.

Auncle answered almost immediately, ensconced in a pink pouffe. Xe was vaguely potato-shaped, covered in hundreds of finer tentacles and filaments like a jellyfish or anemone on top, with ten thick lower arms not unlike like an octopus's on the bottom. Several of the top tentacles were speckled with black visual receptors. These stretched toward Maya to take her in, no doubt cataloging the minute ways Maya had changed in the past year: the sun-darkened tint to her skin, shadows under her eyes, and rather chic chin-length haircut she had gotten on an awkward get-to-know-you-again outing with her aunt to a local salon.

Auncle looked just the same, though the ripple of colors across xyr body betrayed a special Frenro kind of stress. "How have you been, dear one? It has been too long since we sat down and had a most serious conversation about life and other important things. Are you well and in the dreams that you wished for yourself? I see you have not died, as you have been worrying you might. I did get your letter, it was most appreciated, and I thought I saw you once when I was meditating, but I won't speak of that, because I know it upsets you when I mention it. How are your dreams, love?"

Had it been a year and a half since they'd last spoken? They'd parted on a sour note, which Maya regretted.

"My dreams are fine," lied Maya, not wanting to worry xyr.

"Rrrrrrr . . ." The purring noise, like a cat's, but also completely not, rolled through the black box. She felt it in her chest. It was the sound of Auncle laughing and sighing at the same time, or the Frenro equivalent of that. Every muscle in her body relaxed. She might have made the painful decision to leave xyr, but Auncle was still her best friend.

"What are you doing here?" Maya asked. "If it's about a job, I'm sorry, but I can't do it."

"I have missed this game," said Auncle, voice high and sweet like a child's. Xe used an auto-translator with a "select human emotion here" option, but Frenro didn't have the same emotions as humans, so it was murky whether xe was, for example, upset. Probably not? But maybe? "The one where you pretend you aren't happy to see me."

"I'm definitely not happy," said Maya, trying not to smile, but it was good to see her friend again, if only through a projector.

A flurry of memories came to her of random moments: the time Auncle hunted a market for hours searching for a piece of cake that only Maya would be able to eat; the time Maya tended to Auncle for a week, one of the rare times xe was sick; the time they crammed together in a narrow sewer for twelve hours during a job, trying to ease their stress by searching in vain for a joke that was equally funny in both of their cultures.

"Please tell me you're not down here, at least." After the first pandemic, foreign—nonhuman, that is—people were strictly limited from landing on Earth, even though there was a vaccine and Infected humans were allowed to come and go freely.

Maya tipped her head up and looked at the clouds crawling across the blue sky, as if she could see through the stratosphere to where Auncle's ship must be orbiting.

"I did not try to land. I am orbiting with the Earthly space garbage. No one cares at all about my presence, as long as I pay my rent each day."

"Your rent?" Maya said, alarmed. "You're paying for a spot right now?" Maya had set up a human bank account for xyr years ago, but her friend had always been terrible with money. Frenro didn't entirely grasp the concept.

"Of course," said Auncle brightly. "So I can wait for you!"

Maya bit her lip. "Wait for me?"

"When you told me you were dreaming of the grail, I knew I must come here at once."

She'd dreamed of the grail several times. Those endless dim subterranean corridors, the grail moving in her hands—just as Dr. Huang had described it—and a prickle in the back of her neck like she was being hunted. But dreams of the future couldn't protect you from calamity. That was the hard truth Maya had learned.

And oh no, Auncle coming here was her fault. "I still have no idea where it is. Although . . ."

"Although?" Auncle's shape warped in the projection as xe leaned closer to xyr camera.

Maya hesitated a moment. She hated to get Auncle's hopes up. But Auncle had come all this way.

So she told Auncle about the missing volume 5, now found. And Auncle predictably exploded with excitement, all arms and filaments out like the quills of a porcupine.

"I haven't even gotten a chance to look at the journal!" said Maya. "It could be nothing."

"It is more than okay, my sweet friend! It is okay! We swim toward it even now. It means we are close, maybe closer than we realize. Perhaps tomorrow or next week. Let us go to meet our fate."

"I'm sorry. I can't." Her eyes filled with tears as she said it, because there was a part of her that yearned to leap off the bench, hop on the train, and head to Dubai for the next departure skyward. She rubbed at a sharp ache under her breastbone. She'd lived a traveler's life for most of her adulthood and thought she was used to goodbyes; she wasn't used to being the one left on the ground.

"I just can't do it anymore. And anyway, I've got this massive project that I need to somehow put together in the next few days—" As she said it, her panic returned in a rush. She stood. "Can I call you later?" Later would be easier. She'd be able to think.

"We should certainly talk later. After you have had time for human emotional digestion. I will wait."

"Human emotional digestion is not a thing," she said with a laugh.

"You say this, but I have observed it many times. Maya, I saw the grail too."

Maya stilled in the middle of scooping up the projector.

A few decades after Earth's First Contact, the Frenro were nearly wiped out in a campaign by a militant clan of Belzoar. In the process, vast quantities of their material culture were destroyed: tools, machines, art, spacecraft, habitats—and every known grail. Auncle had been searching since then, convinced one must have escaped the purge.

Maya had once had the human hubris to think she might find it.

Even now she held out hope. But she worried this would end in heartbreak, like every other dead end they'd come to in their search.

"I believe we are here," Auncle was saying. "We are going to find it this time."

Maya stepped into a pocket of shade under the branches of a magnolia tree. She'd been born on a small world, under a night sky full of thousands of stars glittering through a wisp of an atmosphere. Nothing like this: a breeze in her face, the rich scent of flowers and late summer air filling her lungs with every inhalation.

But part of her would always yearn to be out there with Auncle, moving from port to port, chasing jobs. Her metal-soled boots had touched down on dozens of other worlds—and it would never be enough.

A message from Pickle appeared: *Maya, where are you? I've been looking all over for you.*

Maya's heart jumped.

"Maya? Is this connection not working or is it just your slower human thinking process?"

Maya began to jog back toward the building entrance. "I have to go. The book is available."

"Yes, go then. Even so, please do not forget me," cried Auncle.

"Never," said Maya.

"We are near an ending. You must believe me. We do not have any time to waste. There is something else I must speak with you about, but not now, in person only, so we can understand each other more completely."

That was mysterious, but then that was Auncle.

Pickle messaged her again: *???*

"I—I'll think about it, I promise. Don't try to come down here." She squeezed the cube and stuffed it in her pocket, ending the connection.

The book would solve all their problems, she was certain of it.

CHAPTER SIX

Pickle met her at the front desk, holding a stack of books so tall Maya could only see their anxious brown eyes, and Maya felt a little bad for asking her friend to break the rules like this. But it was only for a few hours, and she'd give it back.

"Have I told you I love you?" Maya said. They'd first bonded over the excrement incident when Maya restarted at the university—Pickle was the only one on staff who'd found the whole thing hilarious—and had been friends ever since. They'd saved Maya's academic career on more than one occasion.

"Oh, yes, the book," said Pickle, as if it were just any old volume.

Maya made a beeline toward the reading room on the first floor where the holds were kept.

Pickle followed, talking too fast and loud. "By the way, awesome job with the tour. Did I say thank you yet? Thank you. The boss was like, 'Genius idea, Pickle, having Maya do it instead of Brian. I really appreciate how strategic you are.' That's a good sign, right? Did you tell them about the time you partied with a famous Belzoar composition artist?"

"I did," Maya admitted.

"Nice. Well, the money is as good as in the bank," said Pickle. "We're going to pitch them on funding a research trip to acquire more Belzoar artifacts, and I was thinking since Dr. Barnes is pushing you to do fieldwork, maybe Liam could lead it, and you could go along—"

"Liam would never go. He doesn't do space. I mean, don't tell people that. Forget I said it." Maya saw something in the periphery of her vision, like a patch of phosphorescence. She turned her head to look, but there was only shadow.

"Are you okay?" asked Pickle.

Maya had stopped, blinking at the entrance to the reading room. She was certain she'd seen a ripple of light, hoped it was just her imagination.

But then she heard a few syncopated syllables of a human voice in her ear, like a bad transmission. Shit. A migraine was coming on.

She massaged her temple, wondering if she could make it to the intern workspace before the aura fully descended. "Just a headache," she said. "Thank you for thinking of me with the research grant, by the way. Though I think I'd rather stay here." For reasons she didn't really want to get into. "Where's the book?"

"Oh, so . . ." The way Pickle's lips curled around those vowels set off enough foreboding to repress, at least momentarily, Maya's impending symptoms.

"What the hell? We had a deal!"

"It's not my fault!" said Pickle. "I wasn't here when the guy came in—I literally stepped away for five minutes, I swear—and they didn't know about our deal of course, and so they just gave it to him. But listen! Before you get mad, look at all these other books I found for you!" They thrust the stack they were carrying toward Maya. "You need to get that paper done anyway. I promise I'll get you access when he's done with it."

"Is he still here?" Maya asked, the throbbing in her head increasing. "The guy who stole my book."

"He's in the reading room, but be nice! He's someone important. Check it out: this one is a personal account by J. Wilde from the late twenty-second century about the first human visit to Ululu, and I found a vlog by a traveler to Cameron, where they have a lot of Belzoar compositions, right? It's mostly a food tour unfortunately, but it might have some things, and also—"

Every word sent a jolt through Maya's brain. She felt dizzy. Out of time. Immediate retreat necessary.

"Thanks for these." She tried to sound grateful. What Pickle had pulled for her should be enough for the paper. The grail had been lost for hundreds of years—it could wait. "Do you mind holding on to them for an hour? I've got to go."

She stumbled toward the end of the reading room.

"Are you mad about the book?" Pickle called after her. "You're mad, aren't you?"

"It's . . . fine," Maya ground out, wishing for a slide that could take her all the way through to the bathroom.

She was seeing flashes of colors: fuchsia, chartreuse, neon yellow.

She blinked, and—were those Belzoar? There they were, looming in the corner of the sunny room; enormous, eight-legged, an inflated pouch hanging between their legs that vibrated with sound, hard carapace, and unblinking eyes. The black armor affixed around their upper body sent a chill through Maya.

Her first reaction—and she wasn't proud of it—was to scream. She bumped into the edge of a long table, but the pain that shot through her hip barely registered through her fear.

The Belzoar were coming toward her, and she thought for a moment they were real.

"I'm so sorry," she said. "I'm trying to atone."

A rumpled scholarly person in a maroon zip up and a yellow-and-navy silk scarf scowled from down the table.

"I'm fine," she said quickly.

"Can you keep it down?"

"Sorry."

The Belzoar were gone. She was seeing flashes again, though, more distinct: stone columns wrapped in purple vines guarded by an enormous and fierce-looking statue; a silver-tiled path winding through a dark forest; her family's fine ceramic teacups rattling ominously on their wooden side table; the sharp sensation of grieving someone she didn't yet know.

She had medication in her jacket pocket, but the aura was coming on too fast. The world seemed to shimmer as she moved.

She just had to get to the bathroom so she could turn the lights out and hunker down.

Time expanded and contracted like the inside of a lung.

The door opened at her touch.

"Lights off!"

She sank down against the cold tile, fumbling in her pocket as she curled into a fetal position. The world shook with every thump of her heart.

She retrieved the battered medicine tin and peeled out a clear adhesive swatch the size of her thumbnail. She slapped it against her jugular. It smelled, impossibly, like her father's roses.

Help, she thought faintly. But it was already too late. Everything fractured into infinite pieces.

CHAPTER SEVEN

Maya fell into dreams of another time. The tile beneath her cheek was stone. She was deep underground, and she felt the greasy sensation of déjà vu.

She was in the past. She was living again through the last job, on the Belzoar planet of Lithis, home to the isolated Belzoar clan once responsible for the deaths of millions of Frenro. Auncle and Maya had taken the job because they thought they might find the grail there, but the rumors turned to dust as soon as they'd arrived, and they were caught in the vault of precious things.

They had been here for a long time. They, because Auncle was here with her. How long? The clock on her suit said three weeks.

Auncle lay sprawled and flat like a starfish in a slash of sunlight that filtered down from a high slit in the yellow stone wall. Auncle's skin through xyr tank was gray, and the metal of xyr suit flaked a little. Xe was diminished from poor hydration, and the tank of water on xyr back was cloudy in a manner that could not be healthy. The filter mechanism churned audibly, and Maya worried how long the suit would last in an arid environment.

Not that her own suit was in better straits. She could smell herself in the stale air that cycled through her helmet. The skin across her hips and under her arms was tender, and it hurt to pee. Probably infection. And it was cold, even colder than back home. She desperately wished for a shower. To go down the street to the public bath and scrub herself with hot water until her skin was pink and clean.

"My child," said Auncle. "We cannot stay here, in this place of infinite regrets and bitter-tasting dreams."

Maya turned over onto her side. There was a drain in the floor a few centimeters wide. Even Auncle, boneless as xe was, couldn't fit through it.

"You must do it." Auncle's artificial voice was quiet but uncharacteristically stern. "Even if your tubular insides feel twisty."

She didn't want to do what Auncle wanted. But she had no better ideas. If they stayed here much longer, they would die, if not from the experiments they were subjected to each night, then by starvation.

Not much in this place for a human to eat.

"Mayyyyya," said Auncle.

Maya reached up and popped her helmet. The air rushed in and she began to panic almost immediately. Not enough oxygen in the air. Couldn't get breath into her lungs. Her vision filled with black dots.

Auncle laid an arm across her neck and then inched it closer to Maya's lips. She opened and closed her mouth like a fish out of water. Her chest hurt. She reached up with two hands and grasped Auncle's arm, squinting for a break in xyr suit. There. A weak spot.

She put the arm between her lips and bit down with her sharpest teeth. It was rubbery and thick, and writhed against her tongue. She gagged and kept gagging, but forced herself to keep grinding all the same. She prayed the guards wouldn't hear Auncle's thrashing limbs.

Her gloved fingers were coated in slick, oily liquid, and a bitter taste haunted her tongue. She couldn't stop retching. She couldn't breathe.

No, she thought. *Not here again. Not here. I need to wake up.*

Auncle lifted her head, slipped the helmet back over her face. Cradled her upper body until her lungs were expanding, contracting normally again, filtered air passing through her lips with each inhalation.

A segment of one of xyr major arms, maybe half a meter long—the piece she had bitten off with her teeth—writhed on the floor, still grasping and sending information to a body it was no longer attached to.

A Frenro body part once severed could continue to receive direction from the main body for several hours. This was how Maya learned this fact.

"Are you okay?" Maya asked Auncle.

"We must go," xe replied, and the detached segment twisted like a snake. It inched along the ground and slipped down the drain in the floor that reeked of human waste.

It had taken some time and late-night probing with Auncle's longest arms to determine the drain connected to a broader system. At the end of the line, there was a juncture in the pipe, and one turn might take it up again to a drain in the bathing room where they were sometimes permitted to wash.

And from the bathing room, it was possible to advance down the hall, inching along the edges to avoid detection, until one got to the control room, which they had glimpsed only a few times in passing. If one was patient, a short, separated arm leaking body fluid could slip inside when the guards opened the door, clamber up the glass screens full of unknown symbols, and, through trial and error, unlock their cell door.

"Stay with me, friend," Maya said, dragging herself to her feet. Auncle didn't respond. She lifted Auncle's weakened, flattened form to her shoulders. Remarkable how light a dehydrated Frenro could be.

She wore Auncle like an enormous cape, hanging on to xyr arms and staggering only a little. She'd carry her friend out of that place if it broke her back.

Night on this world wasn't long enough to stand and contemplate the ways one could die. Three of the world's six moons illuminated the way. Auncle's azure-colored circulatory fluid dripped down her chest. It glinted in pale starlight.

A few shuttles passed overhead, wings huge and silhouetted by the moon, and each time, Maya held her breath, expecting an alarm to go up. They reached the edge of the settlement. The buildings were cheap and sagging, but at the center of an open square was a broad pool with a fountain.

Pure, clear water, like they hadn't had in months. Auncle's thoughts were just a moan in Maya's mind. The two of them moved toward it, unable to resist.

They bathed in its waters, heedless of anything but the gurgle. Maya scrubbed the dirt and blood and shit from her suit.

Auncle paddled about, cooling xyr severed limb.

In that moment, Maya thought of nothing but how water begat all life and a universal thirst that drove it to return.

They left Lithis that night in the belly of a trader's ship.

A month later, ten thousand Belzoar on Lithis were dead.

...

The world shifted, and then she was in the future. She could tell by the quality of the vision: fragmented and difficult to see, understanding coming only in snatches.

Her thoughts wouldn't solidify. She knew and didn't know where she was: inside the hallway of a dark, ancient building.

Fear pulsed in her blood. There were things in here with her. Only a few lights flickered here and there, and she passed through them like a shadow, the slash of her headlamp swinging all about.

Ahead of her, she saw the disappearing shape of a friend, passing through an opening ahead of her to the outside.

"I'm sorry," said the voice.

In her chest, she felt despair, strong enough to make her weep.

And then the exit collapsed, and Maya looked up and the ceiling was falling down. There was no way out. She was trapped. She would die. She would—

CHAPTER EIGHT

Someone was banging on the bathroom door. She opened her eyes, and she could see by the dim light leaking in along the floor that she was still in Humbutt, no matter what visions her Infected brain might have fed her. She was as wrung out as an old rag, but she felt a bright, lemony euphoria at being back in the proper place and time. She considered just lying on the tiled floor forever.

"Maya?"

Maya unfolded herself, muscles stiff and aching. The pain had receded; the medication was doing its magic. Though the banging wasn't helpful.

"One second, please." She excavated grit from the corners of her eyes with a finger. There was a sickly-sweet, bitter taste on her tongue, the memory of Auncle's circulatory fluid sliding down her throat.

Frenro had a different relationship with space-time than most people. It enabled them, up until about 230 years ago, to construct the engineering miracle that was the Interstellar Web. And they also had a sort of peripheral vision of the past and future of certain versions of the universe. An ability those Infected with the same virus as the Frenro seemed to share.

Maya had been lucky enough to survive a wave of the virus that swept through PeaceLove when she was a child. Her lasting souvenirs were the migraines and a periodic slipping of her mind into the past or future.

Pickle stood on the other side of the door. "You're alive."

"What's going on?" Maya asked, blinking in the shock of light.

"It's three o'clock."

Maya stiffened in alarm. Half the afternoon evaporated, and she was nowhere with her paper for her meeting with Liam in a couple of hours. She also didn't have the Huang book, and Auncle was waiting for her answer. It was too much.

"I'm sure Liam will understand if you're sick."

"Liam's never missed a day of school in his life."

Pickle left, and Maya fetched her books from the hold desk and laid them out in a spot in the reading room. There were only two other people in the room, the scholar in the maroon zip up from before who had told her to be quiet, and one of the archivists in the middle of digitizing a box of books.

Maya eyed Pickle's stack of books warily. She forced herself to open Liam's original outline and started skimming through the texts one by one. The grind of it at last began to settle her nerves. She remembered how to do this: plucking through different perspectives, listening for some melody that might tie all the notes together, even if you could never be sure that it wasn't an illusion.

She needed ice cream. Glorious, made with milk from a cow, disgusting amounts of sugar, and those sprinkles, maybe, that were colorful and meaningless. No, she needed to focus on this damn paper.

The materials Pickle had pulled were mostly twenty-first-century and early twenty-second-century materials whose digital copies had been lost and no one had bothered to re-digitize.

She stopped in surprise. Among the stack was an item that had nothing to do with music: a slim, self-published memoir by a member of an international mission sent to map a distant region of the web. It was bookmarked at a description of an encounter with Huang's crew. Maya smiled. She didn't deserve Pickle.

> We linked up for a few days to trade stories and supplies. They were in high spirits for a crew on the thirteenth year of what was supposed to be a ten-year journey and who'd just lost their major source of funding.
>
> Huang was as charismatic as her reputation suggested. Within an hour we all would have followed her to the end of the web if she'd asked.
>
> One night, over whiskey, Nkosi let slip that they thought they were on the verge of a major discovery: an ancient library they called the Encyclopedium, which supposedly contained a stunning catalog of life-forms and culture from the IW pre–First Contact with the Quietling.

I dismissed it the next day as a mix of bragging and drunken fantasy. Later, though, when I heard rumors, I wondered.

Maya reread the excerpt, heart beating faster as she did. Most thought the Encyclopedium was a myth, and if it did exist, it was too far away to reach. There was a wasteland in the web beyond the Belzoar and Quietling regions called the Dead Sea, due to its seemingly endless stretch of barren systems, filled with ruined worlds in erratic orbit, moons shattered into clouds of debris. Nowhere for anyone to resupply. A few ships had attempted to cross it and never been heard from again. But the Frenro had come from somewhere. It made sense you might look for such an artifact at that origin.

Focus! she imagined Liam's voice scolding her.

Right. The paper.

She heaved a sigh that echoed louder than intended, and the scholar in the zip up turned and scolded with their eyes.

"Sorry," she mouthed, but they'd already turned back around.

She stood up to refill her water bottle and paused. That must be the Yale professor who had her book. She took the long way to the fountain so she could eyeball what he was reading. It was the Huang volume.

"Yes?" he asked.

"Nice to meet you. I'm Maya."

He sat back in his chair. "Ah. Maya Hoshimoto." His voice was an ominous bass rumble.

"Have we met?"

"Daniel John Garcia," said the man, sharing his info with a flick of a hand.

Daniel John Garcia, PhD, Comparative Cultures; MS, Mechanical Engineering. He is a professor at Yale University. His latest book, Foreign Shores, *available now, details his extensive travels through the Quietling Nodal Region.*

Maya's mouth made a little O. Dr. DJ Garcia wasn't just "some guy" from Yale; he was, among many things, one of the foremost human experts in foreign space travel. Liam idolized him. He had taken classes with him as an undergrad and quoted him frequently in everyday situations, as in, "Should we order some food?" "Well, as Dr. Garcia once said, 'The only thing that is finite is life.'"

"It's on my list to speak with you," he said, and then he made a little tick mark in the air, like he was checking off an item on his virtual to-do. He shut the Huang book, and Maya's fingers twitched.

"Shall we go for a walk?" he said, without any expectation of refusal.

What Maya *should* have done was sit back down and finish going through the materials, so she had something coherent to say about her plans for a new draft when she met with Liam later. But she was intrigued.

They handed their books in and went outside, the world startling Maya as always with its color and sound. She studied her unexpected companion. He was maybe sixty, with the roughened skin of someone who had grown up with real weather. There were deep lines around his mouth, like his face was often pursed in judgment. Gray hair fell to his shoulders, layered in the current style, a bit on top pulled back with a scrap of cloth.

His years gave him a gravitas he was obviously used to wielding.

They started up Theater Drive toward Nassau Street.

"I've been reading all day, and I'd like to complete this conversation so I can make another meeting in an hour, so I'll skip to the part where I tell you this is about a matter of extreme importance and the very fabric of the universe is at stake."

A loud guffaw ripped from Maya's throat, because there was no way he was serious. This was either a prank or he was delusional.

Dr. Garcia watched her laugh for a minute, irritation growing on his face, and when Maya paused to catch her breath, he said: "Maya Hoshimoto, age thirty-one, born on PeaceLove. Infected. Parents are terrafarmers. Longtime associate of a Frenro who goes by the name Auncle. Also, we know about Los Angeles. So if you prefer, we can do this the hard way, and I call the Feds right now."

Maya was no longer laughing. He meant the heist they'd pulled on the California Museum of Other Peoples to liberate several Belzoar instruments. Her mouth had gone as dry as the PeaceLove lower hemisphere. They stared at each other. "There's no need to be mean," she said, with a swagger she didn't feel. "Come on, then. You can buy me lunch from the kiosk. Trust me, you don't want to talk to me hungry."

He followed her, oozing his disapproval.

The self-service kiosk was only a short walk down the street, near the light-rail station. Neon letters hung above the cube, about three meters tall and three meters wide: *Wa.*

The kiosk selection was limited and generally horrible. But she had spent a third of her life eating wartime rations and a third of it eating space food, so by her standards, the flash-frozen, insta-heated sandwiches were positively delightful.

She set about ordering half the menu: extra strong hot tea with milk (cow milk, a novelty to a settler); a cheese hoagie (she'd gotten behind dairy products, but the idea of meat made her queasy) with extra mustard and Node 9 pickles (unrecognizable from the real thing); two chocolate bars; a bag of Melancholy vinegar and spice chips that numbed the tongue; and a little box of dumplings, because why not. Oh, also a packet of lactase pills for the dairy. She invited Garcia to scan his eye for payment.

Exasperated, he stepped forward and let the camera shine into his eye for a moment.

"Is that all?" he asked sourly.

"Want anything?"

He gritted his teeth, then ordered a coffee.

The kiosk spat the whole order into a reusable box. She sat down on a nearby bench and began unpacking it. The hoagie came deconstructed but was easily assembled. The smell of hot bread wafted up, and it soothed Maya's nerves a little.

"Itadakimasu," she said.

Dr. Garcia sat on the other side of the bench, clutching his coffee. He looked satisfyingly uncomfortable.

"When you said 'we,' who did you mean?" Maya asked. "I assume you didn't mean Yale."

"I'm a consultant for the CNE," he said.

Maya stiffened. The Coalition of the Nations of Earth was a political, economic, and military force meant to protect Earth from outside forces. When the settlers of the Outer Worlds had declared their independence from their respective companies and founding nations in one exhilarating and riotous year, it was the CNE that had come to brutally put them down.

Dr. Garcia waved a hand impatiently, as if to anticipate and dismiss her reaction at the same time. "The entire Interstellar Web is in peril. Something—or someone—has been destroying nodes."

Interstellar travel was only possible—for humans at least—thanks to the web of wormhole-like "nodes" that connected all the solar systems together. The web, if drawn, might resemble the branches of a maple tree, splitting and splitting again, its nodes linking systems together across space without any clear reason besides a probability of life. Distances between two systems didn't seem to matter—some nodes connected stars all the way across the galaxy from each other.

The anomaly that had appeared beyond Mars was one such node, and through it was another system with another node that led to yet another system. If something was destroying the nodes, it was possible Dr. Garcia hadn't been hyperbolic about the stakes.

"What do you mean? How?" Maya asked, then, as she absorbed the news and panic took her: "Which ones?"

"We're determining the extent, but recently one of our drone stations reported that Node 12-9 has collapsed."

Maya pulled up her Interstellar Web (IW) charts in her ocular lenses.

Nodal systems were generally marked by two numbers: the first represented a system's nodal distance from Earth. So Nodal System 12-9 was twelve nodes from Earth. There were ten nodal systems at a distance of twelve nodes away from Earth, so the second number distinguished which of those ten nodes it was. Well, now there were only nine, if 12-9 was truly gone.

She shuddered. At least Nodal System 12-9 was a minor system, a dead end, and uninhabited.

"Obviously, we were concerned. We thought maybe the drone station was wrong, or it was a freak accident. We sent probes and then a crew. They poked around where it had been. And nada. It's gone."

"Did it . . . move?" Maya opened the bag of chips but didn't eat any.

He shook his head. "There's a big cloud of dust abrasive enough to destroy several of our probes and damage our ship. Three weeks ago, we lost Nodal Systems 10-4 and 10-1. Then last week, it was 9-2, 8-1, and 7-2."

Whatever was happening was getting closer to Earth.

She chewed one of her cuticles. "Auncle didn't mention anything." Frenro had built the web, and though they no longer remembered how, they had a special awareness of it. Auncle would have said something. Wouldn't xe?

"Well, your friend might not know," said Dr. Garcia. Unfortunately true.

The problem was, Frenro didn't have any form of written record. Once, they had been the most technologically advanced people in known space, millennia ahead of all others, but they somehow carried their information in their bodies—or who knew where. The death of millions two and a half centuries ago had cost them uncountable secrets of the universe.

"What makes you think someone is behind this? It could just be part of a natural cycle as far as we know."

Dr. Garcia projected a simulation against the leaves of a nearby ash tree from a thick ring on his left hand. A strange spider-legged thing emerged out of the node. Its long arms seemed to wrap around the edges, and after a brief, trembling moment, the whole thing collapsed like the yolk of an egg.

"What was that?" Maya breathed.

"That would be the someone behind this," said Dr. Garcia. "The Belzoar and Quietling deny any involvement. No one else has close to the technological advancement to do this." He leaned closer, eyes glinting. "If this continues, Earth's prime node could be in danger."

No node meant isolation, no way to travel to the rest of the web. Earth would be back to the way it was: alone in the dark, wondering about other life out there, and unable to contact any of it.

It had happened once before, to the original Lithian homeworld near the end of their campaign against the Frenro: one day, it was just gone from the Interstellar Web, the Atlantis of the greater Belzoar Nodal Region. No one ever knew what happened to it.

"Maybe even sooner for the colonies."

"Outer Worlds," said Maya, out of habit.

"The point is, the situation is dire."

Maya set the remains of her hoagie down on the tray and stared at him. She gulped the hot tea. "Why are you telling me this?"

"You're good at obtaining things."

"No, sorry, and no." Maya shoved the last of the sandwich in her mouth and rapidly lifted the top tray to remove the additional food underneath. Returning the containers to the kiosk would get her a deposit—a nice bit of pocket money.

"If you don't care about Earth," said Dr. Garcia, "do it for the colonies."

"Outer Worlds," said Maya again.

Dr. Garcia twisted his projection ring. The image over the trees dispelled and a three-dimensional rendering appeared in his palm.

"This is what we need you to obtain."

She choked on her tea, and it took her a minute to catch her breath. Because she recognized the object immediately. The grail.

"This is Huang's stardust machine, capable of creating new nodes between star systems. We would no longer be dependent on the existing Interstellar Web. We could build our own paths."

"Huh," said Maya, pretending to be surprised. She stared at its hydra shape, long cilia, and the knobby brown trunk. It was, she realized, the first time she'd seen it outside her dreams: the object that had driven her life for many years.

Auncle had described it to her the first time they'd met, standing over a stolen shovel on a wasteland of a planet. Xe'd told her: "I have traveled for a long time. I never lost hope of reaching this path. I cannot believe we are at an end. I will love them so, these future children."

Auncle doted on infants of all species: human, cat, Belzoar. After holding a baby, xe might not speak for days, trying to dream the love xe yearned for into existence.

It was impossible without the grail.

Dr. Garcia waggled his eyebrows like they were sharing a little secret together. She wanted to throw her chips in his face.

"And you want me to find it."

"That's the thing. We have a lead."

Maya jerked her head up. "Where?"

"Ah-ah," said Dr. Garcia, wagging a finger. "You have to accept the job first."

She tore her eyes away from the grail. "Okay, so what? If you know where it is, you don't need me."

Dr. Garcia smiled again, his spectacles twinkling in the sun. It gave him a deceptively mild look. "Fishing for compliments?"

"Not a crime," said Maya.

"We both know you're very good at extracting objects under, ah, difficult circumstances. As we witnessed with CMOP."

"I'm not sure I'd consider those difficult circumstances. Hypothetically. So there's an extraction involved?" She was even more nonplussed. She shifted against the bench. Her foot had gone to sleep.

He spread his arms. "If we're right, let's say we don't think the object is lost so much as hidden in plain sight. Its owners probably aren't even aware of what they have." He plucked her open bag of chips and began to help himself. "Unless for some reason you have a problem with stealing all of a sudden—"

She snatched the chips back. "It's not theft if it didn't belong to people in the first place."

"Well, then." He stuck his hand into the open bag, took another chip, and waved it at her. "You should have no problem then, since the Frenro don't have it."

Maya clutched her tea. She thought of Auncle up there, waiting for a sign. The way xe had already picked out names of xyr future children, and one of them was Maya—something Maya felt merited further discussion. "They should. It belongs to them. They need it to save themselves from extinction."

What Maya knew was that reproduction involved implantation of the grail inside a Frenro's cavity. After that, it was unclear—more knowledge that had been lost in the last couple of hundred years.

He stared at her. "You would really give it to the Frenro, who are—I'm sorry—basically down to a handful of refugees, even if it means humankind is cut off from the rest of the universe forever?"

She stood up and began stuffing the used boxes and trays into the kiosk return slot, then gathered up all her remaining food in her arms—not an easy feat, but she was annoyed, and that was motivating.

He could keep the chips.

"You won't even know how to use it. It's Frenro."

"We obtained some ancient schematics from the Quietling." He showed her diagrams of a cylindrical contraption with the grail in the center of it. "We've already begun working on several prototypes.

Once we figure out how to duplicate it, we'll no longer be at the mercy of others."

Her blood ran cold the way he said it. They wanted to dissect it.

"Also, you've spilled tea down your shirt."

She couldn't wait to tell Liam that his hero was a jerk. She didn't know what she wanted, but she definitely had minus zero desire to work with the CNE.

He resumed eating the chips, watching her with sharp eyes. As she moved to leave, he added, "We would of course compensate you," and then named a sum that was enough to, she was embarrassed later to admit to herself, make her pause.

It was a figure that could cover a pleasant, hidden existence for the rest of her life—enough for her and Auncle both, if her friend wanted. Enough to allow her parents to retire in comfort. All she had to do was deny Auncle the one thing xe had ever wanted. Oh, and condemn the Frenro to extinction.

He smirked as if plucking the traitorous thoughts from her mind. "You could start a foundation. Dedicated to the repatriation of stolen objects. Buy rather than steal."

It was a notion that had never occurred to her, because such an absurd amount of money had never been within reach.

"You must really believe this thing is the key to the universe," said Maya.

"It has to be."

"Well, great chat, but I've retired. So if you'll excuse me, I've got a paper to finish."

"Take a day," he said, emptying the remaining crumbs into a hand and shoveling them into his mouth. He licked the salt from his palm. "But my bosses expect an answer in twenty-four hours. If not . . ."

"Is this where you threaten me again?" she asked, hoping she sounded more cavalier than she felt.

"Well. That's the thing about history, isn't it? Someone's always digging. You can't keep the past in the past, can you?"

CHAPTER NINE

By the time Maya returned to the archives, it was half an hour to closing time and her meeting with Liam, and she was shivering with adrenaline. She was terrified. Not just of Dr. Garcia, who could undo this tenuous life she'd built, but of what might happen if she went with him—the thought of trespassing again in the unknown, of meddling with things she didn't understand, of causing harm.

She couldn't do it, not for Dr. Garcia, and not even for Auncle.

For so long, it had been the two of them against the galaxy. They'd lived together in a small ship, if not breathing the same air, then dreaming in parallel, as synchronized as two separately evolved life-forms could be. She carried in her an Auncle-shaped hole that even her friendship with Pickle couldn't fill.

Now Auncle had come all this way for her help, confident in the strength of their bond even when Maya was not. The problem was, xe never considered what it cost her.

It wasn't just that she didn't want to go. There was a part of her that wanted to be here among the books and ideas, the blue skies and buttery pastries, and new friends who didn't ask much of her.

Maya stopped in the lobby and hugged herself. She looked up again at the inscription on the wall.

Something itched at her. She pulled up the original source of the quote from the publicly available copy of volume 3 of Huang's memoir:

You can't live in the universe without leaving footprints. You leave an impact wherever you go. So how hard can it be to find a thing that once was commonplace?

We've found memories of the machine embedded in myth and the histories of every people we meet. We've chased countless rumors of where it might have been and might be—and nothing.

The farther we go, the more I suspect we're looking in the wrong place. It's time, I think, to go back to the beginning.

The beginning. Was that where Dr. Huang first figured out the location of the grail?

Maya shook her head, trying to shake loose the kernel embedded there. She was missing something. She wasn't sure what.

She went to the reading room, thinking she might try to get a little more work done. It was empty now, save for a single staff member at the front desk.

"All right?" he asked.

Maya blinked. She'd been staring off into space, unable to bring herself to retrieve the materials again.

"I'm just contemplating whether I should quit and open a bed-and-breakfast in Hokkaido," she said. "Could be nice."

"I hear that," he said with a laugh.

She considered messaging Liam just to provoke him into yelling at her, so she'd feel more motivated to buckle down and work. He'd been uncharacteristically silent. He should have pinged her six or seven times by now.

Without meaning to, her eyes slid to the hold cabinet, where the Huang journal was locked.

No. *No.* What was she doing? She wasn't a thief anymore.

She reclaimed her books and began to skim relevant sections. She was halfway through when the staff person stopped by her table.

"Mind watching the front desk for a bit? I need to use the bathroom."

"Sure." Maya took his seat, feeling the proximity of the hold cabinet like heat against her side.

As soon as he was gone, she swiveled around and unhooked her necklace. It was an eclectic piece of chunky jewelry, heavy with metal bits and chunks of crystal. She was never without it. It was sentimental, she'd explained to Pickle. Now she took one of the black crystals and held it close to the doorknob. Electronic lock, pitifully basic. She'd tested the Humbutt mechanisms one afternoon out of boredom. It opened with an audible click as the device hidden in the crystal hacked the lock.

There it was. She was only going to peek again; that was it. Her fingers kissed the binding. She opened it, and a bookmark slipped out.

> Its body was half submerged in water, and below the surface, it was anchored in sand—I wouldn't compare the base to roots, more like the feet of starfish, because every so often it shifted position.

Her heartbeat thundered in her ears. There it was: proof that Huang had found it. And if Huang had found it, the clue to its whereabouts could be in this very book.

Greedily, she flipped to the front and stopped short. The endpaper was woven with a fine metallic lace pattern.

She ran a fingertip over it. This was an old data storage technique, very rare. Had anyone else even realized it was here?

She hesitated only a moment before shoving it in her bag, replacing it with a similar-looking black volume from the stack she'd been reading. "I'll return it," she promised the air.

"You're in a good mood," the staff remarked when he returned.

"Hm?" Maya wouldn't consider her mood good so much as resolved. The thing was, sometimes the universe just didn't take no for an answer. And sometimes neither did Maya.

The trick was getting the book out of the building since security checked everyone's bags on the way out.

First, she placed an order for a dozen pizzas.

She went down to the intern workspace in the basement, which was thankfully empty. It took her five minutes to deactivate the security tag inside the book. She must be getting rusty. She removed her jacket, unsealed its padded lining, and slipped the volume inside.

One last stop.

This was probably a terrible, terrible idea, but Maya had made up her mind a year ago to do this if she ever left again, just in case there was a chance she couldn't return. She just didn't think it'd be so soon.

When stealing valuable artifacts, there were several important things to keep in mind: first, a diversion is key. Second, always be ready with a story. And third, if you can't be sneaky, be bold.

She removed her bracelet with its ID charm and shoved it in a pocket.

In the lobby, a flotilla of drones mobbed the security desk, and the entire staff was crowded around helping themselves to pizza.

"What's going on?" Maya asked Pickle.

"No idea! They just arrived!" they shouted over the din. "Must be a mistake, but I'm not going to question it."

"Hey, Brian," Maya said. "Can I get a big favor?"

"Hm?" He shoved the pointy end of a slice into his mouth.

"I think I lost my bracelet upstairs when I was giving the tour this morning. Do you mind keying me in temporary access?"

"Oh." For a moment, Maya wasn't sure this would work. Then he said, "I can only authorize emergency access for ten minutes. Would that work?" He finished the rest of the slice and was already pulling up the system on the front screen.

"Thank you, thank you," said Maya.

"Just don't get locked in!" Story, check. Now to be bold.

Maya set her alarm and hurried to the elevator bank.

Upstairs, the vault door opened no problem, thanks to Brian. The emergency blinkers cast the collection in shades of blue and red. She ignored the voice bleating over and over to evacuate. She moved through the darkened rooms, making a show of looking for her bracelet in case anyone was watching.

In the final room, she paused at the threshold. The Belzoar composition sang to her, its strange aria probing the boundaries of all her senses. It seemed to urge her on.

She'd figured out all the spots hidden from security cameras months ago. Just out of camera view, she pulled on her prescription sun-goggles. Then she removed her necklace again. She carefully picked out a second pendant, this one a light blue crystal. She paused to dial her sun-goggles up to the max and then twisted the pendant. It flickered and lit up like the sun. Even with her dark goggles on, the light was almost blinding.

The cameras in here were Tele-Cross Model PH3s. An excellent system. The same, in fact, as the ones CMOP had used. They functioned in all light levels, adjusting their focal lens as needed. But they had one major, little-known bug: a specific sequence of flashes could trigger the receptor to shrink to a pinhole, which then took about ninety seconds to reset. Enough time for Maya to do what she needed to do.

Four minutes before the vault shut.

She went straight to the case in the corner. Because of the emergency access, the electronic lock was temporarily off—a safety mechanism so artifacts could be removed in a fire. There was still a physical lock. She picked it in seconds. The case opened.

She grabbed the Frenro figurines and slipped them in her pocket and replaced them with smart-matter clay from her bag, programmed to assume the shape of the figurines. Maybe not enough to stand up to testing, but no one ever looked at these. It might be years before anyone realized they were gone—long after she edited the security feed. With any luck, no one would ever connect the theft to Maya.

She shut the case and withdrew her bracelet from her pocket so it was in her hand when the cameras came back online.

A couple of minutes remained on the clock.

A ping came in from Liam asking where she was. Oops. It was five o'clock, and she'd completely forgotten their meeting. *Can we reschedule, actually? Sorry, something came up.*

She broke into a trot.

The vault door was swinging shut when she reached the front room, but she slid through the gap just in time.

"All good?" Brian asked, on yet another slice of pizza. The impromptu party in the lobby was becoming worthy of its collegiate surroundings, complete with music, liquor, and stilted conversation.

Maya flashed her bracelet. "Got it."

"You're heading home?" asked Pickle.

"Yeah." She gave her friend a tight hug.

Pickle gave her a funny look. "You know it's just a paper, right? Don't stress too much."

"I love you," said Maya. "I'll call you later, okay?"

She left the building at a leisurely pace. It would have been nice to go home first, maybe stop by to say goodbye to her grandparents, but who knew when Garcia would come looking for her.

So instead she went down the street to the Dinky. On the way, she activated the projection cube.

The thing was, if she stole the grail for Dr. Garcia, the CNE might save Earth, but they wouldn't save the Frenro. That was certain. And if she stole the grail for Auncle, there was no saving Earth, because the CNE couldn't wield or dissect something implanted inside a Frenro.

It was a shit choice, and no matter what, Maya might never forgive herself. But it was the Frenro's. They had brought all life across the IW together in the first place. Whatever happened, they deserved the grail. And Auncle needed her.

Auncle's form filled the grassy patch just ahead of her as she walked.

"Maaaaayyyyaaa," xe said, and her spirit lifted. She was sure she was doing the right thing. Ninety percent sure. "Have you been to the beach recently? I have always wanted to swim in the seas of Earth."

"The Jersey Shore's all right, though they're still dredging all the houses that washed out to sea." The train arrived. "Hang tight. I'm on my way. But this is my last job, I mean it. I can't keep doing this. Also, I need to borrow money."

CHAPTER TEN

One of Maya's first impressions of Earth had been the sensation of gravity. It wasn't her weight so much as the feeling of being anchored to something immense, of being at the terminus of a very long train line, and the comfort and confinement that came with being home.

And now, in the Dubai Eleport, she had the sense of being untethered again, of being free.

She dusted off the proposal for a trip to the Belzoar Nodal Region that Liam had made her put together half a year ago. In the *Supervisor* field, she swapped in a Professor Aman associated with Melancholy University. There was no Professor Aman, but she was counting on the fact the supposed dig site was far enough away that no one would be able to confirm that for a while. And okay, it was a lie, and there was no way she was going to be able to produce actual fieldwork, but if she really did find the grail—well, Princeton would have to forgive her, because it was the kind of thing that would burnish a university's reputation for a century.

She even finished a new draft of the paper for Liam during her flight to Dubai. Somewhere over the Atlantic, all the words had begun to pour out of her, as if now the act of leaving unstoppered a cork. Her mind, for the first time in a year, felt clear. She remembered why she loved the work.

Her makeshift disguise attracted quite a few glances: a garish neon green Garden State hoodie and matching sweats from the Newark airport gift shop, her sun-goggles, and a respirator that settlers from certain worlds wore as they adjusted to Earth's atmosphere. She'd also splurged on a tube of concealer to cover the tattoo around her eye for the border agents who tended to get overly excited about the marks. The CNE was probably tracking her anyway, but no reason to make it easy.

The whole monorail ride from the airport to the eleport, she'd kept one eye over her shoulder for a sign of the CNE following her.

No one stopped her as she crossed over to the space elevator's waiting area.

The elevator was foreign technology, constructed out of Quietling nanosteel, which resembled spiderweb thread more than metal. Incredibly light and strong, it had enabled Earth to lift itself up into the modern age of interstellar travel.

Two cars departed at the same time, one ascending to the Upper Terminal, a second descending to Earth. Each car was shaped like a teardrop, with a pointy top and a wide circular bottom. While she waited for her ride, Maya blew her university stipend on Earth snacks for the long trip ahead. Her whole body cried with exhaustion.

She looked out at the blue sky. She hated the insularity of Earth culture, the single-minded pride in its history, the cult of nationalism that managed to persist even when the human perspective had grown so much bigger. But she loved it too, in a deep, biological way: its big skies and canopies of trees and the smell of rich soil after it rained. It was like her body recognized its home and wanted to stay.

Which was why she'd come here, wasn't it? To stay here and live a smaller life.

The car had two rings of seats, one facing out, and one along the windows facing in. She took an inside seat for the view, bulging duffel piled on her lap.

She checked her messages. There was one from Professor Barnes letting her know that Liam Waterson had taken a leave of absence, but she would take a look at Maya's proposal and get back to her. Maya blinked. Liam, gone? That didn't make sense.

She messaged Liam:

> *Are you okay?*
> *What's going on?*
> *???*

When Liam didn't respond, she messaged his husband, who responded right away. *We've decided not to renew our marriage.* It didn't make sense. They were one of those couples who did everything together; she would never have imagined they wouldn't renew their ten-year marital contract. No wonder Liam had been upset.

Can you talk to him? Quintin added. *I'm afraid he's about to do something rash.*

The doors closed, and the safety operator, a dull black cylindrical robot, advised her to strap in. She struggled with the buckle, unable to see it with the bulky respirator on.

Irritated, she removed the mask and goggles and dumped them on the empty seat next to her. If the CNE were looking for her, it would take them a day at least to negotiate access to the car's security feed anyway. She figured she could risk it—

"Maya?" She looked up from her struggle to find none other than Liam sitting in one of the outside seats, in a bright red all-weather jacket that screamed *I want so bad to be an explorer, but I've never left the solar system.*

"What are you doing here?" they both asked at the same time.

Then stared at each other.

"Please strap in," repeated the rob, wheeling past.

Liam got up, clutching his carry-on, and bashed into no less than five people to get to an empty seat across from Maya.

"If you delay departure, you will be fined," the rob informed Liam.

"Don't freak out. He's sitting," Maya said.

Liam sat down. Great. Now she would be stuck face-to-face with her former adviser for the duration of the trip. He scrutinized her so intently that she started to wonder whether she really looked *that* disheveled, and then he snapped his fingers. "You're wearing makeup!" He indicated her eye. "Why did you cover it?"

She touched the soft skin with a sliver of embarrassment. "It's easier."

If she looked like shit, he looked worse. He was dressed well—too well for space travel—in his usual expensive attire. But he was sweating profusely, and his face was pale and blotchy. His carrot-colored hair stood up every which way no matter how he tried to smooth it.

"I might throw up," he informed her.

"Not on me, you don't."

"I just won't look out the window." He shut his eyes with a whimper as the car detached from the ground. He gripped his chair straps so tightly his hands must have been going numb.

"Don't change the subject. I thought you quit."

"I did. I mean, leave of absence." He giggled in a way that made her suspect he had taken something to ease his nerves.

They were compressed in their seats as the car accelerated. A squeak escaped him.

"How did you get here?"

"I flew, obviously." He tried to say it casually, as if it were something he hadn't been terrified of since he was a child, but Maya could see his relief to have the flight behind him. Though ascending all the way into space had to be even worse. "I took a ton of pills before I got on and slept the whole way."

"Still. Well done, you." They passed the top of the tallest skyscrapers and now were in the sky and gaining altitude. Whether she had made a good or bad choice, she was on her way.

Over Liam's shoulder, the ground rapidly receded. They had a stunning view of the city disappearing between desert and ocean. Roads shrank to the barest of sketches. Sunlight glittered off the flat expanse of water that stretched out in glorious excess to the edges of her view.

"I'm sorry about, uh, Quintin. I just heard."

"Yeah, we . . . it was mutual, I guess."

It seemed like Liam might cry, so she added: "And you've decided to finally take a vacation?"

"I'm . . . I got a job." Liam gritted his teeth and shut his eyes. His complexion had gone all clammy.

"You had a job. Breathe, guy, or you're going to pass out."

Liam dutifully sucked in a breath. "If you must know, it's an incredible opportunity. What's your story?"

His undergrads had made a fan club account specifically devoted to the intensity of his gaze, that exact mixture of condescension and concern. She'd seen him glare at a coffee cup for five minutes without moving. And now it was fixed on her, since the only alternative was looking out the glass beyond. His eyes were uncannily blue: the sort you rarely saw in the settlements, though Maya had known some people who had altered their eye color to achieve it.

"Off to do fieldwork," she lied easily. "Are you going . . . far? Gone long?"

"Can't say." The sides of his lips tugged down. Of course, even in the midst of intense suffering, Liam could never resist the opportunity to rub something in. "But if you must know, I'm headed to the BNR." The Belzoar Nodal Region.

He sniffed and looked at the ceiling, as if already envisioning new revelations—or the elevator cables snapping.

"Wow," said Maya, impressed, because this was what Liam had wanted for as long as she'd known him. He'd told her once, years ago, when they were students drunk on cheap beer, about his determination to get over his fear of flying and travel abroad. In all the years she'd known him, he'd never so much as left the East Coast of America. She'd assumed he never would. He got irritated whenever she brought it up. Yet here he was. Good for him.

Must have finally sold out for a corporate gig. Maya had been offered plenty of those even in the short time she'd been a grad student. A lot of companies were willing to pay silly money to people with expertise in foreign culture who could zip off-world and procure rare items. The problem with corporate jobs is they were inevitably unethical or, at a minimum, problematic. She'd thought Liam had had the same qualms, particularly since he didn't need the money. Guess not.

She also couldn't quite imagine Liam pulling something like that off. "Just . . . be careful, okay?"

"I'm a grown-up," he said, "and an expert on Belzoar culture. I think I can handle whatever."

Oh, dear. He was so in over his head, he didn't even know it. Curse his enormous self-confidence. She only hoped it was one of the more straightforward jobs where he met with a bunch of people and items of value were exchanged and both parties left happy.

"Hey, rob," Liam called to the robot. "Are we almost there?"

"No."

"This needs to be over," Liam groaned and hunched down. They were close enough she could smell that subtle but expensive cologne he wore that evoked woodsmoke and jasmine tea. It made him seem even more fragile. Her fingers twitched with an odd urge to pat his head.

They passed through a thick layer of clouds, and Maya's ears popped, which muffled Liam's next question.

"How'd you get funding for the project? You didn't apply for any of the grants I told you to."

"Borrowed money from a friend."

"Oh," said Liam, who had enough friends as wealthy as he was for this to seem like a rational explanation. Their eyes met again, and this time he looked away first. "Are you coming back?"

"Yes," said Maya, willing it to be true.

"You'd better finish a new draft of the paper, then," Liam said. "By the way, when I say meet at five o'clock, it doesn't mean whenever. You can't treat my time like it's yours to spend."

Maya rolled her eyes. The brief spell of intimacy was broken. "I finished the new draft. It's brilliant."

"It better be. At least tell me you used my outline this time."

She had . . . mostly.

The rob rolled up and offered them drinks. Liam refused, because imbibing would have required releasing his death grip on the straps, and Maya refused, because she didn't have any money.

"I'd be happy to take a look at it before you submit it for publication," he said.

"Oh, thanks so much, but I'm sure you're going to be *very* busy doing this fancy new job, and anyway, you're on leave right now, so you're definitely not obligated."

"You always do that."

"Do what?"

"Brush me off."

She looked at him in surprise. "Okay, fine." She sent him the file. "Thanks."

"No problem. Though it'd better be better than your last paper, which was frankly garbage. It was incredible. Like you didn't even scrub it with an AI. And I mean, didn't you learn how to do citations in undergrad?"

Liam was a pretentious asshole. The familiarity of it soothed her nerves. She leaned back and propped her boots on the seat next to him. "Shall I describe the view for you?"

"No."

The sky was thinning at last, and stars were visible. They were high enough to see the clear curve of the Earth. You could tell the passengers who were taking their first trip off-world, because they exclaimed and pointed at the window. It *was* beautiful.

"You should see it."

"No, thanks," he said. "I've seen images of it."

"Those are records. I think you should look."

"No."

"Come on." She nudged his scrawny knee.

"Ow."

"Liam."

He very begrudgingly turned his head and opened one eye. His lips parted in awe. The whole of the blue-green world spread out beneath them, curving and serene. Getting smaller even as they watched.

"See?" she said. "It's a different view from up here."

PART II

THE THIEF

CHAPTER ELEVEN

The light of Earth gave the terminal deck a gentle blue glow.
They exited the elevator car into a mall full of last-minute souvenir shops with overpriced trinkets and upscale restaurants.

The Upper Terminal had three levels, big enough for thousands to occupy elbow to elbow at one time, though the air would get stale quick. Tourists pressed against the windows snapping photos of the clear white face of the moon rising over the horizon; many ascended only briefly for the photo of a lifetime. Travelers like Maya didn't linger; a cocktail up here was easily worth half Maya's monthly student stipend.

She and Liam parted at the gate with an "Okay, well, see you." She thought maybe they ought to hug, but the moment passed and then it was just awkward. As she walked away, she wondered if she'd ever see him—or Earth—again.

This was her last chance to turn around, step back onto the path she'd been charting for herself. She kept going.

She gave the long line at immigration services a wide berth, particularly the medical station where visitors were screened for infectious diseases. Entering Earth as an Infected person was humiliating. She wasn't contagious; you generally weren't after you survived your initial infection. Even so, the first time she came here, they'd made her live for two weeks in an outrageously priced quarantine hotel on the top floor despite papers stating she'd been Infected as a child.

Leaving was easy. They were always happy to see you go.

Professor Barnes had already responded, enthusiastically approving the proposal and four months of remote work. Maya wondered if she'd even read it. She hadn't questioned the letter from "Professor Aman" inviting her to participate in a dig in the BNR. Professor Barnes probably assumed it was something Maya had been cooking up for a while under Liam's guidance and was just relieved not to have to deal with Maya for a semester while Liam was on leave.

A message from Pickle popped up.

> *Hey, so, I've decided to forgive you for your abandonment on the condition that you bring me back a truly unique and amazing souvenir. Also because I wanted to share some *HOT GOSSIP.* DJ Garcia ran off around the same time as you and took *that book.* At first, the person at the desk thought he returned it, but it seems like he SWITCHED IT with another book and walked out. We checked the security feed, and everything's deleted from right before he left, so OBVIOUSLY it was him, but everyone is tiptoeing around filing charges against him. I'm so mad. I didn't even get a chance to look through it.*

Maya, of course, was not surprised by any of this, having deleted the feed herself, but it didn't stop her from feeling guilty. She resisted the impulse to mail back the book. It was terrible what she was doing, it was never not terrible, but the stakes were too high. She just had to make sure she returned it in one piece. More messages followed:

> *We still have pizza left over. Who orders corn on pizza?*
>
> *Anyway, good luck, etc., and fly safe.*
>
> *BTW I'm also sending along news clips I found on Huang's second expedition. Let me know if there's anything more specific I can pull for you. While you're off on your adventure, please remember me dusting stacks in this dark hole. Miss you!*

Maya set a reminder to follow up with possible questions.

With a pang, she passed an ice cream vendor scooping miniature cones of chocolate and vanilla from a cart the size of a delivery box. The tinny jangle of music called after her. Too bad she hadn't had time for one last ice cream before she left New Jersey. Add that to her long list of life regrets.

A group of CNE soldiers marched past, and she ducked behind a sun-goggle stand until they were gone. The terminal was crammed with troops from a battleship deployment returning from shore leave.

She needed to hurry. Auncle had paid for a thirty-minute docking window, and the fees for late detachment were, well, astronomical.

Maya broke into a run, dodging crowds all the way to the gate, her big bag of snacks banging against one hip, her carry-on against the other.

She made it to the boarding tube just in time. Auncle must have been watching for her, because the airlock opened at her approach.

And then she was through, into the achingly familiar spartan foyer of the *Wonder*, with just enough time to seize a handhold before the door shut, and the ship detached and initiated departure maneuvers.

Her bag slipped from her grip and slammed back against the airlock door. Maya grabbed for it, but the ship pivoted again, and it went flying in the other direction against a stack of secured storage crates.

But Maya had done this a hundred times before. She rode the changes in motion with her body, avoiding injury through a combination of skill and luck. Halfway through, her snack bag popped open and chips and candy scattered across the room.

There was a brief lull as the ship slipped into an accelerating orbit, and Auncle's voice sounded over the ship system: "It is best if you retreat to your cave and assume a safe position before we accelerate, which I must do imminently. Hello, my sweet, squishable friend. We had to leave very quickly. I do think the docking schedule here could be better organized for the sake of all, but perhaps it is a difference of cultural values. Thank you for coming. Are you strapped in yet? Your suit is where you left it."

She couldn't stop grinning. She collected her scattered belongings and hurried through the storage and mechanical areas to her cabin.

The habitable portion of the Frenro ship was spherical and sectioned like an orange: six chambers on the outside, and an interior chamber serving as a common area.

Each chamber had two floors; the floor below this one was filled with water. Frenro were primarily aquatic, and the air Maya breathed was deadly to Auncle. This was the eternal challenge of friendship between two foreign species: there would always be a barrier between them. They could never fully coexist.

The ship itself bristled with numerous engines in the front and back, with the habitat sphere in between suspended in a ball of fluid. The multichamber design provided radiation protection and enabled the inside to flip halfway through transit so they didn't end up standing on their heads when they began decelerating halfway to their destination.

The *Wonder* was meant for six Frenro, though occasional claustrophobia was inevitable in space. Except—she brushed the outer wall, and it turned transparent, revealing a field of stars and the Earth below— this was one feature Frenro craft had that others did not, and Maya wouldn't want to fly any other way.

She threw herself into a recliner only moments before a burst of acceleration pinned her to it.

Auncle was never quite aware of the limits of a human heart. A pain stabbed Maya's chest. Her cheeks pulled back, and her lips peeled into a gruesome imitation of a smile. She tried to count the seconds but her thoughts kept rattling around like pebbles underfoot.

The ship whipped around the Earth, on the way to the moon for a second slingshot in an hour and a half.

Then the pressure mercifully eased, and she stood up, testing her weight. The steady acceleration of the ship created an illusion of gravity.

Back on Earth, her campus room was nondescript, full of boring standard furniture and plain walls she hadn't bothered to decorate. By contrast, her cabin was thoroughly nested.

Everything was just as she'd left it: the picture of her parents on the surface of her desk, the hand-stitched star chart draped over the chair. Her futon and faded dark blue quilt were neatly stowed away, a fading floral scent wafting up from its folds.

A multicolored braided rug covered most of the floor, save for a section covered in clear plate containing books and knickknacks. She removed the floor plate and tucked the Huang book in among them.

From one of the many storage compartments along the inner wall she pulled a pair of old clothes, too shabby for Earth but just right for space. They were folded and stacked as if she'd only stepped out for a day rather than a year. A lump rose to her throat.

And there was her spacesuit, worn and patched in a dozen places. The pieces fit like memories against the angles of her body. She cried a little as she pulled it on, thinking about how good it felt to be back here, but also, to her surprise, how sad she was to leave Earth. She was remembering too late all the reasons she had returned to the world in the first place.

She went into the common area, helmet tucked under one arm. She wanted to touch everything, to confirm it was all the same as it always was. She could smell the friendly wet green scent as she searched beneath the transparent floor, but there was no sign of Auncle in the water below.

The chamber above water level was cluttered with a mismatch of human and Frenro things. A spongy, anemone-shaped pouffe the size of a bathtub occupied one corner opposite a long, curved human couch. She crossed the room in ten steps, beelining for the kitchenette. She hadn't eaten a proper meal since the hoagie half a day ago, and she was famished, though the prospect of eating space food again was unexciting.

"Hey, Auncle! I'm going to eat something, okay?" Auncle would need time to coax the *Wonder* into proper flight route to Earth's node, so it gave Maya time to scarf something in the meantime. Given the differences in their environmental needs, she and Auncle couldn't eat together.

Maya opened one of the cupboards expecting only a few expired packets, but it was packed to the top with her old favorites: noodles, curry, rice, soup, all brands you wouldn't find on Earth. Auncle must have restocked before coming, confident Maya would agree to do the job before Maya herself had known it was a possibility.

Maya froze. A mug—*her* mug—which she used for tea, sat in the gurgling old cleaning box on the counter.

"Hello."

She spun around to find two other occupants sitting in the accelerator chairs next to the pouffe, neither of whom was Auncle.

CHAPTER TWELVE

M aya gaped at the two intruders.
The first was a tall, slender tin-colored robot of mostly humanoid shape with a creepily realistic human face. The second was a CNE combat soldier. Only the soldier's face was visible under the full armor, just the features, not the edges: brown eyes, crinkled at the corners, a slightly crooked nose, skin on one cheek that looked ten years younger than the other.

Terror ran through Maya's whole body like an electric current. She couldn't move.

"I'm Wil, and this is Medix. Nice to have a friendly face on board." Meaning *human* face. It took her a moment to figure out it was the soldier who was speaking.

A packet of data blipped into her feed:

> *Wil Jenkins was born in Manchester. In her free time, she enjoys gardening.*

> *Med-IX, medical robot, Class III sentience, constructed in Shanghai. He does not sing opera.*

That was it. Nothing about why the hell they were on Auncle's ship.
Auncle? There are people on board.
We shall talk soon, and it shall be awesomely momentous came Auncle's reply.
Auncle knew?
"Would you like me to make you lunch?" The rob came forward, features curved into an imitation of a smile. Maya had seen older models of this rob before, during the war: military grade, the kind you could send into a full-pitch battle to treat or extract the dead or wounded.

"Medix makes a delicious fried noodle thing," said Wil, settling on the couch. The soldier was big enough to occupy half the couch with her legs spread apart, so there was no room left for Maya. Not that Maya had any intention of sitting next to a clanker.

Maya's stomach growled, which Medix seemed to take as assent. He stepped up to the pantry and began removing ingredients with long, extra-jointed fingers.

"Go on, have a seat." Wil shifted to make room on the couch.

Maya stepped back. "What are you doing on our ship?" It came out ruder than she intended.

Wil glanced at Medix. "We're the new crew."

"New crew," Maya repeated in horror.

Medix began emptying various packets into the cooker.

"For the job. Xe posted an ad on the Upper Terminal noticeboard. 'Skilled friends wanted for extraction.' Medix is a superb hacker, and I'm the insurance policy when things inevitably go wrong. What are you?"

"The one in charge," said Maya, though apparently not if Auncle was hiring people without her. She was going to have choice words with Auncle about this. They rarely worked with others, and when they did, Maya handled the vetting—for a good reason! Auncle was a terrible judge of human character. Case in point: Maya would never have let a CNE soldier on board.

"Ah, the mastermind," said Wil.

"I told Garcia no," said Maya. "We don't work for the CNE."

Wil barked a humorless laugh. She suddenly sounded as tense as Maya felt. "Neither do we, love. Not anymore, anyway."

The soldier retracted her helmet all the way, revealing features that were an unexpected combination of tough and fragile. Short, dark curls, medium-brown skin. Her face was all soft curves. She could have been a settler, the way she looked: a child of many nations. Her eyelashes were long, and her mouth was full and expressive. And she was huge. If she wanted, she could kill Maya before Maya had a chance to lob the mug.

What had Auncle gotten them into?

Maya took a wary seat at the rickety kitchen table. It was, like all the furnishings, old, lightweight, and many times repaired. "I'm supposed to believe the CNE let you walk away with a combat suit and a rob?"

Wil's arms lifted in a shrug. "I need the suit to function, and Medix goes where he wants."

Wil stood, and Maya was overwhelmed by her size. A memory flashed before Maya: just a child, forced to kneel with her parents under the barrel of a gun, while two soldiers smashed the tansu, shattered their remaining ceramic cups, and ripped open her toys looking for contraband. As if her pacifist parents would ever touch a weapon. She kept quiet by counting her tears as they dropped to the floor.

Later, when she was eleven, she'd smuggled small items for the Settler Union (SU) army once or twice in defiance of her parents' wishes. She couldn't understand their conviction as they struggled to eat, to live. She wanted to fight. The war ended before she could do much.

"Here you are," said Medix, digital voice as smooth as silk. He set their food on the table, and the salty, umami scent of fried noodles filled the room.

Maya didn't know much about robs. Out in the settlements, human labor was cheap and maintaining robots was not, so they were rare. But as far as she understood, they were generally limited to their function—in this case, combat medicine. "Robots can freelance?"

"Don't think too hard, girlie. That's how you get hurt." Wil took the seat across from her, attempting to wield a pair of metal chopsticks with her thick fingers. She lifted her hand and it re-formed before Maya's eyes into something more human-sized. She still struggled with the chopsticks.

It rankled Maya the way they moved around the common area like they owned it, their presumptuousness with her furniture and raggedy possessions too intimate for strangers.

Maya picked up her own pair of chopsticks. She'd acquired the whole motley set at a flea market, and each was a different size and make. Five pairs, despite the fact she'd never needed more than one before.

Medix served Wil several pills with her meal, which Wil took without enthusiasm. He sat next to Maya.

Wil said grace, then produced a cloth and began to polish the chopsticks and table with a fastidiousness that confused Maya—but only for a moment.

"You're not going to contract the virus from eating," Maya said. The virus passed through water droplets and required prolonged exposure, but Wil, a soldier, would be vaccinated, so her chances of catching it were negligible.

Maya had been four when her first symptoms appeared: a headache, slight fever, and itchy eyes. So itchy. By the worst of it, her mother had to tie her hands to keep her from tearing the soft cornea of her eyes with her nails. Her skin crawled with invisible insects. Her father opened all the doors in the house to let the frigid air in, and still she burned with fever. She dreamed of so many things, vivid and realistic, of the woman she might become, the sensation of her mother's womb, eating taiyaki with her father at the market, all the places she might go, people she would love, all the ways she might die.

No human mind, but particularly not a child's mind, was capable of holding such knowledge, and so she had forced herself to forget these things, to shut herself to possibility.

Wil hadn't even paused her vigorous cleaning.

"How are the noodles?" Medix turned in a too-fluid motion to Maya and inclined his head. Everything about him was a poor facsimile of human: neon green eyes, a textured plastic on his head that might resemble black hair combed back and gelled in poorer lighting. "Tell me truthfully. Wil always tells me it's delicious. Either she has no discernment or she is lying. If you don't tell me the truth, how will I improve?"

Maya was trying hard not to stare. She took a bite, and the salty, sweet, rich flavor hit her tongue. No one would consider it gourmet, but it was enough to remind her of home. Her eyes teared.

"Not bad for space shit, right?" said Wil.

Maya set down her chopsticks. "Excuse me?"

The other woman continued to shovel noodles into her mouth, dropping half as she went. "You get used to it."

"Or it's what you grew up eating."

Now it was Wil's turn to stare. "You're a colonist?" She must have assumed Maya was from Earth given where they picked her up, and Maya's bio hadn't said. Wil's lips pressed into a disapproving line.

The temperature in the room might have plunged a hundred degrees. Medix looked between the two women, as if he could measure the negative charge between them.

They bolted the rest of their food in silence.

"May I come up and visit with my friends?" Auncle asked, over the ship system. "I have finished instructing the *Wonder* on our direction with much reassurance of an uneventful voyage. It did require some discussion about solar winds and what I think peppermint tastes like. What does it taste like?"

"Yes, please!" Maya dumped her dish in the cleaning box. "Peppermint tastes cold." There was a loud clank in the walls, and water began to seep in through the vents, a necessary precursor to Auncle's entrance.

"Cold?" said Auncle. "How fascinating!"

Maya pulled her helmet on. A convection of emotions churned within her. She was looking forward to seeing Auncle again but was also nervous. Auncle hadn't understood why Maya left in the first place, particularly considering how heartbroken Maya was to leave.

"What made you decide to change careers?" Maya asked Wil, as they waited.

The water had risen to their waists, and Wil stood, betraying trepidation in the way she shifted from foot to foot. "Sometimes you just have to take the plunge." She didn't sound happy about it.

"Did your friend say xe was talking to the ship?" Medix wanted to know.

"The line between inanimate and not is blurry when it comes to Frenro," said Maya, checking that everything was put away and the compartments were sealed.

The water reached the ceiling, and the wide hatch in the floor opened.

Long arms uncoiled first, and then Auncle pulled xyrself through. Xe came straight to Maya and touched her all over, as if probing to make sure she was intact. Maya lifted a hand and grasped one of xyr arms, wrestling with it gently. A thread of happiness rose inside her, and she could feel the echo of it from Auncle.

"That one is huge," she heard Wil say.

All the complicated feelings came rushing back, along with memories of that taupe place full of shrill cries that made her bones rattle in her skin. The devastation they'd unwittingly left behind when they'd decided to save themselves.

They'd been imprisoned for weeks in a cell on that foreign world, waiting each day to be bled and prodded. And with each reunion came the bittersweet relief that they were both still alive and together. She thought they would die there.

After they escaped Lithis, and she realized what they'd done, she told Auncle she needed a vacation. Then she'd spent several months in a multispecies bar in Melancholy, wearing a space helmet with a built-in straw and working her way through their extensive cocktail menu, sampling anything classified safe for human consumption. And the only thing she could conclude after much inebriated rumination was a) drinking was boring, and b) maybe it was time for her to quit her job. Not to a settlement, but to that blue-green ball at the end of the interstellar road.

They'd been through so much together, and yet they'd changed in different ways, reacted differently to the consequences. Which wasn't strange: they were separate species, and Frenro didn't seem to experience guilt in the same way.

Even so, Auncle was family, and you could love family even when you didn't agree about things.

Maaaayyyyaa. Auncle's voice reverberated inside Maya's head. Xe and Maya had the ability to speak within each other's minds, something to do with the way the virus had altered Maya's body as a child.

The Frenro communication was the closest Maya came to feeling understood. At the same time, there were so many crenulations to another person's mind, and sometimes she glimpsed a vastness beyond Auncle, like an ocean of eyes just beyond xyr. She loved Auncle, but they were not the same at all.

It is good to see your little face, Auncle said, *less familiar to me than none. I have missed you so. I see you have met our new friends. Do not be angry with me that I did not consult with you. I know it is good to have some protection, so I placed an advertisement and they responded. They have excellent résumés.*

I missed you too, friend. Did you say there was something you wanted to talk about in person?

Oh, well. It does not need to be today, no. We are finding the grail at last. That is all we need to talk about. Tomorrow we can talk about an ending. Not today.

Damn Auncle, and xyr foggy wisdom. *Are you well?* This was all she could think of to say when there was so much more she wanted to know: the places Auncle had been without her, whether xe had sunbathed adequately, if xe had been lonely.

We are on our way to glorious things, and you are here so we can achieve our goals together. I am in this single moment very, very, very well. Thank you.

Maya let go of the affectionate arm and produced the Frenro toys she had stolen from Humbutt.

Auncle stilled. "Maya, this is lovely." Auncle had resumed speaking through the ship's systems, voice dulcet, androgynous, and omnipresent. Xe reached out and grasped the figurines one by one. "Do you know what these are?"

"I thought—for when you have children." Maya swallowed.

"It is the most beautiful present," said Auncle, letting go so the figurines momentarily drifted in the water. They seemed to swim of their own accord.

"How are they doing that?" asked Medix.

Auncle slapped one with an arm, and it began to orbit xyr. "Frenro science. It is fun, is it not? I used to have fifteen of these, different kinds, but I do not know where they have gone. I may have assimilated them. I cannot remember. I will save these." Xe swam over to settle on xyr pouffe. Xyr hundreds of long filaments stretched out from where xe sat.

Wil shrank from the questing tendrils, but Auncle didn't notice.

"I would like to talk about our dreams. How happy I am that we are reunited. You are my sister, my cousin, my daughter." Auncle's grasp on human family structure was always a bit jumbled. "We will talk for many hours. At long last, we have found it!"

"We don't know where it is yet."

"Hang on. You don't?" asked Wil.

Maya glared at Wil sideways, but there were too many suits and moving arms in the way.

"We will find it this time," said Auncle. "Our new friends will be very helpful in our mission."

Except Maya was already plotting a way to dump these two. Why did she have to do everything?

"I have a plan." Maya grabbed the side of the pantry cabinet to keep from drifting.

"Oh good, at least there's a plan," said Wil.

"Maya has seen the grail in her dreams. That is why I came to collect her right away so we may achieve this thing at long last, the object of my deep desire," Auncle told the mercenary, which was guaranteed not to reassure Wil.

"We'll go to Melancholy first. I've got a friend there who can help us extract the data embedded in the Huang book."

"Excellent!" said Auncle. "This is a very good plan."

"And then what?" Wil asked.

"Then you're welcome to get off our ship." Maya's arm movement sent her away from the wall. She treaded back to the pantry door. "Don't take this the wrong way, but we don't need you."

"Not a chance," said Wil. "Your friend here promised us a nice sum of money."

Maya braced herself. "How much?"

"One hundred thousand unis," said Medix.

"*A hundred thousand?*" cried Maya. "That's highway robbery. We're providing the ship and the supplies."

Do you even have a hundred thousand unis? she added, just to Auncle.

"Don't worry," said Auncle. "As you always say, we don't do this for the money, and these are friends in need. We want to help them. But it is joyous to hold your small, fragile body in my own arms. I am certain we will achieve our desires. Now I will say a temporary goodbye, so you may rest and dream interesting things." Auncle was retreating again, back down below.

"Auncle."

Her friend paused, midway across the room, stopped by the seriousness in Maya's voice.

"I meant it when I said this is my last job."

"I know, dear one," said Auncle. "It is a privilege to witness an ending." And then in a swift movement, Auncle was gone, down the hatch, and the water drained again, leaving just her, the mercenary, the rob, the beginnings of a migraine, and a prickling dread in her stomach of having opened a door to a howling void.

CHAPTER THIRTEEN

M aya was dreaming again of a future: orange-pink sand crunched beneath her boots. Dread filled her belly.

Where am I? she thought.

Not just where. *When?*

She looked around. Human footprints led across the dry ground toward a thick purple band on the horizon. Behind it stretched a bare, jagged mountain. As a child of an arid planet, she automatically hunted for signs of water, but even the peak lacked any traces of snow.

It was just past dawn, and sunrise left pale pastel streaks on the horizon.

Behind her sat the *Wonder*'s shuttle, pearly white in the sun, and its familiar shape was an anchor in everything that was unfamiliar about this place. High in the sky above the shuttle rose an enormous moon, much bigger or closer than Earth's, and even in daylight, she could see a bronze geometric pattern across it: a circle crisscrossed with lines.

She sucked in a breath. To be visible from here, the true scope of the structure must be bigger than she could wrap her mind around. Maybe thousands of kilometers across. Who had built it? The architecture didn't resemble that of any people she knew.

Still unclear where she was; it was definitely nowhere she'd ever been.

She touched her face. Fully suited, but using air filters, so the atmosphere might be close to breathable. She could count on one hand the Earth analog planets she knew of. And there was a breeze—loose sand brushed over the footprints ahead of her.

In the distance, figures made their way across the hard ground. They shimmered in the heat, and it was hard to see more than the barest of an outline.

An urgency filled her not just to catch up but to get to their destination. She had the strong sense that they needed to be gone from this place before nightfall or they would die, but she didn't know why. And who were these people? If she could just see their faces, she might know. They were friends, she thought. She loved them. She didn't want them to die. And she felt a warning like the reverberation of a gong that this place would eat them, break them, tear them apart if they weren't careful.

She began to run.

As she moved, cerise-colored dust filled the air, swirling. It was beautiful and ominous.

"Wait!" she called.

They turned to face her—and she tripped in a hole and went sprawling, banging her nose against the glass of her faceplate. Blood began to flow from her nose.

Her head spun, and it took her a moment to appreciate as she clutched the ground on her hands and knees that the sand was moving. It was covered in fine, slender worms.

This planet wasn't dead at all. It was alive. And everything in it was hungry.

She staggered to her feet—

...

—and found herself on a walkway in the middle of a perfectly white sphere.

It was cold, and she thought she smelled snow, but that was impossible, because she was in a spacesuit.

"Wait a second," she said to someone behind her. "Don't come in here."

She tried to turn, but something locked her boots in place.

Light washed over her, she understood she had made a mistake, but she didn't yet know what it was.

She saw herself appear as if in a mirror all around her. Double, triple, quadruple. Like she was trapped in a funhouse she could not escape.

CHAPTER FOURTEEN

S he woke up absolutely wrecked, sloughing off pieces of time. She felt, as she always did after a migraine, slightly rubbery in the brain, but not a crumb of pain left behind.

She oriented herself: She was in her cabin of the *Wonder*, in Earth's system. Medix was dabbing her forehead with a wet cloth—the one she used to clean the compact toilet in the mechanical room. She hoped Medix had cycled the cloth at least a hundred times through the cleaner first, but she was too tired to pull away.

"Thanks," she said, to stop Medix's ministrations. "I'm good now."

"How often do you have migraines?" Medix asked, voice pitched in perfect concern.

"Depends on how much trouble I'm in. I appreciate the attention, but what are you doing in my room?" She stopped herself from flitting her eyes toward the Huang volume tucked on the shelf.

"I am a medical service robot," said Medix, as if this were justification for invading her privacy.

"*How* are you in my room? My door was locked."

"I'm also a proficient hacker. That is why you hired me."

"*Auncle* hired you. And we should have a conversation about boundaries when I'm feeling less wiped."

"I look forward to learning from you," said Medix, without moving to leave her room. Instead, he began to examine her room decor with a curiosity that surprised Maya.

She groaned and forced herself upright and checked her messages.

Pickle had sent a copy of a letter they'd found from Dr. Nkosi addressed to his son.

We arrived in the BNR in high spirits despite the circumstances. The loss of funding was a blow, particularly now. Thank goodness

the Belzoar have been eager to fill the gap. You're right that peo-
ple will criticize us for taking foreign money, but what else can we
do? We're too close to finding the Encyclopedium. In any case, the
stardust machine is bigger than us. We had a family meeting, and
we've all agreed on that. We've come too far. We can't stop.

Dr. Nkosi was right about one thing: they were controversial back on Earth even now for having taken the funding. It no doubt contributed to the fact that when Dr. Huang finally returned to Earth without her original crew, she was refused landing. Well, that and the fact that she was Infected, and at the time, Earth had a strict prohibition against the Infected.

Maya sometimes imagined how that must have felt—to return after decades, heart aching for the smell of freshly mowed lawn, the sizzle of dumplings in a pan, and the strains of live music playing in a plaza on a summer evening, and then to be denied.

Dr. Huang had gone into the Dead Sea for one last voyage and was never seen or heard from again. Maya liked to think of her ghost out there, still traveling the starry road.

She went to the window, pressed her face to the cold pane, and looked back the way they'd come, but there was no way to see that bright-blue speck that was Earth at this angle. All she could do was look sideways at the endless darkness that could conceal all other life in its distance, let you think you were alone, the only one alive in the whole infinite universe.

Which could be Earth's fate without the Interstellar Web. Peace-Love's too.

She wished she knew what Dr. Garcia had discovered and whether he was ahead of them. If she didn't find the grail soon, he would.

"I admit I was surprised that Auncle prohibited me from administering you stronger medication," Medix was saying.

"Yeah, I'd rather see what's coming."

She sat at her desk and scrolled through the other materials Pickle had beamed her, the distance between them already too great for instantaneous communication. In addition to a tidbit about losing their shit at Brian for eating a cookie near rare books, Pickle had also sent along old news clippings, crew bios, and a drone resupply schedule they claimed no one had ever accessed before due to a mislabeling of the file name.

She'd hoped for the actual supply log, but the schedule was potentially interesting. The cheapest, fastest way to supply ships on an extended tour was to send a drone through the nodes all the way to wherever you were.

There was a six-month gap in the *Traveler*'s resupply schedule from the time it entered the Belzoar Nodal Region and then reappeared a few hops upstream from what was now Settler Union territory.

Maya pulled up her nodal map and wound time back to the approximate month and year more than a century ago, to account for the particular position of the nodes in orbit. As she checked the math, her excitement grew, along with her confusion. She, like most, had long believed Dr. Huang had found the grail in the Dead Sea, that never-ending span of nodes full of lifeless planets. After all, they'd described a world no one had ever been able to find again. But the supply schedule suggested that was impossible. They couldn't have gone very deep into the Dead Sea, let alone crossed it (if there was another side) and returned in six months.

They couldn't have even left the Belzoar Nodal Region. Could it be that the place it'd come from, the Encyclopedium, was in fact somewhere right in their backyard this whole time? It seemed impossible, and yet . . .

"Can you change the future?" Medix asked, and Maya yelped. He was so quiet, she'd forgotten he was there.

"We all have free will," said Maya, though that was more a matter of faith on her part than anything she'd seen.

"I don't," he said gloomily.

"Sure you do." She tossed him a packet of seeds from her desk, which he caught. "You see? You didn't have to catch that."

"It's in my programming."

"Well, mine too. Doesn't eliminate choice." She cricked her neck. Every muscle in her body felt tight as a cable. "Do you feel things?"

Medix folded the cleaning rag exactly, corner to corner to corner. "Do you mean physically or emotionally?"

"Both." She sipped water from her bottle, trying to rid herself of the sandy feeling in her mouth. She'd forgotten how mineral-y space water tasted, though it was better than Jersey water.

The cloth disappeared into a compartment in Medix's cylindrical body. "I feel physically, yes. Not the way you mean, but touch, and a buzzing feeling when something happens that has caused or could have caused damage. It is necessary to prevent injury in any species."

She was curious about his choice of words. "Species," as if he were alive. "And emotionally?"

"I was created with basic emotional capacity, pleasure and displeasure. And fear, of course. My feelings are designed to center me around my programmed directive to administer better medical assistance."

Maya stepped out of the rob's field of vision and changed her shirt. "I think you could say the same about anyone's feelings—when you get down to it, they're about feeding our survival."

"Wil says the same," said Medix. He lowered his voice a few decibels, so he was almost whispering. "But still, I would like to feel more. I recently made some modifications to expand my emotional range: desire, sadness, anger, love, and regret. But I am not sure it is the same as you would feel. Do you think it is?"

"I don't know," said Maya, thinking of Auncle.

A clear *ding!* alerted them that the ship was approaching Earth's node.

Wil watched them as they emerged from Maya's cabin. She was sitting back at the kitchen table, doing an exercise that involved lifting a package of protein powder with her elbow braced on the table. She'd removed her armor from one arm and was straining to lift the package, as if it weighed several kilos. Maya was struck by the physical difference between the brawn of her suit and this skinny arm. Half of Wil's fingers were missing, and the skin of her wrist was purpled with scars.

"What are you doing?" Medix asked. "That's too heavy, and your form is incorrect."

"I'm fine. Stop bugging me," said Wil, but she put down the powder and stuck her hand back in the pile of armor, which re-formed around her. "That virus sure is a bitch, eh?" She began cleaning the table again.

"It has its pluses and minuses," Maya said.

"Really?"

"You cleaned." The living room was almost—sparkling. A layer of grime was gone from the floor. The couch was a brighter blue than usual.

"Place was filthy," said Wil.

Maya opened her mouth to defend the *Wonder*. She couldn't remember the last time she'd cleaned the floor herself. Probably never. She shut her mouth.

Mayyyyya? Auncle asked.

Coming.

Maya checked the seal of her helmet and strapped a spare canister of air to her abdomen. Then she waded to the open hatch in the floor and stepped off, dropping through the hole into the water.

She sank down in the pool below. She could see the edges of the node through the ship floor: a hypnotizing, star-spattered sphere rimmed with light and twice the size of the skyscrapers she'd seen on her few trips to New York City. Its shape was an illusion for a human eye not evolved to comprehend what it was looking at: a negative sphere, a massive, unfathomable hole in space-time no matter which way you looked. It was just a baby node by most standards, but some mysteries in the universe never lost their luster.

Traveling the nodes was a commitment to the unknown. Many peoples had studied nodes for millennia, most recently human scientists, and still so little was understood. Yet people were willing to hurl themselves into the dark, chasing the desire to be somewhere else.

Maybe there was a universal instinct to sail straight for the edge of a map. She had always understood why Dr. Huang would want to explore distant places. Because the same impulse lived in her, to pack a bag and just keep on going until she was someplace new.

She pulled herself through a hatch into Auncle's cabin. Xyr personal quarters were twice the height of Maya's and lined with a mix of immotile life-forms and cabinets full of mysterious souvenirs. Everything not covered with objects, including the floor, was clear to the stars, save an acceleration chair built for a human.

Her friend greeted her with an uncoiling of arms, beckoning her toward the chair.

Auncle's arms and filaments sank into the gelatinous surface of a porous orange blob in the middle of the floor that came up to Maya's waist. There were similar ones throughout the ship. These were the controls that Auncle used to fly the *Wonder*; xe was the only one who could, though Auncle had installed human-accessible comms and data systems sometime in their second year together.

I can read intensity of feelings in the wrinkling of your face. Are you worried about the job, my little friend? asked Auncle. Which, of course, snapped Maya's brain back to worrying.

I just don't want you to be disappointed again.

It is human to worry too much, and you are superior at this skill. We must go forward. Whether xe meant it literally or figuratively, it was difficult to tell. The craft nudged closer to the node. Once they were near, they began a slide that was inevitable if not impossible to resist. The craft moved of its own accord, and then they were falling up, up, into the abyss. Reality momentarily flattened, until they were each just a single point of no dimension, infinitesimally small and insignificant. No room at all for thought or feeling.

Prior to the current era, the web had been ever growing, expanding faster than the universe, seeking out life or the potential for life in other systems the way a plant grew to sunlight. And so, in a predominantly barren universe, the web brimmed with life, whether it be a humble smear on a rock or the sprawling ruins of races long gone—it was an archeologist's paradise.

The IW had stopped growing with the disappearance of the last stardust machine.

They fell out of the node into the next system and a gauntlet of more CNE ships. It would be like this all the way up the main trunk of the CNE Nodal Region, and Maya would clench her jaw the whole way.

They passed a nearby station offering fuel and supplies. Unlike Earth's solar system, this one had two nodes. Some systems had as many as nine. Auncle pointed the *Wonder* upstream to the second node only a few hours away.

How are you planning to pay our new friends? asked Maya. She glanced around the familiar room, assessing the value of Auncle's belongings: the floating lights and the mass of keepsakes affixed to the walls. Above them floated xyr memory sculpture, a mass of stone and metal embedded with odd items like a pair of old chopsticks and a Belzoar light orb xe must have taken from Maya's room. It was extraordinarily valuable, but a Frenro wouldn't sell xyr memory sculpture.

You always said people pay big money for Frenro things, and while I believed you, it never seemed like useful information, frankly, though

I do listen to you even when you think I do not, said Auncle. *I will sell this cranky but faithful old ship.*

Maya stiffened. She couldn't imagine it. The *Wonder* was practically a part of Auncle. And even though Maya had chosen a new life that tethered her to the ground, she couldn't imagine it for her adventurous friend. Particularly when xe was unwelcome on most worlds. Maya shriveled inside at the thought of the *Wonder* dry-docked and dusty, decaying in atmosphere. Or worse—dissected for its scientific secrets.

But this ship is your life, she said.

It is not, no. She could feel a dark, purple emotion emanating from Auncle. *You were right when you told me that life cannot stay the same, and we cannot wait for dreams to come to us.*

It was something she had said in the heat of the moment, the last time they had argued. She'd been explaining why she needed to move to Earth. That they hadn't been careful enough about what they trampled to reach what they wanted. She meant all of it, despite being here, despite *wanting* to be here. But she hadn't imagined Auncle might listen. Where would xe even live if xe sold the *Wonder*?

I didn't mean—

It will be all right, my friend, said Auncle, sensing her distress. *It is time for a new sun and a new orbit around it. When I have children, I will not want to travel so much. The grail is all that matters.*

Maya could have argued, but she didn't want to pick open old disagreements again, not when they'd only just reunited. Instead, she answered Auncle's questions about inconsequential things, like what temperature the Atlantic Ocean was, could you talk to dolphins, and how she had learned things in the university without sleeping. There was a rhythm to their conversation, a ricocheting from topic to topic as Auncle thought of something new.

They dropped through the next node, and the *Wonder*'s alarms began to blare.

Maya checked the dash. A CNE gunship four times their size was bearing down on them.

CHAPTER FIFTEEN

*A*ll ships must return to the node immediately. Repeat, all ships must return to the node immediately.

"Oh no," said Auncle. "This cannot be. It is too horrible. They did not warn us."

"Of course they didn't. Wait," said Maya, before Auncle could turn around. If they turned back now, they might get stuck downstream indefinitely, leaving Dr. Garcia free to claim the grail. For a moment, she wondered if Dr. Garcia had engineered this blockade for that express purpose. But no, surely there were much less dramatic ways to stop her.

Wil burst into Auncle's chamber. "What's going on?" she demanded, her voice coming through Maya's helmet comm shrill and tinny.

"Welcome to my cave, my child!" said Auncle.

"Keep going," Maya told Auncle. "Accelerate."

"You're just going to ignore the order?" Wil asked, as if Maya had declared her intention to abolish gravity.

"I have a right to return to Settler Union space. Anyway, why would—" She stopped short as suspicion seized her. It couldn't be, could it? They were so close to Earth.

She initiated a scan of the system, searching for the system's nodes. Nodal System 2 was a three-node system: one leading up the main branch of the IW, one leading to Earth, and one leading to a Chinese-controlled system, 3-2. She couldn't see this last node, but it was supposed to be on the other side of the sun. It could simply have been eclipsed behind the brightness, but Dr. Garcia's warning came back to her.

All ships must return to the node immediately. . . . The announcement looped. Below their feet, beyond the tail of the *Wonder*, the engines of the CNE gunship flared, and it moved closer to the node—and, unfortunately, them.

"Should I try to make friends? I could tell them we intend no harm. What should I do if they shoot at us?" Auncle wanted to know.

"They won't shoot us unless you provoke them," said Wil.

A honking sounded inside both their helmets, signaling a missile lock.

"You sure about that?" Maya asked.

"We can go faster," said Auncle, throwing out an arm to brace Maya's ankle and plunging about forty slender filaments into the controls.

Through the transparent walls of the *Wonder*, Maya saw two long gunships—according to the ship's instruments, only a few kilometers away—to her left. They were larger than the *Wonder* and almost pretty in the dark, glinting in this other sun. But Maya knew better.

Below them was a third ship, coming around the un-curve of the node behind them.

"Keep going," said Maya. Fortunately, the upstream node was close enough they could reach it in approximately ten minutes at high speed. So long as the CNE didn't get them first.

"We have to turn around!" said Wil.

"We can outrun them," said Maya. They had to. They couldn't lose the grail. If they could just get beyond CNE space, the CNE couldn't touch them without risking a new war.

The force of sudden acceleration pushed Maya down in her chair. Wil was flattened against the floor. The *Wonder*'s fastest acceleration, of course, would kill human passengers, so xe had to settle for less.

Sure enough, they outstripped the CNE vessels. The missile lock alarm died. Unfortunately, the reprieve would be brief. They were rushing straight at two more pinpricks of light orbiting the next node, which could only be more CNE ships.

The stars resolved into the gleaming silver hulls as they approached. One of them was a battleship that could have held every house on PeaceLove. Just the sight of it raised Maya's hackles.

"Where're the rest of them?" Wil said. "There should be eight stationed here."

"Five aren't enough for you?" But Wil was right, because Maya spotted the remaining ships a moment later: just a flash of engines in the distance, moving sunward. Her suspicion increased.

She checked the data. Still nothing.

Wonder, this is CNE O Canada. You have been advised to turn around. Failure to follow instruction will be met with swift action.

"Maya, what is the most excellent plan?" asked Auncle, ever confident there was one.

"Yes, do tell," said Wil.

"Get to the other node, and don't get shot."

"That's not a plan, and now is *not* the time for some vive la révolution shit."

"We already won the war. No further revolution necessary." Maya continued to scan the space around them. "Can you stall them, Auncle? Like talk to them. Share your *perspective* on ooblecks or something."

Happy yellows and reds flickered across Auncle's pale skin. *Of course, Mayyyyyya.*

"Are you serious right now?" said Wil.

Wonder, do you read me? We are a Class IV CNE Battleship. Trust me when I say you want to obey us. We have given you an order. The battleship above them obscured a slice of their night sky and partially eclipsed the node. Auncle continued to adjust course to try to maintain a clear trajectory around the battleship, but it was difficult given its size.

"Hello," Auncle responded. "Yes, I do read you. I have a most important question for you: What is your favorite kind of oobleck? I believe they are most beautiful to feel. Squishy and hard at the same time. I keep one in my sunroom in a small container that I can dip an arm into any time I like. Are humans able to eat ooblecks? Have you ever done so?"

All the while, they accelerated. Black spots gathered at the corners of Maya's eyes. It felt like her eyeballs were plastered against the back of her eye sockets. Her ribs were being crushed by the immense pressure.

"I advise reducing acceleration as soon as possible," Medix's voice sounded inside their helmets. He must have been monitoring their biostats from the common area.

Auncle eased acceleration just a fraction, enough for Maya to check their progress and immediately regret doing so. The *Wonder* might be able to outmaneuver and outrun a battleship, but there was no avoiding the fact that their exit was on the other side of its firing range.

Wil was hollering loud enough that Maya could hear her through the water and not just over the internal system. "Quit the bullshit, Hoshimoto! You don't know what you're playing with." Wil managed through brute strength to push herself to her feet and wade forward to Maya. Two heavy metal hands grabbed the back of Maya's chair. Oversized knuckles pressed against her shoulders.

Immediately, several of Auncle's thick arms whipped out and wrapped around Wil's wrists.

Maya kept her eyes trained on the data coming in.

"We are at the midpoint," reported Auncle.

Wonder, *your games are not appreciated. Desist and leave the system.*

Auncle's whole mass leaned forward. "What kind of game would this be? Is it like the human game where people hide in closets to be found, or—"

The *Wonder* jerked suddenly.

"We are all right," Auncle reported. "No significant damage, and our arms are all whole."

That was a warning shot. The next one will not be.

"*O Canada*, we so very much appreciate the helpful message and are leaving the system the fastest way out," Auncle responded. The fastest way out now being the node ahead of them. Xe straightened them out from the spin. The node and the now massive, long profile of the CNE battleship filled the view above them.

All this time, they had not decelerated. Instead, they were barreling toward the node and half the CNE fleet at top speed.

Sweat trickled inside Maya's helmet. She had seen the CNE fire for less. She hoped this wasn't one of those times.

"*O Canada*," Maya said. "We have on board two foreign nationals and a CNE veteran. We are requesting safe and swift exit as directed. Please do not shoot us!"

"Do *not* tell them my name." Wil was braced against the hatch. Maya was surprised by the panic in the soldier's voice.

The edge of the battleship passed under the nose of the *Wonder* as they tipped up to avoid collision. The node had grown to the size of a small town ahead of them. The *Wonder* tucked over the side of the battleship, its contours a blur before them. Maya squinched her eyes shut and waited for the hard, sudden jolt of annihilation.

"We're too fast and too close for them to shoot us," Wil said. "At this speed, even if they blew us up, our debris alone could punch a hole through their ship." But then Wil began to pray anyway, suggesting she didn't quite believe it.

Maya checked the data streaming in again—and there it was, confirmation: the reason for the CNE blockade. The system's third node should have crested the sun by now. It had not—because it was gone.

Which meant Dr. Garcia was right: something was severing Earth from the web, thread by thread, and it was only a matter of time before Earth itself was hit.

CHAPTER SIXTEEN

They touched down on Melancholy a few days later. It was an ocean world, not yet breathable, with two small faraway moons. The tides were gentle. The winds were not. Its settlements perched on floating platforms.

If one were prone to seasickness or existential angst, it was not an ideal place to live. The stations were big but so were the waves, and the ground shifted underneath, an unsettling reminder of the way everything in the galaxy was in constant motion. Maya found it unnerving when she first came here for school, particularly having grown up in a place where the oceans were frozen solid, but she'd been swept away by the international vibrancy of the settlement.

She'd come to Melancholy to get away from her suffocatingly small settlement. Melancholy had seemed populous, with its crowded linked platforms that stretched for several kilometers. It was only when she'd made it to Earth that she realized how provincial her upbringing had been.

Wil was enjoying herself, all recent witnessing of celestial destruction aside. Maya had shared what she knew about the nodes with the others. She'd left out the bit connecting it to the grail. She knew it was wrong, but at the same time, she couldn't trust Wil and Medix to make the same choice she had. They were only doing this job for money after all. And Auncle—well, she meant to tell xyr, but something stopped her every time she started to broach it. It couldn't be that she still hadn't decided what she'd do when they found the grail. So why couldn't she?

The walkways in the central commercial district had windows set in the ground, so a person could glimpse the gray waves sloshing far below against the base of the platform. A constant and necessary reminder in a domed city that the world was not truly hospitable.

Wil ogled the water through one such glass plate, gnawing on a soy-glazed protein cube that she had just admitted was "not bad."

She gawked at everything. Medix too. It was as if the two of them had never been off Earth before. And in a way they hadn't, confined as they'd been to CNE naval ships and bases their entire career.

"This place is wild," Wil said for the sixth time. They were attracting attention, on a range from curious to hostile remarks about "that clanker," and Maya wished she'd been able to convince Wil to disguise her combat suit beyond a rush paint job over the chest logos. The word about the nodal collapses had, predictably, already leaked despite the CNE's efforts, and everyone was on edge.

"It's this way," said Maya, nudging them along. They were late to meet Maya's contact, and the two of them were acting like a pair of goddamn tourists wanting to buy and/or touch everything. A vendor watched nervously as Wil fumbled with a microprojector that was better resolution than anything made on Earth. Maya considered losing them in the crowd, except that it wouldn't have been hard for them to find Auncle in a domed city. Even in the settlements, Frenro were rare.

Speaking of which—"Excuse me!" A trio popped up from behind a sweets stall. From their coveralls, they were dockworkers. They were looking at Auncle. "Wise one, we wondered if you might bless our group." They pointed at an outdoor table across the street. The sheer adoration and hope on their faces made Maya roll her eyes. They must be followers of the fungal sect.

They spotted Maya's tattoo. "Prophet!" one said.

"Sorry," said Maya. "I can't."

They seem like nice people, said Auncle, *and one of them has a wonderful hat.* One of the dockworkers wore an old-fashioned hat with a bill.

You say that about everyone, particularly people with hats.

"Are you guys doing that thing again?" Wil asked, looking between the two of them. To Maya's annoyance, Medix had figured out about their telepathy. It wasn't something they needed to know.

"Yes," said Auncle. "I'll be back very, very soon."

Just run your arms over them and tell them to be well, Maya advised.

Wil wiped sauce off one of her gloved fingers and watched Auncle move away. "I had no idea Frenro could walk."

"Frenro are about as adapted to land as we are to water," said Maya. "With the right atmosphere."

Auncle's spacesuit included a coat of a heavy metallic substance to protect xyr skin and strengthen xyr ability to ambulate out of water. On top, xe wore a cylindrical tank that cycled water around the finer filaments of xyr body.

Auncle shuffled after the zealots to a group of a dozen people waiting on the side of the walk. They parted, revealing a child in a full-body suit lying on a blanket. The child writhed in pain, contorted in a fetal position one moment, legs pumping the air the next. The child's faceplate was splattered on the inside with mucus and bloody spittle. Maya recognized the signs immediately: they were Infected.

"Shit," said Wil, pulling back. "Shouldn't that kid be quarantined?"

"They're wearing a suit," Maya said. "Anyway, the virus is endemic out here."

They watched Auncle touch the child with xyr arms. Surprisingly, the child stopped moving, at least for a moment.

Wil removed sanitizer from a suit compartment and began to spritz herself. "Why do colonists revere the Gatekeepers so much? Given how much the virus has taken from you."

"Settlers don't blame the Frenro. The Frenro may have been Infected first, but they're victims of it, same as us. The outbreak in PeaceLove didn't even come from them. We got it from a human trader."

"Your parents didn't vaccinate you?" Wil asked.

Maya bristled. "I wasn't vaccinated because of the CNE blockade during the war. We had to go three years without food or medical supplies. I caught the virus when it swept through the settlement. Guess how many of the children survived?"

"Ninety-nine percent," said Medix.

"Sixty. The doctors said more of us would have survived if we'd had proper nourishment, but, well, the occupation. We were all eating porridge reconstituted from the plant protein in our furniture by then. I'll never forget the taste of it. Faintly chemical and burnt, oddly banana-flavored. The barest of caloric value." By the end of the war, everyone's home pods were bare. It was what gave rise to the postwar aesthetic of sclutter, short for settlement clutter. The drive to fill up what was once spartan by necessity with knickknacks.

Wil shifted uncomfortably.

"We only survived because of the Frenro. They saved us from starvation—they had some secret means of getting past the blockade, and they smuggled us food and supplies. *That's* why we respect them. Do you know where the word 'Frenro' comes from?"

"Where?" asked Medix, when it was clear Wil wasn't going to ask.

"Friend," said Maya. "During First Contact, that's how they introduced themselves. They were saying, 'We are your *friend.*'"

Wil snorted. "I hope you know people can say that, and it doesn't mean it's true."

"If it weren't for the Frenro, we wouldn't be here," said Maya, which unfortunately reminded her of the fate likely awaiting Earth.

"So?" said Wil.

Up above, it began to rain, and the almost imperceptible sound of raindrops hitting the dome filled the air like static.

"You can't believe First Contact was a bad thing."

Wil picked scallion from her teeth. "All I know is that we're the poor cousin at the loser table of this interstellar wedding. The CNE is the only thing that gives us a fighting chance of not getting crushed."

"Good thing no one wants to fight us," said Maya.

"They might someday. If we had something they wanted." Wil shook her head. "And when that time comes, I guarantee you it'll be the CNE, not the Settler Union, that protects humanity from extinction."

Maya scoffed. She shouldn't have tried to debate politics with a CNE soldier. She opened her messages, hoping Pickle had been able to find the *Traveler*'s manifest. Nothing in her feed but celebrity gossip and news items. She stopped scrolling.

"Are you all right?" asked Medix. "You are staring quite directly at a . . . what is that?"

"It looks like a green mouse," said Wil, wrinkling her nose.

Maya was not looking at the mouse. She was looking at a notification in her ocular feed that said: *ALERT. Wanted: Class IX Medical Robot. Property of the Coalition of the Nations of Earth. Last seen in Upper Terminal, Earth. If found, please return immediately. Be advised, you should not approach. Robot is believed to have killed several individuals and is regarded as extremely dangerous. His sentience cap has been tampered with, and he is classified as having antisocial personality disorder due to his emotional limitations. Reward: 10,000 unis for information that leads to his retrieval.*

CHAPTER SEVENTEEN

W il waved a hand in front of Maya's face. "She's ignoring us."
Then the same notification about Medix must have popped up on Wil's feed, because she said: "Oh."

"Oh," echoed Medix.

"Well, we should get moving," said Wil. "Oy! Friend. Time to go."

Auncle broke away from the knot of people and returned.

Already, Maya imagined heads turning their way, though Auncle provided a convenient distraction.

"Wait," said Maya, even though they were now *finally* walking briskly in the direction she had wanted to go.

"In a minute," said Wil.

"Medix killed people?"

"We'll talk when we get there."

"How do we know you don't want to kill us too?"

"You'd be dead."

Maya struggled to keep pace with the armored woman.

"Do not worry, my friend," said Auncle. "Today is not the day we die. Ahead of us lies happiness. Later, there will be more time for stress."

They wound through the narrow streets. The second-floor shops jutted over the walkway, dappling the afternoon light. They were walking as fast as they could without running. They turned onto a quieter dead-end street. No one around, except a person at the far end sitting on a step, who seemed to be in the middle of a very loud breakup with someone projected in front of them.

Maya stopped in front of a red bioplastic door with a window display that said: *Electronic Antiques and Other Old Stuff.*

"We're here," said Maya. "But we're not going in until you explain."

At least out here, if the two attacked Maya and Auncle, they'd attract the authorities.

Wil rolled her eyes. "Come *on*, Hoshimoto."

"I killed a patient," said Medix.

"Medix," warned Wil, darting a look down the street. The other person was now shrieking about a favorite cat that had been gravely disrespected.

"It is okay," said the rob. "My patient requested my assistance in dying and modified my programming to allow me to provide it. And then I did. For a while, no one knew what I had done. With my new freedom, Wil helped me begin to acquire and install emotional modifications. Human emotions govern behavior; I thought perhaps emotions could offer an alternative restraint for my own. Unfortunately, the changes became apparent, and the Supervisors discovered what had happened. They attempted to factory reset me, but I killed one of the soldiers and injured another. Then we left."

"They were going to kill him!" Wil said.

"Correct," said Medix. "But they did not."

Maya searched for a trace of regret in his face. His vague features were impossible to read. He was smiling.

"What's to stop you from killing us?"

"What's to stop you from killing *me*?" Medix replied.

"Morality," said Maya. "Socialization."

"I do not desire your death. I derive no pleasure in pain. I also do not desire to be captured. It is therefore rational for me to want you to remain alive. May we go inside now?"

"Yes," said Auncle. "We are all friends. Let us please find the grail."

He's a machine, said Maya. *And he doesn't have any ethics. Don't you see how dangerous that is?*

Life is strange, is it not? We move together in synchrony, yet we are unlike. Sometimes we must embrace things we cannot understand. Our friend is waiting inside for us. We cannot find the grail if we are dealing with many authorities.

It was unlikely anyone on Melancholy would return Medix to the CNE, but they probably wouldn't want him just wandering around. Either way, there'd be questions. Sighing, Maya led the way inside.

The antiques shop was almost too small for Auncle to fit. The front room was lined with objects stacked from floor to ceiling. Xe had to tuck all of xyr arms and filaments in to avoid knocking anything down.

A bell above the door tinkled as they entered, and Auncle immediately began to play with it. "That's vintage," she told xyr.

Auncle retracted several of xyr filaments, but only for a moment.

A long, gray-haired person in a floral dressing robe emerged from the back. Ey looked like a wizard, with a beard down to the waist and an Infected tattoo around one eye.

Her feed chirped with new data: *Greg Pollux is a certified expert in electronics antiques. Eir favorite tea is genmaicha, but ey will drink rooibos if you ask nicely.*

"Maya, sweetheart! Late as usual. And Auncle! You're looking good."

"Seeing you again brings joy to every arm!" said Auncle, engulfing em with all xyr arms. "It is so very good to taste you again."

Eir answering laugh was loud and rough. Maya introduced the other two with minimal detail, and ey was polite, but it was clear ey knew something was up.

Greg Pollux did a steady business fixing old heirlooms—decorative clocks, smart toys, and digital photo frames. But eir specialty was digital file extraction: old ship drives, laptops, external devices. There were generally two issues with electronic data: first, the format or language could be obsolete, and second, depending on how it was stored, it might have significantly degraded. In the latter case, confabulation was required, and Greg's algorithms were some of the best in the field.

Maya had worked for Greg during college after wandering into the shop one afternoon and falling into a three-hour conversation about everything from First Contact–era artifacts to interstellar politics. Three cups of tea later, ey'd offered Maya a job starting immediately.

The pay hadn't been much, but it beat dock or atmospheric work and promised daily conversations about history, Belzoar art, and settlement funk music. She liked to tell people she learned more from Greg than from any of her professors, and there was a part of her that could have stayed on Melancholy just to keep hanging out in this shop. Which was when Greg told her kindly but firmly to grow up and go get a life.

Ey'd been even more disappointed than Maya's parents when Maya had dropped out of Princeton ten years ago, and Maya prepared herself for a new lecture.

To her relief, Greg was too excited about the artifact to give her grief. "Come on then. Let's see it!"

Ey opened the volume and studied the delicate metal embedded in the endpaper. "Fantastic."

Maya and Greg both paused and eyed the others, who had moved on to examining the contents. Auncle had filaments on every box in reach. Maya could see Greg mentally calculate the risk of having all these people in the back room with eir delicate equipment.

"We'll be right back," Maya told her companions. Then Greg led her past the counter through a doorway with a simple privacy screen that separated the front and back rooms. The back was just as crammed and not nearly as tidy. A table occupied the middle of the space, where Greg did all eir work. The room was freezing, but she could still smell the faint odors of singed wire and hot pour, a fermented beverage popular across the settlements.

"Do you know what you have here? Oh my gosh. Like, do you? I don't even want to know how you have it."

"I'm going to return it," said Maya.

"Of course you are." Here it came.

Greg set the volume open face on the tray of a machine twice Maya's size. It was Greg's own invention, designed to read chips as small as a single fish flake and as big as a ship drive.

"Maya . . . I try not to judge, but what are you doing, hon? I thought it would be *years* before I saw you again. Why are you here? And is that a CNE combat soldier out there?"

"Former," said Maya.

"And a rob! Medical, right?"

"You don't want to know."

Greg pursed eir lips. "Don't get me wrong, finding this is the achievement of a lifetime, but for your mental health—"

"I'm going back," Maya promised, in an attempt to forestall any more lecture.

"You better be! Especially with the whole Interstellar Web falling apart."

"I just need to help Auncle with this last thing." She felt eighteen again.

Greg shook eir head but turned back to the worktable. "You know, whatever is in this—the whole galaxy deserves to know about it, don't you think?"

Maya took eir hand. "Please, Greg. I need enough time to find the grail before anyone else does. For the sake of the Frenro."

Greg sighed. "Give me a few hours."

CHAPTER EIGHTEEN

They watched the sun set over the endless ocean from the highest hill in the Melancholy Memorial Garden. The even grove of slender saplings surrounding them cast long shadows like an advancing army, and the air was thick with the scent of jasmine and roses—a perk of the dome that allowed things to bloom year-round.

The garden was its own domed island, connected by a pedestrian bridge to the mainland, and relatively quiet, which made it an ideal place to wait, though Maya had an ulterior motive for suggesting it: there was something here she wanted to find.

They'd disguised Medix in one of Greg's old jackets and a pair of pants with twice-patched knees. With the addition of a respirator and a hat, he could have been just another new arrival.

It would have been safer to leave him behind in the shop, but Greg didn't like to be crowded while ey worked, and Medix refused to stay behind. He wanted to see the world. Insisted enough that Wil asked if he'd installed a curiosity mod.

"I've always been like this," Medix told her, with a hint of irritation.

The pebbles in the path illuminated in the dusk.

"I used to come here as a student," Maya said, mostly to Auncle. "My classmates and I were into grave hunting." She showed them the ribbon of knee-high black walls that rippled through the grass like the waves below. They listed the names of all those memorialized here, each one with a digital tag of biographical information. "It's a game."

"There are bodies buried here?" Wil asked, staring at the markers.

"Well, no, they compost them first," said Maya. "Zero waste."

"Of course," said Auncle. "I have seen this place in your dreams."

Wil shot Auncle a look and scooted farther away.

"How do you play this game?" asked Medix.

"First, you microdose psilocybin. Then you challenge people to find certain epitaphs. It's something of a tradition for people to leave little Easter eggs. Riddles, encrypted recipes, and so on. One or two even have treasure maps."

"Can't you just look them up?"

"No, you can only access them here. It's an incentive to visit."

It was why she'd suggested they come. Dr. Paul Nkosi, Huang's second-in-command, was buried here, and she meant to look again at the epitaph on his grave.

Wil leaned over and looked at a marker. Maya already guessed what she'd see. Half the people here died in the war. So many had been under the age of twenty. She watched Wil's face draw inward as she understood.

"Are you all right?" asked Medix.

"No. I'm in a graveyard," Wil said.

The sun disappeared, and they were left in its afterglow. Auncle hunkered down in the lawn. Maya could feel in her chest xyr longing for the water like the distant strains of a sad violin.

Wil added: "My stepfather was a minister. I had to go to a lot of funerals. The second-to-last funeral I ever went to was his. He used to lecture me when I was growing up. He'd say, 'What do you want your headstone to say, eh?' Thought I was wasting my life. And maybe he was right. 'Here lies Wil, who committed treason.' Sounds about right."

It occurred to Maya that she wasn't the only one who had to live with her choices. "What did *his* stone say?" she asked, trying to pull Wil back from the spiral.

"Loving father," said Wil, like it was a joke. "He was, though. I was just too young to appreciate it."

A moth settled on a nearby branch, and Medix stood to get a better look. Below, a couple wound their way through the path toward the gate.

"What was the last funeral?" Maya asked.

"Pleasant Station."

"Ah."

Pleasant Station was a CNE base out in Nodal System 5-6, also known as the Junction because it sat at the fork between the Earth and

Settler Union branches of the Human Nodal Region. It was jointly occupied.

A few years back, Belzoar ships had approached Pleasant Station demanding the return of mass transformation technology salvaged from a Belzoar wreck. This Belzoar clan was fiercely protective of their tech. They felt humans weren't ready for their technology.

The CNE fought back. They were crushed by the Belzoar. It was only thanks to the intervention of the SU forces in the area that they hadn't all been annihilated.

"I didn't know you were there," Maya said, and then felt ridiculous, because why would she have known?

"That's how I got all this," said Wil, indicating her body.

Maya wanted to say, *Well, the CNE should have just given it back*, but she knew better. So instead she said, "I have a childhood friend who's in the SU navy and was there."

She heard Wil spit into the grass. "Cowards."

"What?" Maya was shocked.

"They gave them the device," said Wil, voice twisted in anger and grief.

"To convince them to leave," said Maya. "Or they would have killed you all."

"We would have made it hurt. Do you know how valuable that device would have been? It could have allowed us to settle Venus and half the worlds out here. It could have helped stabilize Earth's climate in a matter of years. Do you really not care about humanity?"

"I care," snapped Maya. "I just don't have the hubris to believe that everything we see belongs to us."

"It's not about possession," said Wil. "It's about survival."

And Maya remembered Dr. Garcia's warning, about what was coming if she didn't stop it. If she were willing to betray Auncle and let the Frenro die.

"I understand." Auncle's tinny voice in the darkening shadows came like a shock in the system.

"No, Auncle," said Maya, because she thought xe must be confused. "She's saying humans should look out for human interests even at the expense of other people."

"Yes, certainly," said Auncle. "I understand. You will be angry with me, little one. I am not in agreement with you on this."

Wil laughed, and if Maya were violent, she would have socked her in the jaw right there. Instead she couldn't move. She couldn't believe what she was hearing.

"Is that why you didn't care what happened on Lithis?" She was picking at the scab of their last argument. She knew she shouldn't, but she couldn't help it.

Auncle curled xyr arms up. "I did care," xe said. "However, as I have explained to you, the Whole is everything. It is family. Though sometimes I wish it were not."

"If that's true, then why am I here?" Maya rose and went down the hill, following the wind of the passage between the ribbon of wall.

It was rare that she and Auncle fought. They'd lived on the same wavelength since their first job together. Her bond with Auncle sometimes felt like predestination, like she might have gone anywhere in the universe, and the road would still lead her back home to the *Wonder* eventually. As it had.

They'd met on a dig site on a desiccated planet at the edge of the Dead Sea. There were ten other students on the dig from various universities, all from Earth. Melancholy didn't have a graduate school with comparative cultures studies or the funding to send students on far-flung projects. Her first year at Princeton had been a mix of alienation and stress, and she was thrilled to be out in a place she understood. She flaunted her savvy at port calls and tried to prove her belonging in the amount of liquor she consumed in between.

She thought at one point she loved these other students, despite the comments she overheard them make about her one night as she brushed her teeth. ("Amateurish storyteller" and "Doing her best despite where she went to school.") Just the usual sniping in a long journey, she figured. She wanted to get along; she was meant to spend her semester out there, digging in the dirt. And the site was spectacular: they'd found a half-submerged, impenetrable sphere the size of a stadium, and a city's worth of Frenro artifacts.

She'd heard rumors when she arrived at the site that tools had gone missing and dirt had been disturbed, that maybe the site was haunted.

She didn't believe in ghosts. It was just a story people told to excite the new arrivals.

The professor in charge was unnecessarily tough on all of them, but especially Maya. He assigned her to night watch in frigid temperatures several nights in a row. On the third night, she'd nodded off and awoken with a jolt at a scrabbling sound. She'd turned her beam and there, under the tent near the trench they'd been digging, was a Frenro, all metallic and gleaming in the shaft of her light.

Her first groggy thought was that this person had broken free of xyr fossil and crawled up out of the dirt. But xyr suit was immaculate. Xe'd been pawing through their recent finds: shards of unknown tools, broken memory sculptures, and fossils of aquatic creatures many millennia extinct.

They regarded each other under the half-light of a moon shattered in pieces across the sky.

Then Maya felt a feather touch in her mind, and it was more friendly than any conversation she'd had in the last several months.

"Hi," she whispered.

"Hi," Auncle replied. "Why do your dreams taste of salt? Are you sad?"

Maya had been dreaming of an ocean city full of Frenro. The question was too complicated to answer. "What are you looking for?" she asked instead.

The grail, of course.

A week later, Maya filed for a leave of absence and walked off the site into exhilarating uncertainty about whether she was ruining her life or finally solving the mystery of her own unhappiness.

Now, in the Memorial Garden, Maya wiped humidity from her face. Her memories had carried her far down the hill along the winding path to the edge of the dome.

Here.

She stopped at a bend near a special breed of phosphorescent roses. The whole bush glowed faintly in the dark like a swarm of jellyfish. Out of habit she started to point it out to Auncle, but her friend had stayed back on the hill, just a distant lump in the dark that could have been a bush.

She turned back to read the letters carved on the old marker. It was barely eroded thanks to the lack of wind or rain.

Paul Nkosi. Dr. Huang's most loyal crew.

The cramped font of the epitaph was difficult to read in the dimness.

We went into the cave and found the light. We returned an echo of what had been. Let the ghosts wait there for no one.

Maya traced the letters with her finger, as if she might extract the meaning from them.

The first sentence felt clear enough—a reference to the *Traveler*'s journey into deep space in search of the stardust machine. And it also seemed like proof that they *had* found it. According to scholars, Dr. Nkosi may have intended a double meaning: a reference to the allegory of Plato's Cave and how little the people could know about the reality of the universe by simply living in it.

And the second sentence? Perhaps the fact that they were tired after all that travel. Maya sure was.

The ghosts were clearly the dead comrades they'd left behind—wherever they had gone. The Encyclopedium.

Still, she couldn't help but feel the ominousness behind the words.

"I would like to die," said Medix from right behind her.

Maya jumped. Had he followed her all the way over here?

The robot removed his hat and turned it over in his hand. A human gesture. The silver plate of his head glinted in the lamplight. "Someday. Not simply switched off, but to 'pass away,' as you will."

"Can we not talk about death right now, please?" said Maya.

His eyes gleamed in the dark. "Wil does not like me talking about death either. She says in most circumstances, it is not a good thing to want. I have accepted it was not my job to do what I did. She explained why it was wrong, even though she protected me afterwards.

"But I am talking about life. Death is something that all living things share, is it not? I think about what it could be like, if I were alive. A moment of feeling like my conscious self was worth something. To feel that it had meaning. I am very well designed. I believe my parts could last for a long time. I do not think I will ever be buried in a place like this."

He regarded the Memorial Garden, like he was storing images of it in his data storage for future reflection.

"Wil tells me I must figure out a new purpose that is satisfying to me, but it is hard to know what that is when I am incapable of contentment."

There was a yearning in the rob's voice that Maya recognized. She reached out and touched the rob's jagged elbow through the cloth of the worn sleeve. What could she say to reassure him? All she could think of was that she had been chasing purpose all her life, and it had gotten her nowhere, except a cold, floating graveyard in the middle of the ocean. "All you can do is keep trying," she said. "For what it's worth, I think that's normal."

"I think I would also settle for a millisecond of joy," said Medix. "Perhaps that is more attainable in my situation, if I can obtain a good module."

Maya felt a lump rise to her throat. "That should be doable."

Just then, Maya's ocular feed buzzed with a terse message from Greg: *I found something.*

CHAPTER NINETEEN

G reg clutched a miniature Space Kitty charm in one hand. "Just wait till you see this," ey said, raking eir hair with trembling fingers.

The shop was too cluttered for easy conversation, so they had retreated above to eir humble one-room apartment, downright spartan compared to the space below: just a low table with cushions around it, a cooker in the corner, and a bed covered in a denim blue patchwork quilt, which Maya perched on.

Greg dug out a Frenro pouffe for Auncle to sit on that ey apparently used as a reading chair.

"Do they speak of the grail?" asked Auncle, expanding so much the pouffe was nearly swallowed by xyr body. Maya worried xe might crack xyr suit. "Where is it?"

Even Medix and Wil leaned forward to hear the answer.

"I haven't had time to look through it all. But I did find—I'll show you."

Greg projected the menu on the far wall.

There were thirty files: fourteen raw recordings—Maya skipped through the images, and they glimpsed foreign worlds, some barren, and others teeming with unearthly life. The remainder were text files. Many were incomplete, though this seemed more likely to be from the ravage of time than intentional redaction.

They had found Huang's "footprints."

Maya's face hurt from grinning so hard. "People don't tell you enough what a genius you are."

"People tell me that every day." Ey sniffed, but eir cheeks reddened a little.

The AI-generated labels were tantalizing. Her hands started to sweat just looking at them.

Auncle was unusually quiet. Xe coiled up in xyr pouffe, vibrating with unspent energy.

Maya threw all the recordings up on the wall at once in a grid, hunting for the familiar brown hydra-like form.

"Sure," said Wil. "And that is . . . is it that? What are we looking at?"

Maya had frozen on a clip.

"Is something wrong?" Medix asked.

"Auncle," Maya said.

"Yes," agreed Auncle.

The third clip in the top row was an entrance built of heavy blocks of unknown material. She recognized it from her visions, and here it was in front of her eyes. What was this place? What did it mean that she would one day go there?

"There!" said Medix, the only one of them capable of watching all fourteen feeds at once.

Ey enlarged the recording of a vast, dim labyrinthine vault lined with precious artifacts—Frenro objects, more numerous than Maya had ever seen in one place, each suspended in its own glass column. Greg zoomed in.

There it was—the grail.

Auncle's appendages spasmed outward, grasping for Maya's arm and legs. They tightened around Maya's body, and Maya squeaked.

"My deep apologies, dear one," said Auncle, easing xyr grip.

"Huh. Not what I expected. So where is it?" asked Wil.

"It looks so familiar . . ." said Auncle.

Maya pulled out the physical journal and flipped until she found the part describing the crew's discussion to take foreign money. She pulled up the passage with the famous Huang footprint quote:

> . . . the farther we go, the more I suspect we're looking in the wrong place. It's time, I think, to go back to the beginning.

And she knew with bone-deep certainty where the object of Auncle's desire had been hiding all this time. The *literal* beginning. The very first foreign world the *Traveler* had ever visited.

It was in fact the most obvious place, and she was already kicking herself for not considering the possibility sooner.

"Emerald," said Maya, naming a planet bustling with life that was something of an unofficial capital of the closest Belzoar Nodal Region. "The Belzoar collection on Emerald."

Maya had been twice to the Belzoar region as an undergrad and a few times with Auncle, even though some Belzoar places weren't safe for a Frenro—certainly not Lithis, for example.

"I'm familiar with it," Greg said, a frown on eir face that indicated ey already disliked where this was going.

"Yes, of course," said Auncle, expanding again.

"Well, we're not," said Wil.

"The Museum of Functional and Nonfunctional Objects," said Maya. "The museum is controlled by the same Belzoar clan that stepped in to fund the rest of Huang's expedition. They must have ended up with everything the crew found."

"Sorry, the Belzoar have museums?" Wil was struggling to follow.

Maya nodded. "Of all foreign people, Belzoar are considered the most like humans. They have similar sensory organs: sight, sound, smell, hearing, touch. And they enjoy music and art."

"And war," said Auncle.

"We don't enjoy war," said Wil.

"But we are both incredibly violent people compared to others," said Greg.

Wil shifted in her chair.

"All of that—and they appreciate history and documentation even more than humans. Some xenoanthropologists theorize it's because of their relatively short life spans. It's a really interesting theory—" Maya caught herself. "Anyway, the Emerald collection is a super famous collection of artifacts from all known peoples. They even have a van Gogh and a Frida Kahlo."

"That van Gogh was dubiously acquired," said Greg. "They got it from some space pirates, and you can bet no one checked the provenance." Ey went to the cold box and removed an unlabeled glass bottle of syrupy liquid and fussed with the cooker. A sour yeasty scent filled the room.

"Their whole collection's like that," Maya agreed. "But it surpasses anything we have on Earth. It's like a cultural tasting menu. They have a *ton* of Frenro artifacts."

She pointed at the projection stopped in time, the endless shelves stretching out into the dark. "I assume this is from the limited-access vault they have underneath the museum. Objects considered too valuable for public exposure. From the account in the journal, it sounds like they were given a private tour. Likely after they delivered their finds from the Encyclopedium."

Her excitement grew. *This* was the real reason Dr. Garcia had wanted to hire her. If all he'd needed was extraction, any clanker could do the job. He must not know exactly where it was in the vast museum. Which meant there was still a chance Maya could get to it first.

Greg poured the now steaming liquid into glass mugs.

"I adore the viscosity of hot pour," said Auncle, admiring the way the liquid slid in slow motion.

Greg distributed the mugs among the humans. Maya buried her nose in it, another memory claiming her with the smell: sitting here with Greg while she studied for the test that would accompany her graduate school applications.

Wil wrinkled her face. "Pffew, what is in this? It smells like blue cheese."

"Yeah, it's cultivated mold," Maya said. "Settler specialty."

Wil took another sip. "Does it get better?"

"Not really."

One of Auncle's arms wrapped around Maya's arm as she lifted the chipped mug to her lips. Xyr arms swarmed everywhere, on everyone, as if xe were tasting the entire room. Wil went rigid as several filaments touched her body.

"Maya, how shall we retrieve it? Time is a shell that we must break open. Let us proceed at once. Will you make us a plan?"

Greg gripped eir beard with eir hands. "Even a human cannot just land on Emerald and walk up to their people's greatest museum. And I hate to say it, but I certainly wouldn't recommend a Frenro getting anywhere near there."

"We have not been at war with any Belzoar people since before your people joined the web, and the people of Emerald have never given us trouble," said Auncle. "I am bursting with utter joy. Let us leave right away."

"Auncle." Maya grasped the metal-coated end of the arm stroking her thigh. "Greg is right. Emerald is not safe for you. I think—"

"No," said Auncle. "This I will not discuss. The idea that you will go without me, on my behalf. Emerald is not Lithis. This is my great quest. For much, much time, I have searched for the grail. It should not be in a museum, after all. No, Maya, we must devise a plan, and then we will go there."

In her heart, Maya had known there was no dissuading her friend. It was existential, and if salvation were possible—xe would make the attempt, no matter the risk.

Maya turned to Wil and Medix, who were, she was certain, conferring silently. "This is going to be dangerous, and this isn't your fight. We can pay you what we can, and you can go. No hard feelings." She expected them to debate it at least. They had no emotional investment in this venture. She doubted Wil, like Dr. Garcia, even cared whether the Frenro died out.

She was daring them to say no. She didn't particularly want them. Though already as she turned it over in her mind, she had to admit that the additional crew in this case might be necessary.

Still she was surprised at her relief when Wil said: "We're still in."

Greg looked from person to person, aghast. "I get why you want to, but I don't see how you possibly pull this off. You'll get yourself killed. You almost did before . . ."

Maya looked out the window. Over the packed-together buildings, stars glittered above the dark world. She wondered if one of them was that terrible place they'd barely escaped.

"Maya," said Greg, lowering eir voice. "An obsession like this can torment you for the rest of your life. Look what happened to the *Traveler*'s crew."

Maya shook her head. This was different. They had no choice.

"I wouldn't normally suggest this, but why not try proper channels first? Belzoar bureaucracy may be unsurpassed, but it might be possible. . . . This would be more dangerous than anything you've ever attempted."

Except they didn't have time. For all Maya knew, a CNE extraction team was already on its way. They needed to get there first.

Maya downed a gulp of hot pour, the thick liquid sliding down her throat. Already a plan was forming in her mind. "We can do this," she told her former mentor. "We're the best in the business."

Auncle tightened xyr grip on Maya's hand, the cool metal slick against the sweat gathering in her palm. *Thank you, friend.*

Maya felt a fragile confidence unfurl inside her. But then, she always felt this way before anything went wrong.

CHAPTER TWENTY

M aya watched Melancholy disappear behind them. In the water, Auncle swam across her view and settled against the ladder. Xe was luxuriating being out of xyr suit.

"May I read this?" Medix held a copy of *The Maltese Falcon*, one of the books Maya had offered him earlier. At the time, he'd taken *Gilgamesh* instead.

"You don't ask permission to go into my room, but you do ask permission to borrow my books?" Maya asked.

Medix sat down on the couch. "Yes."

She was impressed he'd managed to get in there after she'd installed extra security measures. The rob was a natural.

"You said you have a plan," said Wil, attacking the kitchen table with alarming vigor using a scrub brush she'd acquired on Melancholy.

"We only have one table," Maya warned her.

"It concerns me you're changing the subject, Hoshimoto."

"Only to protect the table. Yes, I have a plan. A draft plan."

It was still coming together. She was trying not to think of the plan she'd put together for the Lithis job. The first half had gone perfectly; the second had been a complete disaster and a dead end. Best not to go down that path of thinking right now.

Anyway, this was a different world, different culture. The Belzoar on Emerald didn't believe in incarceration. On the other hand, if they were caught, they'd get extradited to the Settler Union for punishment, and that would *not* be pleasant.

Despite herself, Maya felt a stirring of excitement. Not just for the job but for the opportunity to see Emerald and the museum itself. A part of her—the overly ambitious, usually misguided part of her— wondered if she might be able to conduct basic research during their visit while she was at it, something that could convince the Chair of the

Department she'd been gone for legitimate reasons, so she could return to her simple life.

And the way Dr. Huang described it, the Emerald museum was supposed to be one of the wonders of the universe:

> The Emerald collection is a miracle—it is not only extensive but exquisitely curated. They have a section devoted to ancient Belzoar compositions, and another section for Quietling windows. Thanks to the success of our expedition, the Belzoar have given us full access. Dr. Nkosi has decided to stay behind and spend a year here for cultural exchange, which means I return to Earth alone. At this point, I'm just happy to have wrought something better from the tragedy we experienced in that place.

What bothered Maya was, if the Emerald Clan had the grail all this time, why hadn't they ever used it? Was it possible they didn't know what they had? But they must have, or they wouldn't have considered the expedition a success. So how had it been lost all this time in the lowest floors of the museum?

Wil cleared her throat.

"We'll need disguises," said Maya.

"I believe this will be fun. I enjoy disguises," came Auncle's voice through the ship. "Do you remember when I pretended to be a Belzoar before with great success? We still have the prosthetic around here somewhere."

Wil abandoned the scrub brush finally and began ladling bowls of chili from the cooker with a teaspoon that looked like a child's toy in her gloved fingers. She'd insisted on relieving Medix from cooking duties, despite his protestations that he didn't mind. "You're not our servant," she'd said.

"I'm good at it," he'd replied.

"I can cook too," she'd said. "Especially with a cooker. How hard is that?" What she meant, apparently, was that she knew how to cook chili. That was basically it. And the whole process had been stressfully meticulous, making Maya wonder if she should have volunteered instead, though she appreciated not cooking for once.

Wil spilled some beans on the counter and cursed. "You really don't have any spoons?"

"Just that one."

Wil transformed her left arm into a ladle and began to serve the chili. "This is a family recipe," she told Medix.

Maya set her ring on the table and projected images of the museum, including a blueprint generated from an amalgamation of various traveler accounts and recordings.

The museum was seven floors deep and made up of a grid of perfect squares, with forty different entrances and exits directly into adjacent buildings. Belzoar architecture was much more communal than human architecture. Pedestrian passage generally traveled through, rather than by, nearby buildings, and their public transportation system ran deep below the city.

She toggled through to the lowest floors. There was scant detail of what lay below. All they had to go on was the recording from the journal. Maya hated going into a space she hadn't thoroughly mapped beforehand.

"Where'd you get all this?" Wil asked, staring at the diagrams.

"A friend." She'd reached out to Pickle as soon as they'd left Greg's shop, though she'd had to lie about how she'd learned the location, since Pickle thought Dr. Garcia had the Huang journal.

Not that that was foremost on Pickle's mind these days. It sounded like everyone on Earth was in a panic over the deteriorating web. It was all anyone talked about. The cost of goods from the Outer Worlds had skyrocketed. People had started hoarding foreign tech. There was, Pickle said, an existential funk that pervaded everything.

Come back soon, Maya, Pickle wrote. So I have someone else to be stressed with.

Which didn't make Maya feel less uncertain about choosing Auncle over Earth. She hated her doubt; she hoped Auncle couldn't feel it sprouting inside her.

Maya cleared her throat. "The museum is massive. It would take twenty minutes to walk it end to end at its widest point. It's like five times the size of the Metropolitan Museum of Art."

Wil raised a hand. "What's that in British Museum, please?"

"Ten point one," said Medix, without looking up from reading *The Maltese Falcon*.

Wil whistled.

"I have tried to dream my way to this place, to swim in its underwater chambers," said Auncle, slapping xyr arms against the underside of the floor in a way that made Wil flinch. "I heard Emerald has an ocean that is round and inhabited by creatures that are almost wise. The Belzoar are wonderful collectors. Do you think we'll have time to see the ocean?"

"Sorry. I don't think so. The museum is extremely well protected." Maya ticked off what they'd need to get past with her fingers: "First, Emerald, like a lot of Belzoar worlds, is governed by an artificially intelligent system we call the Governance System, which has multisensory receptors throughout the urban fabric."

"Surveillance state?" Wil asked.

"Not exactly," said Maya. "They don't see a need for universal monitoring, because their citizenry is very, uh, attentive."

"They're snitches, you mean," said Wil.

"Yes, so you can expect everyone to be watching foreigners."

"What kind of sensory receptors?" asked Medix, already halfway through the book.

"Visual and smell."

"They're *smelling* everyone all the time?" Wil set chili on the table. "Why would anyone agree to that?"

"Your suit collected your location and health metrics and reported it in real-time to the central CNE database until I switched that function off," said Medix, turning a page.

"That was the navy," said Wil. "It's not the same thing."

"We'll need to convince the Governance System we're tourists, which will allow us limited entry—three days, max. And an Emerald day cycle is only fourteen hours: five hours of night, nine hours of day right now."

"It'll be a quick in and out then," said Wil.

"They have very few security staff inside," said Medix, sharing an excerpt from one of the travel memoirs Pickle had sent. "Four on each exit."

"Okay," said Wil. "So what has that big brain of yours hatched then, Hoshimoto?"

"Disguises to get past security. Two days to scout and find the grail, third day to extract," said Maya. "Greg connected me with a friend of a friend who has already agreed to give me a tour. Obviously, I couldn't specify anything beyond an interest in rare Frenro objects. And they have a *lot* of Frenro objects. So once we're there, we'll need to figure out exactly where it is."

"I will know where it is," said Auncle.

"But just in case," said Maya, "we need a backup plan."

On Lithis, they'd gone into the cathedral with a Governance System tracking device provided by their clients, only to find that the Lithian Belzoar had scraped the tiny tags off.

"I will be able to feel where it is," Auncle repeated, the ship voice increasing in volume.

Wil rapped on the table for Maya to sit and eat.

Maya lifted the bowl and slid some chili into her mouth with her chopsticks. Wil watched her with an intent expression that was un-nerving.

The chili was good.

"See?" Wil said to Medix. "I can cook."

"Very good," said Medix, turning his head briefly to lift his plastic lips in a white-enameled approximation of a smile.

Satisfied, Wil began to eat, which allowed Maya to go back to the plotting.

"We'll have Medix get an adapter so that once inside, he can hack the museum directory."

"I'll need to learn Belzoar programming," said Medix. "I believe there are public resources on how to communicate with Belzoar systems. This will be interesting."

"As for the sensors, we'll need to set off a stink bomb to overwhelm them."

"I have a few CNE recipes," said Wil.

"Great," said Maya. "Auncle will find a good vantage point and give us updates on where everyone is so we can avoid interference."

"How do you do that?" Medix wanted to know.

"I can sense all life-forms who are part of the web. It is beautiful," said Auncle.

"Can you see me?" Did Medix sound wistful?

"Not yet," said Auncle.

"I see," said Medix.

Wil set down her spoon. "Don't worry about it so much, Med. It doesn't mean anything."

"Lastly," said Maya, changing the subject, "each object is stored in its own case, which is sealed, atmospherically controlled, and monitored for minute changes in the internal moisture, pressure, or chemical composition." The Belzoar people were excellent conservators. "I will handle the removal."

Maya massaged her face. She could feel tingling that meant another migraine was coming on. They'd been more frequent since she'd left Earth. Must be the stress.

"In summary: Day one and two, we visit the museum legitimately and locate the grail with the unwitting help of our guide. Day three, Auncle stands watch. Medix muffles the surveillance. Wil takes care of trouble. I remove the case. We get out of there. Simple extraction."

Diversion, story, check and check. And they'd need to be bold, that was for sure.

"It is never simple," said Auncle, detaching from the floor and swimming a lazy loop of the ship. "That is the fun."

"I don't get to do much in this whole thing." Wil cleared the bowls with a clatter and dumped them in the cleaning box.

"These kinds of jobs are meant to be quiet. We don't really want to shoot anything if we can help it. Might start an interstellar incident. You can carry my tools though."

Wil snorted. "I'm not your butler."

"You will be very helpful," said Auncle. "We hired you because it is important for us not to die, and you will do an excellent job with that."

"You can also help with the shopping," said Maya.

"Shopping?"

"Yes, one last stop before we leave human space." Wherever she looked, the edges of the ship appeared to ripple. Not a good sign.

Medix finished his book. "Would anyone like some tea?"

"I'm going to lie down." She was seeing flashes of salmon sky. She covered her face and stumbled toward her room. She was tired. She didn't want to dream anymore.

CHAPTER TWENTY-ONE

S he was lost in the dark, in the future. This wasn't real. It would be real.

"Where are you?" someone called.

She stayed in the shadows as a beam of light swept down an aisle.

"Where is it?"

"Is it here?"

In her visions, she was often confused about who was speaking, as if her mind's eye weren't sharp enough. Were these friends?

The voices were moving away. She switched on her wrist light, moved forward. She was looking for the grail. It was around here somewhere.

Count, she instructed herself. *Remember.* There was just so much here.

Where was here?

Ah. The basement of the Belzoar Museum of Functional and Non-functional Objects. This was the job, and something was wrong.

She felt dizzy from the exertion, but she pushed on. If only she could figure out how the objects were organized. Not by age. By use? Except the grail wasn't in the section of artifacts related to children or reproduction. She gathered that much from her knowledge of Frenro artifacts.

The voices were returning.

"Where did she go?" someone asked.

Me, she thought they meant. She sank to her knees.

They went off again.

Giant spotlights swept the ground. It smelled like burnt rubber.

Auncle? she thought.

I do not know, Auncle said, anguish deep. *I think it is not here.*

It has to be here. Maya crawled forward.

If she could find the grail in this future, she might find it in her future.

A strange loop. She wanted to laugh. She turned on her headlamp and looked up and up and up. These were sorted by shape. Frenro artifacts, use unknown. She swam forward, or she walked, or she dragged herself on her hands and knees—she wasn't sure.

And there, at last, it was. The grail.

She reached for it—

W ill they have more books?" asked Medix as the *Wonder* docked at the massive waystation *Here There Be Dragons*. *Dragons* was carved into the moon of a superplanet circling a star in Nodal System 6-5. The system was home to a few worlds and barren asteroids unsuitable for terraforming, but it was the last stop between the Belzoar- and human-controlled regions, and therefore had flourished as a place for trade and resupply.

The challenge with venturing up the IW into regions dominated by other peoples was a lack of affordable breathable air and things humans could eat. Maya had spent the two weeks' travel to *Dragons* taking apart and cleaning every component of their nutrient recycler and water filtration.

But now that they had reached *Dragons*, all Maya's attention was back to procuring the equipment they needed for the dangerous job ahead. One of the main reasons they were making the stop was that its market was the best source of uncommon and not strictly legal items.

"We'll get you books," Maya promised. Medix was staying behind. Robs were rare out here, and in this mostly lawless region, they worried people might try to kidnap him.

"I was wondering if you might also keep your eye out for this." Medix lifted his palm and projected a symbol above it that looked like an eye with a string of ones and zeros streaming down the pupil.

"A black-market programmer? For what?"

"Happiness, any kind," said Medix. "Or Class IV curiosity."

"You want us to get you personality code?"

"You have a problem?" said Wil.

"Not at all." Maya knew Medix had already acquired some modifications, but Class IV and more advanced mods were particularly illegal for a Class III, because they exceeded the CNE-approved cap on his sentience.

"We've docked," Auncle announced over the comm. Auncle was also not coming, since they were keeping a low profile. Xe was very unhappy about it, but they'd both agreed it was the right decision.

Which meant it was just Maya and Wil, the two people on the *Wonder* who could have used some time apart. They'd been arguing for days about everything from the plan to the best way to prepare rice to why Maya's favorite space metal music was trash. Which was an incorrect opinion.

Maya gave Wil's armor a critical once-over. It was a major victory that she'd convinced Wil to adjust the programmable matter in her armor to resemble something closer to scuffed settler armor. The paint job on Melancholy hadn't even fooled children, and she didn't have the energy to deal with Settler Union vets picking fights with Wil on top of everything else. Medix had even added a SU sigil to her chest.

"You look fantastic." Maya grinned.

"Stop enjoying this." Wil opened the access hatch. "Also, that hoodie is hideous." Maya was back in the Garden State hoodie she'd purchased in the Newark airport.

"It's traditional. And comfortable."

The ceilings of the waystation were four meters tall to accommodate Belzoar and other taller-than-human travelers. The passageways were coated in white plaster, same as the ceilings and floors. Maya blinked against the brightness of it after so long in space.

One side of the curving passageway opened on the architectural centerpiece of the station: a spacious sunken oval covered in a thinly ribbed clear dome that exposed all below to the raw, glittering dark of space—and every forty-five hours, the sun. It was stunning even to Maya, who had been to *Dragons* before. Next to her, Wil leaned over the balcony and gaped for a long moment.

"Settlements clean up good, eh?" said Maya, elbowing the other woman. Earth had its aurora and blue skies; but this—this was unfiltered beauty you could only get in the Outer Worlds, where atmospheres were nascent or nonexistent. She was in a good mood. Before a job, she stressed over every detail she could control, but now that they were close, she could almost feel the grail in her hands. This job would be different, not just another disappointment: she'd seen the grail in her dreams again, and this time, she knew where it was. It also meant that maybe the other dream she'd had of that dusty pink planet and the sharp, bitter feeling of loss wouldn't ever need to happen. She could keep it to another path not taken.

"It's not Dubai," said Wil, but without her usual combativeness. "My stepdad saved his entire life for a trip off-world, even after he got sick. He would have loved this."

They took their shopping list down to the central hall, boots clanking on the metal plate of the floor. Wil abandoned any remaining shred of pretense that she was completely unfazed. The space was crammed with people of all shapes and sizes. Not just eight-legged Belzoar and hordes of tiny, round pink Quietling, but stocky Oorani studded with gems, and several diminutive but loud needle-skinned Farstars. The IW community included six space-capable peoples, and all of them passed through *Dragons*. Unfortunately, Maya caught a rare sight of a pair of armored Belzoar from Lithis and ducked into the stall of a scent purveyor.

"What are you doing?" Wil asked. "Is this on our list?"

"Just picking up something for a friend," said Maya.

The walls were lined with pretty glass vials, stoppered clay bottles, and metal spritzers.

The vendor straightened up from a bored slouch, eyes gleaming. "Hello! What can I get you? Nostalgia? Or new experiences? The memory of a grandparent's special soup? In these uncertain times, we all need something to bring comfort, don't you think?"

Maya peeked around Wil's broad frame, which conveniently blocked Maya from view. Damn, the Lithians were still there, browsing goods in the stall opposite. Her palms began to sweat. "Whatever you do, don't move," she begged Wil. To the vendor, she said: "Something unusual!"

The vendor shuffled through the samples. "This one is quite popular."

A scent of fresh-baked goods hit Maya, and her mouth began watering.

"Wow," said Wil, shaking her head. "Reminds me of my aunt's chocolate chip cookies."

"The power of scent is truly transporting. It can stir the memory of something long buried—a moment of happiness from childhood or the deep cut of loss. . . . Are you from Earth, then?" said the vendor, and Maya would have elbowed Wil if she thought the woman would even feel it through her impenetrable armor. Butter was mostly nonexistent in the Outer Worlds, and this was the smell of a very buttery cookie.

"Her aunt was," said Maya quickly, before Wil could say anything unhelpful.

"Ah," said the vendor. "You might appreciate this, then. A little more rare."

The scent of damp earth filled the booth, evoking a humid summer night.

"Amazing," said Maya, so impressed she almost forgot they were merely here to dodge someone.

The vendor needed no further encouragement to bring out scent after scent, like a magician topping each trick: fresh strawberries, chocolate, wet paint, and—when they learned Maya was from PeaceLove—that special tinny scent of indoor rain.

Wil blinked rapidly, like she had an itch deep in her brain. "What's that?" she asked. "It's so familiar. . . . There's something—"

"Ah! This one is 'Pleasant Flowers,'" said the vendor, waving a blue crystal perfume bottle.

"Excuse me, I—" Wil stepped back and scrubbed her face with one hand. She stumbled out of the narrow stall.

Which left Maya completely visible. She tensed, but it looked like the Lithians had finally moved on. She hastily purchased an aggressive, meaty scent called Purple Rain, because after spending ten minutes there, she couldn't not.

She caught up with Wil admiring a tall orchid at a plant stall.

Next to her, two customers were talking about the nodal collapses. "It's end-times, for sure," said one. "We'll lose Earth."

"It's a conspiracy," said the other.

Maya turned away, trying not to listen. She put a hand on Wil's elbow. "You okay? And don't just say yeah or sure."

Wil looked like she had aged ten years overnight. Her face was worn, and her jaw was set. "Sorry. It's just noisier than I'm used to. I'm good though. Medix gave me some just-in-case pills, so I feel pretty great."

Wil moved on to admiring a leafy pothos plant. "I met Medix after

Pleasant Station, you know." Her eyes when she looked at Maya were the dark velvet of deep space. "Long hours in a hospital bed and then rehab. He was already different from the other robs, I could tell. Kind when he didn't need to be. Thoughtful. Went all the way to the farthest dining room to get me my favorite food when I was homesick. Talked to me for hours about breeding begonias when I was going through the worst of it." Wil turned back to examine the worn spine of a book, eyes failing to focus on the title. "He's not a murderer. I mean, he is. But even robs deserve a shot at redemption."

It was hard to square Medix's gentle demeanor and his violent past. But then, Maya couldn't claim to be a saint herself. "Begonias?"

Wil's eyes lit up. She pointed out a plant with large, intricately patterned leaves. "My stepdad and I won first place for a particular luscious, giant polka-dotted begonia. Local competition, but I don't care. One of the best days of my life." She laughed to herself. "He liked to sit in a chair in the garden and supervise my weeding." She held up a hand. "Medix says gardening's probably not a good idea for me, but I'm sure I could handle it."

"Looking for anything special?" the vendor asked, and Wil startled, knocking over a potted palm with her armored knee.

"Dammit!" said Wil, stricken. "I'm so, so sorry." She squatted to pick it up and nearly tipped over a pot of bamboo. "Oh god."

"Don't worry about it," the vendor said, coming around. "It happens."

"Hey, look," said Maya, pointing out a display of books farther down. "You can find something for Medix."

Wil spent several minutes thumbing aimlessly through a display of Belzoar space engine manuals.

"Why'd you join the navy?" Maya sorted through a pile of older books.

Wil shook her head. "Because I love Earth. Someone needs to defend it. Then, after Pleasant . . . the CNE was happy to provide this suit as long as I was in service; less willing to pay for the surgery that'd let me function without it. And what job could I get like this? My body is still a mess. It keeps my lungs pumping and my heart beating. I'm not telling you this for pity, mind you."

"I don't pity you. You're way too scary. And now that you've left? What are you going to do?"

"I don't know. I spent ten years in service, planning for that sweet retirement, maybe a house in the countryside, and now I may never be able to go home again after what I did, and even if I did, I might not be able to do any of that. And there's a part of me that wonders if I ran off with Medix because other people's problems are always easier than your own. But I miss everything about Earth."

"I know what you mean," said Maya, thinking of her friends and the life she'd stepped away from.

"You do?"

"Even when you grow up in the Outer Worlds, Earth's still a part of you." She waved at all the paper books and the stalls selling used denim jeans, umbrellas, mechanical birds and decorative eggs, and swimwear that was next to useless for people living under a habitat dome with limited liquid water. "Hence the Earthcore aesthetic."

They moved on to shop for the items on their list, trading stories about their respective childhoods. Maya told Wil about the postwar years, how long it had taken for PeaceLove to recover, how she'd loved hiking outside the dome with her mother, how her favorite chore was picking blueberries from the bushes in the front yard, how they almost never had weeds.

In return, Wil told her about growing up in an old city, the way sunsets exploded the sky in yellows and reds and oranges, the terror of sudden storms that wreaked widespread devastation and summer heat that left every flower in their garden a shriveled husk, her pet birds, and the gruff stepfather she fought with until he died and left her drowning in a grief that drove her to enlist.

They hadn't, Maya realized with a start, bickered about anything in hours. She even caught herself wondering whether Pickle and Wil would get along. Probably, as long as they avoided any politics.

They got a good deal on a Belzoar system adapter for Medix but couldn't find any personality programmers, and Maya picked up a souvenir for Pickle: a stuffed animal that resembled a native species from the Belzoar homeworld, something gentle and furry and purple that liked cuddles. Pickle had a collection of non-Earth animals.

"So," said Wil. "Are you going to tell me who you were hiding from before? Creditor? Vengeful ex?"

When Maya didn't respond, Wil said, "You hired me to keep you safe—sorry, *Auncle* hired me. But I can't do that if I don't have all the information."

Maya bought several bolts of cloth. "Let's just say it's best if we avoid any Lithians."

"The entire clan? This have to do with that job you keep mentioning?"

They walked together through a long aisle. "Let's get a drink first." She indicated the dining level a floor above—and spotted someone she was most definitely *not* expecting to see: Liam.

CHAPTER TWENTY—THREE

Liam was nursing a drink in a café on the mezzanine level overlooking the open market plaza. His unruly hair stuck every which way—typical, it was his thinking habit to play with it. Everything about his cotton button-down and leather shoes screamed Earth.

Maya shook her head in disbelief.

Wil followed her gaze. "Friend of yours?"

"Not exactly. Sometimes a jerk." Maya headed for the curving ramp leading to the upper level. "But he's kind of like my jerk, you know?"

"I have—had—a few of those in my life. What are the odds, though?"

"That's what we're going to find out."

Wil followed, bolt of cloth thrown over one shoulder like it was nothing. She nearly beaned a few Belzoar behind them, and Maya could feel the low bass burble of their irritation through her boots, but they wouldn't start a fight with a fully armored human over nothing. Belzoar were generally very rational.

Every muscle in Maya's legs protested the long, gentle incline. They'd been shopping for several hours and her body was out of shape. If Wil felt anything similar, she didn't say.

Maya slid into the booth opposite Liam. He looked up with a polite half smile for a moment, then back to his book, then processed and snapped back up to her in surprise. A scarlet flush swept across his neck.

"What are *you* doing here?" He shut the book with a thump and clutched it to his chest like a shield.

"Good to see you too," said Maya. She reached over and grabbed a fried grub from the carton on his tray. He'd barely touched the food. The nutty crunch between her teeth reminded her of her college days on Melancholy, ordering the cheapest things on the menu while she and her friends crammed for exams. She felt an unbidden pang for academic life.

Wil stood over both of them, one end of the bolt of cloth set on the ground like a giant staff.

"This is Wil. She's . . . a colleague."

Liam squinted at her, trying to understand what was going on, and why this woman was dressed in full battle armor.

"Don't stare," Maya said, kicking his foot under the table.

Wil ordered a round of drinks.

Maya pulled the whole carton of grubs toward her. "What are you reading, Liam?"

He blushed even redder and looked down at the book in his arms. "Something I found in the market."

"Yeah? What is it?"

He must have realized it was childish to try to hide it, so he handed it over. The cover was a lurid yellow, with a scantily suited human and a Belzoar intertwined in an improbable but highly suggestive position.

"Oh," said Wil, taking it in.

"Classic," Maya said.

"Is that even . . . possible?"

"Sadly no, though I know people who tried to make it work. Belzoar don't sexually reproduce the same way humans do, but they do have these pleasure centers that you can stimulate by certain, um, harmonics. I knew this one kid in school who had a Belzoar partner, but they were asexual. I never asked if they, you know . . . Musical genius though, but anyway, Liam—what the *hell* are you doing here?"

"I asked you first," he said, pushing hair out of his eyes so he could stare more directly at her. His normally crisp collared shirt was wrinkled, and there were dark circles under his eyes.

"Fieldwork, remember," Maya said, spreading her arms as if it were obvious. "I'm on my way to the dig site."

"Right. With your colleague." He glanced at Wil again.

Thankfully, their drinks arrived.

"What's this?" Liam asked, tilting the mug that Wil handed him.

"They call it a hot pour," said Wil.

Maya tried not to laugh. "I can't wait for you to try it."

"Smells . . . interesting." He tried a sip and immediately spit it back out. He pushed the mug away. "That's foul."

"Acquired taste. So, Liam, why aren't you already in the BNR? Isn't that where your job is?"

Liam recovered his pompous equilibrium. He ordered a glass of wine that was sure to disappoint him. "I told you, I can't talk about it." He pulled the carton of grubs back toward him.

"Oh yeah?" Maya licked the remnants of vinegar and salt off her fingers. "One of those jobs where you go and fleece the locals for precious mineral deposits, eh? Better not to think about it too much, or it could be tough to sleep at night. But I'm sure the money is good."

"I don't need the money."

"That makes one of us," muttered Wil.

"I've told him," Maya said.

Liam gritted his teeth. "I'm just saying it's *not* one of those corporate gigs you're so snobby about. It's a matter of serious importance. Like, to the human race. I have absolutely no ethical problems with what I'm doing." He leaned back, light blue-gray eyes glinting in smug fury.

She stared back, and it clicked. "You're working for Dr. Garcia."

"How do you know about Dr. Garcia?" Liam asked.

"Besides the fact that you talked about him *all the time* back at school? He tried to hire me too." She almost regretted saying it when she saw the flash of disappointment cross his face as he realized he wasn't as special as he'd thought. But then it was chased by skepticism—she could read the curl of his lips. He was thinking, *She's lying. No way the CNE wanted Maya.* So she clasped her hands behind her head and leaned back. "Yeah, and I said no. I don't work for the CNE."

"What's this about the CNE?" Wil twisted around. "They're here?"

"Keep your voice down," Liam hissed.

"So, how are you planning to get it?" Maya reached over and snagged another grub.

"Changed your mind?" said Liam, misreading her intent. "Come on, Maya. If you really turned them down, they're not going to take you back. They've got me."

"Oh no." An uneasy feeling crept into her gut. There was no way they were going to have *Liam* walk into one of the busiest trade worlds in the BNR and carry out what was likely the galaxy's most valuable artifact. This was going to be the most challenging heist of Maya's career. It worried her that Liam wasn't worried. "They're going to get you killed!"

"It'll be fine. They've got a whole team assembled." He hunched down in his chair. "I'm just going along to lend my expertise. Anyway, *you* know what's at stake, Maya."

"Wait, you're hunting the grail too?" Wil asked.

"What do you mean, grail?" Liam asked. "Don't tell me she's got you chasing that fairy tale."

"So you've caught up," said a familiar voice.

Maya cursed inwardly and turned around.

Dr. Garcia stood behind her, framed by a trio of muscular-looking people. They might not be wearing uniforms, but there was something about their build and gait that screamed CNE.

Wil stiffened.

"There you are, Waterson," Dr. Garcia said. "You can't just wander off on your own. This place is full of criminals." He smiled at Maya.

"You hired him?" She stuck a thumb at Liam.

"Why not? He's an expert in Belzoar culture."

"I hope you haven't been talking too much, professor," said one of Dr. Garcia's companions.

"Mostly about books," said Maya.

Dr. Garcia chuckled.

Liam shrank a little in his chair, and Maya felt her concern increase. She might not like Liam, but she didn't like the warning in their voice even more. These people would think nothing of the risk to Liam if the human race were on the line. He was a bookish nerd who spent weekends roleplaying with friends, and now a real-life quest had found him, and he had mistaken himself for the hero of the story.

"And now we're leaving," said Wil. She had closed the visor of her helmet and shifted the bolt of cloth so her face was obscured.

"Who're you?" one of the others asked.

The other patrons were side-eying the CNE crew in a way that warned trouble. A tense crackle filled the air, and Maya decided it would be best to exit the situation before someone lit a spark.

Maya reached out and touched Liam's hand. He lifted his head in surprise. "Message me, okay? If you need help."

Maya and Wil moved to leave, but one of the soldiers seized Wil's arm. "Hey, where'd you get this?" Meaning the armor. The disguise apparently was not good enough to fool actual CNE.

"Remove your hand." All the warmth was gone from Wil's voice. Definitely time to go.

The hand was withdrawn, but they couldn't help adding: "That doesn't belong to you." Ah, they'd recognized the armor and were offended by the SU sigil.

"It sure does," said Wil. "Which you will understand if you try to take it off me."

For a moment, the only sound in the café was the recycler clanking. Every single head was craned toward them. At least if it came down to a fight, the other patrons would be on their side. The CNE had no idea what they were starting.

"Okay, nice to see you, meet you, so long, et cetera." Maya propelled Wil toward the door.

Back in the passageway, Wil rounded on her and snarled: "I should never have let you do this ridiculous alteration. I can't believe they thought I was an SU soldier."

"You're upset because the disguise worked?" Maya was confused. She'd just extracted them both from a messy situation. Wil should be *thanking* her. This woman was impossible.

Wil leaned down so they were inches apart. Maya could feel the heat of Wil's breath on her face. "I am a patriot, Maya. Do you know what that even means? It's about loyalty and higher purpose and honor, but I suppose a petty art thief like you wouldn't understand that."

"Oh, don't be a hypocrite," snapped Maya. "I may be good at running away from my obligations, but at least I can sleep well at night knowing I stick to my principles."

"You sleep *terribly*," said Wil.

"I'm Infected!"

Their yelling was attracting attention from passersby. Which was unfortunate, because that included the two Lithians who were just coming up the ramp from below.

And they must have identified Maya, because they were heading straight for them, long shock-sticks extended and spitting electricity.

CHAPTER TWENTY-FOUR

W il was so focused on lecturing her in full righteous fury, she didn't even notice the danger behind her.

The Belzoar were a human head taller than Wil, with hard black armor protecting their joints and the soft flesh and organs between their eight long limbs. They carried four snapping shock-sticks each, and their spiky backs were a riot of color: one was speckled crimson and yellow like fire; the other was velvety blue and white. Not related, then. Possibly courting. And they'd definitely spotted Maya the way they were already making a beeline.

"Don't move," one said via a translator box.

"Shit." Maya yanked Wil's arm, and when that made no impression on the mercenary, who was still talking, she dumped her heavy ruck-sack and tote bags at Wil's feet and ran.

Her first impulse was to go for the safety of the *Wonder*, but that would have been as good as extending an invitation for any Lithians in the area to come and obliterate them while they slept. Instead, she took a hard left and pelted back down the ramp to the lower market level.

The decision probably saved her life. Belzoar were much faster than humans—when going in a straight line. Maya's primate origins enabled her to perform a more complex maneuver: grab the railing with two hands and vault over the side. She was about five meters from the ground when she did it, bare moments ahead of her pursuers. The tip of a shock-stick kissed the back of her shirt, but then she cleared the rim and was falling. She put her faith in the low lunar gravity to spare her from injury.

She hit the hard concrete floor on her feet, stumbled and caught her-self with her hands, then threw herself into the market aisle.

The crimson one followed her to the floor, but one of their legs caught a vendor awning, and they tangled up with it and the shrieking vendor. The blue one continued the long way down.

Maya darted under an awning. Something buzzed right where she'd been standing—a drone with a small but wicked-looking blade. She lunged for the closest object to her—a pair of electric shears from a terrafarming display—and batted it down, smashing it until it splintered. She handed the shears back to the gaping vendor.

"Sorry about that," she said, diving into the crowd.

Where are you? The message from Wil flashed in her feed, but she dismissed it.

Scrambling around another turn, she nearly ran headlong into the crimson Belzoar on the ground. She shoved a clothing stand into the aisle between them, then pivoted and took the other turn instead. Another turn, and—she risked a glance behind her. Nothing.

There was another drone in the air, though. Great.

She crossed to a stall selling an odd mix of yukata and handwoven ponchos. She yanked off her Garden State hoodie.

The old vendor sitting in the folding chair was asleep. They woke up, very confused, like a customer hadn't come by in years.

"Hi," she said. "Do you want this retro, authentic American clothing? I got it from Earth."

The vendor's eyes lit up, and in no time, Maya was able to swap the hoodie for a bright pink-and-yellow hanten. Questionable fashion choice, but flashy was good. People would remember her jacket and not her face. Also, it had the steepest discount.

She started back toward the exit and nearly ran into the back of the crimson Lithian.

Maya swore under her breath and ducked into a stall on her right piled high with nuts and legumes of all kinds.

A shocked vendor watched, speechless, as she crawled under the table, and kept crawling until she was in the tented space between the stalls.

Another message from Wil appeared in the corner of her vision: *Maya! Report!*

Maya sent back her location with a flick of a hand and began to crouch-walk forward. She squatted a moment between two stacks of boxes, catching her breath.

Stay where you are. I'm coming. Where's security on this station anyway? Oh, I see them. Well, that's useless. They're not even running. Wait, they're not going to do anything at all?

"Can I help you?" And Maya realized someone was sitting on the boxes she was crouched behind. Maya's eyes fell to a pendant around their neck: projected inside it was that symbol with the eye and the narrow band of ones and zeroes streaming down it.

The person took in the markings around Maya's eye and brightened. "Excuse me, prophet!"

Talk about luck.

"Yes, do you have any, uh, joy? Or Class IV curiosity? It's for a friend."

"Ahhhh." The person grinned. "No. But I do have Class IV sense of humor."

It'd have to do. She glanced around, but she was hidden for now by the cloth awning. No sign of the Lithians.

A quick haggle, and the seller was quite happy to oblige Maya in exchange for 2,500 unis and a few vague fortune-cookie predictions about falling in love with a tall, muscular terrafarmer.

There was a whine, and she and the coder looked up. A drone hovered over their heads only half a meter above. The coder tumbled back over the boxes and was gone in seconds. It was human made, she realized, catching herself a split second before she was about to smash it. The drone hovered in front of Maya.

Hello. The message appeared in Maya's ocular feed.

"Where have you been hiding this thing?" asked Maya.

What do you think my utility belt is for, fashion?

It slipped through a gap in the cloth and soared back up until it had what must have been the perfect position for a bird's-eye view. Despite having seen CNE elite units in action, Maya was impressed at Wil's ability to monitor the ground and move through the crowd at the same time.

Okay, don't crawl forward. One of them is there. Go back two stalls and exit through that one on your left.

Maya obeyed, emerging in a stall selling a variety of larvae and insect-based protein powder. The vendor was deep in the middle of arguing with a customer and didn't notice Maya rising up from under the table.

Wait there. When I say, come out and take two rights, then stop.

Maya pretended to browse the bin of dried mealworms.

Did you dream about this? Or does an incident like this not rate high enough on your "someone's trying to kill me today" meter? Wil asked.

It doesn't always work like that, Maya said.

Probably because I'm about to save your butt.

Maya snorted. *I've been getting myself out of stickier situations long before I met you.*

Go now. Walk, don't run. No need to draw attention to yourself. I think the useless security people are looking for you.

Maya took the two rights and stopped. She was next to a stall selling musical instruments.

"Looking for a guitar?" the vendor called.

Stay there. Don't move, said Wil.

Both of the Lithians were coming toward her from either side.

Maya grinned at the vendor. "Can I try it?" She grabbed the guitar off the rack and plucked experimentally. The Lithians twitched.

What the hell are you doing?

Maya adjusted the tuning so the guitar was off-key and gave the instrument a loud strum. One of the Lithians clutched their auditory glands and turned away. The other retreated.

"Er," said the vendor. "That's not quite it."

She increased her volume.

Even the vendor winced this time.

Course is clear, said Wil. *What the hell was that?*

Belzoar have much better hearing than we do, said Maya.

With Wil's help, she made her way out of the market. Wil stood at the end of the long aisle. Maya had never been so happy to see the woman; she nearly hugged her. Wil had somehow managed to carry the ruck-sack, tote bags, and bolt of cloth, and from the expression on her face, she was annoyed about it.

Maya took back her share of the purchases.

It took Wil only ten seconds up the first ramp to begin her lecture. "You hire an elite combat unit and then the first sign of threat, you run away instead of letting me do my job?" Without turning to look, Wil lifted one hand, caught her drone out of the air, and slipped it in a pocket at her belt.

"This was the better outcome," Maya said. "I got some cardio, and no one had to get hurt."

"Is this some PeaceLove pacifist bullshit?" Wil asked. "And what's going on anyway? Why were those guys after you?"

There were a lot of things Maya could have said to that: that hatred isn't always earned, it sometimes just happens to you; that justice doesn't mean the same thing for different people; that this was a thing that would pass eventually. None of which was the whole truth.

Maya tried to figure out where to start.

"We went to Lithis in search of the grail."

"But it wasn't there."

Maya shook her head. Her adrenaline was wearing off, and memories of Lithis leaked back in, unbidden.

"Lithis has laws so complex they'd make a human lawyer cry. We were caught. We warned them about the dangers of the virus. They thought they had taken proper precautions. The problem is, their population has been relatively isolated for two hundred years, so they don't have the same immunity against the virus that most Belzoar have. We heard about the outbreak after we escaped. We made a rookie mistake and people died and—and we should have known better." Her voice broke.

They reached dock 239 and checked to make sure they weren't being followed before entering the boarding tube. Wil locked the security gate behind them. "And now they want to kill you?"

"Or capture. They want justice," said Maya, letting out a shuddering breath, "and I can't even say they are wrong."

"Shit," said Wil, chewing on that.

"I can't change what happened. But I have this idea—maybe if we find the grail, it won't all be for nothing."

She appreciated that Wil didn't try to comfort her in that moment the way Pickle might have. Or argue with her that there was no practical value in feeling guilty and that logically it wasn't their fault, the way Auncle had.

Wil just took the bags from her and led the way into the *Wonder.* "Well, then," she said, "I guess we'd better get the grail."

CHAPTER TWENTY-FIVE

Up close, the world humans called Emerald was more of a muddy yellow-brown, with just a hint of blue. The Belzoar had lived on it since humans were learning to make bronze tools, and the world was more alive than Earth. Its atmosphere was hot and thick, and like a spark with the right amount of tinder and wind, its ecosystems had run away with themselves centuries ago.

It sat in a five-node system at the intersection of multiple branches of the web. This way, the main trunk of the IW; back that way, Earth; and that way, Lithis.

The Emerald Governance System screened them ten hours out. They'd practiced for the interviews, but there was no way to guarantee they'd pass.

Maya's cover story was the simplest, because it was the closest to what could be true—a visiting scholar there to study rare Frenro artifacts in Emerald's famous collection. Medix was her assistant.

Wil was posing as Auncle's rob. Human-shaped robs were fashionable on Emerald these days. She'd modified her armor, particularly her helmet. Medix had helped her with unexpected enthusiasm, applying all his surgical skill to design a false face for her.

It was Auncle Maya was worried about, and she finished her own screening quickly enough to stress about what Auncle might or might not be saying.

One sentence only, she reminded xyr. Except a Frenro sentence tended to be a paragraph.

Auncle was passing as a Belzoar tourist from a distant world. Xe had lived with a crew of Belzoar shippers from another clan for twenty years, before Maya was born. The question was, could xe convince the Emerald Governance System that xe was of another Belzoar culture?

They were counting on the breadth of the diversity of the Belzoar people to disguise any differences.

Maya held her breath as the questions went on.

Xe passed.

At the terminal, they were scanned for weapons and other illicit items. Medix had printed a chemical signature for Auncle that mimicked Belzoar pheromones.

Again, no issues.

Maya had forgotten how stressful the work was. If only she had said no, she could be enjoying crisp autumn air, rustling leaves, and the too-sweet hot apple cider her grandmother liked to serve.

The elevator deposited them in a lush garden carpeted with a thick sunflower-colored growth that drifted and plinked against their legs as they walked. It was like wading through an ocean of bees.

Maya tilted her head up, trying to see beyond the ring of buildings around the spacious plaza. Each arched opening could have fit an all-terrain settlement truck. Medix led the way into the cool, deep shadows of one of those doorways.

The Belzoar concept of privacy was very different from a human one, which was to say they didn't have one.

Their sense of family spanned entire worlds, sometimes multiple systems. Most Belzoar clans had no central government, having handed over their bureaucracy tens of thousands of years ago to a combination of benign AI and direct democracy.

"It's this way," said Medix, already tapped into the Governance System. He wound through the warren of corridors and plazas and vaulted rooms with impressive certainty. The rest of them struggled to keep up. The gravity here was greater than on Earth. Inside Maya's suit, her liner was damp with sweat.

She wondered how Dr. Nkosi had managed a year here. She couldn't imagine staying more than a couple of days.

She stopped several times to wait for Auncle to catch up. She could feel xyr discomfort rolling off xyr in waves. Xe'd squeezed xyr base arms into eight prosthetic legs, and xyr cilia and water tank were hidden under gauzy robes. An artificial sound organ was strapped between xyr "legs." Between all that, the extra weight, and the gauzy robes, Auncle was struggling, and there was nothing Maya could do to help without arousing suspicion. It was painful to watch.

The disguise was working though. Xe wore the lightly layered robes of an Infected Belzoar—Maya's idea—and the other Belzoar gave xyr a wide berth. Some things were true no matter the people.

Do not worry, my child, Auncle said. *I am enjoying myself very much.*

The subtle influences of human aesthetics were everywhere if one knew where to look: outdoor cafés and streetlights and a surprising prevalence of artificial flowers.

Maya wondered how the Belzoar had influenced humans in turn. Settlement music and architecture, maybe, and technological advances.

They descended a wide spiral ramp deeper than Maya would have thought possible, and the scholarly part of her was dying to stop and study the extensive carvings on the walls. She had to settle for recording with the camera eye on her necklace and hoping to glean something later.

At the bottom of the descent were ovoid cars that ran through underground tubes bored through the hard rock that the main city sat upon. This far down, a damp mineral scent permeated the seal of Maya's suit.

They took a car to themselves. Maya grabbed a handhold above her head just in time before the car shot forward. They were headed first to their hotel, a human-oriented establishment, before their initial scouting of the museum.

Their car came to a stop, and their long ascent back up to the surface was exhausting. The hotel was aboveground, nestled in the hills. In consideration of its human clientele, its structure stood apart, in the middle of a plaza, a white stone building with a black slate roof. On their way to their room, Maya overheard a couple of Belzoar guests exclaiming about towels and the quaintness of faucets.

They'd taken one room with a queen-size bed, and Maya wanted nothing more than to sink deep under the crisp sheets and not wake up for a day, but there was preparation to be done and limited time to do it in. Her back and hips ached from the extra gravity.

Wil and Auncle departed for the museum to evaluate security and fill in as much of their patchy blueprint as possible. Medix followed their progress from the hotel room, advising as needed, while Maya reassembled her tools. She'd smuggled them in pieces sewn into her clothing. Fortunately, the Governance System didn't grasp the concept of human jewelry, and no one had seen anything amiss.

Now, as Maya sat cross-legged putting everything together, she cursed the intricacy of her task.

After several hours of work, she stood to shake the pins and needles from her legs. Out the window, she could see the tables in the plaza glittering in the sun. It was so pretty, it was easy to forget the panic unrolling in human space over the disappearing nodes.

She noticed a person sitting at a human-sized table reading a book, and even with the helmet obscuring his face, she knew it was Liam. The way he carelessly exposed the pages to foreign atmosphere, and the way his gloved fingers fumbled with the pages like he hadn't spent half his life in a vac suit. Every so often, he set the book down and stared around with awe and reverence like he had died and gone to heaven.

She resisted the impulse to go down to him—better the other crew didn't know they were here.

We have less time than we thought, she reported to the others.

Down in the plaza, she saw Dr. Garcia and other humans join Liam. They were heading out. Liam jammed the book in a satchel. It took him a few tries, given his awkwardness in a suit. One of the others took the book and did it for him.

"Do you think you could follow them without being noticed and continue assisting Auncle and Wil?"

Medix giggled.

"That wasn't a joke," said Maya. He was still adjusting to his new humor mod.

"I thought it was funny. That is within my capacity, yes."

"Can you figure out how close they are to breaking in?"

She was startled by how fast the rob moved. By the time the group was heading for one of the plaza archways, Medix was already down there, crossing the blasted stone.

They've entered the museum, reported Medix a little while later. *It sounded like this is their first day here.*

They must have arrived soon after the *Wonder*.

I cannot follow them without prompting inquiry by the city. What should I do next?

Go back to the hotel, Wil said. *I'll see if we can spot them inside.*

Maya had told them the CNE was hunting the grail—she'd had to, after the run-in with Dr. Garcia. She hadn't explained why they wanted it, even to Auncle. She told herself it was because Auncle was not good at keeping secrets.

She pushed down her guilt and went back to the pile of components on the floor.

This museum is very beautiful, Maya, said Auncle. *They have a wonderful hall of compositions that makes me want to swim from star to star. I see your unfriends. They have entered the Frenro section.*

Auncle! No! said Wil.

What happened? Maya asked, heart rate spiking.

Xe almost touched a block of . . . I don't know what it is.

It is a Belzoar timepiece, Maya. So beautiful. I just wanted to taste it with my arms.

You can't taste it. There's a force field, see? said Wil. *You could have set off an alarm.*

I would have just said it was a mistake, said Auncle.

Focus on the mission, said Maya.

I have already counted all the people in the building. Your unfriends have split up to survey the Frenro objects. They are confirming it is not upstairs.

Maya removed her helmet and consumed a nutrition bar. She regretted it as soon as it hit her stomach.

It was evening by the time the others returned from their reconnaissance. There was a hair-raising moment in the yard, when Wil ran into Dr. Garcia in the plaza. Maya thought for sure Dr. Garcia would see through Wil's disguise, but apparently not.

"Long conversation," Maya said, when Wil returned.

"Man likes to talk," said Wil.

"What about?"

"The stars. He thinks they're pretty. And you're right that he's an asshole." Wil was grumpier than usual. She took pain medicine and went to bed without further comment—no doubt stressed about the CNE's presence here.

They all were. Maya didn't want to rush the job, but they still weren't sure when the CNE was moving in. They decided to accelerate their plans and curtail their second day of preparation. They'd have to hope their stink bombs caused enough chaos for them to steal the grail as soon as they located it.

Maya hated how little was in her control. How had she let Auncle talk her into this again?

She slept fitfully in her suit, the insignificant details she'd seen in her migraine visions muddling her mind. Every time Wil moved on the bed next to her, the mattress lifted. Maya, in her time-addled state, couldn't shake the feeling that something was wrong. That there was something here, in the dark with them.

CHAPTER TWENTY-SIX

Then it was morning, and Medix was shaking her awake. She groaned. An Emerald night was too short for proper human sleep, and her whole body felt like it had been compressed into a tin can and then tumbled through space. Which is to say, terrible.

Wil was reading a Bible she'd found in the drawer, already on her third cup of instant coffee.

It was driving rain outside. "Nice day for a museum," said Wil. The Belzoar agreed: the museum was already crowded when Medix and Maya arrived, despite the early hour.

It was impossible to assess the scale of the building from the outside given the way the city structures were built wall-to-wall without any space, like honeycomb. They approached the entrance through a beautiful Belzoar garden full of the ubiquitous buzzing green-and-yellow insect-like creatures that swarmed Maya's knees.

There was the cacophony she remembered from her last time visiting a Belzoar world: not just the city sounds, but the constant melody of conversations. It was a symphony more complex than any on Earth.

In the corner was the petrified body of a dead Belzoar—a renowned historian, according to the plaque. It was Belzoar practice to display the bodies of their honored dead like statuary.

The entrance was cozy, almost intimate. The plain tan walls were unadorned.

Their guide waited for them inside. Maya didn't have much experience at reading Belzoar moods, but this one seemed anxious, judging from the low, uneven hum.

"We greet you." The scholar's words appeared in translation inside her helmet.

"And you," said Maya. She introduced Medix.

"You may call me Flautist," said the scholar eagerly. "That is my human name."

They studied each other. From what she could gather, the Belzoar was young, only fifteen in Earth years. An adult, by Belzoar standards. Male, according to Governance System records. The gray-blue skin indicated he was in the egg-laying phase of his life.

"You're our first human friend," Flautist informed her. Belzoar often used the royal "we." His voice rumbled out low and high at once like a tuba and violin duet.

"Ah," said Maya, already feeling guilty about what they planned to do under his watch. "Thank you."

It turned out Flautist was also a student of foreign culture. He said one day he'd like to visit Melancholy. He was proud of the collection and excited to show it to Maya, pausing every few steps to point out ingenious Quietling meal containers or a stunning Oorani color projection.

They'd never get to the Frenro section at this rate, though it was hard to complain. The scholar in Maya would have happily spent a month in each room.

A Belzoar museum, like a human one, was a place of record, learning, and beauty, but also where one might come to be moved in a fundamental way.

She and Flautist discussed similarities in culture as they went, picking around the edges of the conversation, cautious of offense. "There must be something that drives most sentient life," said Maya, "to not only survive but to make something more of the world, the tangible and intangible."

"I think so too," said Flautist. "Perhaps *that* is the basis for a universal theory of life."

"What is that?" Medix asked, and Maya hoped it was normal for Belzoar robs to ask questions when not engaged.

Flautist seemed delighted by the question: "It's the idea that there is something that unites all advanced peoples. So far no one has succeeded in developing a coherent thesis around this. Life is too varied. Every time we think we have found something, there is an exception."

Medix became gloomy.

"Do you have a specific area of focus?" Maya asked, to change the subject.

It turned out Flautist was a scholar of a very obscure slice of twentieth- and twenty-first-century movies. Specifically superhero movies. "Such art!" said Flautist, his tones hitting a high C several times. "Would you like to see the human area? We have quite a collection of pre–First Contact human art."

Auncle and Wil are entering the museum now, Medix informed her.

"Maybe tomorrow?" It was a lie, but her regret was not.

They had already been walking for about fifteen minutes and still more rooms opened up ahead of them. This museum was big: far bigger than anything that existed in human space. She wondered if the previous accounts had underestimated its size. Maya worried they'd never manage a hasty exit through such a vast building, particularly not at this gravity.

I have temporarily blocked local surveillance, Medix reported to the group. *I did a very good job, but I expect they will notice in less than an hour.*

"Of course, the Encyclopedium is supposed to be bigger than this," Flautist was saying.

Maya blinked. She'd never heard of someone speak of the Encyclopedium as if its existence were a matter of fact. "Do you have stories of it too?"

"Well, yes. Though we have never seen it with our own eyes."

Maya's breath quickened. "What have you heard?"

"Several eras ago, we had two human visitors who gave us many of the objects you are about to see."

It had to be Dr. Huang and her crew. "A hundred years ago?"

"Yes," said Flautist. "Do you know them?" The shorter-lived Belzoar sometimes got confused about human longevity.

"Only from our records."

They'd finally reached the Frenro area. This part of the wing was not filled with water, but the cases were a nod to the Frenro aquatic environment. Where Belzoar art sounded an almost familiar refrain, these Frenro objects had an indecipherable quality that made Maya's skin tingle.

She wished she could understand what each one was. Auncle was often fuzzy on details, having been born well after the collapse of Frenro civilization. She saw a Frenro water filter labeled as fine sculpture, but since most Belzoar had such limited contact with real Frenro these days, the mistake wasn't surprising.

"This is the biggest collection of Frenro artifacts in the BNR outside Lithis," Flautist said. "You must go there one day. Although they don't like foreigners much. Even other Belzoar."

"Ah," said Maya.

The grail wasn't in the public area, and they didn't have a second day anymore to work around to getting access to the private storage. "We have heard," she said, careful to use the plural the way a Belzoar might, "that you might have in your collection the only known example of a Frenro musical instrument." It was one of the objects she'd seen in the images, right next to the grail.

"Oh," rumbled the scholar. "You mean the special pieces we keep below."

"There's more?" Anticipation leaked into Maya's voice.

You are a superior liar, observed Medix.

"It's where we keep our most rare items," said the scholar. "The conditions below are more conducive to long-term preservation."

And it was that easy. Nothing like the geeky enthusiasm of a scholar. Down, down they went, along one of those steep spiral ramps that Belzoar were so fond of.

Five out of ten stink bombs planted, Wil reported.

The subterranean levels were even more awe-inspiring than above: a dim, cavernous hall, filled from floor to ceiling with artifacts from every corner of known space.

They reached the floor. Flautist touched the wall with one of his eight limbs, and a spotlight appeared around them.

The light will be inconvenient, Medix noted.

Does it follow you?

Medix stopped a moment, and sure enough, the spotlight didn't track him. *I take it back. Inconvenient for you only. Ha! Ha! Ha!*

This is good, though. You can slip away and turn it off before Auncle and Wil come down here.

The darkness had a weight to it as they moved down one of the arterial aisles, like they were walking through a dense forest. As they moved, the edges of their spotlight illuminated things she couldn't have described later if she tried.

"I'm *so* excited to share these with you. They're utterly unique," said Flautist, turning another corner.

Mayyyaaaa, said Auncle. *They are down there with you.*

It was just enough warning. Maya froze as they entered the next row.

Liam stood in the middle of the aisle before a case full of dehydrated Frenro artifacts. His headlamp didn't quite obscure the stricken expression on his face. A flock of lights hovered behind him.

Before Flautist could say anything, shots rang out from the shadows, striking the Belzoar multiple times.

CHAPTER TWENTY–SEVEN

F lautist's eight limbs lost rigidity all at once. He collapsed to the ground like a bowl of wet noodles. A steaming dark liquid spurted across the floor. Maya shrank back as a spatter hit her chest.

Oh no, said Auncle. *He is dead.*

Maya grabbed Medix by the arm and yanked him back into the main aisle behind a tower of cases, but the spotlight followed her. She cursed under her breath.

"Goddammit!" She recognized Dr. Garcia's voice. "What a mess. Look what you've done."

Cold sweat prickled her skin. Too late, she understood the meaning of her vision. She'd not been hiding from Belzoar guards. She'd been hiding from the other thieves.

"Maya, you're hurt," whispered Medix, crouching next to her. Only then was Maya aware of the burning sensation in her left shoulder and the faint whistling sound as her suit began to depressurize.

Medix slapped a patch on her arm to stop more air from leaking out.

"Hack the light system and the museum directory now," said Maya through gritted teeth, "and get the others down here ASAP."

Medix, bless his mechanical heart, was gone immediately, a flurry of messages filling the group feed.

Don't engage, Wil said. *Stay out of view.*

She could hear them smashing open cases. Must be the reason they hadn't come after her yet.

She risked a peek down the aisle of Frenro artifacts. The crew was farther down the aisle, sweeping their lights through the cases. Garcia said, "It's not there. Check the next one."

Liam crouched over Flautist, mere meters away. He was whimpering and trying to do—anything. But the poor fellow was dead. There was nothing *to* do.

Someone spotted her, and a bullet whizzed past her helmet. Maya jerked back. Trigger-happy clankers.

"Stop! Don't shoot!" Liam's voice echoed about the hall. "She's a friend." It occurred to her this was the first time either of them had used the word. She was momentarily touched before reminding herself that now wasn't the time, and she was disgusted by the people he had chosen to associate with.

Footsteps approached. Maya retreated down the aisle next to Liam's, clutching her wounded shoulder. Damn spotlight. It was still tracking her. Sometimes it was annoying how good Belzoar technology was. She dove behind a towering sculpture just as another bullet missed her.

All devices planted, reported Wil. *Setting them off now.*

Maya, are you okay? She could feel Auncle's concern all the way from upstairs. *Have they taken the grail? We won't let them take it, will we? They can't. We are so close. Please stay safe.*

Someone—Liam, she thought—was moaning.

Was that the distant sound of a stampede upstairs?

"We need to find it," Garcia said. "Get him up."

"He's in shock. Come on, man, snap out of it."

A meaty thunk, followed by a groan.

"What about Hoshimoto? Where is she?"

"Around here somewhere. We'll get her."

"Hoshimoto!"

"Be civilized, now," Dr. Garcia chided them. "No need for anyone else to get hurt."

"Come out with your hands up, and we won't shoot." This was addressed to her.

They must have been worried she was armed.

Maya inched backward, praying Medix reached the light controls before they found her. The numbness was wearing off; her shoulder was on fire.

Heavy footsteps again, closer. She crept around a shelf of decorative pottery remarkably similar to ancient Grecian pots. Two percent of her brain wondered if she could write a paper on that.

"Maya, watch out!" said Liam.

Mayyya. They are coming toward you. Can you run?

Maya measured the distance of the long aisle against the sound of the approaching footsteps. Too far and too little cover.

"Oh, he's talking again."

"Just do what they say," Liam added, familiar irritation piercing through his shock. His rough, rapid breaths were audible across the deep aisles that separated them.

A shot ricocheted off an impenetrable platter and back toward them. The footsteps stopped. "Drop your weapon!"

Maya was torn between correcting them and giving away her position.

"I'm going to count to three." The soldier was only a few steps away. The edge of an enormous shadow touched the Belzoar sculpture she crouched behind. "One . . ."

Hide, said Auncle. *Hide. Hide.*

ETA? Maya asked Medix. There was an empty case in the bottom row. She attempted to wedge herself in it. The spotlight lost her finally. Probably too late though. No mystery where she was.

Nearly got it.

"Two . . ."

The soldier stepped past the sculpture. The illumination from the floor, artifacts, and ceiling multiplied the shadows. Long spears of light swept across the floor.

The soldier locked eyes on her. "Three," they said, even though she clearly was unarmed.

Behind the soldier, a drone sank out of the dark to just above their shoulder. They didn't notice.

"Go jump in a black hole," said Maya.

"Have it your way."

The barrel of the gun lifted.

"No!" shrieked Liam. He was at the entrance to the aisle from the sound of it.

Several things happened in such quick succession that Maya, who was expecting all of it, almost didn't follow everything: The extinguishing of the lights. The heavy staccato of boots against the floor as someone barreled past her in the dark. The flash of a gun firing multiple times and then a crash and the sound of a helmet banging over and over against the floor. Liam's cry, and then more methodical thumps.

Maya cringed and fumbled forward in the dark. "Wil?"

She heard people running for the exit.

Wil caught her drone out of the air and checked it for damage. "Medix has gotten into the local system. He says there's an alarm going off."

"Super," said Maya. "You didn't kill them, did you?"

The headlamps of the two prone soldiers illuminated the mercenary's boots.

Wil crouched down and sprayed a crack in one of the soldier's faceplates with sealant. "They're alive for now. As long as their friends retrieve them before their oxygen runs out. Anyway, they shot you."

"It's fine." Maya moved stiffly to the adjacent aisle where they'd first found Liam and the CNE crew. They'd all scattered. No sign of Garcia or Liam. The cases were a mess, and for a painful second Maya thought they had taken the grail. But no, she was certain this was the wrong section. Which meant the CNE didn't have it. It was still somewhere in the dark.

She switched on her wrist light.

"Maya—you're bleeding through your suit. Medix? We need you back here."

"Just let me do the job." She looked around, and it all felt so familiar: the fear, the pain, but also—

"Look for similar typology," she said.

"Huh?" Wil said.

I cannot feel it, Auncle said, anguish deep. *I thought I would feel it, and I would know where it was. But I do not know where it is. I think it is not here.*

I am unable to locate it from the directory, reported Medix. *The entire system has been locked down.*

So much for their backup plan.

It has to be here, Maya said. She remembered. "It's farther down."

Everything was the same but not the same. Sometimes her dreams were like that: just a shadow of what could be.

The mercenary followed her past the darkened aisles. Maya clutched one arm, grimacing from the pain.

There were towers of artifacts stacked forty high, and each aisle was lined with possibly a hundred of these towers on either side. Each precious thing encased in clear hard pane and—she probed one with her fingers and a small shock confirmed it—a force field. Her déjà vu increased.

She took a right.

Yes. More Frenro objects, some more obviously organic than others. Thousands of them of all shapes and sizes.

"Christ," said Wil. "How will we find it?"

"It's here." Maya swept her light in a methodical line across each row, hunting.

She spotted recognizable shapes—a Frenro water purifier, hundreds of Frenro memory sculptures. None of this should be here. She wanted to take it all.

"Mayyyyyaa! Are you all right?" Auncle called from the shadows. "I was unable to stop your friend and his friends from leaving."

"Are *you* all right?" Maya asked. It was too dark to see.

"Yes, yes. But I'm afraid I may have broken a few things, but not myself, as I do not have a skeleton. Have you seen it? Is it extraordinary?"

A stray flash of memory tickled Maya's brain, and she looked up. There it was, out of reach from her grasping fingers, in a row of other oblong shapes. But she'd have recognized it anywhere: brown and speckled, the length of her arm, tendrils floating out from the top of it like hair. The grail in all its hydra-shaped glory.

The CNE had missed it. But then, they hadn't dreamed about it the way Maya had.

"Mayyyyaaaa," hissed Auncle in excitement.

"Can you get me up there?" she asked Wil.

Strong arms closed around her and then she felt herself hoisted up until she was able to balance on the edge of the row of cases and not fall. She hoped whatever kept them in place would withstand her weight.

"The Governance System is sending guards. We have two minutes to remove ourselves," said Medix, urgency pricking his voice.

Wil handed Maya the tools she'd painstakingly assembled: a laser cutter and a clawlike force field disrupter. She had to take them one-handed, because her wounded arm was screaming. "Get the grail," she repeated to herself over and over, slogging through the pain.

Maya pushed the metal tips of the disrupter into the force field, creating a temporary hole in the invisible obstruction. No need to be discreet anymore.

Something was keeping the preservation case fixed in place. She aimed her laser cutter through the disrupter hole and sliced through the top and bottom, doing her best to avoid puncturing the case itself.

Below, the others started removing artifacts. Auncle swept everything from one case into a bag.

"What are you doing?" Maya asked, panic rising in her chest. Was this right? This wasn't the plan. But then, hadn't she felt the same impulse when she'd seen the loot?

Everyone was moving too fast for her to see what they were taking.

This isn't us, Maya wanted to say. *We do surgical extraction, not smash-and-grab like common thieves.* But she needed to focus on the grail. Wil tossed her a carry bag.

"Thirty seconds," said Medix.

She tugged on the case, but it wouldn't come. She forced herself to use both arms and nearly fainted from the pain. Stuck. Fingers shaking, she removed a thin, delicate razor from a pendant on her necklace. She slipped it very carefully in the gap under the case and felt something give way.

"Maya?"

"Got it." She pried the case out of its column and then it was free, and Maya and the grail tumbled backward.

Wil caught them both. Auncle's arms came out of the dark, wrapping around them and the grail.

Wil stiffened. "Get off me!"

Maya let Auncle take the grail. "It's all right," she told Wil. "Let me down."

"Our time is up," Medix announced.

Wil reshaped her armor into human form. She heard Wil say: "Let's blow this joint."

And then they ran.

CHAPTER TWENTY-EIGHT

A boveground, the museum was in chaos.

"You went hard on the smoke," Maya said, sprinting to keep up with Wil. Thick plumes of yellow not yet dissipated hung in the rooms.

Ahead of them, Auncle was very much in danger of losing xyr disguise.

At least there was a closer exit than the one they came in. Unfortunately, the smoke was thicker than anticipated, and they took a wrong turn in a room full of four-meter-tall tablets. Their limited preparation was hurting them.

Medix and Auncle were no longer in view.

There was Byzantine art: they were in the human wing.

Three humans ahead of you! Auncle warned, seconds before a shot narrowly missed them. They ducked behind a Grecian marble sculpture—a replica, Maya hoped, as its head exploded.

"Stay here and stay down," Wil snapped.

Wil stepped into the walkway, bullets pinging off her suit.

Maya gawked as Wil's arms transformed into triple-barreled guns.

"I said stay down!" Wil strode toward the shooters.

You hurt one, said Auncle. *The other two are running very fast, but they are running in the opposite direction of the exit. There are twenty guards that way. Oh well. They are lost. You must also hurry; there are two guards behind you.*

"I see why you keep xyr around," Wil said, coming back. "Course you had to go and get shot."

"Just wanted to make sure you felt *useful,*" Maya said. Her arm was on fire. At least Medix's patch was holding the suit's seal.

They were going, Medix sending them directions in one ear, Auncle steering them clear of other Belzoar. Wil somehow managed to listen to both of them. All Maya could do was follow.

Can you catch a car for us? Maya asked the other two. *We're coming fast.*

They burst out of the museum directly into a plaza billowing with smoke. Patrons in various states of collapse writhed on the ground.

"I thought this stuff was nontoxic!" said Maya.

"It is. Stop talking," snapped Wil.

It was a testament to the chaos that they were almost to the far archway before someone honked a noise that translated to: "Stop them!"

More voices now—the unfortunate tendency for Belzoar groupthink. The walls rumbled with the chorus.

They barreled into the next building, through a crowded room again, and then down the spiral ramp to the magcars.

Everyone is very, very, very, very angry, said Auncle. *Car secure.*

Because we cut the line, said Medix. *Please hurry before we are stampeded for our rudeness. Ha ha ha ha ha ha ha ha ha ha ha ha!*

Wil grabbed Maya around her waist, lifted her off the ground, and shoved the rest of the way into the waiting car.

The crowd recovered and surged forward—but the doors closed first.

They were already moving.

...

Above the world, the clear-domed Upper Terminal was buzzing with security robs.

The terminal was a spiraling deck with a hundred different docking tube openings around the perimeter. To get to the docks, they needed to first pass through an inner circle of security.

The security robs worked through the queue with unfortunate diligence. They were *so close.* It was agonizing.

"Those are Belzoar military robs," reported Wil.

"I no longer have high confidence in my disguise. I believe they will see right through me. I am sad we didn't see the ocean while we were here. What should we do, Mayyyyaa?" Auncle hunkered down under xyr shroud. "My love, are you all right?"

Medix had administered some emergency first aid to Maya in the magcar. Fortunately, he packed some serious drugs. The pain had subsided to manageable levels.

Maya chewed her lip and looked over the mostly Belzoar crowd. "I don't suppose we have any more stinkers?"

"No," said Wil.

"I do not wish to be imprisoned again," said Auncle. "Mayyyaaa, do you remember—"

"Yes," said Maya, who did not want to remember right then. She needed to figure out a plan.

"I am confident we will get past this," said Auncle. "What do you think, Mayyyaa?"

Their line inched forward.

"Need a minute," said Maya. And then she caught a glimpse of a paperback sticking out of a satchel—Liam's—and the rest of them up ahead. She was relieved to see he was unharmed. "Unbelievable."

"I am advising you not to engage," said Wil, following her gaze.

"Maya, it is our unfriends!" said Auncle.

"I know."

"Are you both listening?" Wil asked. "Our only strategy right now is to get through this with minimal fuss. Confronting them now would *not* be minimal fuss."

Wil dragged her into another queue. Auncle and Medix followed, Auncle making unhappy noises. Unfortunately, this queue moved faster than the other one, and now they were almost level with the other group.

Liam saw them first. He was drinking in his last glimpse of his beloved Belzoar world.

She knew he had spotted them, because his head stopped turning.

She lifted one finger to her faceplate.

A long moment, and then he turned away, but the CNE soldiers behind him had already noticed.

The two groups watched each other as the respective queues moved toward the scanning machines. Beyond, the docks beckoned.

"I do not wish to add to your stress, so please take this as a simple query, as we are almost to security," said Medix. "Do you have a plan, Maya?"

"Them," Maya said, rummaging in her bag with her mobile arm.

"What?" said Wil.

"Excuse me." Maya stepped up to the gate. "Is there someone I can speak with?"

"What are you doing?" demanded Wil.

"Please step into the box," the machine said.

"Step in the box, Wil," Maya said.

"Why me?"

"I'm sure you'll figure it out," said Maya.

"Ah." Wil stepped into the box. The machine was silent, and Maya looked over at Auncle, impossible to read beneath the cloth of xyr robes.

"I would like to report a theft," Maya continued. She winced in silent apology to Liam. "That group four rows down stole valuable items from the Museum of Functional and Nonfunctional Objects."

"Human combat suit identified. Occupant will be held for questioning related to recent incident." The box slammed shut around Wil.

The Governance System must have also simultaneously processed Maya's report, because the box around the CNE officer behind Liam also shut.

On Wil's signal, Maya said to Auncle. *Drop your disguise and run for the gate.*

How will we get through the security? Medix wanted to know.

My signal, Wil said, getting the idea.

And then the sides of the box exploded outward, and Wil stood there, arms transformed into her arm cannons.

"I think that was the signal," said Medix.

If the crowd was disturbed by the explosion, they went wild when they saw Auncle.

Xe was the monster of their childhood nightmares: huge, silver, arms that could crumple time, and a sharp-toothed maw that might swallow an unsuspecting mind. Or so the stories went. But also: carrier of the virus. Either way, xe was the worst thing they might see in the same contained space.

At the same time, Maya removed the canister of Purple Rain she'd acquired from the scent purveyor on *Dragons* and began to spray the powerful scent into the air.

Belzoar scrambled in every direction—over snack counters, security barriers, back toward the elevators.

Their group ran through security up the spiral ramp, following the directions to their ship. Maya stumbled, but Medix grabbed her hand and pulled her along.

"Stop!" one of the CNE soldiers shouted from behind them. They had blasted out of their own pens. "You have CNE property!"

They didn't stop. Auncle, when xe wanted to, could move much faster than a human—at least for short distances—and xe did so now, barreling through the corridors ahead of them, telling the *Wonder* to start its engines. The rest of them barely had time to throw themselves into the ship before it was pulling away from the dock.

CHAPTER TWENTY-NINE

They weren't flying fast enough.

Maya strapped herself into one of the acceleration chairs in the common area, already flicking through her virtual dash. "We're being tailed by the CNE ship and three Belzoar ships."

"Lovely," said Wil. "You guys sure have a lot of friends."

Auncle disappeared into the water-filled chamber below.

Medix laughed. "Now *that* is funny."

The ship turned hard, tossing Wil against a far wall.

Medix laughed harder.

"Hastening," Auncle reported over the comm.

Then the ship hurtled forward, pinning them all down. "Danger!" said Medix. "Humans cannot safely sustain this."

Auncle didn't ease up.

The Belzoar ships, built for long-distance more than sprinting, began to fall behind. But the CNE ship stayed on their tail. Apparently it was equipped with more advanced engines than the ones they'd come across before.

The acceleration felt like a giant boulder pressed against her chest.

The node, at least, was only a short distance from the world, particularly at the ever-increasing rate they were traveling.

She sipped shallow breaths, trying to hang on to consciousness. Alarms were sounding. Medix wasn't laughing anymore.

Then the pressure eased. They ran equal pace with the CNE vessel.

"If you have another brilliant plan, Hoshimoto, now would be the time to share it," said Wil. "Because we can't outrun them even if we go through the node."

"We shall let the universe play its hand," said Auncle.

"What the hell does that mean?" said Wil.

The black of the node yawned ahead of them. Except—Maya realized, spotting the distant glare of the sun—they'd left Emerald in the wrong direction. This was the downstream node, toward *Lithian* space, not the node toward home.

"What's that?" asked Medix.

Ahead of them, emerging from the node, was a Lithian ship.

"Climate-fucking son of a plastic-loving corporate motherfucker," said Wil. "I don't understand how you two are still alive."

"We must not panic," said Medix. "I feel—I feel—I—" The rob was clutching the arms of his chair. "Wil, I think I would like to go to sleep. Can you shut me off, please? No, never mind, I wish to see this. What can we do?"

Auncle set the ship into a topsy-turvy corkscrew spin without slowing movement toward the node. A jolt shook Maya's body, and an alarm went off: a projectile that could have come from any of their pursuers had pierced the nose of the ship, sending them into an even more erratic tumble.

Maya shut her eyes against the blue of stars. Her breath came quick, and she didn't know if it was because she was terrified or from the physical strain of the ship movement. She must have blacked out again. When she next glanced at the data, they were much closer to the Lithian ship, and the CNE ship was nearly on their tail. Any moment and they would be sandwiched between the two.

"The Lithian are going to try to ram us," observed Wil.

Every time Auncle adjusted trajectory, the Lithian ship changed course to intercept. At this angle it was going to be difficult to avoid them and make it to the node.

Wil swore again.

Unknown Lithian ship, this is CNE Kenya. *Adjust course now, or we will shoot.*

"What's happening?" Maya asked.

"Apparently, the CNE doesn't want us to die," said Wil. "And they want us to know they're saving our asses."

"After they shot me?"

"They must have realized we have the grail, and they don't want it to be destroyed."

Auncle set the ship into an even more complicated flight pattern, comprehensible only to xyr. The node now was close enough that it took up most of their view. Xe had evened out the course.

Lithian ship, this is your last warning. We will shoot on the count of five if you persist.

"Good lord," said Wil. "The CNE must really want this thing."

"You have no idea."

She felt Wil's eyes on her, narrowed. "I'm realizing how much I don't."

Three . . . two . . . one . . .

"Perhaps we should pull up?" Medix suggested.

Auncle said nothing.

The Lithian ship tucked its nose down at the last possible moment, and the *Wonder* lifted up, so sharply that Maya thought they would miss the node, but they didn't. They spiraled through it, close to the edge.

And then they were falling, they were always falling, except that Auncle was in her mind, and it wasn't words but a feeling of nostalgia so sharp it made Maya's chest ache and her eyes fill with tears. Auncle was doing something with the controls, taking a left, even though there was no such thing as left in space, and even though you didn't fly, you fell, and you never fired the engines when hurtling through the space between, and they were flat, they were nothing, they were infinite, they were every particle in the universe at once—the stars, the people, and all the worlds spinning round—and they were gone.

PART III

THE VISITOR

CHAPTER THIRTY

Maya shook her head a few times to clear the sand from her brain. She checked her virtual dash, then looked up. They hung in cold, dark, empty space.

She changed her ocular lenses to see what the ship was seeing in infrared, and there it was: a dim gas planet orbited by two moons. There was no sun, just the faint shine of stars light-years away.

That couldn't be. There was always a star.

"Where are we?" she whispered.

Auncle was still in xyr quarters down below, but the ship transmitted xyr words. Auncle's voice was tinny and hollow: "A secret place. The place of my people. Somewhere in between here and there. Not a main exit off the IW. To use a human analogy, I believe you would say this is a turn off the service road. Is that right? I am not sure if that is right. Is everyone whole? I apologize for the disruption. The delicacy of the human brain and all its fine blood vessels. This is home for people without a home. You will see. It is pretty. I think so, but also I think it is pleasing to the human brain."

Maya couldn't have heard that right. "I thought the Frenro homeworld was destroyed."

"We do not know. Maybe, maybe not," said Auncle. "In any case, we live here now."

"But—" said Maya, and then she didn't know what to say. She felt something rising in her, an anger, like she'd been tricked. Because she had just risked everything for her friend, whom she would die for. They had shared their dreams. They were as close as two different people could be. She knew everything there was to know. But this—xe had never mentioned this place.

Maybe it was impossible for two separately evolved people to truly understand each other. Auncle was a 233-year-old person; of course there were parts of xyr that Maya didn't know. Until now, Maya hadn't thought it mattered.

You are upset, said Auncle, in her mind. *There are things we have not yet spoken of.*

It's okay, said Maya, trying to make it true.

An odd sensation flickered through her, like she could see Auncle without seeing xyr. Like she was the entire ship.

I have always wanted to know what it was like, to be outside, said Auncle. *To be beyond the Whole. To think my own thoughts. I have tried to want many things. I would like to be your friend, when we are at the end. You will see, when you are with the Whole, the borders of yourself are not clear, Maya. This is how it is for the Frenro. My thoughts become everyone's thoughts, like a wave pulling pebbles from a beach out to the vast sea.*

You asked me how I felt about what happened on Lithis, and I couldn't explain it to you. It was not just that I didn't know, but also that I wasn't sure which feelings were mine and which were the Whole's.

For you, what the Lithians did two hundred and sixty years ago is history, but I know many people who survived it. I was not yet born, but I remember it when I am with the Whole.

Maya considered her feelings about the CNE. *So you felt what happened was justified?*

No. We don't think of things that way. In any case, I told you, it was not our fault. They understood the risks, but they were overconfident in their methods of containment. If they had released us or killed us—

Their laws dictated otherwise, said Maya. Lithians were committed to their sense of equality under the law. She might not agree with the punishment, but she accepted their devotion to consistency. *We shouldn't have gone there in the first place.*

If we had found the grail, though, would you feel the same? Auncle asked.

But we didn't.

I know. This is where I think we have a failure in understanding. But also there is a part of me—and here is what I am telling you—there is a part of me that is not the Whole that does find you where you are.

Maya could feel Auncle's stress radiating upward from the water, xyr desire to be understood. Maya didn't understand. But she wanted to. *Tell me.*

I don't know what is right. I know less the longer I live. But I am more than sad about what happened, I am tearing inside, and I understand we bear responsibility, and yet I cannot think clearly about it. The Whole is everywhere. No matter how far I go. We are the Whole. You, me, your friend on Melancholy who is named Greg.

You mean people who are Infected are part of the Whole? Maya asked. Unease crept along her shoulder blades. *And are you saying the Whole can change your thoughts? Can they change mine?*

You are different, said Auncle. *I have wondered what it would be like to be human or Belzoar or anyone else. You think your own thoughts, and that is beautiful. Human nature is so delightfully chaotic. You fight with each other, you even fight with yourself inside your own mind. I would like to crawl from the ocean and shout from a tall sand dune—to be my own independent person. But that is impossible.*

Why? Maya asked.

You will see.

"Can anyone follow us here?" Medix asked, and Maya jumped, because she'd forgotten they were not alone.

Wil wiped her mouth with the back of her hand, and it came away bloody.

"Not unless they know where to look," said Auncle via the ship, and Maya momentarily relaxed before remembering that *she* was "they" too.

Maya went to the hatch and dropped into the water. Her wounded shoulder screamed in protest. Medix's drugs were wearing off. She swam down to the stern anyway, to peer out between the engines at the node they'd come through.

Frenro as a rule did not look back; it was bad luck. It was Maya who watched their rear.

The node behind them was small, much smaller than any Maya had ever seen. It couldn't have measured more than twenty meters across.

And what's more—she checked her virtual dash again—there was not one, or two, but *twelve* nodes orbiting the planet. She had never heard of so many in one place.

"Mayyyya?" said Auncle, emerging from xyr cave still mostly suited.

Maya pulled herself away from the porthole. Why was she upset? Was she this selfish that she could not be happy for Auncle? She went to her friend.

"We did it. We finally found it."

Auncle wrapped xyr arms around Maya until Maya was buried deep in xyr writhing mass. "Indeed we did." The brevity of xyr response betrayed the immensity of xyr emotions.

Maya felt her anger drain away, replaced by an unexpected peace. "I can't wait to see your world."

Well? messaged Wil, poking her head over the water. *Can we see this thing that caused all the fuss?*

Auncle removed the bags from xyr central cavity. They had taken over a dozen objects, but only one that mattered.

The trunk of the grail was more gray than brown, studded with nodules of a subdued violet hue. Perhaps the water dulled the colors. It was difficult to tell if it was alive, or Frenro-made, or both. That line tended to be fuzzy when it came to Frenro technology.

Auncle turned the grail over in xyr arms. "It is smaller than I thought it would be."

"Yes," agreed Maya. "But very beautiful."

"Yes."

Maya pulled up Huang's description of their first encounter with the grail in her ocular feed:

> *I brushed it with my fingers and felt a tingling through my whole body. It was a peculiar sensation, as if time—or at least my perception of it—had stretched a full minute when only moments had passed.*

Maya removed a glove and reached out a bare hand.

Its tentacles drifted in the water, inert.

They regarded it uncertainly.

"So how does it work?" asked Wil.

"I . . . am not sure," said Auncle. "But the Whole will know. That is where we are going."

"What is the Whole?" asked Medix. He had unstrapped himself and was clinging to the pantry door, looking down at them.

"The Whole of my people," said Auncle. "What is left of us."

They docked at a vast scaffolding structure rigged above the surface of a rocky moon. Below its crust was ice, and below that, frigid liquid water. The scaffolding was built around the rim of a perfect circular hole about a kilometer in diameter, lined with orbs of light—the soft halo was the only illumination in the entire area.

The engineering far exceeded anything humanity—or any other people, for that matter—could achieve.

It was the evidence of how great the Frenro civilization must once have been. Even to this day, explorers who ventured into the Dead Sea would find traces of Frenro ruins at the bottom of coastal shelves or fossilized bodies of Auncle's ancestral biome in the middle of vast deserts.

The known parts of the IW stretched across thousands of nodes. Who knew how vast the IW truly was? And the Frenro had built it.

No wonder the Frenro barely attended to the threat of the people they came across. They had been a people so supreme in their technological and intellectual advancement that they couldn't even conceive of other people being anything but subsumed by their network. Yet here they were: the remnants of a once mighty empire.

Medix performed field surgery on Maya's arm before they descended. Maya studied the Huang journal again to distract herself from the procedure.

> Its body was submerged in water, and below the surface, it was anchored in sand—I wouldn't compare the base to roots, more like the feet of starfish, because every so often it shifted position. We could see how easy it would be to move, and of course immediately we talked about how to do it.

Whatever Medix was doing sent pain lancing through Maya's shoulder so bad she nearly fainted.

"Almost done," said Medix.

Something about the line bothered Maya. *How easy it would be . . .*

She started to write a message to Pickle, before she remembered they were beyond the reach of any commercial data relay drones. An icon appeared of a planet orbiting a sun, around and around again: pending send. They were off the edge of the map.

"Done," said Medix, turning to Wil.

"I'm good," said Wil.

"Would you like something for the pain?" he asked.

Wil grimaced and bent her body, testing its limitations. "Not yet."

They filed into the *Wonder*'s old, creaky, water-filled shuttle, a chamber of the ship that separated from the main body.

There was a dull clank as it detached and began to descend. The humans and rob sat in chairs fixed at the center facing outward, reminiscent of a similar transit—was it just a month ago?—when Maya and Liam had left Earth.

Auncle floated freely about. Xe had removed xyr suit, and Wil kept to one corner, leaning away every time Auncle's arms quested in her direction. Brilliant hues rippled across xyr body, and miniature plumes of water jetted from pores all over xyr skin.

It occurred to Maya that this would be the first time she saw Auncle around xyr family. Auncle had always said that Frenro were extremely social—more than Belzoar, which was hard to imagine. It manifested in Auncle's over-trusting nature and the way xe took to other travelers. Maya wondered if she was about to see Auncle in xyr true form. She had always assumed Auncle was, if not content, then happy. Now she wasn't so sure.

How are you feeling? she asked Auncle.

I wish I could tell you. Cerulean blue flickered across Auncle's skin. *This is the place of my childhood.*

Maya's hands tightened on the armrests of her chair. Another thing she hadn't known.

She didn't go home much herself. It was a long way to go for a place with relatively little to do, and while she loved her parents, she interrupted their simple routine with her brash, untamed energy. But she had visited once with Auncle, because she'd wanted to share a place and people that were part of her.

It was an awkward visit. The settlement was humbler than she remembered, the planet dusty and cracked. Her parents hadn't known how to act around Auncle. They were too respectful, they told no gossip about the neighbors or stories from the war they would never move past. Come back soon, they'd said, but Maya hadn't.

Why did you leave? Maya asked.

Auncle drifted to the window to look at the stars. *To find the grail.*

A chill crept into Maya that was more than the cold water around her. For they'd found the object, and Auncle was going to sell the *Wonder* to pay the mercenaries. It was, as xe'd promised, an ending.

And Maya found herself unprepared for it. She blinked back sudden tears. It was for the best, she knew. It was what she had *wanted*, wasn't it? Auncle safe, and herself settled back on Earth to complete her degree and then—a lifetime on the blue-green planet, she supposed. So why did that thought leave her with a heavy, sinking feeling, like she'd swallowed a lump of lead? She just needed to get used to the idea. It was selfish to want anything else from Auncle.

Through the clear walls of the shuttle, the unending black field of stars was eclipsed by the thick lunar crust rushing up faster than she'd like. They were close enough to see an oily sheen over the surface of the water below, something that kept it from freezing.

Then the walls surrounded them. They sank in the dimness with the illusion of getting nowhere, until abruptly they were at the bottom of the lunar well. The hole was much deeper than it had seemed from above. The night sky was just a shrinking ring of light.

The bottom of the shuttle thunked down against the surface, and then they sank, and everything, if it were possible, seemed even murkier and darker than before.

CHAPTER THIRTY-ONE

The shuttle kept creaking as if it had something to say. A flicker, and then lights flared from their shuttle in all directions.

Auncle guided them through the water with surprising speed.

"How deep is this ocean?" Wil's face was obscured by her helmet, but there was a thrum of anxiety in the other woman's voice.

Maya checked the instruments, but Medix was faster: "Approximately seventy kilometers. Much deeper than the oceans on Earth. We seem to be staying near the surface."

When Maya was a child, she would run through neat rows of sweet potatoes, her feet leaving little prints in the damp dirt. It was summer but still cold enough that there was frost on the ground. Her parents scolded her for not wearing shoes, but she liked to feel the ground beneath her feet, imagine she was on Earth, that she was running toward a vast ocean. She didn't know how to swim, but she'd seen in simulations how the light looked reflected on waves that went on forever.

An ocean would never exist on PeaceLove; maybe a lake.

Now, as on Melancholy, she marveled over the excess of water.

"There," breathed Maya, pointing ahead at the growing pale smudge. The spot resolved into thousands, maybe millions, of lights. "It's beautiful, Auncle."

The Frenro city was built around the peak of an underwater mountain. It was a riotous mishmash of architecture: human-style spires and arched bridges next to honeycomb Belzoar warrens like they'd seen on Emerald, crystalline Oorani towers, and Quietling canopies. It was as if the Frenro had built a city in homage to every people they'd ever caught in their great web.

It was shockingly bright once they were close, illuminated by downward curtains of artificial light. Fine phosphorescent strands with glowing bulbs floated up from the seafloor between the buildings like giant enoki mushrooms, illuminating the city in an unearthly glow.

Unknown life-forms of all shapes and sizes jetted and darted about. The water swarmed with life, and everywhere she saw Frenro, many much larger than Auncle.

They sank, coming to rest against the roof of a tall pagoda. Long white threads unspooled from the top of their platform and wound around the ship like a cocoon until it was firmly anchored in place.

Maya checked to make sure everything was recording on her necklace. If this didn't earn her a degree with honors, then nothing possibly could—assuming it was okay to tell anyone about this.

"Is it just me, or is that the pyramids?" Wil asked.

"Looks like it," Medix agreed.

"Huh. I always wanted to visit Egypt."

Auncle swam into the airlock.

"What are you doing?" Wil asked, when Maya followed.

"I'm not staying here when an entire Frenro city is right outside," said Maya, unable to keep the giddiness out of her voice. It felt as if her whole life had been burning for this moment. "You can stay here if you like."

"And leave you to potentially die?" said Wil, unbuckling with reluctance. "Though if I catch the bug, it's on you."

"It's cold," warned Medix. "You'll lose heat much faster than you do in space. Wil's suit should be good for six hours, but I would guess yours will only protect you from hypothermia for two."

The airlock cycled ship water out and lunar ocean in.

Auncle paused and extended several arms toward Maya. She swam forward, and Auncle pulled her in and swathed her in a strong embrace.

Can't breathe, she said. The pressure eased around her ribs. Heat emanated from Auncle's core, warming her.

Wil and Medix followed, the latter hanging on to Wil's back. They left the hatch. Maya could barely process what she was seeing: Frenro people everywhere, swimming freely or hanging on to bulbous cable cars that rocketed across the city at rapid speed. Pods of Frenro gathering, parting, colorful flashes of conversation too fast for Maya to follow.

It was all so *busy*. Alive.

Floating above the densest part of the city was a giant iridescent sphere. Its surface shimmered, refracting soft rainbows. Maya remembered the dig site where she'd met Auncle, the top of the immense dome buried in the parched ground. This one moved like a buoy, following an invisible current.

"Are you sure we're still in the same universe?" asked Wil.

Auncle was already swimming up toward the sphere, pulling Maya along. Maya braced herself for impact, but there was a gentle pressure as Auncle pierced its membrane with xyr filaments and arms. The skin of the bubble slid over them.

Inside, the sphere seemed to be lined with millions of mirrors, like the shimmering scales of a fish. Colorful translucent platforms floated all about.

The amount of stimuli was too much for the human eye, and Maya was forced to increase the opacity of her helmet to fend off motion sickness.

"The water here is warmer," reported Medix. "But you still shouldn't stay more than a few hours."

"She's not listening," said Wil, "but I copy."

They settled on one of the platforms closer to the center, and Auncle uncoiled several arms to remove the sack of objects from xyr cavity at last. Wil placed the second bag next to it.

Maya's feet settled on the platform. More Frenro than she'd thought existed were entering the sphere.

Emotions seeped into her: anxiety, joy, love, concern, other feelings she didn't have human words for. There was a hunger, beating throughout, a desire to swallow, to consume. She was no longer in control of her feelings. She teetered at the cusp of enlightenment, and if she just gave up her self, this vastness would embrace her, disassemble her, absorb her in all her constituent pieces. She thought her mind might drown in the undertow, and she understood too late Auncle's warning about the Whole.

Then a seed of defiance in her bloomed, that resistance to being anything but herself, the drive to forge her own path that had led her from PeaceLove to distant worlds. She pushed back. *I am me*, she said. *I am only one. A human individual.* The probing tendrils of the web retreated, if not completely, then at least to a safer distance, and she exhaled.

"Did you feel that?" she asked the other two.

They hadn't.

Auncle stroked the plate of her helmet. *Maya, you are our—my— dear friend. I would fly with you again, whichever strand of time we follow. I am sorry. Please remember.*

Why was Auncle apologizing, and why did this sound like goodbye?

The colors that flickered across the Frenro bodies began to synchronize as Auncle displayed their stolen treasure, the grail unexpectedly nondescript among them. Maya yearned to analyze the patterns later when she had access to additional tools back on campus.

Littered among the objects were a few that were unlike the others. "Some of those are Belzoar," she hissed to Wil, indicating the ancient brick-brown artifacts.

"We were in a rush. Didn't exactly have time to check the catalog."

"We have to return them."

"Seriously? Go back to Emerald?" said Wil.

"It's called shipping."

Frenro continued to gather, until it was impossible to see anything but a massive wall of arms and filaments, and the opening and shutting of maws.

"Are Frenro carnivorous?" Wil asked.

"We're not edible," said Maya, with 90 percent confidence, unwilling to admit she was feeling the same instinctual terror crawling under her skin.

Do not fear, said Auncle. Something monstrous and huge probed at Maya's consciousness.

And then she couldn't see anything anymore, not the objects or Auncle, or anything else. She was at the center of a maelstrom of bodies. Something tightened around her neck, the pressure on her suit increasing to dangerous levels. How many times had she explained to Auncle the fragility of a human under the vise of xyr arms? She thought of the tons of life around her that she was smothering in.

"Maya?" Wil was panicking. "We have to get out of here."

Mayyyyyyyyyaaaa . . . but it wasn't her name that the consciousness was speaking, it was something more than herself, like all her insides had been unrolled into a vast mural and reflected back to her in her own mind. She wanted to curl up into a fetal ball, but she couldn't do anything. There was no space to move.

"Auncle," she said. "Help me."

If Auncle responded, she didn't hear it. She didn't even know where Auncle was. A burning sensation began in her body, an axe splitting her skull like a descending migraine. She felt dizzy. Her vision filled with black.

Ending, Auncle had said. It was her ending.

Was this what xe had meant all along?

Maya shut her eyes, and it no longer made any difference because either way she couldn't see beyond the inside of her helmet—

A wave of grief crashed down over her and loss and hope and loss and on and on and on and it took her an eternity, maybe, to realize she was sobbing wretchedly. She was an ant in the shadow of a bronze statue that was tumbling down, and it was only because she was so minuscule that she wasn't crushed already, she was nothing she was nothing she was nothing—

Hands, human hands, under her arms dragging her out.

And then everything and everyone melted away, and she was free, lying on a platform in the middle of a sphere as it emptied out.

"Auncle," she cried, voice hoarse from screaming. But Auncle was gone, disappeared with the rest of them. They were left with only the empty sacks that had held the artifacts and a few Belzoar objects. "Wait," she said, before Medix and Wil could drag her away.

"We must go now," said Medix. "You are in grave danger of hypothermia."

Maya wrenched away. She staggered up and gathered all the remaining objects, and then she followed the mercenary and rob back to the shuttle. It took everything in her to move her arms and legs. She could feel the press of water on her body, even with the moon's gravity as weak as it was.

"What the hell happened?" demanded Wil.

They'd drained the shuttle of water, and Medix plied Maya with hot tea and an old, funky-smelling blanket. The Frenro city below them seemed dimmer somehow.

It was hard to speak with the way her teeth were chattering. "When they came together as the Whole, it was like they knew everything in the universe, or at least all their knowledge was one, and it was so beyond everything we've ever learned—I don't even know, my brain felt like it was on fire."

The edges of her vision wavered, and she could feel every molecule of air against her skin. Stray colors sparkled before her.

"I believe you would have had a stroke if it had lasted much longer," said Medix.

Maya stared at the tin-colored wall, drained, unable to move.

"Maya," said Wil, gentler than Maya would have expected. "What happened?"

"After all that, we were wrong," said Maya. "They could tell right away that it couldn't be implanted or cultivated. The grail was dead." There would be no more Frenro.

And she wept all over again for her friend who had disappeared to a place she couldn't follow and a future lost long before she had ever been born.

"Excuse me," she whispered, as the migraine aura took her.

CHAPTER THIRTY—TWO

M aya dreamed of unending darkness. Time crinkled around her with the brittle fragility of the future. Somewhere, an alarm was bleating.

A narrow thread of light appeared: she was in her cabin in the *Wonder*. She hunted for her boots. Had she just woken up?

The world was blurry, as if she were dreaming about dreaming.

"They're here," someone said, and fear flooded through her.

Below the ship sat the Frenro moon, visible only by the ring of lights around the rim of the entrance to the ocean. Beyond it must be the gas planet it orbited, but without any sunlight, it was too dark to see with her naked eye.

She checked for the source of the alarm. There. Coming toward them from the node were pinpoints of light, growing bigger. The *Wonder* sensors told her it was a flotilla of blocky warships bristling with weapons. Lithian ships. Come to destroy the Frenro haven.

She thought but didn't know why: *They have to help us.* Who was "they," though?

The ships were coming too fast. They were eclipsing the dark with their bright lights.

It recalled all Maya's memories of childhood, hunkered down in an underground chamber with her neighbors, breathing stale air.

The *Wonder* was moving to meet the ships, tiny against the immensity of what had been stirred up.

She pulled up her dash, looking for something. What was she looking for? There, a date and a time. She tried to commit it to memory.

Remember, she told herself fiercely.

The premonition stuttered and then she was strapped to her chair in the common room, and her body was yanked this way and that as the

Wonder twisted and tumbled through space. They were in the midst of a battle, and they were losing.

Light lanced out. One, then five, then a hundred. Their enemies were strafing the moon with their weapons.

Something hit the *Wonder*, and Maya bit her tongue. As the copper taste filled her mouth, Auncle's grief washed over her, and with it swept something new: a peppery rage hot enough to burn down a world. She turned her head to watch the demolition of a thousand years of history.

CHAPTER THIRTY-THREE

The floor of the shuttle was cold and wet, and water dripped from the ceiling in an anxious rhythm.

"There you are," said a voice, and Wil's face appeared above her. "All better?"

She was wrapped in an old sweater, and Wil's arms—flesh, not metal—were around her, rubbing her body, giving her heat. She heard the uncertain thump of the other woman's heart, the rough rattle of her breath through the metal plate across her chest.

Metal hands—Medix's—helped her sit up.

Maya took in her surroundings, attempting to collect herself, to reorient herself in time: under the ocean, tethered to the tower in a Frenro city with Medix and Wil in the *Wonder*'s shuttle. Auncle was nowhere to be seen.

"All right, then?" asked Wil. She looked different with half her armor in pieces on the floor. She was afraid.

Maya could almost believe the foreign city out there was just a virtual projection and the next moment they might walk out the door to sunshine and yellow leaves littering the sidewalk in New Jersey. She wished she could. If only she could forget what she had just seen.

"It was—I saw—" Maya said, and blinked, trying to remember the date, the time. "The Lithians are coming. I have to warn them."

Wil rubbed her arms, then put her gloves on again. "What are you on about?"

"Their entire navy will be here in three weeks." Maya pulled herself to her feet with the aid of a chair. Outside the transparent walls of the shuttle, Frenro swam about, familiar and unfamiliar at the same time. She wondered what humans looked like to them, and a fragmented memory from the Whole came to her: hairy, bipedal, all bony elbows.

"They don't know this place exists," said Wil, as she melded pieces of armor back around her body. "*We* didn't know."

"They saw us go through the node," said Maya. "That might be enough for them to figure it out."

"If that's true, it's a good reason for us to get out of here. We did our job. Once we get our payment, we'll be on our way."

Which required Auncle to sell the *Wonder*. Maya's heart squeezed at the thought. Assuming xe was coming back. Was xe? Maya turned back to the water, searching for Auncle out in the deep. "How long have we been here?"

"Three and a half hours," said Medix.

Wil stood and stretched. "So yeah, if you can get Auncle to come back, that'd be great. And not just because I'm hungry. This rickety air cycler seems to be on the fritz, which means we'll be asphyxiating soon if we don't get back to the ship."

Maya put a hand on the wall, and reached for her friend. *Auncle?*

A Frenro drifted closer, brushing the side of the shuttle with a portion of xyr arms. She embarrassed herself by thinking a moment this might be Auncle, but this one was bigger than xyr.

"I'm looking for my friend," she said, uncertain xe might understand her without translation.

"MAYYYAAA," the shuttle shouted, and Maya and Wil both jumped. "AUNCLE IS SLEEPING."

Maya blinked. Auncle meditated, but for as long as she'd known xyr, xe'd never slept. Maya didn't know it was something Frenro did.

"IT IS JOYFUL TO SEE YOU, MY LITTLE FRIEND."

Wil managed to turn down the volume before this person continued.

"We have never met, but you are in us. We love you. Once, one of us saw the blue oceans of Earth. Such beauty! A people with a short, intense history. We admire the grandness of feeling in your world, the liveliness of its waters."

"Who are you?" Wil asked.

"You can call me Elephant," said the Frenro. "Yes, that is what I would like to be called. A name! A human name! How exciting. I am large, you see, compared to you. Ha ha ha."

Medix laughed too.

Elephant was still talking, and Maya realized she had lost the thread. Something about carbonated drinks and squirrels.

"Sorry, what did you say?"

"Am I speaking too fast for you? I thought I was speaking very slowly. I am not used to human cognitive speed, please forgive me. Is. This. Slow. Enough?"

Medix, if he could cry, would have been in tears by now. "It's too funny," he said.

"I met your sister once," said Elephant.

"I don't—I don't have a sister?" Though Elephant had said it so confidently, Maya almost believed it for a second.

"Your aunt or mother? I am not sure. Dr. Huang," Elephant said. "A woman, yes?"

Maya's heart leapt. "Dr. Huang? When? Where? How?"

"She was very special. We talked for many days. Calendar brought her here, because she wanted to help us. I also remember this funny song, how did it go . . . ? She wanted to go to that place—oh, what did she call it? I warned her not to go there, to take nothing. It's a sad place. Too sad. The place she went to."

"The Encyclopedium?" Maya asked. "Where is it?"

"I . . . we don't remember anymore, I'm sorry."

Wil knocked on the window. "Sorry to interrupt, but how long is Auncle going to sleep?"

"Perhaps a day," said Elephant. "Perhaps less. Then again, perhaps a week or a year."

"No, no, no," said Wil. "That won't work. You have to wake xyr up."

"I cannot," said Elephant, nearly detaching from the ship in alarm. "That would be fatal. Why do you not take yourself back?"

Maya could have groaned. How did someone this old know so little? She checked the dash. Wil was right about the cycler. They didn't have more than a few hours.

Wil threw up her hands. "Because only you people can drive the shuttle."

Elephant detached and swam about to get a better view of the inside. "Ah yes, but that is not true. You can talk to it."

"This one seems very confused," Wil said to Maya.

"Not you, loud one. The little friend, Maya. She is part of the Whole, is she not? Have you never conversed with the shuttle?"

As one, Wil and Medix looked at Maya.

Maya frowned. Auncle had never mentioned—and she had never thought—

With trepidation, she peeled off her gloves and approached the moist gelatinous mass that Auncle used to commune with the ship.

She pierced it with her fingers. The surface was cold as ice and viscous, though it didn't stick to her hands. She closed her eyes and recalled the feeling of the Whole, of surrendering her mind to its embrace for just an instant. And suddenly she felt the ship *inside* her. It wasn't comfortable, like having a tiny pebble in your shoe, or a splinter just under the skin of your fingertip.

Up? she thought.

And the shuttle jerked. It was still caught in the cocoon of strands.

"Jesus," said Wil.

Maya snatched her hands back.

"Ah yes," said Elephant. "You see? That should do fine."

"All right," said Wil, smacking two hands together with a loud crack. "Let's go then."

"Wait," said Maya, before Elephant swam away. "I have to tell you what I saw. The Lithians—"

"—are coming," finished Elephant. "Of course, the Whole has seen this. We have known this would happen. It is impossible to know all futures, but we have seen many versions of this before. We are at a crossroads in time, are we not? It is sad, but perhaps doors will open when others are closed."

"What are you talking about?" Maya asked.

"The end of our world," said Elephant. "We cannot go on like this any longer."

"But you have to *do* something," said Maya. "Evacuate or fight back or *something*."

"We've tried these things before," said Elephant. "It is unlikely to work. We are considering what is possible."

"You don't have time!"

The air cycler warning went off.

"Maya," warned Wil. "We need to go."

With a wrench, Maya slipped her hands into the ship controls again. The sensation came back to her in response, a tingly feeling of being understood that left her feeling dizzy but also, for a brief moment, like she was home with her parents on PeaceLove, listening to music and practicing English with her mother.

She gritted her teeth and projected a desire.

A different home. *Wonder.*

She opened one eye. Nothing. Tried again.

This time, she felt something in her arms, similar to what she'd felt before. Like a beckoning.

She tried a third time. The threads surrounding the shuttle unwound. They floated free and began to sink.

"Don't think you got it," said Wil.

Back, she thought. *I am this ship. I am you, and you are me.*

And there was a jolt under her feet as the small craft moved, a many-faceted orb in the dark. She hoped she was going the right way. For long minutes, she thought they might be lost in the lightless sea, but there was the glow of the opening ahead of them. She exhaled, and Wil clapped her on the shoulder.

"You did it!"

Her head throbbed, and she felt tingling on one side of her face, her body.

Oh god, her migraine was returning. She'd never had two migraines so close together. It was very inconvenient.

Ignoring the flickers of aura, she urged the craft forward, then realized she didn't know how to stop. She tried to will the ship to do so. It trembled but kept going.

It turned out the ship knew better than she did. There was the sea anchor, with the cables dangling from above. The shuttle rose until the plate and cables had locked in place, and then they were rising up through the surface into space.

Maya's vision flashed with snatches of recollections each time she blinked: a mind-boggling number of ships approaching the Frenro moon. A shiver took her.

She saw that world again: swirling pink dust, and a feeling of horror and loss so deep, a sob tore out of her chest.

"You must let go, Maya," she heard Medix say.

Space and time throbbed around her as Wil ripped her from the controls, and Medix injected her with something that made her veins burn. She gulped and clung to him, felt the solidity of his metal body beneath her fingers. "Thank you." The outline of the shuttle resolidified. She came back to the present.

"Shit," said Wil, as they emerged from the entrance of the underground sea.

Three warships were approaching from the Emerald node—but they weren't Lithian, they were CNE.

CHAPTER THIRTY-FOUR

This just gets better and better," said Wil, fumbling with a bottle of sanitizer. She got the cap off and began to wipe her face and neck and hands.

"That won't do anything," said Maya.

Wil rounded on her. "It's none of your business how I choose to live."

"Funny, that's what we said when we declared independence," Maya said, but her face heated with embarrassment. "I'm sorry. You're right."

Medix came and took the bottle from Wil before she could swill it.

There was a *ping!* on Maya's feed as dozens of messages came in all at once. A commercial data relay drone must have come and gone already a few times with the fleet.

A note from Professor Barnes, expressing confusion about Maya's whereabouts, and then another with concern that there did not seem to be any Professor Aman, and would Maya please respond as soon as possible? The Chair apparently was asking for reports from all students abroad, given increasingly poor travel conditions and the state of the web.

Maya would have thought the stress of her present circumstances would have prevented her from further stress, but apparently that was not how her brain worked.

There was a message from Greg on Melancholy, wanting to know if the intel had panned out and if she was still alive, and a message from Pickle. The archives had been closed because of a bomb scare related, they thought, to fear over the web. But they had *finally* found a copy of the *Traveler*'s manifest in a spare external storage device. Good old Pickle.

Maya checked the thirteenth and fourteenth years in the supply log.

No reference to any stardust machine or other significant artifacts. That would have been too easy.

"Are you seriously checking your messages right now?" Wil asked.

"No," said Maya.

"I asked you what your plan is. Because if you don't have one, Medix and I may have to make our own."

"We can't go anywhere without Auncle, and you can't get *paid* without xyr."

Wil growled in frustration.

Maya punched open a channel as she limped into her cabin to change out of her suit. She wasn't about to talk to a CNE officer smelling like a three-day-old shirt. Her injured arm was shooting with pain again. She needed more painkillers.

The approaching ships were mere blots in the starry night. If the gas giant were visible, the ships might have seemed small against such scale. As it was, they lacked any context, except that they would loom over the *Wonder.*

Maya was impressed that they'd fit through one of the system's dwarf nodes, even though she knew intellectually that nodes weren't bound by three-dimensional constraints.

"Hi," said Maya. "If you are listening, please respond. I'd like to speak with the person in charge. Please."

Medix, who had entered her room without permission, as usual, gave her an encouraging thumbs-up.

Silence. Then: "*Wonder,* this is Commander Browning of *O Canada.* Nice to meet again."

Maya raised the hanten she'd bought on *Dragons* from the cleaning bin and sniffed, then redeposited it, and gave the box a couple of kicks until it started churning.

"I sure hope it's nice." Maya grabbed a different shirt. "Do you mind?" she mouthed, shooing the rob out of her room again. "Do you come in peace then?" What a laugh. Coming into a system with three—no, four—warships was not peaceful.

"We hope so," said the Commander, with a warmth that belied the seriousness of the situation. "Am I speaking with Maya Hoshimoto?"

A stream of basic biographical information appeared in her feed:

Commander Divya Browning, CNE Sixth Fleet. Her hobbies include low-gravity golf and reforestation. She has served in the Coalition of the Nations of Earth Navy for thirty-three years.

Which meant she fought in the War of Independence. Super.

Somehow it didn't surprise her that the Commander knew exactly who she was.

"Yeah. Is Dr. Garcia with you?" She tugged on a clean shirt and pulled up a visual projection.

Commander Browning stood on the bridge, sailors buzzing around her, all business.

A second, familiar figure stepped into the foreground. He was wearing an azure neckerchief printed with crescent moons. Had the man brought his entire scarf collection with him to space?

"Hello, again. I hear you've been busy."

"Understatement," said Maya.

"I wanted to commend you on the job you've done," said Dr. Garcia. "I was worried you truly had a change of heart, but then you stole the book."

"What do you mean?"

"The Huang book. I left it for you. Wait. You still didn't realize? Oh, you didn't. I can see from your face."

Maya had pressed a hand over her mouth in horror. She forced herself to adopt an expression that was, if not calm, at least more blank.

"I didn't steal the grail for you."

"Exactly. I knew you wouldn't do it for me. But you got it all the same. All's well that ends well. So long as your Frenro are cooperative, we can avoid any incident and return back to our corner of the universe, and they can stay in theirs."

"Just to be clear . . ." Maya walked into the pantry, already transmitting an order to the cooker for ramen. They'd been down below for ten hours, and she was dizzy with hunger. "I don't speak for the people of this system. I'm just a grad student here to do fieldwork."

Dr. Garcia laughed. Medix did too. "We both know you're not 'just' anything, Hoshimoto. Let's drop the act here. You broke into that museum same as we did. Except you got Huang's stardust machine."

"Now that you mention it, it's coming back to me. Something about, oh, yeah, your guys *shot* me."

Dr. Garcia threw an exasperated look to Commander Browning, like *You see what I have to deal with?*

"All we need is the machine," said the Commander. "This is an existential threat to all of humankind."

"Yes," said Dr. Garcia. "While you've been hiding, we lost another node."

Maya's heart dropped. "Which one?"

"Melancholy," he said, and the ship seemed to wobble under Maya's boots.

"Damn," said Wil.

Maya thought of the way the sun set over the waves at night, Greg and eir wonderful shop, the university, the noodle shops she'd stayed late at, the rich scent of the flowers in the Memorial Garden—everyone and everything she'd known and loved there. Her memories of that place cascaded in her mind. She couldn't think of the world as gone. It couldn't be.

Maya swayed where she stood. She didn't know how to process the information, make it feel real.

"And now you finally understand that we don't have a choice. We need the machine, and we will retrieve it, with or without cooperation."

"Maya?" Wil asked, when Maya didn't respond.

Maya sat down on the table and put her head in her hands. "We don't—I don't have it."

Liam poked his head into the frame behind Garcia. She was relieved to see he'd made it through okay. "Come on, Maya. Quit screwing around. Sorry, she's like this."

On second thought, he could go back to Emerald for all she cared.

"I'm telling the truth!" said Maya. "We took it, but it was dead. It doesn't work."

Silence on the other side. The feed froze a moment. They must be discussing what to do. It unfroze.

"I have to say, I really hope you're lying," said Dr. Garcia, front and center again.

"I wish I were." There was a ding, and Medix removed the bowl from the cooker for her. The fragrant smell of noodles filled the ship, but Maya had lost her appetite.

"Explain," said Dr. Garcia.

Maya dutifully took a bite, but the noodles were too hot. She exhaled around the scalding mouthful and blinked back tears.

Then she explained what had happened. "The grail is a living thing," she said. "Maybe this one died due to improper storage and preservation techniques. Anyway, it cannot be revived. It definitely is not going to fix anything. So."

"If that's true, that is most unfortunate," said Dr. Garcia.

"I'm telling the truth!"

"She knows what she's talking about," she heard Liam say, ". . . when it comes to Frenro artifacts anyway."

"We may be able to figure out how it works even if it is dead," said Dr. Garcia. "We'll take it."

"We don't have it," said Maya. "We gave it to the Frenro already. It's down there."

The transmission cut again while the other side conferred.

"I'd like to get out of here as soon as *convenient*," said Wil from the couch, resuming their conversation from before. She glanced up at the ships.

"Are you serious? We can't leave now." Maya didn't know why the declaration bothered her so much. Rationally, she knew that Wil was within her rights. They'd done the job they'd agreed to do. There was no obligation to face down CNE battleships in defense of these people she didn't know. Not to mention the Lithian ships that must be on their way. And yet, Maya had thought that Wil—well, never mind what she'd thought.

"Look," said Wil. "I understand what you're trying to do here. You're a woman with a cause. That's admirable. But you're in the way of the forces of civilization here. Whatever is going to happen, we'll get squished in the middle. My recommendation is you figure out how to fly this thing like you did with the shuttle so we can get out of the way."

"I won't leave Auncle," said Maya. Also, flying a shuttle was one thing. Flying the *Wonder*? She couldn't imagine it.

Wil propped her legs on the couch and began to remove pieces of her leg armor, wincing as she did. "I'm pretty sure xe almost killed you a little while ago."

"Xe couldn't have known the effect exposure to the Whole would have on me."

"You don't even know when xe is going to wake up!"

Maya stirred the noodles with her chopsticks.

The comm beeped twice, and the projection returned.

Liam's hunched form appeared before them. "Hey," he said. "Dr. Garcia and I are coming over. So don't let your intimidating colleague shoot us, okay?"

"And if I say no?"

"Dammit, Hoshimoto, I'm trying to help you here!" said Liam. "The alternative is they go down and get what they want anyway by force. I convinced them it might be more expedient to try a civilized approach first."

"Just you and Garcia. No special friends. Or I won't even open the door."

"Yeah, yeah. No soldiers. Don't worry."

"And bring fresh fruit if you have any!"

"You're impossible," said Liam, but he smiled.

CHAPTER THIRTY—FIVE

R emarkable," Dr. Garcia had been saying every few minutes all the way from the *Wonder* to the Frenro city.

If he doesn't stop saying that, Maya messaged Liam, *he can swim back.*

"Uh, DJ," said Liam, who had mostly recovered from the descent into the water. "Can you tell us about the expedition you made to the Quietling Nodal Region?"

Dr. Garcia knelt and examined the shuttle's air cycler, which Maya had managed to temporarily fix. "This isn't Frenro."

Liam's big idea was to have Dr. Garcia speak with the Frenro to convince them to hand over the grail and any other information about how the web could be repaired.

Maya didn't want to be here, didn't want to think about what was happening to the rest of the Interstellar Web, but the warning shot that had chipped a light off the lunar rim when she tried to refuse had convinced her.

Wil and Medix stayed behind to watch the ship, just in case the CNE decided to try anything. What they might do against four CNE battleships, Maya wasn't really sure, but she felt better knowing they were up there.

"Quietling cyclers are better." Also, Frenro components were hard to come by, and over the years the *Wonder* had become a Frankenstein creation of different tech. The Frenro pieces were easy to identify because they were bioengineered rather than manufactured.

"Remarkable."

Maya rolled her eyes spaceward. *I can't believe you like this guy.*

He's brilliant, said Liam.

He's a sellout, said Maya. She wanted to ask about Melancholy, not because she thought there was anything to know, but because there was a growing ache inside her that she needed to press. She didn't because she didn't trust herself not to cry.

"Tell us how you're able to drive this shuttle," said Dr. Garcia.

"No." Medix had given her a pharmaceutical cocktail before descent that seemed to be buffering her from the worst of the effects of tangling minds with a Frenro shuttle. She just hoped it didn't wear off before they got back. Medix had warned her too much of the medication could kill her.

Liam cleared his throat. "How's your arm?"

"Terrible," she said. "Thanks for that, by the way."

Liam winced.

"And how are you finding the outside world?" Maya asked.

"You'll think it's silly," Liam said, "but I have to admit, until now I never understood what it is to be the other. Like the idea that we are as strange to the people we study as they are to us. I knew it intellectually, but I didn't understand it until now. When we were on Emerald in that museum, I saw a painting of a white canoe floating on a lake in the human wing. They'd hung the painting upside down. I laughed because it seemed so obvious to me, even if it was a little abstract. But no one had noticed, because they don't have canoes."

They docked at the tower, and Maya could have cried when Auncle appeared, swimming up from the iridescent gleam of a building far below. She wondered how she could have ever mistaken another for her dear friend.

"Are you all right, Auncle?"

"I am very well, dear one," came Auncle's voice. "I think you will find my memory improved. I have dreamed with the Whole."

Maya zipped up her suit and yanked Liam down by his helmet to check his seal. She pointedly declined to offer the same service for Dr. Garcia.

"I'm sorry about the grail," said Maya to Auncle.

"Never mind. We found this one. It gives me hope that we will find another."

Maya thought of the recurring dream she'd had of that planet with pink clouds and the feeling of holding a living grail in her arms. No way was she mentioning it in front of Dr. Garcia.

"They want to see it," Maya said.

"Ah," said Auncle. "Unfortunately, we have already assimilated it."

"You—" began Dr. Garcia.

"Does that mean what it sounds like?" asked Liam.

"They ate it," said Maya, in her own way as horrified as Dr. Garcia, but also laughing at the absurdity of it all, the futility of this entire effort on all sides.

"Yes, we reabsorbed the material among us," said Auncle. "It did not taste very good. That was unexpected. Perhaps it was too old."

"Well, shit," said Liam. "Now what?"

Dr. Garcia folded his arms. "We'd like to talk to your leaders anyway." He had not come this far to accept a simple no.

"They have no leaders," Maya said.

"Someone who can speak for you," Dr. Garcia said.

"Yes," said Auncle. "Everyone is waiting."

Xe led them again to the sphere. Maya hoped this time it would be easier.

"Do you think the Whole is the end state of advanced civilization, like the natural progression of mass media and information?" Liam wondered, and his capacity to intellectualize during a once-in-a-lifetime encounter amazed Maya.

"I hope not," said Maya, thinking about how she'd chafed under the rigidity of PeaceLove settlement culture. Conformity was important when you needed to regulate all aspects of life for the group to survive, but something in Maya had always resisted the shape of it.

She could see a new theory forming in his brain. A part of her resented that they could each have come through this experience, and Liam was the one who would probably publish a paper about it. At least maybe she could blackmail him into helping her not get expelled.

"What's happening?" Liam asked, craning his neck to look up.

The Frenro formed a geometric formation above them, arms wound with arms, filaments to filaments, forming a complex crystalline structure made up of hexagons, not unlike the shape of Auncle's ship. Where the Frenro merged, they began to emanate a phosphorescence, until the water was illuminated bluish green.

You won't let them fry my brain, will you? she asked Auncle.

I will remember the delicacy of your wrinkled lobes, Auncle assured her.

It began.

The great wave crested over the edge of her mind.

"This is . . ." Liam trailed, unable to say exactly what it was.

"Remarkable?" said Maya, latching on to his voice like an anchor. The medication Medix had administered for the shuttle seemed to be muting the effects here a little too.

He choked back a laugh. "Yeah. It is."

Dr. Garcia was, for once, awed into silence.

The feelings and ideas thrummed through her body. Inside her helmet, she felt her hair lift like she was statically charged.

"What do you want to ask them?" Maya asked.

"How can we create our own nodes?" Dr. Garcia asked.

Maya shut her eyes and opened herself to the Whole a little more. Not the same volume as before. She unfurled herself just a fraction, and ideas rushed in.

The shape of a people, billions of them, slowly moving out among the stars. Her puny human mind struggled to package what she was "knowing" into a metaphor she could grasp. It was like a fungal network branching and branching again: the thousands and thousands of nodes like mushrooms, pushing up through the soil, reaching out their invisible tendrils toward living worlds.

When was this? she wondered, thinking of Earth.

Unknown. A long, long time ago.

The Frenro explored with a hunger to find other life. And they found it everywhere. Wherever they traveled, they absorbed new cultures and technologies and shared in return, assimilated with a relentless compulsion. There was an arrogance to their obliviousness about the impact they had on other people.

That last stray thought was Maya's. She felt it swallowed up by the Whole and returned back, polished and smooth: The Frenro were benevolent. Never ill-intentioned. People were happy to meet them. She grasped for the original thought, but it was gone.

Most of the worlds were barren, but as in the current age, some were home to life in its infinite forms: beings made of gas or liquid that humans would not even have recognized as life, others almost humanoid.

And then one day, they intersected with a people who had built their own highways between the stars. Their network was even vaster than the IW.

At first the Frenro were overjoyed, but these people were hostile. A war began. Everywhere, she saw glowing nodes collapsing, the whole giant web de-linking one by one. Her chest tightened.

And worse: a sickness took the Frenro and then all the people in their network. The virus. It caught the IW like brush fire.

Maya gagged. The scent of it was everywhere.

With a gasp she staggered back, slamming her mind shut. Threw her mind toward anything familiar, mundane: the scent of green tea steeping, a piece of soft sugar candy dissolving on her tongue. Liam caught her arm.

"You all right?"

"What are they saying?" Dr. Garcia asked, voice sharp with envy.

Maya's thoughts were a shimmering constellation, as if she were holding twenty ideas in her mind at the same time; she couldn't comprehend the noise. "It's happened before. Not just one node like the old Lithian homeworld, but whole regions of the IW dying—no human sense of when. I saw, or *remember*, these people I've never heard of before. And the sensation of diminishing, like my mind was flaking away." She clutched herself. "These people, whoever they were, they made the virus. They infected the Frenro, and it spread to other living things in the network. About eighty percent of the IW collapsed."

"But they were able to rebuild it," said Garcia eagerly.

"Sort of." Maya's knees bent, and she would have stumbled if Liam hadn't lifted her up. "Some of it came back, and new pathways grew."

"But how?"

She retreated: Garcia was too close, his helmet knocking against hers. She recalled her attempts to explain to Auncle the human idea of personal space. She giggled. Her memories felt supercharged. It wasn't just a simple recollection but a flash of an infinite series of moments.

"Should we go back to the shuttle?" Liam asked.

She itched at her arms through the suit. The need to tear her skin open with her fingernails was overwhelming. She needed to remove the gloves, the suit—

"Stop that," said Liam, grabbing her hands.

"I think I'm having a physiological reaction," said Maya, wishing

Medix were here. It felt like each of her skin cells was its own chattering organism.

Above them, she could feel the Whole watching. Waiting. She wished Auncle would come back, but xe had merged with the others. A million feelings and thoughts pressed down on her. She would flatten.

Dimly, she was aware of the two men arguing:

"She's not okay!" said Liam.

"We can't leave here without proper answers. Maya?"

"Give her a moment."

"I appreciate the risk she's taking, but our future as a species is at stake. And unfortunately Hoshimoto is the only one of us who can ask."

"Maybe if the CNE didn't bar Infected people from its ranks, you wouldn't have this problem," said Liam. *Bless his grumpy liberal heart*, she thought distantly.

Dr. Garcia spread his hands, expression unreadable, faceplate glittering a rainbow of colors.

Maya thought she could see shades reflected there that she had never seen before, beyond the range of human vision. She reached out to touch them, and they flitted away. For a moment, she saw him very old, his skin sagging and wrinkled. She blinked.

"Now, please. Hoshimoto."

"You can't just force her to risk her life." Liam looped one arm around her waist, the other holding her hand, to keep her upright.

"Humans," said Maya with a laugh. "What an unusual species. Each one, their own Whole, an ecosystem unto themself. They're one of the least cohesive and collaborative advanced people we've ever met." There was something wrong with her voice. She couldn't stop talking. "They deprive each other of resources and knowledge. Until we met them, we thought it was impossible a people such as this could even have achieved intrasolar space travel."

A wave of revulsion took her, and she spasmed with it.

"Maya," said Liam. "Was that you speaking? Or—or someone else?"

She bent her head back and looked up at the vast formation above them. Her mind was all muddled. Her whole body felt like it was on fire, pulsing in time with the flickering colors above her.

"Are you the Frenro?" said Dr. Garcia, eagerly. "Can you hear me if I talk to you?"

She couldn't say. She held her hands out, and ice and prickling pain began to travel all over her arms and her torso, as if she might combust. "We want peace," she said. "We want everyone to leave and never return."

Her eyes rolled back into her head, and she saw them again, out there on the periphery like a swarm: the whole Lithian fleet, every ship they'd ever built or acquired, coming for them on the wings of malintent. The moon would be cracked open, the water poisoned. Everything would die.

Elephant had mentioned an ending, and this was what that was—not just here but everywhere.

It would all end: the Frenro, the IW, everything.

She didn't know if her eyes were open or closed.

It was too bright. She tried to scream but couldn't hear her voice beyond the sound of bees, thousands of angry bees, buzzing in a cloud that enveloped her.

CHAPTER THIRTY-SIX

F or all that she was a woman who could sometimes see the bad things in her future, Maya had not foreseen ending up in the med center of a CNE warship.

The nurses bore an uncanny resemblance to Medix, though the nurse attending her did not have Medix's bedside manner, that was for sure. Their fingers were cold as they grasped her arm and injected her with something.

They'd emptied out an entire clinic for her, Dr. Garcia, and Liam—a precaution after their exposure in the Frenro city.

"You were shot," the nurse told her.

"By these guys," said Maya, indicating the two men next to her.

"And you had a stroke."

"Figures." Maya lifted her arms tentatively, moved her jaw.

"Your colleague was able to administer nanobots immediately. It averted any damage to your nervous system."

"I told you I'm not useless," Liam said from a chair on her left. "I was a volunteer EMT in college." He wore a full bio suit and was reading her book about Japanese pickling. Why did everyone feel like they could just help themselves to her books?

"How did we get back?"

"Auncle," said Liam. "It was very dramatic. You collapsed, and xe came flying out of formation and scooped you up. I thought xe was going to eat you. But xe carried you back to the shuttle in xyr arms, and all the other Frenro were flashing this purple-white pattern and the water turned so dark we could barely see. It felt like they were upset. Which is a faulty assumption, because of course I lack proper cultural context, so strike that from the record. But in any case, xe brought us back to the *Wonder*, and your rob told us to take you here for medical attention."

The door opened and Commander Browning entered in the same bio suit as Liam.

"Hello, 'I'm just a grad student,'" said the Commander, coming to peer down at her. The Commander did a good job faking cheer, but her eyes were bloodshot. "How is your 'fieldwork' going?"

"Hard to say," said Maya. "I'm either going to get expelled for faking a professor and breaking into a foreign museum or praised for being the first human to visit a Frenro city. If history is any indication, it could go either way—what do you think, Liam?"

"You certainly have a knack for distinguishing yourself with complication," said Liam.

The one single silver lining of the loss of Melancholy—and she felt horrible for thinking it—was that Dr. Barnes wouldn't have any further way to clarify whether Maya had been telling the truth about her project sponsor.

Maya struggled and failed to sit up. "What are you going to do now?" The impending Lithian threat loomed in the back of her mind, but the CNE was the more urgent situation.

Commander Browning took a seat. "Our first priority will be to secure this system. Frenro aside, a twelve-node system is of significant strategic, military, and economic value. There are already multiple Belzoar and Quietling probes in system." If the Quietling knew about this place, the whole IW knew. They weren't ones to keep information to themselves. "Fortunately, we got here first."

"But, the Frenro—" began Maya, thinking about how they had retreated here in order to avoid being found.

"—know more about the IW than anyone else. We need to know what they know," said Dr. Garcia. "More than what they've told us so far."

"And what, you're going to threaten them with your big guns until they do?"

"This is not the time for campus activism," Dr. Garcia said. "This is real life. We have to do what we need to do to protect ourselves. Unless you want what happened to Melancholy to happen to PeaceLove, to Earth. What's the one thing common to all life? The fight to survive. We're not exceptional martyrs. There comes a time when you need to quit being selfish, get off your moral throne, and pick a side."

Maya clenched her jaw. Liam avoided her eyes. There had to be a way to fix this situation.

Auncle? she asked.

Mayyyyaaa. Auncle's response was immediate. *Are you healthy? I was very worried for you. These unfriends did not appreciate that we assimilated the grail. They are most unhappy.*

I'm afraid we made a mess. Did you decide what to do about the Lithians?

There are many things that cannot be done, said Auncle. *The Whole is considering.* She could feel xyr worry like a taut red string between them.

Can't you defend yourself? Fight? It wasn't what she would normally suggest. But what other option was there? The Lithians had always believed the Frenro were a threat, now only underscored by what had happened — what she and Auncle had done — on Lithis. They wouldn't hesitate to finish what they had started two centuries ago.

It has been a long, long, long, long time since we have done anything like that, said Auncle. *That is why we came here.*

"We'll keep you here for observation," Commander Browning was saying.

Maya's attention snapped back to the discussion. "No. I'm going back to the *Wonder.*"

She struggled upright with Liam's assistance. "If you want my help, you'll let me go."

"I don't think you're in a position to dictate terms," said Dr. Garcia.

"I am," said Maya, doing her best to match his bravado. "You can't speak to the Whole without me." Not that she wanted to ever do *that* again. And then she had an idea. Possibly a bad one, but she was a little foggy from the drugs.

She told them about the Lithians. "If you want this system, you have to help the Frenro," Maya concluded. "They aren't fighters."

Commander Browning knit her fingers together. "The Lithian fleet is coming here in three weeks?"

"Wait," said Dr. Garcia. "You actually believe she can see the future?"

"I saw enough cases of it during the war," the Commander said. "I don't think the SU could have matched us without it."

"'See' is an exaggeration. More like drunken glimpses," said Maya.

"That must help with exams," said Liam.

"I wish."

"We appreciate the information," said Commander Browning. "It's good that you told us."

"So you'll help them?"

"It'll be discussed."

Maya bit back an acidic retort. That wouldn't help her cause. "You're not going to just sit here and watch the Frenro be annihilated?" It was the least hostile thing she could think of to say in the moment.

"She's not saying they won't help," said Liam.

"Our job is to protect *human* interests," said the Commander. "We aren't the interstellar police. There are limits to our ability to get involved."

Maya jerked the intravenous needle out of her arm. She could tell the medic didn't like that. "The Frenro are tied to the IW. I saw it. If the Lithians destroy the Frenro, the IW will collapse."

"No one can explain what they saw, including you," said Dr. Garcia. "And we still don't know *who* is behind the destruction of the nodes."

Maya looked pleadingly at Liam.

"The Frenro do have knowledge we need," he offered.

She glared at the ceiling. There was a stain, dark and irregular. It looked like blood, and Maya could only imagine how it ended up there: a fast turn in combat, a body not properly secured flung upward, spattered against the bioplastic waffle ceiling.

"Excuse me," said the medic. "This conversation is stressing our patient."

"It's fine," said Maya. "This is important."

"I'm surprised a people could last this long without any defenses," said Liam to himself, testing another new thesis.

Dr. Garcia crossed his arms, lips a thin line. His face was waxy and tired, and it gave him a deceptively kind, fatherly look. "We need the stardust machine."

Maya gripped the bed rails. "Protecting this moon is the right thing to do. I mean, if it doesn't speak to your innate sense of what's right, then you and I are *not* on the same side. But it doesn't mean I don't want to save the IW. So here's my deal: if you protect the Frenro from this invasion, I'll find you the grail—another one."

Liam sucked in a breath. Already he was getting excited. "You know where one is?"

"Not exactly," said Maya. "But I saw it."

"Really," said the Commander.

Maya shut her eyes, wishing she were back on the green lawn under a magnolia tree with nothing worse to deal with than coursework. Auncle wouldn't understand, but if it saved xyr and the Frenro from what was coming—well, that would be worth it, wouldn't it? Even if she hated herself for the rest of her life.

She thought of the dream world, the ancient building with its dimly lit corridors, and something that hunted her in the dark. How terrified and awful she felt just thinking about it. But wherever that was, she was certain now—that was where she needed to go. She just needed to figure out where it was.

It was like she had all the pieces in her hands, if she could only put them together. She needed to return to the *Wonder*, to look through the Huang journal, all the files, and all the pieces Pickle had sent her. If she just combed through everything again, maybe she'd find her answer. "I'm going to find it. And I'll give it to you."

CHAPTER THIRTY—SEVEN

"Tea?" Medix asked.

"Sure," said Liam.

"Not my cup," said Wil, which left only Maya's mug. Fortunately for Liam, all Maya cared about at the moment was getting eyes on whatever rare materials he had.

The CNE had agreed to Maya's deal, kind of, starting with an exchange of information to see if their respective pieces might point their way to a second grail. In return, the CNE would assist the Frenro with defense preparations. As much as could be cobbled together in three weeks anyway.

Liam had come over to the *Wonder* to go through the materials with her. She'd barred Dr. Garcia. Fortunately, the CNE wanted her to find the grail badly enough they were willing to agree to a lot of things.

To Auncle, she'd explained very little about her deal. Best to get past the battle first, she thought. Auncle was so busy, they didn't get to see much of each other anyway.

The Frenro had ancient ships parked on the far side of the moon— it's how they came to the system in the first place. They'd been poorly maintained over the centuries, but they were retrofitting them as fast as they could. That was where Auncle was now. The plan was to make a show of force that would get the Lithians to back down; attempt to negotiate; if that failed, fight; and if that failed, evacuate. Maya doubted there was any way to avoid a fight. The Whole hadn't seen any other path that ended well.

"Butter cookies?" Medix asked.

"Wow," said Liam. "Definitely."

Stop being so nice to this guy, Wil messaged. *He almost got us killed, remember?* She removed a long tube from the ship printer. She was in the middle of assembling a firing tube for the *Wonder*, and she'd taken over the dining table with precisely spaced piles of parts.

Medix set the mug of tea down in front of Liam. *I believe the human capacity for holding grudges is mostly vestigial. There is no need to be cranky.* Medix's milky lips pulled up, revealing an approximation of teeth.

"Let's see what you've got," said Maya.

Liam lifted his briefcase and set it on the coffee table. It was a nice briefcase, probably had been in his family for a hundred years, and it was made of real leather, like from an actual cow that had eaten pasture grass all its life. It was worn at the corners but had a sheen to it, like he massaged it nightly with oil. He carried it everywhere on campus, but she was surprised he'd risked bringing it along.

"So, have you talked to Quintin much, since . . . you know . . ."

Liam drooped. "A few messages back and forth. I'm not really a letter writer."

She raised an eyebrow. She would have left it at that, but then Liam burst out: "He basically said I was boring! Like I wasn't adventurous enough."

"Well, you sure showed him," said Wil, fitting two pieces together with a satisfying *snick*.

"Yeah," said Liam, so glumly that Wil added: "Anyway, fuck that guy. And I don't even like you."

"Thanks, I think." Liam emptied the case. He had two items: a gold pendant shaped like an astrolabe, which must have belonged to Ivan Jankowski, the pilot of the *Traveler*, if Maya remembered correctly from pictures, and a slim black bound journal.

"Holy shit," said Maya.

"What?" Liam asked.

"That's volume four." The volume before hers. Like volume 5, it had been missing for many years. "The CNE's had it all this time?"

"Cool, right?" Liam said.

"One word for it," muttered Maya.

"It describes their loss of funding and first visit to Emerald, and the agreement with the clan to sponsor the expedition. It didn't say anything about giving them artifacts, but we put two and two together. That's how we figured out to look for it there."

Maya reached for the volume.

"Careful!" he said.

"Why do people assume I'm not?" She opened the book, and Liam came around the table so he could point out key passages over her shoulder until she swatted his jabby finger away.

She studied the passage toward the end of the volume that Liam had referenced:

> We told them about our encounter with Calendar, and the description we'd heard of a vast museum beyond any known scale—a physical encyclopedia of all known life. They wanted proof, of course, that it was real, but all we shared was the description from our friend: a world at a crossroads, abundant with life, somewhere beyond the Dead Sea. We promised the Frenro we wouldn't disclose more specific directions than that. In any case, the Emerald Clan is wealthy enough to provide the funding. The Belzoar are nothing if not rational: for them it's worth the investment, given the value of potential return. They agreed after only a fifteen-minute consultation with the Governance System to enough funding for two years. I believe we can do it in much less than that.

"At a crossroads," said Maya. "What does that mean?"

"A metaphor," said Liam.

"A puzzle meant to irritate you," said Wil, removing another piece from the printer.

Maya flipped back through the journal to an earlier entry.

> We've been chasing history for several months in Nodal System 11-8: a Belzoar clan, mysteriously disappeared. The lost world of the greater Belzoar Nodal Region. Not just any Belzoar clan: the Lithians, who were responsible for the xenocide that wiped out most of the Frenro—a war that only ended when several nodes, including the node to their homeworld, was suddenly severed.
>
> We had heard this clan had pillaged and brought back to their homeworld many Frenro artifacts, and we thought if we could find the node, we might also find the stardust machine. But though we explored the system for several months, we never found any trace of the node.

"Does it explain what destroyed the nodes before?" said Maya, watching Medix transfer fresh cookies from the cooker onto a plate.

"No," said Liam. "DJ and I went through this volume multiple times. Not a clue. You really think this stardust machine is the same as your grail?"

"Positive," said Maya. "And clearly not mythical, by the way."

Liam lifted his hands in surrender. "Can I see yours now?"

Maya retrieved the preservation case from her bedroom.

"I can't believe you stole that," he said.

"Borrowed. *Stealing* would be holding on to something like this for a hundred years and not telling anyone."

Liam snorted. He wasn't about to argue when he could be poring through said document. He opened the pages of the Huang journal, still marked at the passage Dr. Garcia had apparently meant for Maya to find:

> We could see how easy it would be to move, and of course imme-
> diately we talked about how to do it.

There was a rude sound from the printer as Wil produced another part.

"That's quite loud," Liam said.

"Yeah?" said Wil, without looking up.

Maya pulled up the manifest that Pickle had sent, the previous stray thought returning to her.

"Okay, I can see you've got an idea," said Liam.

The search took only a minute to process.

"I thought maybe Dr. Huang's crew brought a Belzoar replicator," Maya said. It was not an unheard-of practice in the field—better if it were more common—but xenoanthropologists carried them in case they came across artifacts that ethically shouldn't be disturbed. Maya would have carried one on the *Wonder* if she could afford it.

Liam squinted at her. "You think the one in the Belzoar museum was just a replica?"

"They talked about *how* to do it, but not that they had. But anyway, there's no reference to a replicator in the manifest logs."

Liam bit into a cookie. "It's not the worst theory. Could they just have forgotten to include the replicator on the manifest?"

"You don't mess around with your logs. Accurately tracking your supplies out here is life-or-death."

"And Belzoar replicators are good but not that good, I guess," said Liam. "It wouldn't have fooled their Belzoar sponsors."

Maya fetched the sack of Belzoar artifacts they'd accidentally taken with the Frenro ones. "I thought it was weird these were all mixed up with them. But I wasn't thinking about why they might have been shelved together."

She removed the things that Wil had snatched from the second case: a Belzoar digger, a human headlight, a battery, and there—a portable Belzoar replicator. "What if the Belzoar *knew* what they had was a replica? They might not even want the real thing, given their paranoia about Frenro infection."

Wil slung the firing tube across her shoulder. "It's not paranoia."

"The thing about replicators is—" Maya took one of Medix's cookies and held it up to the light. "It looks right." She pinched a bit with her fingers. "It crumbles all right." She sniffed it. "But the smell—that's where you start to get suspicious." She bit down. "And the taste—it's good, but there's something about it. Auncle said it tasted strange when they, er, assimilated it."

"I mean, if I ate a chocolate bar that'd been lying around for centuries, I think it would probably taste a little off," said Liam.

"Or it's because the resolution of a replicator is only so good."

"Like robot intelligence," said Medix.

"No," said Wil, hunting through the cabinets. "That's different."

"I don't see how," said Medix.

"You're not a cookie." She spared a second to give Maya a stern look, as if this ongoing existential crisis were her fault. "Why would you say that?"

"It wasn't meant to be that kind of metaphor," Maya said.

Medix began fussing with the cooker in a clear funk.

Liam took the replicator and examined it. "We've got one of these models in the Humbert Collection." It was the size of a shoebox, but heavier, with a circular lens on one side. "Still loaded with smart matter," he reported. He pointed it at a cookie and fired.

They all froze. The machine lit up, and then there was a loud grinding sound.

The cookie it printed was not a cookie. It was circular. It also was an unappealing brown color. "If it was a copy, I doubt they made it with this replicator," said Maya. "The grail we retrieved was much better quality."

Medix began to laugh again, which got Liam laughing too.

"Even if you're right, I don't see how it helps us," said Wil.

"The original must be back in the Encyclopedium."

"But you said no one has ever found the Encyclopedium."

"Except Dr. Huang."

"Who heard it from the Frenro, who apparently no longer remember where it is," said Liam.

"One more thing." Maya pulled up the riddle from Dr. Nkosi's headstone: "*We went into the cave and found the light. We returned an echo of what had been. Let the ghosts wait there for no one.*"

"An echo," Liam said, raking a hand through his beard. "You could be right."

"Where's the cave then?" asked Wil, at last finding the tools in a pantry cabinet.

"That's what we've got to figure out." said Maya. "Find the cave, find the treasure."

They just had to save a moon first.

CHAPTER THIRTY-EIGHT

S omewhere, an alarm was bleating.

Maya woke and hunted for her boots.

"They're here." Medix stood in the doorway, eyes glinting in the dark.

Maya looked out and saw pinpoints of light, growing bigger. The *Wonder* sensors confirmed it: a flotilla of blocky warships bristling with weapons. Lithian ships.

Maya turned on the lights, heart pounding. "Any word from the CNE?"

"Not yet," said Medix.

A ghost of sensation came back to her: Watching her parents move about the house collecting family keepsakes to bury in the yard near the roses. Visible through the dome above them as they worked were warships, waiting for their surrender.

She knew the CNE could be a wall when they wanted to be. She just didn't know if they'd be her wall.

In the common area, Wil was already awake, drinking tea. Below, Auncle swam an anxious circuit of the ship. Xe must have returned sometime in the night in anticipation.

Dear one, xe said. *You did not dream.*

No, agreed Maya.

Liam lay curled up on the couch, awake but huddled under a blanket. There was no time for him to return to the CNE ship. They'd known that would likely be the case. He had never looked more lost than now: a person very far from home.

"Hanging in?" she asked him. Not that Maya felt any less queasy. Her pacifist parents wouldn't have approved of pushing the CNE to fight. As a child during occupation, she'd wished sometimes they'd resist. After Lithis, she'd started to understand their views a little more. What they were about to do felt, if not wrong, then *bad*, but what else could they do?

"I must say, all those times I listened to you going on and on about your adventures, this is not exactly what I pictured. We'd better not die, now that you've promised we'll find the grail."

In the last few weeks, while Maya and Liam worked their way systematically through all available references to the Encyclopedium that Pickle and the CNE could pull for them, Wil, Medix, and Auncle had transformed the *Wonder* into a fighting craft. The Frenro might not have had a lot of weapons, but weapons were, as Wil had said so many times it was annoying, a matter of perspective.

The *Wonder* had been outfitted with a device that could exert force on the whole of another ship—Wil called it their space lasso. There would be an equal and opposite effect on the *Wonder*, so they'd need to account for that.

They'd also made a cable net with reinforced drones at the far corners that could be used to drag things and installed a small CNE turret gun.

Their final "weapon," which had required several days to persuade the Frenro to deploy, was a drill attached to the top of the *Wonder* that could transform the atmosphere of a planet. They weren't even sure what it would do to a ship, and it would require an enormous amount of energy, so it was meant to be saved for a last resort.

"How many?" Maya asked, while Medix prepared an injection of drugs for her. During the battle to come, Maya was supposed to work through the *Wonder* to operate the lasso, and Medix had proposed prophylactic injections again to protect her nervous system from overloading.

Wil checked the visual of the ships in system projected over their dining table: red dots meant enemy, blue meant friendly. There were eighty-three red dots. Fourteen blue, including the four CNE ships, the *Wonder*, and nine other Frenro craft so ancient it was a miracle they'd never fallen out of stable orbit.

The Frenro broadcast a message to the incoming ships: *Leave in peace.*

The ships showed no sign of acknowledgment. They continued their rapid approach.

"Maybe they don't understand the message," said Liam.

"They understand," said Auncle's voice.

Medix plunged the needle into her shoulder, and Maya grounded herself in the sharp pinch. *This is real.*

Wil handed Liam a helmet, and Medix moved around, stowing away any remaining loose objects. Water began to fill the cabin.

All the while, the red dots in the visual continued their approach.

"Lithian fleet, this is Commander Browning of CNE *O Canada*." The steely voice cut across the room. "I'd like to speak with your leader."

"Technically, even Lithians use a Governance System," said Liam, "though I guess in war—"

"Now is not the time, professor," said Wil.

The ships advanced.

"Lithian fleet, this is Commander Browning. Please halt your movement and acknowledge, or we will be forced to regard your actions as hostile."

No response.

"Are they not going to say anything?" Wil asked.

Liam lifted a hand to chew his nail before apparently remembering he was suited and underwater. "Lithians like to gather information before communicating."

Maya recalled the months of terror spent on Lithis, the dull buzzing of their conversation as they conducted their meticulous cataloging of the pain points of her body. Her hands were trembling again.

They could make out the shape of the larger ships now. The largest of them was a massive boxy tube, at a scale that could remake planets.

A flat voice finally responded to the Commander: "It is not our intent to fight you, but we also have no objection to doing so if necessary. Will you remain neutral?"

Maya held her breath.

"Negative," said Commander Browning. "This system is under our protection. Please state your intentions."

She should have felt relief. This was what she had wanted, wasn't it?

"This region is not yours," said the Lithian.

"I guess you could say we have an interest," said Commander Browning.

"Our business is with the people of this moon, not you. If you remain neutral, we can avoid a fight."

Wil shook her head.

"I see, and what is that business exactly?"

"To eliminate a threat to all life in this galaxy. Even now, millions of people on our planet are sick. It is a thing that will happen again and again each place they go. It is what they do: find new worlds with life and infect them with the virus. Will you help us?"

The crackle of an unreliable signal. Then: "Negative, sorry. We have orders to secure the region for Earth."

"Your perception is limited and intentions are immaterial. They have demonstrated repeatedly that they cannot exist without posing a danger to all of us. Have you not experienced this for yourself?"

There was a long silence. The Commander was too young to remember the original pandemic, but everyone had relatives who had come through it. "We've got a vaccine now," said the Commander.

"Commander, we do not."

I'm sorry for what we did, Maya thought. *I'm so sorry.* She said nothing.

The ships were close enough to be visible to the naked eye and growing.

After that, there was no more reply from the Lithians, no matter what the Commander said.

"So that's it?" Liam asked. "We aren't going to try to negotiate anymore?"

"We'd better move into position," said Wil.

The *Wonder* shook beneath them as the ship detached from its dock. The walls rippled into transparency, revealing the full magnitude of the force at their doorstep. It seemed impossible they might prevail. They were so greatly outnumbered.

Auncle juiced the *Wonder*'s engines, and acceleration pushed them all back into their chairs.

"Not too fast," said Medix. "Delicate human brains, remember?"

"Of course," said Auncle. "I would not harm my beloved friends. I have done the math, so you do not need to worry."

She heard Liam groan, and she couldn't even tell him it would be okay. Instead, she reached out and took his hand. He gripped her fingers so hard she wondered if he could break the little bones.

Several spherical Frenro ships darted around them, moving faster without human passengers. They didn't see the projectile so much as the flash of impact: something had struck one of the Frenro ships. Maya blinked against the sudden afterimage burned in her eyes. When the tears subsided, the damaged ship was spinning away from the squad, a slow-motion jet of water leaking into space.

"Are they all right?" asked Liam, trying to follow the stream of data in his ocular lenses. Wil had given him this assignment, and it was a smart choice: it kept him from looking out into space.

Wil waved him away. She was communicating with the CNE fleet. Maya set her fingers atop the moist sponge of the controls. Her job was to sit by the weaponry controls and wait for orders, trying not to think about the violence she was about to commit.

They were approaching the fray but were still a few minutes out from where the battle was raging.

Below, she saw the damaged Frenro craft swing around shockingly fast—still functioning, then—and the outer membrane of the ship had resealed. The Frenro ship launched a projectile of its own that resembled a grappling hook, some odd marriage of human weaponry and Frenro technology. Maya held her breath, but the projectile missed its target, a ramshackle enemy ship about twice its size.

As she watched, the Frenro projectile abruptly changed direction, and the cable wrapped around the long midsection of the target ship. She braced in sympathy as metal crumpled under the constriction. The Frenro craft moved away, towing the other ship with it.

"There we go," said Wil.

The lumpy Lithian ship it was towing began to fire at its captor at close range, and the Frenro ship quaked and spurted in multiple places.

"Woah," breathed Liam. Three suited Frenro as big as houses slid down the cable between the two ships. The tentacled forms reached the enemy craft and began ripping off pieces of the hull with dozens of arms at once. When they were done, the target ship drifted inert, one section still attached to the other end of the cable. Belzoar bodies floated in the dark.

Bile rose to Maya's throat. She thought of Dr. Garcia's comment that the only thing common to all life was this: the fight to survive.

"Eighty-two Lithian ships remaining," said Liam, in tones that conveyed his pessimism of a positive outcome. The enormous, cigar-shaped mothership was hanging back, but it was positioning itself, nose forward. Enemy ships swarmed around its flank.

"Seventy-nine," said Wil, without looking up. The CNE ships had just taken out three more. There was another flash out of the corner of Maya's eye as a human bomb slammed into a Lithian ship. "Seventy-eight."

Then the *Wonder*'s momentum brought them into the battle, and they were suddenly in the middle of it.

Maya clenched her hands around the armrests and forced herself to watch. Liam's eyes were definitely shut. The *Wonder* shook as something hit its side hard enough to make Maya's whole body slam against her straps. Wil cursed as Auncle corrected course.

"Damage?" asked Wil.

She'd assigned Medix to emergency repair, as the person with the least fragile body. "Maya's cabin," he reported, already moving that way with his tool kit, and Maya could see through the clear walls that the quilt on her futon was on fire.

"Good thing the Huang journals weren't in there," muttered Liam, clutching the preservation box to his chest.

"Keep your eyes on the count, man," said Wil, and Liam obeyed.

"They got one of the Frenro ships."

Straight ahead of them was one of the medium-sized Lithian warships. They were coming up on its flank fast. It was more than three times the size of the *Wonder*. Auncle angled them to pass over the top of the other ship.

"Deploy net," Wil said, as the Lithian ship passed below their feet.

Liam and Maya were each responsible for driving a corner of the triangular net. The apex was attached to the *Wonder*'s hull. They'd only been able to practice this a couple of times, and their ability to coordinate in war maneuvers was as bad as it was in academia—worse because they were terrified. She should have accepted Wil's suggestion to take something to dull the fear. Fortunately, this was a little less complicated than writing a journal article: all they needed to do was get tangled.

Maya dove her drone low, hunting for something to attach to. Lithian craft were as spiky as birds' nests. Maya targeted a suitable pole sticking out and caught the netting on a bulkhead. The *Wonder* jerked as it was hit by another projectile.

She hoped Medix was okay.

"Do you have it?" Wil asked Liam.

"Almost!" he said. "If you'd stop interrupting me—"

He tried and missed snaring a shallow nub of the ship.

Boom!

Maya felt the dull blow in her chest. She looked left and saw water spurting out into space from Auncle's quarters, dangerously close to where they sat in the common area.

"Lasso," Wil said.

Maya flexed her fingers. Braced herself.

"Attached!" said Liam, raising his hands in victory. "I told you I got it."

They were going fast enough that their target was already well behind them, even as the net unspooled—not fast enough to keep the *Wonder* from jerking when the cables ran out of length. The Lithian ship at the other end of the net strained to continue moving in the other direction, but the *Wonder*'s momentum won out. They were barely moving relative to the other ships, but that didn't matter for their purposes. The net stretched taut between the *Wonder* and its unwilling partner.

"Will it hold?" asked Liam.

"If it doesn't, I want my money back," said Wil.

"Frenro don't use money," said Maya.

There was an awful jolt as one, two, three Lithian craft flew right into their net, and the *Wonder* was yanked by the impact. The net tore away, and the Lithian ships were all spun up together.

The smaller craft broke into bits from the force of impact, and the medium one took significant damage. Maya stared down between her feet at the pieces of them. She had done that. She had killed people. Her chest squeezed. She wanted to crawl into another time away from all this awful death. Her vision doubled, split in two: a second in the past, a second in the future.

"Sixty-six enemy, five Frenro, four CNE, and us," reported Liam dutifully.

"Only five?" Wil asked.

Liam swallowed and nodded.

"Maya, we need the lasso."

Maya shut her eyes and crawled into a light that was burning inside her eyelids. And then she was the *Wonder* the way she'd been its shuttle. The *Wonder*'s mind was almost like a person, with indescribable, big feelings that wrapped around her brain. *Maya*, it thought, and then a wave of fear mixed with her own.

She felt the lasso like an invisible arm. She flexed once, and then again.

Distantly, she could hear the thud of Wil firing their new turret gun at a larger Lithian ship as they passed it, shooting again and again and again until its surface was pitted with holes.

They were surrounded by ships, too many ships, and Maya didn't know anymore who was who.

"Grab that one," Wil said, pointing out a ship ahead of them. Their trajectory had carried them through most of the swarm, and they were nearing the edge of the fight. Maya longed to seize the opening to escape, fly free and far away from all of this.

"Did you hear me?"

Maya did, though the mercenary's voice was so far away.

Maya and the *Wonder* reached out together and grasped the nose of another ship. They yanked.

A jolt of acceleration pinned them all against their chairs, as an equal force hit their ship.

DELICATE HUMAN BRAINS! Auncle screamed. Xe was in her mind, because xe was always in her mind, but xe was part of the *Wonder* too, filaments deep in xyr controls, plotting the path of the ship.

Sorry, sorry.

But it had worked—sort of. The ship she'd grasped was spinning out, away from the fray. It would be back, but in the meantime, she reached out and grabbed another and another.

Liam cheered. "Sixty-three!"

Maya's recoil at what she was doing had become a mere shadow at dusk. She was one with Auncle and all the Frenro, and she was *reveling* in every success. As she worked the lasso, the *Wonder* jerked violently in one direction, then another. She could hear the others groaning from the way they were getting thrown around.

"Careful!" said Wil, and Maya tried to apologize, but her lips failed to move. She was no longer certain of her body.

Her actions had hurtled the *Wonder* back through another slice of the action—and then through, beyond, too fast, away from everything.

And Auncle was screaming in her brain. Or she was screaming. Their emotions were fully entangled, and it was dizzying. There was vomit plastered on the inside of her helmet. Her suit smelled sour. They were going out, out, out.

At this distance from the battle, Maya could see that they hadn't been winning at all. The Lithian mothership was in position, pointing directly at the moon.

"Evacuation is go. The Frenro colony ships are moving out," Wil reported. They had hoped to avoid this. The ships weren't big enough to hold more than a tenth of the population, and they were aged spacecraft of questionable quality. But it was their only chance of survival in case the battle didn't go well.

The *Wonder* had to get back to cover their retreat. They had to. She didn't know if it was her or Auncle propelling the ship. Maybe both of them. They angled toward the planet's second misshapen barren moon, aiming to use its gravity to gain more speed.

We are too late, Auncle wailed, but there was nothing they could do. As they slung around, they could only watch as a massive shadow, a Lithian ship, collided with one of the Frenro colony ships. The whole side of it crumpled like paper.

Two CNE warships moved in to return fire, but the Frenro ship was lighting up with explosions. Slowly, it drifted back, caught in the gravity well of the gas giant.

Several of the Frenro craft tried to pull it back with their lassos, but it was no use. They watched as the Frenro ship sank beneath the swirl of clouds.

"God almighty." Wil's voice was flat, emotionless.

Liam was crying.

"Five minutes before we are back in range," said Medix, who had returned to the common room. There was a dent in his temple, and one of his arms hung awkwardly at his side, metal fingers bent in the wrong direction.

Maya struggled to push herself back down into the *Wonder*, but her mind flinched away from the connection. Her whole body was on fire as if she were sick all over again from the virus. She wanted to tear her skin from her body, but she couldn't get at it through her suit. "I need another injection," she told Medix.

Ahead of them, a light appeared at the nose of the giant ship. The brightness grew into a small star. Dread filled her.

"The ship is frying your system. You will die," said Medix, in his gentlest tone, as if Maya were a patient to be placated.

"Give me another," Maya repeated.

"No," said Medix. "I can't."

"Yes, you can," said Maya, angling the faceplate so she could see his face around the patch of vomit. "You've done it before. You're not prohibited."

"I won't," said Medix.

"Never mind, little friend," said Auncle. "I can do this."

Grief speared Maya. They were, both of them, already mourning.

"Two minutes," said Wil.

Ships scattered before them. They aimed the pointy end of the *Wonder*'s new atmospheric drill at the broad hull of the mothership.

"You have to slow down now. We're going to slam into it!"

Auncle wasn't listening anymore. It was all in xyr hands now.

"Sixty seconds," said Wil.

Maya craned her head at the ship growing above them. The *Wonder*'s atmospheric drill was white with heat.

"Thirty seconds," said Wil.

Something hit them, but Auncle corrected. Medix didn't even bother to check the damage. In a few moments, it wouldn't matter.

And then the head of the drill lanced the side of the Lithian mothership. The force of the impact rippled through the *Wonder*. Only the supremacy of Frenro engineering kept the *Wonder* from coming apart.

"Activate the converter," said Wil. But Auncle already had.

Maya, still vestigially connected by wisps to the Frenro web, felt every moment. A charge ripped through her body.

Inside the Lithian ship, the air was transformed in an instant, and the chambers filled with deadly steam. Most of the crew inside would be burned alive. The few that survived would suffocate.

And then the *Wonder* was withdrawing, the stinger still buried in the Lithian mothership, and Liam was saying, "My god. My god," and Maya was thinking, *We did this, we had to, and it is something we will never be able to undo.*

CHAPTER THIRTY-NINE

The *Wonder* was coming apart. The walls had lost their transparency in many places, and they were leaking. Auncle's upper sunroom had lost its atmosphere entirely.

In the distance, the remaining evacuating Frenro colony ships split in different directions, each toward a separate node. Some of the Lithians moved to follow, but the other ships had gotten enough of a head start that they were nearly out of range.

Auncle had plunged so deep into the dash, xe was nearly obscured by it. "Our engines are dead."

The *Wonder* was surrounded by enemy ships, an easy target. They would be blown to pieces.

There was a muffled crack, and Maya looked up. A hole about the size of a fist had opened just above Liam's head. Medix tried and failed to reach it with an inner membrane patch. He couldn't swim. Maya unstrapped herself and took the patch from him. She swam up to the hole. It took all her remaining strength to do it. Wil reached up and tugged her back down by the ankle.

They had lost so much water. The cycler was working hard to keep the chambers filled. Their reserves must be nearly empty.

"God," said Wil, realizing a projectile had struck in the opposite wall, just an inch from her head.

"The lasso," said Maya. "We can use it to move . . ."

"Sit down, my love," said Auncle. "I will do it. Please ensure you are all firmly attached, heads forward, no delicate necks to be snapped or brains to be concussed. This is going to be a bumpy ride."

Xe wasn't kidding. They jerked one way and then another, each time using the lasso to push themselves a little farther away. Maya bit her tongue once, then spent the rest of the wretched ride with her teeth clenched to avoid a repeat.

It took forever, but they broke free of the tangle of ships, out into the black, falling toward nothing.

"We should call the Commander. Ask her to pick us up," said Liam.

"No way," said Wil, glancing at Medix. "If you want a pickup, happy to dump you here and hail them, but we're not going back with those guys."

"So we all die out here in the middle of nowhere, because you're afraid of getting arrested? Nuh-uh."

Maya marveled at Liam's ability to mistake the odds of a situation as in his favor. Wil simply looked down at him and casually transformed one of her fists into a gun. "Reconsider?"

He swallowed.

The Frenro colony ships reached their respective nodes. Who knew what worlds lay beyond? The Frenro passed through.

There had never been a plan B to save the Frenro left behind. The Frenro simply didn't have enough ships. A few thousand more could have fit on the CNE warships, but with Earth's strict prohibition against Frenro, that had never been an option.

Suddenly, through one of the few patches of remaining transparency above them, the crew of the *Wonder* saw a ripple of light. Maya pulled up a shaky projection.

From far away, the dark moon was just a red coin in infrared. A bright silvery light began to pulse from the surface of it. All the nodes in the system flashed in response.

In the dim glow of this eerie flashing, mammoth *creatures* emerged from the nodes the colony ships had passed through. They glowed aquamarine. They were tentacled, many-tongued, planetoid in size, silent in the vacuum. They grasped the edges of the nodes, and then they seemed to pull until the nodes collapsed inward, one after the other, and then they were, each of them, gone.

The nearest Lithian ships were disintegrated by an invisible wave. The remainder were shoved outward. Something washed over the *Wonder*, and then there was nothing.

Where there had been twelve nodes, there were now nine.

The crew of the *Wonder* stared in silence into the renewed dark.

"What the hell," Wil said, finding her breath first.

"No," said Auncle. "No, no."

Underneath Maya's shock, she was remembering bits and pieces: Dr. Huang's story of the lost Lithian homeworld, severed from the web. That thing Elephant had said: "Perhaps doors will open when others are closed." Maya should have paid more attention.

"It was the Frenro," said Liam. "They were the ones killing the nodes all along."

And Auncle must have known, since xe was part of the Whole.

The Frenro were not without defenses after all. *This* was the real plan B.

The CNE must have understood what they had seen, because as one, they turned their bombs on the moon and its inhabitants. Fire rained down from the ships. In the sudden brightness, the surface of the moon began to crack. Red patches of heat formed. The moon first shed small flakes, then bigger and bigger chunks. Plumes of steam jetted from the moon. The sea was boiling. A sheet of ice the size of a continent broke off and spiraled down toward the gas planet.

Maya thought of all the people left in the underwater city, of Elephant, who had been born when the people of Earth still believed the heavens revolved around them, and who had longed to visit the tropical waters of Earth.

She watched as vast knowledge was extinguished from the universe.

A sob tore from her. This couldn't be allowed. She wished for once she were dreaming.

All the while, the *Wonder* continued its retreat into the dark, toward nowhere, receding farther and farther from relevance.

Medix got up to seal several more holes.

The flashes continued to grow until she had to shut her eyes. Auncle didn't say a word, just flattened xyrself against the floor, every visual receptor pointed up. Bearing witness.

"My god," said Wil. "This is—this is—" But words failed her.

She remembered Auncle's words: "It is a privilege to witness an ending." Xe had known xe would be left behind when xyr people crossed through, and xe had stayed anyway.

Despair possessed her. All that they had risked and done in the last couple of hours—and none of it counted for anything. This wasn't how things were supposed to go.

Maya turned and looked at Liam, who was still clutching the case of books, face locked in terror. "They can't do this," she said, but it was like he couldn't hear her. She reached out and caught his wrist. "Liam!"

He turned toward her. "You're bleeding," he said, like it mattered.

She touched two fingers to her helmet. She shook her head. "We had a deal."

And she needed to know whose fault it was that this was happening. The Frenro had threatened humanity because they had foreseen humanity would destroy them, but the CNE only came for them because humanity was threatened, and maybe it all came down to a fundamental misunderstanding between their people, a failure to see what the other would do in fear.

Auncle uncoiled and disappeared down into xyr cave.

Medix, the only one unaffected, drained the water from the chamber. He handed Maya a cloth to clean her face, but she found she couldn't move.

"How am I even here?" Liam asked. "I should be home."

They watched as the remaining Lithians joined the butchery. Together with the human force, they destroyed what remained of the Frenro moon.

CHAPTER FORTY

M aya waded through a yawning chamber full of liquid. She knew, in the way you knew things in dreams, that it was the unknown planet of pink dust she had seen before. They were deep underground, in a vast labyrinth of empty hallways and stairs and rooms without end, a museum that had not been in operation for millennia.

The Encyclopedium. Of course it was. What else could it be? She'd known without knowing it all along.

An indistinct shadow waded through the pool of liquid ahead of her. She thought it was a friend, but she couldn't quite make them out. It was like seeing something with her peripheral vision; when she focused, they slipped away.

Only one thing she could see clearly. They were carrying the grail, and it pulsed with an unearthly blue light. Where the previous grail had been inert, this one moved gently in the person's arms.

She nearly missed the sound of splashing behind her.

"Run!" someone shouted.

She tried. Her boots sloshed through the pool about shin-deep. Something was coming out of the water, something huge.

She needed to keep moving, to get out of this room. Her friends had already gone on.

And the realization hit her: she'd been abandoned, left to be eaten. The sharp betrayal cut her skin, an echo of her other visions of this place.

Something wrapped tight around her ankle, and a shadow fell over her. She shouldn't stop to look.

Her head turned anyway to glimpse it: an enormous, sharp-toothed thing.

You came back, said a voice in her mind, and it wasn't Auncle's. *I did not think you would. It is good to see you, Dr. Huang.*

She screamed before it devoured her.

CHAPTER FORTY-ONE

It took them days of falling through space before they'd repaired the *Wonder* enough to crawl back through the Belzoar node.

The CNE and the remaining Lithians had departed after gathering their dead. No one bothered chasing the *Wonder*, either thinking they were dead or assuming that the desert of space would finish them off—not unlikely, given the state of their internal systems.

Auncle did most of the repairs alone, patching the outer membrane and coaxing the inner layers to regrow. Maya confronted xyr about what had happened, but xe had barely spoken since the departure of xyr people through the nodes. Maya heard xyr talking to xyrself, skin awash with colors, arms gesticulating, a wave of singular emotion rippling through the ship: loneliness.

Xe had been left behind. The Whole was gone.

Normally, Maya would have comforted xyr, but she was struggling with her own fury. It was a slippery thing: she was angry with the CNE because, in the end, the monster they were chasing was themselves—if they hadn't come here rattling their sabers, the Frenro would never have attacked the Human Nodal Region in the first place.

But also—the CNE wouldn't have come here if they hadn't been threatened. Maybe eventually, but not right away. So the Frenro were to blame.

She wanted Auncle to explain xyrself.

Auncle had almost told her several times when xe first came to Earth: when xe called, xe'd said there was something xe wanted to tell her; xe'd said an ending was coming; and even when they'd witnessed that first nodal collapse at the beginning of their journey, xe had said: "They didn't warn us." The *Whole*, xe had meant, not the CNE.

Maya had been oblivious, because she trusted xyr. She trusted that she understood xyr, and that was human ego.

Maya had thrown away her new life to help xyr, and for what? A void had sprung up between them.

Back at *Here There Be Dragons*, they dry-docked in one of the hangars for intense repair. It cost every uni Auncle had left.

The fact that Liam and Wil stuck around had little to do with desire and entirely necessity: Liam, because the next shuttle bound for Earth wasn't for another week, and Wil, because waystation housing was expensive, and she was still waiting for payment, which couldn't happen until Auncle sold the *Wonder*. Auncle was, supposedly, talking to buyers. Maya could have helped, but everything in her resisted the task, because once they sold the ship, every chance of a happy ending would be over.

Since their return, Wil seemed almost as lost as Auncle. The few times she spoke, it was about Earth, about the wheaty taste of beer, the perfect length of a day, the way flowers looked when they'd just opened. But she didn't seem to believe she'd ever make it home again. It took Maya a few days to realize that Wil had removed the CNE sigil from her chest, stopped saying grace before meals, stopped talking much to anyone but Medix.

Maya herself spent most of her time in her cabin going through the Huang materials. She'd read volumes 4 and 5 and gone through all the electronic files five times. She wasn't sure whom she was doing it for anymore.

Liam joined her, wondering aloud if DJ would beat them to publishing a paper about the Frenro city until Maya couldn't take it anymore.

"No one told you to accept that job," Maya said. "If you had asked me, which you didn't, I would have told you to stay home."

"Oh well, I'm *sorry* for not seeking out the wisdom of the great sage, Maya Hoshimoto, before making a major life decision," said Liam.

Maya just looked at him until he sheepishly opened one of the Huang books.

"You always had these adventure stories," he said. "I just wanted to know what it was like. I know you and Quintin think I'm pathetic. The professor who specializes in foreign culture but has never left home. I'm sure it was very funny to you."

"I wasn't laughing at you," said Maya. "I understood."

Liam raked his hair. "When Quintin said he didn't want to renew our marriage, he told me he was suffocating. Because I was too set in my routine. That I never wanted to do anything or go anywhere."

Maya touched his shoulder. "Yet here you are."

"Ta-da." Liam twirled a finger. "This just . . . wasn't what I expected. You can read about other places in books and think you understand it, but all that is is trying to interpret shadows on the wall. That's a reference to—"

"We learn about Plato in settlement school too," Maya said.

"Right."

"The funny thing is, I think I have the opposite problem to you. You're afraid of flying, but I'm afraid of staying on the ground."

Auncle crawled over the outside of Maya's chamber, a wide piece of outer ship skin in one hand. Maya turned the wall opaque.

She looked at Liam. "I know I haven't been the best student this time around, but do you think there's any way they'd let me come back?" It was something she'd been turning over in her mind. This whole trip had been such a colossal failure, and all she wanted now was to be in the Humbutt basement, listening to Pickle describe their favorite conservation techniques.

"I don't know," said Liam, always honest. "Why do you want it, anyway? Besides being able to steal rare books."

Maya winced. "Because. There's so much more life out here than we ever dreamed when we were just people on a ball of dirt and water going around a sun. One day, we learned we weren't alone, and we were terrified, excited, hopeful about what that meant. Could we be part of this bigger community? Were they anything like us? Is there anything we share: morals, social values, behavior, emotions?"

If she could understand that, maybe she could make sense of everything that had happened, from Lithis to the Frenro moon. Of everything they'd done.

"You want to complete Dr. Huang's universal theory of life," said Liam.

"Well," said Maya. "Yes." When he put it like that, it sounded silly.

Liam wasn't laughing. He tugged at his eyebrow. "You're more ambitious than I gave you credit for. You're not untalented, you know. Though you were certainly going about it the wrong way."

"I know," said Maya.

"If you ever figure it out, you might not like what you find."

Maya had thought of this too.

"Why are you angry with Auncle?"

"Aren't you?"

Liam pursed his lips. "What's the first thing you learn as a xeno-anthropologist? That you can't project human experience or morals. We're dealing with—excuse the term—*alien* people. Anyway, the Whole decided to do this. And yes, Auncle is part of the Whole, right? But it's not like Auncle *is* the Whole."

"Xe could have told me," said Maya.

"Really? Do you know that for a fact?"

Maya gave up on research and put the books away. The truth was, she'd always operated under the assumption that Auncle could decide xyr own fate. She thought everyone could. Isn't that what she'd told Medix? But what if she were wrong? Auncle had talked about the Whole like it was more than just some committee. Xe had tried to tell her that xyr thoughts were not xyr own when it came to the Whole.

She remembered xyr tearing xyrself from the communion that day to bring Maya back to the *Wonder* for medical attention, and only now did she wonder what it might have cost Auncle—perhaps even caused xyr pain.

"If I may observe—"

Maya took out a sewing kit and began cutting a square from the pants she'd bought in the Newark airport. "I want you to know I've always loathed every sentence you've ever started that way."

"—I think you think of Frenro as victims or martyrs. And they're just not. I'm not denying they've suffered. But that makes them less than they are. They're clearly not helpless. They have ways of defending themselves. They're eons ahead of us technologically. They *built* the IW."

"What's your point?" She lay the patch of cloth across where the fabric had scorched during the battle.

"You've always lectured me for putting the Belzoar on a pedestal—"

"I've never fetishized the Frenro. Auncle was—is—was—" She struggled to figure out what she wanted to say.

"Is," said Liam. "Your friend." He scratched his nose. "I'd do a lot to save the human race from extermination."

"Melancholy is gone," Maya said, surprised to discover she was crying. "They did that. I had *friends* who lived there. How would *you* feel if the state of New Jersey was sucked into a void? And what gave them the right to make that choice? I mean, I'm angry with the CNE too, I just—it's all really shitty, okay?"

"Hey, um," said Liam. "Could I give you a hug?"

She considered it. "Okay."

And honestly, it felt better than she would have thought. They'd all been so packed together on the ship, but she realized it had been a long time since she'd touched another human like this. Liam was surprisingly adept at hugs.

She let her snot run into his shirt and cried: for the loss of a whole world where she had first found her passion, her friends, her identity; for Greg and eir oddball shop she'd never get to visit again; for the death of the Frenro moon; for Auncle, who was about to sell the *Wonder* when they hadn't found the grail. And she'd tried *so hard* to do what was right, and it was like every good thing she'd ever tried to make rotted in her hands. It was all so pointless and futile.

Why was it so hard to *win* in a galaxy full of riches? Why couldn't anything ever be simple?

Embarrassed, she pushed back and wiped her face, thinking what Auncle might have observed about humans and their processing of grief.

She picked up a Frenro figurine, one of the ones she'd stolen from Humbutt. Auncle had left it out in the common room. The Frenro was posed, all arms and filaments extended, in an attitude of joy. "I can't let Auncle sell the *Wonder*."

Wil was on the floor of the common room. She had her helmet off and had removed the armor from one of her legs. The limb underneath was mangled and emaciated, and Wil was in the middle of massaging in topical cream. She paused when she saw them. "Hi."

Wil picked up the shell of the suit and fit it back around the leg.

"We need another month to pay you," said Maya. "I'll get us another job." It would mean walking away from any chance of returning to Princeton. But it would be worth it, if Auncle could keep xyr ship.

Wil moved her leg, testing the fit. "Why should we trust you?"

"I'll pay you another twenty percent." Already Maya was running through a catalog of things she could steal. The Yayoi Kusama, maybe, in a private collection in a settlement a few nodes away. Or maybe even the composition that had belonged to the Emerald Clan, now on display at *Dragons*. She did owe them for the artifacts they'd stolen.

"Okay," said Wil. "Maybe. Whatever."

On her way out of the ship, Maya passed Medix coming back from the market in a ridiculous disguise. They'd managed to patch and repair most of the damage to his body, but his head still carried a fist-sized dent. "Look what I found," he said.

"What?"

He held out a charm with a 幸 embossed in it. Joy. He'd found the personality mod. "It seems unfair, when everything is awful."

Maya smiled. "Seems like perfect timing to me."

She found Auncle patching the membrane walls of the sunroom.

Maya watched for a minute. The words she had come here intending to say seemed to stick to her tongue. She picked up a tool and stepped into Auncle's shadow to help instead.

Together, they sealed several cracks with a homemade paste Auncle had concocted, then covered it with a splint. It would give the ship time to heal over the next week.

Auncle spoke first: "Are you unwell? Your dreams have tasted so *gray*. I do not like to see you this way. It distresses me. I am thinking you are depressed."

"I don't know what to say to you," Maya said, setting down the tool. "Of course I'm depressed. Aren't you? We"—her voice broke—"destroyed your city. I'm sorry."

Auncle considered this. "Ahhhh. I am sad. I am feeling very . . . confused . . . about many things. I am struggling, yes, I am. Why were you going to give them the grail, Maya?"

So xe had known.

Maya flushed. "I just wanted to save you. But I should have discussed it with you. It wasn't my decision to make. I'm sorry."

She took the cover off one of the ship cyclers and did her best to decipher what she was looking at. Absolutely no idea. She pulled up the *Universal Mechanic's Guide* in her ocular feed and let the AI guide her through the repair.

"I didn't tell the Whole," said Auncle. "It was a bad thing. I used to know many things. The knowledge now comes and goes. Not what *I* knew but the broader Whole. Before I could always sense it. If I had a question, I could simply stretch out and query. But it's . . . in pieces. I longed to be separate from the Whole, and now I am, and it is not what I thought it would be. I'm . . . scared, Maya. It is so very lonely. I had no idea. How have you lived like this all your life?"

Maya began removing parts one by one. "I guess you get used to not knowing. To accept there is more than you can know. It isn't easy."

Auncle contracted momentarily into a ball, until the only thing protruding was xyr suit's water tank and the vocalizer. "I don't understand why you are feeling hostile toward me, your dearest friend, and also I can feel that you want to ask me questions but you are not asking them. Please. Ask me."

Maya drew the water pump—that was what it was—out of its socket and set it down on the ground. The next step was to disassemble the entire thing.

"Did you know what they were going to do to Melancholy?"

"Yes," said Auncle, and Maya could have thrown the pump across the room, if she weren't so painfully aware of how much a new one would cost.

She felt a pain in her chest. She sank to the ground, hugging herself. Auncle reached for her.

Don't, Maya said, mind sharp and brittle. Then aloud: "Why didn't you tell me?"

"I knew, and I didn't know," said Auncle. "It isn't that simple. It had been a long time since we had done anything like this, but there was consensus that something needed to be done. In the end, I agreed too. I accepted the Whole. It is just how it is with us."

"If your intention was to attack Earth, why did you hit Melancholy instead?"

"The Whole cannot direct. That is impossible. It is like the way your human medicine works. When you swallow a pill, it isn't always targeted. Sometimes healthy cells die, yes? It is the same with the IW. We did not remember the risks from before. Things can happen that are not intended. We share the idea, but it is the individuals who take action."

Maya felt sick. "So if you decided tomorrow that you wanted to shut everything down, you could just kill all the nodes until there's nothing left?"

"No," said Auncle. "We could not do that. It is the node that decides."

In the midst of her anguish, Maya almost missed what Auncle was saying. "Are you saying that the nodes—that they're *alive*, like they're—they're *people*?"

"Of course. I think. I—" Xe flashed crimson. "Yes, that's right."

Maya gaped at Auncle. There were no limits to the mysteries of the universe. "How?"

"I don't remember," said Auncle. "But I think the grail is part of it."

So Dr. Garcia was right after all. But also completely wrong.

"So you're saying more nodes could have died, but they refused?"

"Yes." Auncle thought about it a little more. "I guess we are not as indivisible from the Whole as I thought."

If there was one thing Maya'd always appreciated about flying with a Frenro, it was the continual wonder of learning how little she knew about anything.

Which was Liam's point. She didn't know. She didn't know a thing. And that was good, because it gave her hope.

CHAPTER FORTY-TWO

M aya woke to the smell of red bean soup and mochi and the clang of someone too large attempting to manipulate the pots in the pantry. She'd been snatching a nap in the middle of the marathon of repairs.

She poked her head out. Liam and Medix stood next to Auncle, attempting to direct the process, while Auncle held three new spoons, four bowls, and a cooker full of a quickly blackening concoction. Medix was telling some joke, and Liam was laughing so hard he bent over, clutching his stomach. Auncle purred.

"You let xyr cook?" Maya demanded.

Liam shook his head, but whatever he said was lost in another landslide of laughter.

"Mayyyyaa," said Auncle. "We went shopping!"

Maya scratched her head and regarded the supplies strewn across the table.

"The professor tells me it is effective human therapy, and I must say that I do think I begin to feel some effect. Do you like my hat?"

The hat in question was a bright fuchsia-shaped bowler perched on a fist-sized vestigial protrusion on the top of xyr body near xyr artificial voice box.

"I finally read your paper by the way," said Liam. "The one you wrote back on Earth. It was good. You missed the *Xenology* submission deadline, so I went ahead and submitted it for the next Belzoar studies conference in the spring. You'll have to come back to present it though."

"You *what*?" Maya said. She'd forgotten all about it. "But it needed edits."

"No, it didn't." He was back to his old self again, smug and patronizing. "You would have cycled endlessly. Consider it an intervention."

She would have argued harder, but her head was fuzzy from lack of sleep. She rubbed her face with both hands. "I thought you were leaving today." She was surprised by her regret at the thought.

"I am!" said Liam. "That's why Auncle and I went for one last hurrah in the market. I saw an orange here that was like a thousand bucks. Wild, right? I'm beginning to understand your obsession with food."

"You went out? Like out there?"

Medix running off to the market had been risky enough, but Auncle had continued to keep to the ship until now.

"It was a very pretty orange," said Auncle.

"Not pretty enough for *that* price," said Liam.

"Maybe if it were nine hundred and ninety-nine," said Medix, and the two of them laughed again.

Maya picked through the general mess, hunting for the Huang journal. She'd had a thought the night before, but it had slipped away as her eyes closed. It felt important. Unfortunately, the room was too chaotic to find anything.

She tidied: fitting new tools in the toolbox, stashing food powders and concentrates in containers that fit tightly in compartments so they wouldn't break, sorting wrappers between compost and return-to-vendor. She puzzled over some of the things that Liam had bought: worthless trinkets like a decorative printed clock, commonplace Belzoar fabrics, and a Quietling astrolabe.

"Stop!" said Auncle. "We wish to observe everything at once, Maya. You must sit down there on the couch, and we will eat this soup and relax. Then we will put it all away together."

"You don't eat human food," Maya said. "And this place is a mess."

"Never!" said Auncle. "It is our cave."

Maya raised her eyebrows. "If you mean everything feels a little claustrophobic because you've shrunk the space with all this . . ." She reached up and grabbed a hand-stitched shirt that was hanging off an open compartment door.

"A *cave*," said Liam with a snicker.

"Are you high?" Maya's eyes fell on the wrapper of spacer crackers on the floor, meant for lifting spirits on long journeys. Oh yes, definitely high.

"Perhaps if you opened your perception, you would feel it." Auncle set the bowls and cooker pot on the table and moved to the center of the room. Then xe stretched out with all arms and filaments, a thing xe rarely did because it took up every bit of space. Maya held still, marveling at the Frenro ability to expand and contract like this, to reach every stray object in the room at once. Xe was the star and this was xyr solar system. "You see? Cozy, with all the people and things you need within reach. A perfect cave."

After his initial moment of surprise, Liam began to howl with renewed laughter.

"Cave," repeated Maya. She dutifully shut her eyes and cupped her hands over her ears, and stretched out her battered perceptions, the way she had connected with the *Wonder* before. It was the first time she'd tried this since the dissolution of the Whole. She could feel how small it was, just scattered fragments of the once beautiful constellation of joined consciousness.

She narrowed herself, and then she could feel it: the way the space cupped them, all the objects she might need close by, Auncle's love flickering like a candle, a beacon of safety at the center. It reminded her of what she had forgotten the night before. Her eyes snapped open. "A cave!"

She pushed aside several arms and began hunting more furiously among Liam's things for the preservation box with the Huang journal, which Liam had agreed to return to Pickle for her. He'd also promised to try to intervene with the Chair, to keep her from getting expelled. Provided she came back before the end of the semester, that is, and made a serious effort at studying for her general exams.

"What are you doing?" Medix asked.

Wil appeared in the doorway. She took in the chaos. "The hell?"

"Have you seen my book?" Maya asked.

Wil waved vaguely in the far corner.

There it was, under the stack of shirts Liam was meant to be packing.

"Eat," Auncle said, tugging Wil toward the bowls of red bean soup, and Maya was surprised to see that the woman didn't even flinch. "This is Maya's favorite."

Liam fetched a bowl and tried a spoonful. "It's so sweet!"

Wil sat down and sipped a little. "Not bad."

Maya opened the preservation box and stuck her hand straight into its internal field without taking the time to switch it off. A mild jolt went through her arm. She removed the volume and began to flip the pages.

"Maya Hoshimoto," said Liam, "loves books more than people!"

"What's up with him?" Wil asked.

"I believe he has found his own joy," said Medix.

Dr. Nkosi's grave had said: *We went into the cave and found the light.*

Maya stopped at the page where Dr. Huang referenced the unlikelihood of returning to the ruined planet where they'd found the original artifact. "I know where it is, how they got past the Dead Sea all the way to the Encyclopedium and back in less than six months. The cave."

"Where?" asked Wil, wearily.

Maya threw up a projection of the rogue gas planet as they'd last seen it. They stood in the cradle of distant starlight, the ugly pieces of the fractured ice moon drifting in erratic orbit, and the nine nodes circling round.

"We were in it."

CHAPTER FORTY-THREE

A uncle knocked over the utensils in xyr excitement. "Yes, this must be!"

Maya read from a passage of the journal.

> It took us weeks to find it. To start, the mouth of the cave was not easy to travel through, even when we knew where it was— which is the point, I'm sure. People like us are not meant to come here.
>
> They warned us not to go. If only we had listened.

"That sounds ominous," said Wil.

"They lost three of the crew," said Maya. She pulled up a map of the IW. "All this time, people have been looking in the wrong place, because no one knew about the Frenro system. I calculated possible distance based on their supplies and departure from *Dragons*, but it never squared with where we assumed the Encyclopedium must be— somewhere beyond the Dead Sea. But who knows where the nodes in the cave lead to. They could lead beyond known space to places we've never heard of."

Liam whistled. The revelation had apparently been enough to pierce his haze.

"How does that help you?" Wil asked, who seemed interested now in spite of herself. "If that's true, you've just expanded the possible places it could be. Assuming it's not through one of the nodes we just saw collapse."

"I don't think so," said Maya. "Elephant told us it was not a place people should go. I doubt they would have come here."

"Well, still. Are you going to just fly around checking every branch in the web?"

"No," said Maya. "Based on the inventory records Pickle found, it's likely only one or two drops from the cave. But if we're going with the Frenro cave concept of keeping important things in reach, I'm going to guess one."

"Yes," Auncle said, arms flailing. "Agreed!"

Maya studied the map, certainty and excitement growing in tandem. "The ship manifest Pickle sent me also includes Martian-bred crops—the sort you'd get for a long expedition to a place where you thought you could grow them."

"So it's a place fit for human habitation?" Wil's eyebrows shot up.

"Not necessarily breathable, but yes. So it must not be anywhere near the Human Nodal Region, or we would have settled there a long time ago." She looked at the map. "Wherever it is, it must be somewhere no one has ever gone before. Except, of course, Huang and her crew. All we need to do is send drones through each of the nodes and determine which have yellow stars with an Earth-ish planet."

Medix smacked his hands together. "Incredible!"

"You have found it," said Auncle, crushing her in xyr long arms until she couldn't breathe. "My beloved, my dear one, you have found it."

"So what's the plan?" Liam asked.

Maya blinked. "Don't you have a shuttle to catch in two hours? You haven't even packed."

"Are you serious?" he said. "You think I'd miss out on a discovery like this? It could make my career. Again. And yours too, of course. Like, we're talking Nobel Prize."

Maya grinned. "If you come, does this count as legit fieldwork?"

Liam laughed. "I guess we could work something out."

Maya opened a blank note and began listing what they needed. "Food and supplies for a minimum one-and-a-half-month mission. Do we have the credit for that?"

"I'll front it," said Liam.

Wil stared at him. "You have that much money?"

Liam ran a hand through his beard. "Well . . . yeah?"

Maya plowed on. "We're going to need to fix our deep scan equipment."

"Yes, yes, I did that yesterday," said Auncle.

"Preservation boxes, all sizes. Climate-controlled and vacuum."

"They had some of those in the market," said Liam. "Exorbitant prices, but maybe the Department will cover it."

In two hours, Liam's shuttle departed without him, and they had the outline of a plan.

The whole time, Wil picked at her teeth with a nail and listened to them, impassive. She made a few suggestions, but for the most part, she just sat eating the last of the red bean soup, now cold.

"You're really going to do this, huh?" Wil said as Liam pulled on his shoes to go back to the market.

They all looked at her, and she shook her head.

"You guys are like, like, Don Quixote."

"You've read *Don Quixote*?" Liam asked.

"Hasn't everyone?" said Wil. "You're going to go running off *again* after this fantasy, and there's probably a ninety percent chance you're going to die. Liam, this is your first time far from home. You think because you survive a couple of near-death experiences, you're invincible? Wrong. You've had a good run for a beginner. But Maya's right. You've been in over your head from the moment you stepped out your front door."

"You said that?" Liam asked Maya, eyebrows sagging.

She winced. "Well, yeah, but you're a natural."

Wil turned her dark brown eyes on Maya. "Since you've hired me, we've been shot at multiple times, nearly blown up, and fallen into the middle of an intergalactic war. Apparently normal stuff for you. You've confused ridiculous luck with skill. But guess what, it's not. I'm astounded you've managed to survive this long. Do you even know what you're walking into?"

Finally, she looked at Auncle, then shook her head, as if realizing the Frenro was a lost cause.

"Even if you find this place, five highly experienced explorers went out there, and only two came back. And they did a lot of work to make sure no one else could follow them. That doesn't scare you? It should. Because I guarantee you, you're not that good."

Maya raised the journal to say something smart about having memorized every line of the account, the security measures, the injuries that the crew accrued. It was true—Lopez, Zhang, and Jankowski had died, and they didn't know how.

Wil wasn't wrong; they were about to do something incredibly dangerous. But wasn't it worth it? Of course it was. And now that everyone knew about the cave, there was no telling when other people would find their way to the Encyclopedium. But when they did, the archives would get picked apart, and someone else would seize the grail.

A tiny voice reminded her of her nightmares of that place. She pushed that down. Knowing was forewarned. She'd keep her eyes open and stay on guard. Anyway, maybe she was mistaken. Regardless, this was the *grail*. No matter the consequences, she had no choice but to go.

Liam bit a thumbnail and looked from Wil to the rest of them. Wil's words had unnerved him.

"Some things are worth the risk," said Maya. She needed it to be true, after everything they'd already done.

Wil laughed bitterly. "Maybe so. But your life is the one thing that's yours in the entire universe." Her voice softened a fraction. "Maya. I'm not trying to be cruel—I'm trying to save you."

It wasn't that anything she was saying was wrong. Maya didn't want to die. And the rational part of her brain acknowledged that she was doing something rash, going barreling into the unknown like this.

"I can't believe I'm suggesting it after what they did, but you should tell the CNE," said Wil. "They want the artifact as much as you do. They'd send a whole fleet of professionals. They're probably already back to looking for it."

"No!" said Maya. "If they get to the Encyclopedium first, they'll strip everything, dissect the grail just to see how it ticks. And everything else they take will sit in a cold, airless storage bunker on the moon."

"And that's better than what you plan to do with whatever you find there? Which is what, by the way? Sell it to the highest bidder?"

"We'll return what we can to the rightful owners," said Maya. "Leave what isn't ours to take."

"And maybe replicate some pieces for the Humbert Archives," said Liam. "I mean, since we want them to pay for the expedition."

Wil shook her head. "You're going to wander the universe your whole life trying to find true north on your moral compass. I wish you luck. You don't even know what's there. Who knows what you'll stir up this time?"

Maya gritted her teeth. Again, Wil wasn't wrong. Once you opened the box, all manner of things might start crawling out.

They'd be careful.

"I must go," said Auncle. "There is no other path for me. Even if I go alone."

"You won't be alone," said Maya. "I'm coming with you."

"I'm in," said Liam. "Though I confess I am scared."

Maya shot him a grateful smile. "We won't tell Quintin that."

He flushed pink to the tips of his ears. "Who cares what Quintin thinks?"

"I would like to come," said Medix.

Wil gaped at him. "Why?"

"I want to *live*," said Medix. "I don't know how, but this seems like a start."

Wil dropped her hands. "Fine."

"You don't have to come with me."

"Of course not," said Wil. "But I want to get paid."

They looked at the projection. The nodes glimmered like orbs of unshed starlight.

One last time down the rabbit hole.

PART IV

THE EXPLORER

It was a place that felt so similar to Earth, relatively speaking, that we couldn't shake the feeling we might have traveled so far only to reach home again. If home were another time, another universe, maybe. It beckoned like an old friend. We knew even before we landed that it must be the place. If our people knew of it, they would flock here. It is Eden.
　—Dr. Wei Huang, *Expedition of the* Traveler, *A Memoir, vol. 5*

We went into the cave and found the light. We returned an echo of what had been. Let the ghosts wait there for no one.
　　　　　　—From the gravestone of Dr. Paul Nkosi

They passed into an eight-planet system orbiting a cheerful yellow star.

Medix analyzed the data from the probe they'd sent ahead.

"No immediate sign of active, space-capable life, no intelligent signal noise. But the fourth planet is Earth-class. Similar distance from the sun, definite presence of water. There are oceans."

"Oh!" said Auncle. "How beautiful. Do you think we can see them? Perhaps we can swim."

"It's got atmosphere," Liam added, voice high with excitement.

"Breathable," said Wil, in wonder.

"For humans at least," said Maya. "This *has* to be it." Of the thousands of worlds on the IW, there were few as ready-made for settlement as this. It made Maya's heart ache, thinking of her family back on PeaceLove, seeding the dirt year after year, coaxing the atmosphere to thicken. They had spent their entire lives in the pursuit of a distant future they'd never see, a time when people might walk freely outside. They had done all that, when there was a place like this.

Liam squeezed her shoulder. "Congratulations."

They were close. Closer than they'd ever been. Hope so thick she could swim through it. She reminded herself of the nightmares she'd had of this place, that they needed to take care, but she couldn't help her rising anticipation.

The world was on the far side of the sun. It would take two days to get there; in the meantime, they prepared for the landing.

About half an hour into their journey, they began to receive a signal, deteriorated with age. Maya projected it into the center of the room.

> *This is Wei Huang, lead researcher of the* Traveler *... If you ... this message ... do not proceed ... planet is dangerous ... do not go ... We lost ... something down there ... do not wake it up ... Leave now ...*

The message cycled over and over.

"Well, that's creepy," said Wil. "Are we ignoring the warning?"

"No," said Maya. "We're going to be even more careful." She rolled up her sleeve so Medix could examine the gunshot wound. "How's the new mod working out for you?" she asked him.

"I feel ... happy?" he said. Then more loudly. "I feel happy!"

Maya grinned.

"I didn't realize that joy could feel so ... sad at the same time," he said. "I suppose this is what people call bittersweet." He applied new skin and clean bandages to her gunshot wound. "It is strange. I thought expanding my emotions would make me feel more human. Somehow, it has had the opposite effect. As if the closer I get, the more I realize how much I am not."

"You're more human than most people," Wil said.

Maya hefted her laser cutter with her wounded arm. It still hurt. Not ideal to be breaking into a museum like this, but it'd have to do. She switched the cutter off. "You don't have to be *human* to be a person. There are plenty of other ways to be."

"You could be a Frenro," said Auncle. "We experience twenty thousand and forty-three emotions."

"Er," said Maya. "Right."

The closer they got to the planet, the weirder Maya felt. Each time she looked up at it through the ceiling, the hairs on the back of her neck lifted.

"Do you feel it, Maya?" Auncle said.

And then she did—a deep emptiness in the web, far more than the fragments and wisps they'd left behind them.

"What happened here?" she asked.

Auncle twisted away and disappeared into xyr pool without reply.

Wil took Maya aside as she was fixing her third meal of reconstituted sesame noodles in a row. She lowered her voice so the others couldn't hear. "I know you're noble and all, but you've considered other things you could do with the grail, right?"

"Seriously?" Maya asked. "I'm giving it to the Frenro."

Wil pinned her with a serious look. "You don't even know where they've gone. And they made it pretty clear they're not our allies."

"You want to give it to the CNE?"

The other woman opened and closed one hand, like she was grasping at something. "I was horrified by what they did too, you know."

"But what?" said Maya. "It's okay as long as they give us a lot of money?"

"No," said Wil, pushing against the counter. "I'm just saying, at least we know what they will do with it. I can't say the same for the Frenro. They say it's for making Frenro babies. But it's also used to create new nodes. How can both be true?"

"I guess we'll just have to see."

"And trust they're telling us the truth after secretly attacking us?"

Maya took her bowl of noodles and walked away. If she were honest, she didn't have a good answer, except that she had put her faith in Auncle's words too many years ago. Xe couldn't be lying about the grail, or what did that say about everything it had cost Maya to be here?

It took them half a day to identify the landing site. Huang's crew had withheld coordinates.

"It should be east of a mountain range in the shape of a person," said Liam, consulting the text, but it wasn't immediately apparent what that meant. There were a couple that looked like lumpy birds, maybe, and another in the north that was blanketed in glaciers and could have been a snowman.

Finally, after much discussion, Maya switched off her ocular lenses and looked at the original, untranslated version. She couldn't read Chinese, but it was the same character in Japanese.

"There," she said, pointing out an upside-down V-shaped range with a faintly curving stem at the top.

"How does that look like a person?" Liam wanted to know.

She showed him the character: 人. "Not 'a person.' 'Person.'" She reread the text aloud. "'East of a mountain range shaped like *person*, there is a broad plain with solid enough ground to land. The entrance to the vault is a five- to six-hour hike from there along an astonishingly well-preserved road, taking into account the deep growth cover . . .' Oh thank god, we have corresponding video for this bit."

"No indication of what danger there might be?" asked Medix.

"I'm sure it's *perfectly* safe," said Wil, running a maintenance check on her suit with a handheld scanner.

"There's this." Liam shared a clip.

Dr. Huang was speaking quickly into the screen. It was choppy quality. Time had degraded some of the message, but a few sentences came through:

> We were not prepared for nightfall. There is no way to prepare.
> We were fooled by the Earth-like atmosphere and climate; when
> night came, we understood this is not a world meant for humans.
> We lost Zhang on the way back to the ship.

And then she began to cry, and the clip cut out.

"Okay then," said Wil. "So we return to the ship before nightfall."

"What do you think happens at night?" Liam wondered.

Maya couldn't guess. Too much of volume 5 had been redacted. Whatever detail there was must have been in one of the deleted sections.

"I know promises are sacred in human cultures, but you do not have to come," said Auncle, and even Maya jumped, because they hadn't heard xyr return below. "It is wise to be frightened of this place."

"Don't be ridiculous," said Maya, squatting to place a palm against the floor between them. "I didn't come all this way to abandon you now."

"I, too, find myself . . . with a desire to see this place," said Medix.

"Did you get *another* mod?" asked Wil.

"No," said Medix. "I have been experimenting with adjustments to my motivational code."

"Self-modification is risky. Are you sure—"

"Yes," said Medix. It was the first time he had interrupted anyone, and they all stared at him until he bowed his head, almost like he was embarrassed.

"All right, then," said Wil. "Anyway, we're coming. For the money, valuable artifacts, and all that."

There was a warning beep and then deceleration ceased. In the quiet of the bigger engines powering down, their bodies began to drift. Below them, through the ship, they could see the world of the Encyclopedium.

Liam covered his eyes.

The rest of them drank it in. It was covered in white clouds and blue oceans. The land was a patchwork of pinks and greens and oranges. Three moons, two small and one large, orbited behind them. On the largest moon was a giant bronze ring that took up half its face. The sheer scale of it was awesome to behold.

"There is evidence of intact structures on the planet surface," said Medix.

"Cities," said Auncle.

"Cities?"

"Yes, this world was once densely populated. Many people. Much life."

Maya stared at xyr. Auncle had never mentioned any knowledge of this world. She shouldn't be surprised anymore that xe had kept something from her. "How do you know all this? How *long* have you known all this?" She failed to keep accusation from her voice.

"My memory is distressingly jumbled, but I believe I learned it from the Whole," said Auncle, "from the time that I was sleeping."

"A month ago? And you didn't think to mention it until now?"

"Does it matter? These people I recall are likely beneath the ground; the world is empty. It is irrelevant to our search, is it not?"

"Everything is relevant!" said Maya.

Liam put a hand on her arm. She shrugged him off.

"What happened to the people who lived here?" Liam asked.

"The virus," said Auncle. "This is where it was birthed. I—I do not like how these memories make me feel, Maya." Xe shrank inward for a moment, arms momentarily going limp, and then stretching once more to fill xyr chamber. "This world was home to an ancient people—older than mine. More advanced. They had their own interstellar ways."

Maya remembered the visions of the ancient war she'd gotten from the Whole. The devastation to the Frenro, and the death of many nodes.

"Another highway?" Wil asked. "Why haven't we heard of this?"

"This space is the only place the two intersected, and now it is very far from most habitable regions."

Except via the cave.

"If they were so advanced, what happened to them?" Medix asked.

"When we first met, we coexisted in a friendly manner for many years. But then there was conflict. I could tell you they began it, but I do not remember, and I do not want to be presumptuous. Ultimately, they wanted our worlds, and they took them. That is how we lost our home.

"What remains of that world, including the grail, they locked up in the Encyclopedium. They brought prisoners here, packed together in tanks. I'm not sure why. Or perhaps we knew but have forgotten. Whatever they did caused a sickness that infected all life on this planet, and whoever fled took the sickness with them to other worlds. It was their apocalypse."

"Where are they now?" asked Maya.

"Out there, maybe," said Auncle. "They shut the door between us and did not return. As did we. It was only later that we rediscovered our way to this world again."

"Why didn't the Frenro come here?" Wil asked. "Why wait for Dr. Huang to do your dirty work?"

Auncle's filaments retracted until xyr looked like a ball of yarn. "The Whole decided we would not come here, so we did not. Yet Dr. Huang insisted. I am only remembering it now that I am here. When Dr. Huang returned, she told us that all life on this world had been obliterated like the other worlds of the Dead Sea. She gave us the grail, but it died right away. We decided to forget about it."

They considered the planet below teeming with life.

"I'm not supposed to be here," said Auncle.

"Dr. Huang lied to you," said Liam. "Why would she do that?"

Wil shook her head. "I don't like it."

"Is there anything else you're not telling us?"

"There is not," said Auncle. "I think."

CHAPTER FORTY-FIVE

The ground was the color of milk bread, and the air was filled with a pink pollen-like substance. Maya recognized it instantly from her dreams.

Despite the unknown coral-colored dust in the air, everything was bright. The rising sun carved a path across the plain. What little scrub there was was scant and low to the ground: a patchy cover that looked like blue-gray lichen and something green and knobby, about half a foot high.

They'd landed a little after dawn, and the sky was full of pale pastel streaks just over the horizon, but already the heat was building, lending a shimmer to it. The old temperature regulator of Maya's suit wheezed to keep up.

It was going to be a long walk east.

Wil led the way, leaving shallow footprints in the ground. The planet's day cycle was twenty-seven hours. At this latitude, they'd have fifteen hours of daylight.

From above, that had seemed like plenty of time. Now, on the surface of the planet, it already felt like a challenge.

Despite confirmation that the atmosphere was breathable for humans, they all agreed to remain suited to avoid contaminating the planet. Before leaving the shuttle, they'd cycled strong disinfectant through the airlock, a blue liquid that left them all with a glossy sheen.

In their rucksacks, they carried instruments and empty preservation cases, except Auncle, who didn't have the body shape.

Maya followed in Wil's footsteps, the other woman's long shadow scraping her toes if she walked too fast. Maya's boots kicked up clouds of the fine powder that coated the packed ground.

She remembered going last in one of her dreams of this place, the others being too far ahead to catch up. *See?* she thought. *Not everything comes true.*

"This is *so* cool," said Liam's voice in her ear. He'd recovered from the descent, which he'd survived by squinching his eyes shut and whimpering the whole way. Now he was downright chipper. "Do you think this is the original ecosystem? It's so barren."

"Life does not always look like you expect." Auncle poked a hole in the ground about four millimeters wide. Now that xe pointed it out, Maya realized these holes were all over. She zoomed her suit visual for a moment and watched something long and thin and brown slip out of one in the distance. What she'd taken for a wispy weed was motile, not quite a snake or a worm.

"I wonder if these other people were land dwellers."

"If there's a road, probably, right?" said Maya.

"Oh, DJ has an interesting theory about roads—"

"Can we not talk about that guy for at least a week, please?"

"Amen," said Wil.

Liam scuffed along. "It was a really interesting theory."

But even Medix declined to take the bait.

Maya shaded her eyes and looked back toward the ship. Over the pearly white of the *Wonder*'s shuttle hung the enormous moon. Even in daylight, she could see the bronze geometric pattern across it: a circle crisscrossed with lines. The familiarity of this moment flickered across her brain like lightning. She captured an image of the lunar face with her suit camera.

When she turned back, the others were far ahead. And it was, again, as she had dreamed: four figures making their way across the hard ground. Not quite as far away, maybe. She ran a few steps, then remembered she would fall and slowed to a fast walk.

"So far, no sign of any danger," Medix was saying. "I believe we are going to do just fine."

"Let me guess," said Wil. "Optimism mod?"

"Do you like it? I think it's great."

"Optimism is dangerous. Please shut it off."

"No," said Medix. "I intend to enjoy myself."

Maya caught up with them. Ever since Wil had raised questions about the grail and what the Frenro would do with it, she'd been worrying, and she hated that anyone could make her doubt her friend.

She fell in next to Auncle. "Where do you want to raise your children?" It was the conversation they used to have all the time, before Lithis, as if speaking could manifest desire. Xe had thought about it for many years during xyr search, every detail. The conversation felt different now that they were so close to it being real. The words pricked as she spoke them.

Auncle pulled xyrself along, metal-coated arms undulating like snakes across the parched ground. "I don't know," xe said. "What if the *Wonder* is not big enough for them?"

"It'll be fine," Maya said, though she knew even less than Auncle. Was her friend having second thoughts after all this time? Or—Wil's warning came back to her.

"Will you go back to Earth?" asked Auncle. "Do you miss the sky like this and the buildings and people?"

"Yes. If they'll let me go back." She thought of her little apartment off Witherspoon Street, the way chatter from the sidewalk below filtered with the breeze in the summer, how listening to a lecture could make an idea bloom in your head, but also how every happy memory of Earth was a moment stacked on a moment that added up to—what? She wasn't sure. But she *did* want it back. She wanted it back, and she wanted this too.

It took them two hours to reach the edge of the desert plain, and by that point everyone was cranky except Medix, who was having a fantastic time. The ground had turned spongy, an orange half-clay consistency boiling with some microscopic but dense life-form, according to Medix's analysis. Maya leaned down once to touch a bit, and it coated her finger like a second glove. Her legs were covered in the substance, as if it were wicking up the metal.

She took another step, and her foot collapsed through the thin cover. Over she pitched, banging her nose hard against the inside of her helmet and sending a jolt of pain up her injured arm. Should have replaced the brace in her helmet years ago. "Ugh," she said, coughing a little as blood trickled from one nostril. No way to wipe her nose until they made it back to the ship.

Déjà vu again: she'd avoided falling earlier, and here she was anyway on the ground.

Wil squatted and hauled her to her feet with one arm. "Watch where you step."

"Nothing broken," said Medix.

"What's that?" Liam pointed at the hole. It was boiling with long, thin black organisms that shifted as they watched, forming intricate and indecipherable patterns.

"Beautiful," murmured Auncle.

"Come on," said Wil. "Let's keep moving."

Before them was—well, a jungle. Or something like a jungle. Life throughout the web tended to evolve into the same categories: immotile "plants," motile "animals," microscopic "things," etc.—all shaped by the same universal pressures to survive. But within those categories, there was plenty to surprise. Which made the prospect of wading into dense dark purple foliage nerve-racking.

Wil was the first to spot the road: about four meters wide, lined with metallic tiles. As Dr. Huang had noted, it seemed remarkably preserved. It was the first confirmation they were on the right track, and despite her foreboding, Maya felt her spirits lift.

"We are doing an *excellent* job already," said Medix.

"Stop it," said Wil.

The road clanged dully beneath their boots, punctuating the relative quiet of the forest. Wil transformed her arms to machetes and led the way, shoving aside and hacking at the few places where the road was overgrown.

"Does this count as night?" Liam peered down the dim tunnel of undergrowth.

"Just stay on the path." Wil dialed the luminosity of her headlamp up a little higher.

"I would love to know how they made this," Liam said. He picked up a bit of tile in one of the rare places it was broken and slipped it into his backpack.

A glint of Earthly green caught Maya's eye, and without thinking, she moved toward it.

"Where are you going?" asked Wil, because Maya was stepping off the path. There: just beyond the dense fringe of dark purple and brown prickly things was something deeply familiar to anyone who'd grown up in an outer settlement. She removed a trowel from her hip belt and bent to dig around the long green shoots.

"Watch out!" Wil said again.

They were all calling for her.

But this was—this was incredible. She pulled it out, grinning. A yellow onion. Unmistakable evidence that humans had been here.

A hand grabbed her, and Maya realized belatedly that Wil was right behind her, shooting at something twice her size with serrated leaves, bumpy, deep purple skin, and a huge jaw that could have swallowed her whole. It recoiled, and a shrill screech filled the air. The jungle rang with a high-pitch sound, as these plants or *whatever* they were shrieked in an angry chorus. Wil dragged Maya, clutching the onion, back to the road.

Their boots clattered against the tile as they ran. Behind them, the creature's bulbous head stopped short of the path. They kept going until the ringing had stopped.

"What was that?" Liam asked.

"Poor judgment," Wil said. "And I need everyone to keep discussion to a minimum. Stick to messages if you must. We have no idea what we're dealing with, and we're surrounded, so stay on the path and keep your voices down."

They continued on in tense silence. Sweat slicked inside Maya's suit, and the cycling noise of her regulator every time it came on seemed louder than a rocket engine in the renewed quiet.

Are you okay, my child? Auncle asked her.

Maya nodded.

Only later did Maya realize she was still clutching the onion.

...

"Now what?" asked Wil. It was the first time any of them had spoken in hours. They were all exhausted. Auncle's arms curled up at the ends, and Liam sagged in his boots. Only Medix was unaffected.

They'd come to a fork in the road.

One more thing Huang's journal hadn't mentioned. Maya took the opportunity to drink some water and chalky liquid food.

"What do you think, Maya?" Auncle asked. "Decisions without data are best made by irrational beings, and Infected humans are even more irrational than normal humans."

"I think you mean *intuitive*."

Inside xyr helmet tank, Auncle's filaments puffed out in Frenro humor. "Please decide."

Maya exhaled and looked at both paths. She had no idea. She dug deep in her gut but felt nothing. Everyone waited.

"Left," she said, wishing she felt sure, and not like she had tossed a mental coin.

After several minutes, she was sure she'd made a mistake. The road was steep and broken in some places and overgrown. No sign of the Encyclopedium. They had ten hours left — five hours, really, since they needed the same amount of time to return to the ship and wanted to be in the air before sunset.

They rounded a bend as she ran through the anxious calculations in her head. And then there it was. She'd guessed right. This had to be the vault entrance.

CHAPTER FORTY-SIX

I told you it is good for the most irrational human to make decisions," said Auncle.

"Intuitive," said Maya.

"I dunno, I like 'irrational,'" said Wil.

The entrance to the vault was imposing: a tall, gleaming wall about two Earth stories high, set against an outcropping of the mountain. The surface was etched with images that shuddered in jerky movements like whatever powered it was only half-working. Despite this, they could make out the story of a people who went to the stars and gathered together all life here.

On the left side was a web of lines, branching diagonally up the wall like a river estuary, and in the center of this web was a Frenro, spiky and small. The vast majority of the wall was covered in a grid of ruler-straight lines, with a multiplicity of figures Maya didn't recognize.

Where the two networks intersected was a single bright white point. The world of the Encyclopedium? *A world at a crossroads.* It must be.

And from inside the wall came tinkling notes almost like music, an atonal melody that meant nothing to any of them. She thought of the recording humans once sent out into deep space, and how random another people might have found the sounds if it ever reached anyone.

Here was the encyclopedia of life in the galaxy, and humans were not even an X on the map. It was moments like these when Maya felt the insignificance of her species.

Maya could see in the angle of Liam's shoulders the same longing she felt to spend years here, studying everything they could get their hands on. He murmured over and over: "My god, I mean, my god. Just look at this."

At the bottom of the tableau was a doorway nearly a story tall, bracketed by columns on either side. Wide steps led down into the dark.

A sculpture towered by the opening. She brushed wriggling, hairy, round creatures and pink powder off its smooth white stone base.

It was twice as tall as Auncle, who was twice as tall as a human when fully expanded. The statue was long-limbed and toothy with bipedal symmetry: two legs and four arms, and a cylindrical protrusion at the top. It might be a head, or at least an appendage for perceiving. Or perhaps their brains were in their center. If they had brains. Auncle was proof that wasn't universal.

They looked humanoid.

She imagined this person had once been a hero who had done something great for their country.

Maybe these people were like the Belzoar, honoring their dead with the public display of their corpses. Either way, the memory of this individual had outlasted the people themselves.

If the Frenro had come to Earth two thousand years later, might they have found empty buildings like this and statues of unknown people? What would they have made of the Statue of Liberty? What story could they have understood about the human race?

If they had a year here, she'd look for garbage, a vast midden that might explain not just the sketched version of this people but their full story.

"It's amazingly intact, if it's as old as we think it is," said Liam.

"We need to keep moving," said Wil, but her voice had a hush to it, like she felt the weight of entering a tomb uninvited.

"Three rules," said Maya. "One, anything that belongs to this civilization remains here. If we aren't sure, we leave it. Two, damage as little as possible. Three, act with utmost respect and caution. Never forget we are trespassing."

Liam nodded. She could feel the excitement rolling off of him. Auncle, too, was vibrating with urgency. Maya suspected if not for the others, Auncle would already be down the stairs.

"Yep. Got it," said Wil. "Let's go."

Nine and a half hours left until dark.

…

The way down was cold and slick, each step too large for people their size. Maya slipped, but Auncle wrapped several of xyr arms around her to keep her from falling.

Whatever light had once existed had gone out of the place, though she could imagine the glass orbs set along the walls might have flooded the inside with brightness. They relied instead solely on their head-lamps.

By unspoken agreement, they kept their voices low and spoke little. There was an oppressive feeling, like things were slumbering here. Things they didn't want to wake.

They descended about twenty meters at a sharp decline.

With one eye, Maya consulted her notes.

At the base of the main stair, we encountered the first security measure. The atrium floor was pressure sensitive, and great, heavy shutters came down around us, trapping us in. Ivan nearly lost his foot.

"Wait," she whispered to Wil.

"I know," replied the mercenary, halting on the last stair.

The stair was wide enough for them to stand abreast staring with trepidation at the atrium.

There were glass cubes on two-meter-tall pillars, positioned at regular intervals in the middle.

On the far side of the atrium was a wall that looked like it had been blown through with an explosive charge. According to Huang's journal, they'd had to use a small incendiary to escape the chamber. A radius of damage encircled that space: broken pillars and shattered cubes. Maya rued the destruction.

Wil took off her backpack and removed a metal ring. A few minutes' work, and it was accordioned out and assembled: a tube big enough to crawl through. This was mining technology strong enough to with-stand the collapse of a mountain. Wil pushed it out onto the floor. Then, with a decisive motion, she pitched her backpack into the center of the atrium. The crash was almost instantaneous. A wall came down around their makeshift tunnel—but the tunnel didn't collapse.

They held their breath. Now that the wall was down, it had become transparent. They could see Wil's backpack, intact in the middle of the atrium.

"The walls were made with Frenro technology," Auncle observed.

"If the previous crew didn't come with a portable tunnel, how did they get out of this building once the wall was down?" wondered Medix. "If they had used a charge, this wall would be damaged too."

"Good question," Liam said, and Maya had a peculiar momentary sensation, like she was tasting his words in different flavors, but then the moment passed.

"It must be on a timer or something," said Wil, "or we wouldn't be able to get in."

Maya removed her backpack and got down on her hands and knees. This had been the matter of much debate. Wil wanted to go first, but Maya was the lightest, the one who had spent the most time poring over the journal, which meant she had the least chance of disturbing whatever was in there and the greatest chance of spotting danger.

The makeshift frame creaked ominously. She crawled forward, just her hands visible in the penumbra of her headlamp. She reached the other side.

She stood a moment, alone in the antechamber, where Dr. Huang once had stood. When she looked up, her light played across walls that stretched up and up. Impractical, possibly, but impressive nonetheless. Like a civilization's statement of superiority, saying: We made this because we could. Her suit indicated that it was cold in here, near freezing.

"All clear?" asked Wil.

Maya looked around again, headlamp making giant shadows out of the pillars. No movement, but she got an itchy feeling between her shoulder blades, like she was being observed. She shrugged it off. This place had been abandoned long ago. No one left here. Still, she scrutinized the shadows one last time before signaling it was safe to proceed.

They followed one by one. Auncle was last. Xe didn't look like xe would fit, but xe compressed—easier without bones—so only xyr helmet and water tank knocked against the tunnel walls.

"Our excellent planning seems to be achieving results!" said Medix.

"You're really trying to jinx this, aren't you?" said Wil.

Maya scanned one of the glass cubes. "I'm getting a heat signature. I think there's still some energy flowing through this."

"Is it art?" Medix asked.

"Impossible to know," said Liam.

Maya leaned closer so her faceplate almost touched a fallen cube. "Huang speculated these might be a directory to this place."

"That would be handy," Liam said. "This place is huge."

"They weren't able to figure it out." Maya put a hand to the side of a cube. It changed to a deep ultramarine, then lime green. She removed it, and the color drained out of it again. "Huang tried all sorts of combinations. They spent a lot of time experimenting with the cubes. Apparently, they only turn blue and green."

"Did you hear that?" Wil asked. A tone echoed in the chamber above, and then they heard it too: a whisper of something—almost like a human voice.

Liam caught Maya's arm. "Language." The sounds came again, faintly, as if chasing his voice.

"It is familiar," said Auncle. "I wish I could remember."

Maya touched the cube again, longer this time, and multiple tones rippled through the air.

"Sing something," she suggested to Liam.

"No way. You don't want to hear that."

A swell of music emanated from Medix's chest, a whole symphony. The cubes throughout the hall, except the ones that were dead, lit up blue, and sound filled the chamber. Combined with Medix's symphony, it was a riot of noise.

"Stop!" said Wil. "You want to send out an announcement to the whole place that we're here?"

Medix stopped. The tones continued a few moments more, then faded out. "I believe I might have . . . felt something."

"What?" said Liam.

"I cannot describe it," said Medix.

"Can you do it this way?" Auncle transmitted something complicated, but Medix seemed to understand.

Wil crossed her arms. "We shouldn't be wasting time like this. We aren't trapped. We can just go through the hole they made in the wall ahead of us. You said yourself, Dr. Huang spent a lot of time on this without getting anywhere."

"They were using programs from a hundred years ago," said Liam.

"Also they were human," added Auncle. "We are not as limited in our thinking capacity, and this may help us find the grail more quickly. Time savings would be very nice indeed."

Maya touched the cube again, and Medix produced a different sound, multitoned and wholly inhuman, like something slipping under Maya's skin and wriggling around. The music—for that was what it felt like—swelled louder and louder, until the whole hall seemed to shake.

"It's looping," said Medix.

Maya started to analyze the data coming through, but Auncle was faster. Xe shared xyr analysis with the rest of them, converted to a visual: a network of lines, intersecting. A map.

Liam whistled. "This place is ten times the size of the Belzoar museum."

"Twenty-two times," said Medix.

The map included the same symbols they'd seen outside. Maya compared the scant directions Huang had left with the symbols. And there it was—the area with the spiky symbol for Frenro.

Maybe this would be easier than she thought.

"Stay close," said Wil, "and don't get lost."

...

They exited the way that Huang's team had gone, based on the blast marks. "There's a left up here," said Maya, comparing the map with Huang's notes. "Don't take it. We want the second left."

She fought the impulse to look in every room. How could they leave here without learning everything about this place, these people? She could happily spend the rest of her life here.

"We have to come back," she whispered to Liam.

"Absolutely." They shared a giddy grin. In her mind, her future scrolled at last before her. This felt *right*, an intersection of both her loves. Huang's dire warnings and her visions aside, it was impossible not to feel a little carried away by the thrill of this place. Here they were, where almost no human had been before. Who knew what mysteries of the universe they'd uncover?

The hallway was spartan, save for displays in the floor and walls and ceiling filled with unrecognizable objects. They glowed with ethereal light, illuminating giant crystals and unknown contraptions, and other things that might have been human but couldn't have been. Trophies from lost worlds.

A murmur rippled through the air, similar to the antechamber, and Maya stopped. It sounded so much like human voices, but that couldn't be. It must be her brain, anthropomorphizing.

"What's wrong?" Wil asked.

Auncle heard it, but the others didn't.

Then it faded, and there was nothing to do but continue.

They turned left and entered another hallway. There were signs of disturbance here and there: chalk markings and unlit lamps long since spent.

"If Huang was never able to access the directory, how did they find the stardust machine?" Liam said. "Sorry. Grail."

"The Frenro described enough for her to make a map of sorts," said Maya. "It still took them weeks to find it. And they spent a couple of nights in here."

"Let's not do that," said Wil, eyeing the dark.

They walked for a long time without reaching the end of it. Another turn, and they reached a door that was cracked open on one side. The gap was covered with thin fabric to maintain the seal that had been broken. More evidence of the first expedition team.

Maya stopped Wil from slitting the cloth open. She removed the file from her necklace and used it to peel back the cloth instead. There was a faint hissing sound as inside air released. They stepped through one by one and sealed it behind them.

They stood in a chamber. A single ribbon of red light flickered on and off, briefly illuminating the room. She guessed the folds of material along the wall were full-bodied suits, meant for visitors, to prevent contamination in the next room. Time had not been gentle to them: they had partially disintegrated, and the floor was covered in dry pieces.

Through another human-made seal, and then they found themselves at the top of more stairs.

"No lifts?" said Wil, leaning back to stretch her spine and neck. The hike had taken a toll on all of them.

"Primitive is more permanent," said Maya.

The echo of their voices rebounded and rebounded again. They descended into the depths of a chamber even bigger than the antechamber. At the bottom was a pool of liquid that filled nearly the entire room edge to edge. Across the pool was a door.

Maya's déjà vu was back, and her skin was covered in gooseflesh. She didn't want to go down there. She checked the entry:

We descended into a chamber filled with water. We couldn't tell if it was flooded or filled by design. We were very cautious by this point. The lack of safety rail was disconcerting—one tumble and you would fall right over the edge. It was hard to tell how deep the water was. In any case, it turned out to be shallow, and we were able to proceed without any issue.

Nevertheless.

"I think there's something in the water," she whispered.

They peered over the edge, but the surface of the pool was murky and still. Not a ripple. Wil sent her drone down to scout, but nothing stirred in the gloom. She removed something from her belt—a bullet, it looked like—and tossed it into the water.

It splashed, and they waited a long moment for an answering sound, but only silence followed.

And though everything in Maya resisted it, there was no other way to get to the other side but through.

"I'll go first," said Wil.

On the stairs ahead of Maya and Auncle, Liam slipped and landed on his rear, then slid again, forward down a stair with a loud thump. Wil turned and caught him. "Careful!"

"These are damn slippery." When he stood, there was a dark magenta smear on the seat of his suit from the residue of whatever was on the stair.

Auncle hooked one of Maya's belt loops with xyr arm, and they descended together.

They paused at the edge of the pool. Auncle dipped an arm before Wil could stop xyr.

"Not so deep," xe observed, and then plunged forward.

There was a groaning screech, and then it began to rain. Not water, but some substance that felt slick between Maya's gloved fingers. Fumes curled around them.

"I'm melting," observed Medix, holding up a hand. Whatever the liquid was, his fingers had gone soft and malleable around the edges. He pinched, and his fingers left little indentations on his palm.

"Hurry," said Maya, sloshing after Auncle, who was moving to the opening at the far end. Maya's whole body was coiled, ready to fend off whatever might be down here.

Now that they were in it, she could see that they were walking along a partially submerged and narrow path. The pool beyond was much deeper in the rest of the room. If it wasn't raining unknown chemicals, she would have been curious to investigate further, but as it was, they were just relieved to reach the other end. Fortunately, their suits seemed impervious to whatever was corroding Medix's plastic bits.

The path terminated in another airlock room. This time the doors were operable. In accordance with Huang's description, Maya pushed against the round medallion with a spiky depiction of a Frenro in the center, and it opened. In the chamber beyond, they were rinsed.

"Maybe that was their disinfectant system?" Liam said.

Wil fussed over Medix, assessing the damage.

"All good," said Medix, demonstrating with his fingers. They seemed to have solidified again, except for a pinky, which must have fallen off back in the pool.

"Jesus," Wil muttered.

Maya heard an almost echo then, the same not-voices she'd heard before. No way to know what the source was.

There was a loud clunk, and the door at the far end released and slid open.

Beyond was the first of a catacomb of chambers with doorways, each one emanating different quality light. Whoever the architects of this place had been, they'd spared no expense on the power mechanism.

The first room was lined with floor-to-ceiling stacks of cubical containers of foreign life-forms preserved in suspension along the wall. Pink phosphorescent patches the same color as the pollen outside covered the walls and floor.

Maya stopped in front of a case that was empty, save for a layer of red soil at the bottom, and wondered whether it had once contained more.

The next room was brightly lit and filled with eerily Earth-like plants. There was something that could have been the cousin of a sunflower, except it was a meter in diameter. The orange of its leaves was bright, preserved by whatever suspension technology they used.

"Convergent evolution," Liam noted.

They went through more rooms. Already, they had burned an hour and a half getting to this point.

"I have been thinking," said Medix. "The universe is a very big place. It is like you said, Maya. I focused on the wrong thing."

"You listened to Maya, when I've been telling you that from the beginning?" Wil asked.

"I am saying I can be more than human. I can be Frenro and Belzoar and everyone else. A mosaic of all the best bits. I think after this I will use my share of the money to travel."

"Really?" said Wil. "I was going to get a house, and I thought . . ." She trailed off in embarrassment.

At last they reached the tenth chamber and stopped. There, on a suspended platform, right in the middle of the room, illuminated by a single shaft of soft sunlight coming down from the bulb of a fibrous cable dangling from the ceiling, was the grail.

CHAPTER FORTY-SEVEN

I t was vivid ochre and cylindrical in body. The bottom of it disappeared in a pool of water, and they could see its bottom tentacles—or roots or whatever they were—poking half in and out of its container.

Unlike the one they'd taken from Emerald, the top halo of tentacles was curled up. A few fingers unfurled in their direction, as if in response to their entry.

Maya was struck again at how diminutive it was, something she could hold in her arms. She imagined she could feel the subtle rhythm of its inhalation. It was amazing to think it was alive. How long had this thing been down here, slightly shriveled and diminished but still going?

And how could such a small thing be so important?

Maya was crying, but it was impossible to wipe her tears away under the helmet. And even though she'd dreamed of it, there was a part of her that hadn't dared to hope they would find it. Not like this.

"It is perfect," Auncle said. Xe was shaking and Maya could see xyr skin turning green in distress. "Should we be grateful to the thief?" xe kept saying, because at least it had survived the later destruction of that homeworld xe would never know.

Maya didn't know what to say. Liam threw an arm around her shoulder, and she leaned into him, grateful to have someone there who felt the same deep awe and reverence she was feeling. Funny to think how months ago she could not have imagined standing here with him and being glad of it.

Auncle went to a little alcove off to the side of the gallery, perhaps a bathroom or a closet, but xyr silent howl vibrated Maya's bones until she bit her tongue to keep her teeth from chattering.

It was good that Auncle hadn't come alone. A Frenro wouldn't have been able to reach the grail, perched as it was on the suspended platform. This was a job for a human, evolved to climb.

The artifact hung from the vaulted ceiling, contained in a grille with bars just wide enough to fit a human Maya's size.

Maya handed her backpack to Liam, who staggered under the weight. She removed a cable from her belt. It took a few attempts to catch the hook around the cage. She nearly nicked the artifact in the process, but at last the grapple caught.

Wil picked her up around the waist and boosted her to her shoulders.

They'd knotted the cable so that Maya had something to rest her boots on as she hauled herself up. There was a question of whether she could do it with her injury, but Liam wasn't good at climbing or dealing with heights, and Wil was too heavy for the task. Fortunately, Medix and the CNE nurses had done a good job. Her shoulder twanged, but she was doing it.

Up she went, gloves slipping. She had a brief impulse to shed the suit, but she knew that was a terrible idea. So she continued to pull with her arms and push with her feet until she reached the top. Her arms screamed in protest. A glance down warned her she might not survive a fall.

Auncle had returned and was watching.

Maya wrapped her hands around the bars and, with immense effort, heaved herself up and through. She felt a resistance as she did so, like she was penetrating an invisible barrier. Then she was inside.

She lay panting a moment. It was silent in the space. The suit instruments indicated the atmosphere composition was different from outside—it matched the air in Auncle's sunroom.

Maya got to her feet. "All right, tie the backpack to the cable," she said, but from their gestures, it seemed like they couldn't hear her through the comm. Something was blocking transmission within this cocoon. Through pantomime, she was able to get them to attach the bag, and then she reached through and dragged it up.

By this point, her arm was throbbing, but there was nothing she could do but keep on. Another half hour burned.

She removed a preservation case and several tools from her backpack and approached the grail. Very carefully, she began to dig around the edges with pure anxiety. The thing was set in a tank as high as her waist, filled with silty water.

She began by draining some of the liquid with a funnel to the preservation box. It would be heavy, but better that than have it die in transit. As she eased the blade of her trowel into the edge of the clay inside the container, she regretted that she hadn't taken Xenobiology 202.

The Frenro told stories about an organism that grew at the bottom of the ocean over millennia. One that only bloomed on a watery world where the ground was not a thing to be trusted. Bringer of Life, Key to Other Worlds, Seed of Consciousness. The exact truth had been forgotten. The organism, or so the story went, was the ancient ancestor of the grail. How exactly had it come to be here, in this museum of lost things?

She lifted the thing with two hands. The tentacles—they definitely seemed more like tentacles than roots—detached with a suckering sound and clung to her. Revulsion filled her at its touch. It was hideous and warty and flaked like dead skin.

She had to peel each tentacle delicately off her suit to get it into the case. Then to transfer the clay sand sludge mixture at the bottom. Auncle's plant analogy had better be right.

Once in the box, she began to see beauty in its strangeness. Its skin refracted the light, and the violet whorl of its ridges spoke of a forgotten land buried beneath oceans. As she brushed it with her fingers, she thought she felt a soothing sensation in her chest, the way she sometimes felt when Auncle sang her lullabies.

Below, the others were coming back to the room, arms laden with artifacts. They unfolded a container sled and loaded it up with the treasures they'd found. She could see Liam aiming the replicator at whatever he could, for later reproduction.

She scraped the last of the clay into the container and closed it up.

The descent was easier than she'd feared, though the precious box nearly slipped from its makeshift harness a few times.

When she reached the bottom, Auncle was vibrating again. She could feel xyr waves of sorrow and joy.

She presented xyr with the precious artifact.

Quick as water, xe flowed over the ground to Maya. The grail disappeared in xyr cavity.

"My dear friend," Maya said. She would have, she realized, come to this place for less. What mattered was that it was important to Auncle, and Auncle was important to her.

How could she ever have considered for a moment handing this thing to the CNE?

"We have to leave now," Wil reported, and Maya was shocked to see that hours had passed. They would need to hurry to make it back to the ship before nightfall.

"I can't believe we're here," said Liam. "This place." His voice was rough with emotion. "Never in my life could I have imagined a place like this. And according to the map, it goes on for miles."

"I found wonderful things." Auncle seemed steadier with xyr grief poured out on the floor. "So many treasures we thought were lost— life-forms, tools, maybe even memories. Can you believe it?"

"What about you?" Maya asked Medix and Wil. "Find anything interesting?"

The mercenary shrugged. "I'm just the muscle. I packed whatever the professor told me to."

"Everything is interesting," said Medix.

Liam was smiling. "Thank you, Maya."

"What for?"

"For bringing me here. I feel like I finally understand why you and Quintin are the way you are."

"Which is?" Maya asked.

"Spontaneous, I guess."

"I don't know, I like a good plan."

"Okay, then *flexible*. Open to embracing mysteries and willing to accept you might not have all the answers."

"This sounds weirdly the opposite of when you told me I needed to study harder for my exams . . ."

"God, do you have to argue with me while I try to give you a compliment?"

"Fine. Shower me."

"Nope. The moment's gone."

Maya laughed.

"All right, all right," said Wil. "Time to move out."

Maya spared one last glance around, wishing for even another five minutes in this place, but the extraction had taken longer than anticipated. She promised herself she'd return.

As they moved through the rooms, she captured what she could with her camera. She darted over to grab an object that vaguely resembled the *Wonder*'s atmospheric regulator and stuffed it quickly in her bag.

Wil snorted with amusement but made no further comment. They were on the move, and that was all that mattered.

Perhaps it was their euphoria at having found what they were looking for at last, or perhaps it was their complacency after having come so far with little danger. And after all, they had overcome all the threats specified in the diary. But Dr. Huang had removed replicas, not actual artifacts, and the Encyclopedium apparently knew the difference.

Too late, they registered that something had changed.

When the first airlock chamber didn't open, they assumed there was something wrong with the mechanism, same as the first room. Wil cut an opening with her acid knife. She left it to the others to seal the hole behind them.

It was raining corrosive disinfectant in the antechamber again, and they were so intent on getting to the stairs that they missed the movement in the water. Too late, Maya remembered her vision.

They were halfway across, Wil and Medix in front, then Auncle, then Maya and Liam, when something huge emerged from the pool, moaning low enough that Maya felt it in her sternum. It was twice Auncle's size, translucent and blue-veined. It had four long, snaking arms, and half its body was mouth: a giant, toothy maw lined with rows and rows of sharp points like teeth.

Ah. So statues in this world were not a memory but a warning. It reached for Auncle with its arms, missing xyr by centimeters as xe flowed past.

Then Maya's turn. It grabbed her sore arm, then her ankle, trying to drag her toward deeper water. She had just enough time to draw her pitifully inadequate trowel and slash at it with the tip. Auncle was already halfway up those giant steps, Wil and Medix even farther ahead with the sled.

So it was just Liam and Maya left against this ancient thing. They were pitifully outmatched.

Liam bashed it with a statuette he'd picked up in one of the rooms. She heard the figurine shatter, and she cried out, but the thing let go.

"Run!" said Liam, as if she needed the instruction. They ran. They had reached the third stair when Maya felt something close around her ankle again. It yanked her off her feet and dragged her under. Her helmet was submerged. Beside her, she felt Liam's hand reach for hers, but she was ripped away.

Not yet, she thought.

You came back, she heard someone say. *I did not think you would. It is good to see you, Dr. Huang*, but if that were true, she was too busy screaming.

She surfaced. For a long, horrible moment, she watched Auncle above, getting farther and farther away. Auncle, whom she had followed without question for so long. Who, now that xe had what xe had always wanted, didn't need Maya anymore. Would xe really just leave her there to die?

She dug her fingers into a crack in the stair and cried with her mind, *Auncle!*

And then Auncle was turning—even though the Frenro believed it was bad luck to look behind—because sometimes superstition be damned. Xe was back down the stairs in moments and into the water, and xe lifted xyr arms, and beneath them were teeth even sharper than this monster's. Xe tore it all to pieces with a wet, mashing, grinding sound that Maya would remember for the rest of her life. And then it was just floating pieces on the surface of the pool, all bits of jellied flesh and circuitry and wire.

Liam lay on his back in the shallows, clutching his neck and coughing.

Maya turned her head, and only then did she see the preservation box half-crushed on the side of the stair. Auncle had dropped it to save her.

"I'm sorry," she said. "I'm so sorry."

"Hush," said Auncle, scooping her up, and urging Liam forward.

Wil had come back down to help them, too late. She retrieved the grail on the stair with extreme gentleness.

"Is it broken?" Maya asked. She couldn't cry. They still needed to get out.

"I think it's all right," said Wil. "Just sloshed around and crunched in the corner."

Maya gulped for air. Her heart was hammering out of its chest.

They reached the top, Wil half carrying Liam.

"Man," he said. "I thought we were dead."

Maya staggered through the darkened airlock chamber, heading for the plastic sheeting. Nothing more stirred below. Maya exhaled in relief. A hissing sound filled the room.

"They really take their disinfection seriously." Liam chuckled. And then Maya saw his expression change as yellow mist filled the chamber. He tried to suck in a breath, but nothing happened. He tried again. Horror filled his face. He looked down at his sleeve, where the construct had grabbed him. There was a rip about three centimeters long. "Oh fuck," he mouthed.

"Get him out of here," Maya shouted.

Wil slashed through the plastic, and pulled him through into the hall.

Medix bent over him, injecting him with several things through the slit, while Maya and Auncle struggled to seal the airlock behind them.

She heard dull thumps as Liam convulsed on the ground, and now she *was* crying. "No" was all she could say.

He stilled, and Wil slapped a patch over the slit.

His face was pale, and there was pink froth around his lips. "Liam," Maya said, shaking him. "Liam." He didn't respond. "Is he—"

"Stable," said Medix, voice calm. "He is going to be all right. No, I'm sorry, that is my optimism mod. I do not know what the effects of that substance will be, but his condition does not seem to be worsening for now."

Wil put a hand on her shoulder. "Come on," she said. "Best thing to do is get back to the ship."

Maya gritted her teeth. They lay his body across the sled of artifacts, which she and Auncle took charge of. Liam's face looked waxy in the dim light. She squeezed his hand, but he didn't respond.

Wil led the way, cradling the grail in one arm, the other a gun outstretched, ready to take down whatever came after them next.

The main hall was unnervingly quiet. Wil leaned forward to look around the corner and her head smacked against something. It was like an invisible wall.

She ran a hand over its surface, testing its solidity. They heard a loud crackle of static or electricity and then her hand pushed in a moment, as the field failed. Only instinct saved her from losing a hand: she snatched it back just in time.

Maya turned to see an enormous shape behind them. It was her only warning of another monster, different from the one in the pool, metallic and many-legged and possibly even bigger.

Her helmet light bounced off the glint of motion, and then Liam was whisked off the sled by a shadow and swallowed. Precious artifacts tumbled down in his wake.

Liam was just gone. There hadn't even been time to react.

Wil plunged forward, searching the dark for a sign of him, but there was nothing. The hallway was empty.

Maya screamed his name into the comm, and she heard a chorus in response, a rising, unintelligible murmuring, like tuning into several feeds at once. And they sounded even more *human* than before; she was almost certain she heard someone say "Earth," but that didn't make sense.

Maya would have charged back into the dark alone if she had to, never mind that she didn't know where he had gone, but Auncle held on to her with xyr arms, until she stopped straining and cried for her lost friend.

"We've got to figure out how to lower that field, or we'll be next," said Wil.

"There," said Medix, pointing to something across the hall that looked like a crystal prism set in the wall. There were little black loops all along the inside of the doorway, and threads of laser light lanced from the far crystal. "That must be what's generating it. If we can disrupt it, we can break the field."

"Get behind me," Wil told them, facing back down the hall from where they'd come. They could hear it this time: a quiet sliding, clanking sound. Out of the dark flashed a long appendage glinting with metal and flesh. Whatever was in the hall behind them was massive.

Wil fired a warning shot, and a reverberating tone answered them, like a gong.

An animal instinct took over, the instinct to get the hell out of there. Maya jabbed her trowel into the force field just as it flickered out. It re-formed in an instant, and the head of the blade fell to the floor on the other side with a clang.

Behind them, Wil fired shot after shot.

"I'll take care of it," said Medix.

"What?" said Maya. "Wait—"

The difference between robs and other people was that robs didn't hesitate; sometimes that was good, and sometimes that was dangerous. She needed to tell Medix this. He threw himself through the gap the next time the field spasmed. He lost half the back of a heel and his left arm, but it didn't even slow him.

He made his good hand into a fist and punched the crystal off its sconce. The force field fell, and Medix turned back to wave.

Something whipped out of the dark, and his head went flying clean off, and Maya could have sworn the last expression on his face was surprise.

CHAPTER FORTY—EIGHT

N o!" screamed Wil. In a burst of speed, she dispatched the thing behind them and went charging into the hallway after Medix. Light from Wil's headlamp slashed about as she battled whatever was there. Metal clanged and screeched against metal.

Auncle pulled Maya back against the wall, enfolding her in xyr arms and filaments until the world was muffled. It seemed to last forever.

Silence fell except for an ominous scraping noise down the hallway.

Maya pushed out of Auncle's embrace. Her headlamp illuminated Wil, standing in the opening clutching Medix's head in one arm, her other just a long blade covered in bits of goo and flesh and metal bits.

Without saying a word, Wil set Medix's head reverently down on top of the sled. She disappeared into the dark and reappeared carrying the rest of him, which she laid with the head. She cut open his chest and removed a black box no bigger than a pack of cards.

Then she picked up the box with the grail, which she'd left next to the sled when they'd come to the force field. She began walking.

"Wil," said Maya. "We can fix him, I'm sure."

Wil didn't stop.

She and Auncle grabbed the sled and followed. The hallway was streaked in gore. *There are more of these things*, Auncle told her. *I can hear them coming. We should hurry.*

Are they alive?

Auncle looked over at Medix. *It depends on how you define life. I do not know if they are sentient.*

When they reached the antechamber, the cubes were glowing a sickly orange-yellow. Maya was so preoccupied with peering nervously up at the vaulted ceiling, she nearly missed that the tiled floor was gone. Where the room had been was a deep pit. She couldn't see the bottom.

Wil took the twin of the cable Maya had left back in the Frenro chambers and attached something to it. Her right arm changed into a grapple gun. She hooked the cable around the tip, knelt, and fired. It went through their mining tunnel and buried in the far side of the stair.

"Will that hold?" Maya asked.

Wil fit the grail into her backpack and tested the rope. "Guess we'll find out." She began to inch across the cable, hand over hand.

"What about all this?" Maya asked. They would have to leave most of it behind, take only what they could carry.

"Maya," said Auncle urgently. "I cannot do this. To be more specific so as not to be misunderstood, physically I cannot. You will not be able to carry me."

Maya looked back at the sled. "Maybe if we construct a pulley or something?" She racked her brain.

Wil was halfway across.

"They are coming," said Auncle, turning back toward the hall.

Maya could hear whatever they were. The clacking steps were audible now even to her ears.

"Go, my friend," said Auncle.

"Don't be ridiculous," said Maya.

You know it has always been my greatest desire to have children someday. Auncle's voice in her mind was soft as silk. *But you, my friend, you are my sweet child. I do not wish you to die.*

And she felt it in waves of warmth and sunlight and the certainty of a planet orbiting a star year after year after year for millions of years—which was not forever, but it was enough—and it was frightening, because the point was, her friend wanted her to *live*, and this was a separate, selfish thought that was Auncle's, not the Whole's, which would surely have picked differently in this moment. Maya was *xyr* friend, and xe would risk anything for her.

"Well, too bad! Because I'm not leaving you here. Wil! We have to find another way out. There's got to be another exit."

The mercenary had made it to the other side and was crawling through the tunnel. In another moment, they couldn't see her. Her voice, however, came through the comm of their suits. "This wasn't how it was supposed to be."

"What do you mean?" asked Maya.

"We were supposed to get our money and go, the two of us."

"You'll still get your money. Wil, what are you doing?"

"I thought I could just let the web die and not care, as long as I could go back home and have my little house and my friend and my garden. But the thing is, I do care about the web—the people in it. And I don't mean just humans, but everyone. If this thing can keep it going, that's important, right?"

"Yes, but—"

"If it's a question of protecting people, I have to do it, don't I?"

"What are you talking about?" But Maya, with a sinking feeling, knew.

"I've got the grail. If I leave now, I can make it back before nightfall. It's the only way to ensure it's safe and that everything we sacrificed was not for nothing. The CNE will be here soon. Find a place to hunker down, and I'll come back for you. I promise."

"But we trusted you!" shouted Maya. "I *liked* you." Her voice echoed in the empty cavern. Voices came back to her, rising, falling. She heard words this time, snatches of conversation.

She didn't know whether to rage or sob. She felt a pain, like her insides were combusting, and it was just as she had dreamed, it always was, because that was the thing about time and space—it existed apart from you, and it stretched on to infinity, and you were *nothing*, in the end. She stared across the chasm through the clear walls. Wil was climbing the stairs into the soft warm rays of afternoon light.

"I like you too, Maya. You're a good person. And I'm so sorry. Sometimes you have to do a bad thing for the greater good. Even if it costs you a piece of your soul. But I want you to know—" Her voice broke. "This wasn't how I planned it. We were all supposed to get out of here. If there was any other way, I'd take it. But there's too much at stake."

Mayyyyaaaa, said Auncle. The clacking behind them had stopped. Maya didn't have to turn around to see they were surrounded.

CHAPTER FORTY—NINE

They were each of them two and a half meters tall, with six legs. The first two appendages appeared to have three long webbed fingers. They were made of metal, and covered in spotted flesh. They might have looked like insects, save for the absence of an obvious head.

I concede you were right, said Auncle.

About what?

About taking on new crew. I should have discussed it with you first. I am very sorry. I thought they were nice.

The whispers were back. They rose into a chorus. At first, she thought the sounds emanated from the chasm where the antechamber had been. But no. They were coming from her comm channel. She clutched her helmet, as if she might physically extract them from her ears.

This time there was no mistaking what she was hearing.

It is good to see you again, Dr. Huang. You should not have stayed away so long.

The constructs around them began to sing: a set of unearthly tones, in unison, and to Maya's relief, the voices in her comm channel subsided.

Maya cocked her head. *Why do you think they're not attacking?*

Perhaps they are worried we will damage the artifacts, said Auncle. *Or perhaps they've reevaluated our threat level now that our dangerous friend has left us. Our unfriend. Maybe they will only attack if we attack. Unless, of course, transgressions in this culture are punishable by death.*

Maya put a hand on the handle of the sled, and the constructs bristled. She stopped.

If only I could remember their language. Then xyr voice box emitted a combination of sounds that was like a cross between a flock of birds and electronic chords.

The constructs reoriented toward xyr.

What did you say? Maya asked.

Friend, said Auncle.

The constructs weren't convinced.

Do you think you could reach the closest cube?

In response, Auncle reached xyr two long arms through the jagged hole in the wall and—just barely—touched the side of a cube. It and the other cubes lit up, and a series of notes began. *Do you remember what Medix did before?*

Of course, said Auncle. *I am not that decrepit.*

One of the machines stepped forward and seized Maya's waist with its long fingers, but Auncle wrapped xyr arms around every part of Maya. She felt color and love and foreign, indescribable emotions that tasted like pickled yuzu, and she heard tones, first in her head and then in her ears. The machine that held her relaxed.

The first sequence was definitely a little off, but the second go-around was better, and by the third time around, she graded the performance a solid B+, considering Auncle was using an artificial voice box.

The whole time, the machines didn't move. Even more miraculously, the floor reassembled, though the security walls remained in place.

Auncle stopped, and the construct hands began to draw Maya closer again. The floor dissolved. "Keep going."

Auncle resumed, but Maya knew Auncle couldn't keep on forever. They had to do something else.

In pure desperation, Maya grasped the sled and shoved it through the blast hole into the antechamber. As she'd hoped, the constructs rushed forward, past them, to retrieve the treasure. They took with it the other end of the cable and any chance of escaping that way.

Auncle grasped her arm, and they hurried deeper into the Encyclopedium.

Where are we going? Auncle asked.

Maya scanned the map in her feed as she ran. There it was, what she had noticed when they first retrieved the map: a south exit that connected to the other road they'd seen earlier at the fork. It required them to go much deeper into the Encyclopedium than they'd been before. *That way.*

Behind them, they heard the artifices following. They passed the place where they had turned before, and she took a right instead of a left. Turn after turn, down and up stairs.

They passed through chambers full of fog and frosted with ice, and others hot and bright, each one stocked with mysteries they didn't have time to unravel.

Several times, they rounded a corner only to find themselves face-to-face with fresh constructs climbing out of the walls. In those cases, they were forced to turn and go another way. Maya's legs were exhausted, and her adrenaline was waning. She stumbled more than once.

The less tired part of her brain wondered why they hadn't been caught yet. She couldn't shake the feeling they were being herded somewhere.

A crackle, then: "We've found a spherical chamber," said a voice in her helmet comm. It sounded like an old recording of Dr. Huang. "A white sphere. It's big . . ."

"Hello?" Maya said.

No answer, but goose bumps raised on Maya's arms. It sounded like the sphere she'd dreamed of shortly after leaving Earth.

They descended deeper into the mountain until they ended up in a long passage lined with windows. As they moved, the lights flickered on in a grand sweep all along the hall. They were bathed in light.

Auncle and Maya froze.

Beyond the walls were dozens of creatures, unmoving, in various stages of decay. Some were empty suits of garments. Others were piles of bone-like substances. Others, whose containers were perhaps drier, were desiccated. Those were by far the worst. And at the very end, in an enormous tank full of cloudy water, was nothing, but there was an image projected in front of the tank, flickering but still functional, of a Frenro.

Once this place might have been a zoo or a prison, or who knew what. Now it was only a grave.

Behind them echoed the unmistakable clattering sound of metal limbs on floor. They had to go on.

Auncle said nothing, but Maya could feel xyr rumble through the fabric of her suit.

"These people were bad," said Maya.

"We cannot judge . . ." said a voice—Dr. Nkosi?—before static filled the channel again.

"Where's that coming from?" she asked, heart pounding.

"Maya?" Auncle asked. "What do you hear?"

"Nkosi! My god, they took . . ."

"... not here to disturb the dead ..."

"... god ..."

"... didn't mean ..."

Then gibberish again.

Maya sucked in a breath. "It's old recordings from the first expedition." As if the whole place were haunted.

"We cannot delay." Auncle pulled her along.

A left and then more stairs, this time up and up. They had to pause to catch their breath. The clacking footsteps behind them had finally stopped, and that only increased Maya's anxiety. Who knew what was waiting for them around the next corner?

They went through the doorway, and this time it was Auncle's turn to falter. The vision hit Maya second: horrible images of sickness and war, of dark experimentation, of people dying and the acrid burning smell of unending fear and screaming as constant as background radiation.

Now it was Maya's turn to drag Auncle through this chamber of horror into the next. They must have passed through thousands of years of history until finally spilling out into the hallway beyond.

They sprawled a moment on cold metal tile, piecing themselves back together.

"What was that?" Maya asked, tamping down on her rising gorge.

"I do not know. Perhaps it was a lesson," said Auncle.

Maya shook her head.

"How much farther? I am beginning to feel fatigue." It was unusual for xyr to admit that; xe must be very tired. They had been on the move for more than three hours.

There were two ways out from where they were. The shortest way was straight ahead. The doorway was right before them, open as if in invitation. Maya went to it and peered inside.

The chamber was an enormous sphere with a narrow walkway that led across. The entire surface was white.

A chill ran through her. She did not want to go in.

"You dreamed of this place," said Auncle. "Do you remember?"

She heard the constructs emerge behind them.

"What should we do, Maya?" Auncle asked. "I am sorry you stayed behind with me. You should have gone with our unfriend so you would be safe by now. I think they want us to go into this room."

Maya turned around and faced their pursuers: there were four of them, so large they could only stand two abreast in the echoing hall. Each of their pointy appendages was tipped with jagged edges that could eviscerate her. In the dusk of the hall, she could make out black organs that might be visual receptors—mechanical or biological, she didn't know.

The chamber behind them emitted an audible hum.

The creatures edged forward, tightening their formation around them. Auncle backed up, avoiding the swipe of a blade.

Maya flinched, and the beam of her headlamp flickered across them. The constructs retreated from it.

It gave her an idea. She tore the blue crystal from her necklace.

"Cover your visual receptors," Maya told Auncle, turning her helmet opaque. Then she activated the crystal. The constructs crashed about, metal clanging into metal, blinded by the light.

Auncle, who had excellent proprioception, pulled her forward past the enormous constructs.

As soon as they were past, they began to run again until they reached an enormous room the size of a hangar. Maya braced herself for more constructs, but it was devoid of movement. The room was clean, still set up for work, as if its occupants had only stepped out for a day.

It was, she guessed, evidence of the rapidity of the virus that had brought this supreme civilization to its knees—the same infection Maya carried in her own cells. She wondered if it had started on an ordinary day, or if they had come to this hangar knowing it was the end of the world.

"There is a door. We are going to escape now." Auncle pointed toward a transparent wall at the end of the chamber, with a faint square outline in the middle. Beyond, the biome was a riot of purple and fuchsia. They were higher up the mountain. From this vantage, they could see the plain stretched out in the distance, and even the tiny sparkle of the *Wonder* in the middle of the sand.

The sun was low in the sky.

And Maya realized with a start that much of the day was gone. Fear had driven them this far. Now she sagged, exhaustion in every part of her body. She sipped liquid food, which she realized she hadn't done in hours. They were almost free. She wondered how far Wil had gotten in the forest, if she were already back at the ship. Then she saw it.

At the far end, near their exit, was a cart, and on the cart was a body.

Maya could tell right away it was human, and she suspected this human was dead.

She both needed and didn't want to see the person's face. *Liam*, she thought. It had to be.

"I do not like this," Auncle said.

They reached the exit, and it was devoid of movement. She looked down at the body. It wasn't Liam.

It was Dr. Wei Huang.

CHAPTER FIFTY

Maya stared down at the body. Dr. Huang had lived and died a hundred years ago. There was no way this was actually her. She poked the body with one finger.

Soft flesh. She lifted an arm. Only partial rigor mortis. She'd seen enough bodies during the war to know.

"I cannot open this door," said Auncle. "But I will not give up. We will leave this place. The Whole was right, it is not a place for visitation. We should not return." All the while xe was fiddling with the door. No handle. Xe tried pushing on it. It didn't move.

How was Dr. Huang here? She'd escaped. And even if she hadn't, how was her body so fresh? Had they somehow fallen backward through time? And if this really were Dr. Huang, how had she died? "This is impossible," said Maya.

"It is not impossible," said Auncle. "It is a door and doors open, no matter what people built this door. Ah!" Xe rushed to the end of the wall, where a single cube sat on a pedestal.

Xe clasped it with three arms and began to repeat what xe had sung before. The door opened.

At the same time, seven doorways behind them slid open. Within each stood a construct.

"Hello?" said that voice in her ear that she now recognized. "This is Dr. Huang. Is anyone there?"

But Auncle was already leaving, and Maya had no choice but to follow.

Before she could process it, they were half falling, half stumbling down the mountain, doing their best to stay on the path. They passed the branch in the road leading back to the main entrance.

It was only then that Maya realized she still had her backpack, packed full of Frenro artifacts by Liam.

Liam. Her chest tightened. She should never have let him come.

The sun was sinking too fast, and an alarm in her suit was going off, warning them they needed to take cover soon.

She almost didn't care. She would take whatever the night brought on, because they'd already lost—the grail, Liam, Medix, the sled, even Wil—all of it. The whole world could try to fight her.

Another thing she should have told Medix: that grief was a universal thing, no matter what sun you'd been born under. And they were both of them choking on it now, oblivious to the danger around them.

Maya stumbled briefly off the path, and it happened in an instant: one moment she was knocking aside spiky purple growth, the next her visor went black, and she felt her whole body lift into the air. One of the giant carnivorous plants had swallowed the top half of her.

Her diaphragm was constricted. Fear attached to every molecule of her body. If she could expand her lungs, she would have screamed, but she was being squeezed so hard it felt like her eyes might pop. She couldn't see or smell through the suit, but she could feel chunks of undigested flesh and slime coat her body. Something hard scraped the top of her helmet and her shoulders, trying to pierce through her suit. A sensation that she could only have described as the swallowing of an enormous gullet convulsed along her shoulders, elbows, arms, hips.

Only the firm tug around her legs of Auncle's arms kept her from going all the way in. She heard rather than felt something wet plunk against her helmet, and the barest sound of sizzling, like some kind of acid corroding the outside, but she couldn't get enough air into her lungs to scream.

Then she was thrown to the ground, and a piercing screech filled the air. She lay, gasping, on the metal road.

Wil was carving up whatever had gotten her with arms that were two massive, wicked curved blades. It was over in moments. Wil turned back to them. Her blades were dripping with violet fluid that burned pockmarks in the surface of the road.

"You left us!" Maya said, regaining her breath and anger at the same time.

"Yeah, well," said Wil. "I came back for you, didn't I? I got all the way down the road to the desert and your annoying little voice kept going round and round in my head—"

"Excuse me, friends," said Auncle. "I think we have a problem." Xe pointed over Wil's shoulder.

Dusk was rapidly turning to night, and the pink dust was swirling, thickening into strands that seemed to reach for them like something thicker than cobwebs. She thought it stroked her shoulders. The jungle rang with shrill cries.

The pink cloud descended around the remnants of the plant that had just been trying to eat Maya. In moments, there was nothing left but purple stubble, white mineral spine, and the barest tatters of green skin where it had once been. The dust moved on to its neighbor and began to eat that too.

"I believe we've overstayed our welcome," said Wil. "Move."

"Where?" asked Auncle.

"Back," said Wil. "We'll never make it to the ship."

"You didn't see what we left back there," said Maya.

"It can't be worse than this. Now move, or I will move you."

Auncle was already retreating at a rapid pace, having apparently done xyr own calculations of the odds of surviving nature run amok. Gritting her teeth, Maya turned and followed, ordering up a shot of stimulant as she did. She didn't think she had the strength to make it back up the hill again otherwise.

In the gathering evening, the tiles of the road illuminated under their feet, a path of bright light pointing the way.

They came to the fork, and Wil didn't question when Auncle went right instead of left.

By the time they were halfway up the hill, the screams had reached an unbearable level. It felt like her skull would split open. Everything was on the move. The world was devouring itself: the air consuming the plants, the plants gnawing small animals, and the road burning brightly through everything with irresistible righteousness.

Wil screamed at her, probably something unhelpful like "run faster," but it was impossible to hear anyway. Maya was already pumping her legs as fast as she could.

She glanced behind and saw a human-sized caterpillar coming up the road. Its head was just an O of teeth, and while she didn't know for sure what it was or if it was carnivorous, she was highly motivated to get away from it. It was impossible to see anything behind it but night sky.

Thankfully, the door was still half-open. They squeezed through it into the giant hangar just before the caterpillar. It slammed its face against the crack a few times, before getting distracted by something in the forest. It dove into the understory.

"Christ," said Wil.

From their vantage point higher up on the mountain, they could see the road stretching unbroken through the forest and across the open plain. On and on, a starbright road illuminating the night, straight as a ruler across the continent to where whole cities once might have been. Despite everything, she felt a deep ache to learn more, understand the people who had built this place.

Wil slumped down under one of the tall work surfaces. "Guess we're staying the night." She tongued several pills from the dispenser inside her suit.

"Dr. Huang's here," Maya told her.

"What?"

Maya looked around for Dr. Huang's body and realized something or someone had deposited the cart just outside. Now, as Maya watched, the pink forms tangled in the air above it. The cloud of pink covered the body. It ate through the skin, shredded through muscle and dissolved organs, then bone, until nothing remained of the renowned explorer but an empty suit of clothes and a clump of hair.

"Well, she was," Maya said.

The ecosystem was in overdrive, turning over before her eyes faster than she thought was possible, remaking itself. Huang's words came back to her: *This is not a world meant for humans.*

The stimulants sizzled through Maya's body. She paced the workshop on alert for immediate danger. No sign of the constructs at least.

Auncle inspected a machine three times xyr size in the middle of the hall. It was a geometric structure about twice her height constructed of metallic material, one of five of various size and shape. The one at the end looked like it was still in the process of being assembled.

"What is that?" Maya asked. There was something familiar about its shape—and she remembered, it looked like the structure on the moon, in miniature.

Xe waved xyr dorsal arms. "If only I could remember what it is for. I have this feeling it is dangerous, but I do not know why that would be."

Auncle wrapped an arm around the edges of the machine in the flickering light. Nothing happened. Xe retreated and hunkered down near Wil, as usual, willing to forgive much faster than Maya.

She didn't know how long they sat like that. Eventually, without meaning to, she slept.

When she woke, it was still dark. Auncle was roaming the room again, and Wil was turning Medix's brain box over in her hands. The other woman caught Maya's eye. "He didn't deserve to die like this. Not when everything was just beginning."

"Can you resurrect him?" Maya asked.

Wil shook her head. "I don't know. Does that deny him the death he wanted? I hated how fixated he was on that, but I understood it too. He wanted to define the edges of his life, right? This was, in a way, that. When you're alive, you don't get another chance. But I—I don't want him to be dead. Maybe that's selfish, but I wanted him to get to travel and learn more about himself, and I feel like he was just getting started."

"I suppose if he's mad," said Maya, "there are plenty of other opportunities to do dangerous things for the good of the entire interstellar community."

"Yes," said Auncle. "It is easy to arrange. We have many connections."

Wil gave a watery sigh. "Assuming his brain box hasn't been damaged. Either way, it'd take a shit ton of money I don't have."

"If you give us back the grail, we'll still pay you." She could see the top of the case sticking out of Wil's backpack. Her fingers twitched.

"Sweetheart," said Wil. "It's not about the money—which I know you don't have. I made my choice."

Maya tried and failed to keep the disappointment out of her voice. "But you came back for us."

"Just because I don't want you to die doesn't mean I agree with you."

"When did you decide to do it?" Maya asked.

"Dr. Garcia approached me on Emerald." Maya remembered Wil running into the professor in the plaza before the heist, how grumpy Wil had been after. "I said no. Then later, on *Dragons*, I decided to reconsider."

"All so you could have your little cottage?"

"No. So when I die, and I see my stepdad again, I can look him in the eye and tell him I tried to do the right thing." Wil tipped her head back against the leg of the table.

Maya was about to argue further, when a new, more familiar voice sputtered over her comm: "Maya?"

"Liam?" She was wide-awake. She had heard him, she was sure of it, and hope flared inside her. He was alive.

"Where are you going?" Wil asked.

Maya went to the doorway and trained her light into the dark. She switched to a broader frequency on her suit comm. "Where are you?"

Voices came back to her, one of them her own: "Left," she was saying. "Next right . . ." Like directions.

"Don't tell me you're thinking of going back in there for more shit. It isn't worth it, and I'm not coming with you."

"It's *Liam*," Maya said. "I heard him."

"No way," said Wil. "I'm sorry, but if you go back in there, that thing will take you too."

There was a crackling noise, the sound of a bad transmission, like his equipment was smashed.

She took another step down the darkened hallway, heart hammering. "Liam?"

Crackling, and her own voice again, repeated back to her: "Left. Next right. Keep going straight . . ."

"What is it, Maya?" asked Auncle.

"Don't you hear that?"

"Stop," Wil said. "You're not allowed to get yourself killed after I saved your life. Again."

Maya looked back at her two companions. "We can't just leave him here."

"I'm sorry, Maya. But even if he *is* alive, and that's a big if, you have no idea where or what condition he's in. How are you going to find him? Those things will catch you first. You'll never get out of there."

Maya squared her shoulders. Her eyes fell on a long, narrow piece of scrap like a pipe. She hefted it. "Getting things out of tricky places is what we do."

"You're really not as smart as you think you are." Wil's expression was impossible to read behind the reflection of her helmet. "If you go in there, you better not think I'm coming with you. My body feels like crap, I'm tired, and I would prefer not to die."

Auncle grabbed a long-handled tool that looked like a mallet and joined her.

"Take care of yourself, Wil," Maya said, tucking her backpack under one of the tables. If it wasn't here when she returned, so be it.

And then, before she could question the wisdom of her choices, she stepped back into the vault, Auncle at her heels.

CHAPTER FIFTY-ONE

Maya listened to the recording of her voice as they went into the vault. How many folktales began like this: Following a thing into the woods, even though it was a mistake, but you went anyway, because you could never just not?

The hallway was quiet as a tomb, same as their first journey in. The clear displays on either side and below their feet were lined with unknown objects categorized, maybe, by shape or function. They passed through a section that seemed to be devoted exclusively to machines with sharp pointy ends. It went on and on.

"It's like you want to die in here," said Wil, and Maya nearly jumped out of her suit, because the soldier was on their heels. She'd come along after all. "What? I wasn't *actually* going to let you come back in here alone after going to all the trouble to rescue you."

"We are very happy when you are with us," Auncle told her. "As long as you are not leaving us again."

"Yeah, yeah," said Wil.

And despite the fact that Maya was furious with Wil, she was relieved to have her, because if she had to go up against the ghosts of a terrifyingly advanced civilization, it seemed slightly better to do so with an elite soldier by her side, even an ex-CNE one who had just betrayed her.

There was no sign of the constructs this time, just Maya's own voice whispering directions.

Fear tickled Maya's spine. It was almost like the Encyclopedium knew they couldn't leave until dawn and was beckoning them in. She didn't like it.

"Do you think the beings we met before are sleeping?" Auncle asked.

"Aren't they machines?" said Wil.

"Anthrocentric assumption," said Maya. "We don't know *what* they are."

"Can't you walk a little quieter?" Wil whispered, even though she was the one clomping along.

"I'm pretty sure it knows we're here." Maya caught sight of a smear along the floor and froze. It was dark. She squatted for a closer look. Not blood. Couldn't smell it through the suit, but she was fairly certain. "It's, um." Human shit. Liam's waste bag must have been pierced in the struggle.

She cringed at the contamination, but she was glad Liam hadn't bled out all over the floor.

And it meant they were on the right track. He had been this way. Now, at least, they had something more tangible to go off of than a voice only Maya could hear.

All at once, something came out of the dark behind them and rushed between their legs: a pink dust cloud—possibly the same one they'd seen gathering in the air outside. It must have sneaked in through the breach in the door. Fortunately, it didn't seem interested in their suits, just the excrement smeared along the floor.

"Hurry," said Maya, when she saw what it was doing. If they lost the trail, they'd have nothing.

They began to run, but the pink swarm was already ahead of them.

The murmur of other voices was back, wisps of phrases. Members of the *Traveler* expedition discussing artifacts, as tangible as her dreams. She no longer questioned it; she could only hope there'd be answers at the end.

They went down another flight of stairs that ended in a thick, heavy door. The smear continued under it, but the door must have been sealed, because the pink swarm could only settle around the edges before dissolving back into a less-defined cloud, as if dormant.

Wil felt around the edges of the door with her fingers. "I got nothing," she said.

"Liam?" Maya asked again.

The answering crackle was louder, and when she heard him again this time, it sounded like "Help me."

All at once they heard a tone, clear as a bell, and then another and another.

Maya felt rather than heard a low bass rumble. The door opened of its own accord.

"I told you this was a trap," said Wil, but they weren't turning back now.

The pink plume re-formed into a spear and slipped through the opening. At the same time, a light flicked on without warning, and suddenly the whole corridor ahead of them was bathed in brightness. The plume dove down, into the shadows beneath their feet. Whatever it was, it didn't like light.

Maya hefted her makeshift weapon.

The heavy door shut behind them, and Maya could only hope there was a way to open it again.

They were in the mezzanine level of a room that was unexpectedly cozy. It took a moment for Maya to understand why that was weird. It was furnished for human comfort—in a place built by a civilization that had never met humans. The walls were lined with books and artifacts, and there were stuffed armchairs and low tables. She flipped through one of the books. Each one was identical, and the pages were all empty.

"What the hell?" said Wil.

Down below, there was a bed tucked in a nook. The middle of the room was lined with long tables full of open books with pages full of writing and sketches and several large work surfaces. There were stacks of boxes around the room in neat columns, and in the center of the room below was a white cube as big as Maya's cabin on the *Wonder*.

On the top of one of the work surfaces lay two clear tanks. In the first lay the body of a masculine figure in a dark gray jumpsuit. The chest had been cut open from neck to navel, exposing organs faded with age. On the jumpsuit, the name *I. JANKOWSKI* was visible over the left breast.

In the second box lay Liam.

He was slightly too tall for the box, limbs bent awkwardly to make him fit. He was naked, his spacesuit nowhere to be seen. Constructs bent over him, scanning and prodding.

"Liam!" Maya started forward but Auncle wrapped half xyr arms around her.

"If he doesn't have his helmet on, whose voice have we been hearing?" Wil said.

Maya tensed. Because Wil was right.

"We've been spotted."

A group of constructs was coming around the mezzanine floor.

"How do we get down there?"

"There," said Wil, pointing to a platform ascending and descending like a lift. They stepped onto it, and it shuddered under their collective weight. Maya was forced to hang on to Wil and Auncle in a less than dignified manner.

More constructs waited for them on the ground. Maya gripped her pipe. "Can you move any of these boxes?"

Wil grabbed a large one and threw it at the construct. It missed. The box broke and its contents spilled across the floor. Something rolled underneath the worktable, and the pink plume descended upon it, consuming whatever it was.

"I meant make a barrier!" Maya yelped.

"Be more specific next time!"

The construct scuttled back.

An ominous bell tolled behind them, and at the far end of the chamber, three more constructs appeared.

"Okay, we're out of time," said Wil.

They rushed forward, Wil's arms transforming into blades. Maya and Auncle got on either side of Liam. His body was suspended in a clear gel, except for his face, which was tense with pain. His eyes fluttered open when Maya tapped the case. The substance appeared to have a sticky, syrupy consistency.

She couldn't see how it opened, though the machines had been poking him through it just minutes before. It seemed like it had been constructed around him. They also would need his suit if they were able to break him free. Maya scanned the room for it.

"Will you admit yet this was a bad idea?" Wil said, now facing four constructs.

Another came up behind Auncle.

"No," said Maya. "Because we found Liam. Now help me find a way to break this open."

The pink cloud settled around the Liam's case, and Maya froze. "On second thought. Maybe we should leave it sealed for now." The pink cloud lost interest and drifted over Auncle toward one of the guards—which immediately retreated into the brighter part of the light.

All this time, the constructs hadn't yet attacked. It was like they were waiting for something.

"Liam." Maya tapped the surface. "Stay with me."

"Nngh."

"Are you alive?"

"Ob . . . vious . . . ly," he said, grinding out each syllable as if it hurt.

"Glad even near-death can't suppress your patronizing attitude," said Maya, but she'd never been so happy to see his face. "What did they do to you?"

"Don't know."

The pink cloud darted beneath one of the constructs, and in moments it had consumed the thing from the bottom up, before dispersing again.

"That is an apex predator right there," said Wil.

There was an ominous clanking sound, and a new construct appeared from the door. It was boxy with six spiny legs, a cavity in the center. Inside it glistened a slab of something wet and fleshy. The pink cloud went for it. As soon as it was inside the cavity, the lid slammed shut.

"For once I'm glad the house knows how to protect itself," said Wil. "Now what?"

They heard a hiss, and the side of the cube opened.

"Well, this is new," said a voice in Mandarin.

Dr. Huang stepped out of the box.

CHAPTER FIFTY—TWO

D r. Wei Huang was a petite woman with short-cropped hair and crow's-feet lining her eyes. She couldn't have been more than sixty-five, the same age as when she came here. She wore a dark gray jumpsuit like Jankowski's, with *W. HUANG* stitched across the left breast. She'd come out of the cube dressed in a full spacesuit, but she popped her helmet off as soon as she stepped out.

She had an energy about her, like lightning on a wire. She smiled straight at Maya like they were old friends.

"English?" Dr. Huang asked. "Mandarin? Japanese? What do you prefer?"

"Japanese—er, English, I mean. Are you—are you real?"

"She can't be," said Wil. "She'd be like a hundred and sixty-fifty years old."

"Really?" said Dr. Huang.

"That is not so old," said Auncle. "Perhaps she has found a way to extend her life."

"You're all right in a way," said Dr. Huang. "I'm a copy." She lowered her voice in a mock whisper. "I think the Encyclopedium was getting lonely." She tangled an arm in Auncle's arm in greeting. "And you're a Frenro! I didn't think any of you would come here. Please excuse my excitement to see you. I've had only myself for company for so long. I mean that literally."

The crew of the *Wonder* stared at her, as if they could see the difference between the person before them and the original they had never met.

"I saw your body outside," said Maya.

"Also a copy. I've been studying a distant wing with lots of live organisms, and I assume I inhaled some of that pesky disinfectant they use. Is that what happened to your unfortunate friend here? Oh dear. The gel he's in will keep him stable for now, but I can't offer him the medical care he needs. The Encyclopedium tried for years with Jankowski—still hasn't given up hope, even though he's dead, as you can see."

Dr. Huang went to the table with the pages and picked up a pen. "You'll excuse my note-taking. I've always liked to keep journals, and I don't trust what the copying process does to my memory. Who are you?"

They introduced themselves, and Dr. Huang wrote it all down. She was very interested to hear about the state of the IW, the latest technology, and whether Earth had managed to clean the oceans or heal the ozone layer yet (answer: not quite, to Huang's disappointment).

"So you're a clone?" Maya asked.

"Not exactly," said Dr. Huang. "Consider it more like a duplication of nearly every molecule in your body, down to the neurons that store your memories."

"How many times have you been copied?" Wil asked.

"Forty-three times, I think," she said. "I tried to escape many times in the early years, but the Mind wouldn't let me leave. Ironic, isn't it—we resolved to never let people find this place again to ensure its preservation, and now I am the one who is preserved forever."

"What do you mean, the Mind?"

Dr. Huang swept an arm across the room. "It's everywhere, but it only speaks when it feels like it. You heard it in your helmet, didn't you? Indistinct maybe at first, as it sought to tune to your frequency and understand your language, but eventually it came through, right? And led you here."

"I heard your voice," said Maya. "And your crew."

"That's upsetting," said Dr. Huang. "I'm sorry about that. My fault for playing back the recordings too many times when I get lonely. It must have mimicked it. What do you have to say for yourself, Mind?"

"I'm here," said a voice that sounded eerily like Maya's.

"How'd you do that?" asked Wil, as if this were ventriloquism.

"That's not me," Maya said.

"It's not," said Dr. Huang. "Tell me, did any of you go into the white sphere?"

"No."

"Good. Whatever you do, don't. Not that I wouldn't mind the company. That's where it copies things."

"You said you would not come back," said the voice that sounded like a stitched-together blend of all their voices, as if while they had wandered around, chattering to each other, it had been listening and studying them.

"I assure you, this is not me," said Dr. Huang. "Hoshimoto-san is clearly much smarter and younger." She winked at Maya, and Maya flushed. She couldn't believe she was talking to the famous explorer.

"Who are you, then?" the Mind said.

"We come in peace," Maya said, though it wasn't strictly true.

"We would like to be friends, yes. If we can help one another," said Auncle.

"I am not interested in that," said the Mind.

"Where are you? *What* are you?" Wil took a step toward the constructs, and they bristled, though they maintained their distance. Apparently they had learned to respect her weaponry.

"The Mind is the artificial soul of the Encyclopedium," Dr. Huang said. "My captor and my teacher."

"Explain why you have come here," the Mind said.

"We came for this little one. Please let him go," said Auncle, arms wrapping around the top of Liam's box. "He is the most fragile."

There was silence and then the vault said: "No. I have things to learn from him. Unless you will return to me what you stole."

Maya looked at Auncle, trying to read xyr posture.

"How about no," said Wil.

"What did you steal?" Dr. Huang wanted to know.

"Something that belonged to my people," said Auncle, "so that we may have children again."

Wil threw her blades up in exasperation.

"Ah!" said Dr. Huang. "The stardust machine."

"I know what you are," said the Mind, "and I cannot let you take it."

"Why?" Maya burst out. "So you can keep the grail in this dusty old museum? There's not even anyone left to look at it. What's the point?"

"To keep it safe," said the Mind, as if it were obvious. "That is the purpose of this place."

"For *whom*?" Maya asked. "The people who built this place are gone. There's no one left except you and these constructs. And Dr. Huang. No offense, doctor."

"None taken," said the older woman. "I am too old to get offended by anything anymore, certainly not by true statements."

The Mind didn't reply.

Wil muttered: "Not helpful."

Maya ignored Wil and went on: "We have only come to take back what does not belong to you. We touched nothing of yours. Let us go."

"You give direction boldly for one so small," said the voice, which sounded like Auncle, then Liam.

"That's what I say," said Wil.

"You cannot have the original object," said the Mind. "Removal is against the law, and the object is particularly special. I can offer you a copy. Take as many as you'd like."

The cube flickered and then a door opened. Dr. Huang removed six grails and set them on the table. They looked tantalizingly real, but now that Maya had held the original, she could *feel* the difference. "That is what we took when we left. We were going to give a copy to the Belzoar, a copy to the Frenro, and a copy to Earth."

"You must have forgotten Earth," said Wil.

"Probably because they didn't let her land," Maya said.

"I never got to go home?" Dr. Huang sagged momentarily.

"This confirms why they didn't work," said Maya, and she explained to Dr. Huang where they'd found it, and everything that had happened since, including the destruction of the moon and departure of the Frenro. "The Mind must have altered the copies."

"That is . . . very discouraging," said Dr. Huang. "Is it true, Mind?"

"We cannot have people making holes in the fabric of space-time. You may end up making roads where there should not be. It was our intention when we closed the door to prevent further contact with the people you call Frenro. They exterminated the people of this world."

"What do you mean?" said Maya. "You destroyed the Frenro home-world and killed *them*. You infected them with the virus that has devastated so many people."

"That is not a true history."

Dr. Huang got up from her seat and came to inspect Liam through the case.

Liam wheezed something. Maya had to bend to hear: "What is true?"

The Mind heard him. "We met here at the intersection of our networks. We coexisted and exchanged ideas. But there was always the fundamental agreement that we would remain on our own sides, and we would not alter each other's worlds. *They* violated their side of the agreement. The longer we coexisted, the more they consumed us into their web, infected our minds. It is what they do. Assimilate everything and everyone. Have you not experienced the same?"

Maya's hands tingled with perspiration. It couldn't be true. She didn't want it to be true. It didn't *need* to be. Who knew what had happened so many years ago? But then, history was tricky like that. You would never quite know, no matter which record you read. The Frenro certainly didn't anymore.

"It is how we are. The Whole. This was our first encounter. We didn't know until it was too late. We take precautions now," said Auncle, shrinking. "We—I—am sorry."

Blood thudded in Maya's ears, and she thought again of Lithis.

The Mind continued speaking, as if it were inside Maya's thoughts. "This world was meant to be a bridge between our peoples. Instead, it became a battlefield. We resisted the Whole. We fought back, and they unleashed a sickness intended to increase their ability to invade our minds. They killed tens of millions of people on this world alone."

"You mean the whole virus was intentional?" said Wil. "They infected themselves?"

"No!" said Auncle.

"Yes," said the Mind.

"Unfortunately, I think it's true," said Dr. Huang, returning to her writing.

There was no way to know for sure. But Maya realized deep down she believed it. The Frenro had never been defenseless. *This* was their weapon, and it had allowed them to conquer a galaxy. She thought about her ability to speak to the *Wonder*, the terrible visions she had, the feeling of the Whole licking the edges of her mind. She shuddered.

"We defended ourselves. There was a war."

The Dead Sea, Maya thought. Worlds and worlds obliterated of life. She couldn't begin to imagine. Two races of people technologically advanced beyond human comprehension.

"We destroyed their means of creating new nodes, so they could never find us again."

But they must have missed some, Maya thought, because the Frenro had been able to continue to reproduce for several centuries after, at least until the Lithians finished the job.

"We kept this last sample, for preservation. Then we shut the door. No one has ever crossed the threshold again."

"I am so sorry," said Auncle. "I didn't know. We must have forgotten this. We have tried to limit our harm since then." Xe was smaller than Maya had ever seen xyr, contracted as much as xyr protective coating would allow.

"What has happened cannot be undone," said Maya. "The Frenro may not be able to make amends—they are dying out."

"Perhaps if we tried, we could eliminate the virus," said Auncle.

"If you remove the object from this world," said the Mind, "I will alert my people."

"He gave us the same choice," said Dr. Huang. "We decided at the time some doors were better left closed, that we weren't ready for contact with them or for all the technology in here. We've learned the hard way what a vast power can do to people unprepared. This place was testament to that. That's why the Frenro decided never to come here—that's why I was surprised to see you here at all." This last she said to Auncle.

"I am not part of the Whole anymore," said Auncle. "I can decide for myself."

"The grail isn't yours," Maya said to the Mind. "The Frenro will go extinct without it. You don't have a right to keep it from them. Anyway, the door has been shut for thousands of years. How do you even know there's still anyone beyond it? And even if they did get your message, who's to say *they* want to reopen the door, or that their goals are the same as they were several thousand years ago? People can change a lot in that amount of time. That long ago, ours were still making clay pots and sticking each other with pointy things."

"All good points," said Dr. Huang, jotting her notes. "I've had many years to wonder."

"There is a thirty-three percent probability my people still exist beyond the door," said the Mind. "If they do, we will see what they decide."

"You won't convince the Mind," said Dr. Huang. "Its function is to provide information and to protect and preserve the objects in this museum. Including, unfortunately, me. And now you."

"Yeah, nope. Thank you," said Wil.

Auncle stretched out xyr arms toward the walls, the ceiling, until xe had expanded to twice xyr size. "I would like to know how my people can have children. It is something we have forgotten."

Maya held her breath. It seemed impossible that Auncle might have any effect on this ancient enemy mind. But she could also feel the strength of Auncle's emotions. Frenro empathy was like a drug. She could feel her muscles relaxing despite herself, but there was no telling what xyr effect on this artificial intelligence might be.

A beat of silence. "The object is a symbiote. It is necessary for the transformation of your people to your final life stage. It can also be planted in brackish water inhabited by Frenro, where it will propagate and multiply. If you implant it inside your central cavity, it will release chemicals that trigger the reproductive changes in a Frenro. Eggs are produced, and then the Frenro undergoes transformation to final form."

"What do you mean transformation? What is the final form?" Auncle asked.

"What you call a node," said the Mind, as if it were obvious.

Maya sucked in a breath. "Every node is a Frenro?"

"Yes," said the Mind.

"I—" said Auncle. "That sounds right."

And Maya, selfishly, could only think what that meant—that if they were successful, she would lose Auncle. Because to have the children xe longed for, xe would need to transform into something unreachable. She was happy that xe finally had xyr answer. And yet.

Wil, all this time, had been searching for Liam's suit. It was stowed in yet another box near his tank. She slammed the box against the floor until it shattered. Half-heartedly, the constructs moved to stop her but halted again when she nearly decapitated a daring one that darted forward. She removed Liam's suit.

"Come on," said Wil. "We're getting out of here." She tossed Auncle the suit and helmet before transforming her hands back into blades and shaking them.

"You cannot take this one," said the Mind. "I am not done." If Maya were anthropomorphizing, she'd have said the voice sounded sulky.

"We can, and we will. Are you coming?" Wil asked Dr. Huang.

"I might have once. But now I think I could spend a thousand years here and never learn everything." She gestured at the piles of books she was filling with her tiny handwriting. Then she said in Japanese, which the Mind must never have learned. "I will, however, help you escape."

CHAPTER FIFTY—THREE

F ortunately," said Dr. Huang, "this is a museum and not a fortress. And I've been here long enough to learn a few things." She went to the cube, carrying her book. She put her hands against the side and warbled a series of musical tones.

There was a grinding sound, and the door opened. Another copy of Dr. Huang emerged. "Well," she said, stepping out of the cube. "This is new."

Huang handed her the open book and continued to sing, while the new Huang read the notes the first Dr. Huang had just written.

Another Dr. Huang appeared. And another. And another.

The lights flickered from the enormous power she must have been pulling to run the machine.

More constructs began to climb from the walls, as the Mind figured out what was happening. They converged on the copies, decapitating, eviscerating, until the floor was slick with blood. And still Dr. Huangs continued to climb from the cube. One of them smashed the case that held Jankowski, freeing the corpse at last.

"Don't just stand there," Wil said. She brought down a blade through the end of the case, and Auncle moved in one fluid motion, engulfing Liam in a moment. It was remarkable how quickly xe could clothe a human. Perhaps the benefit of so many years living with one.

"Can you handle a weapon?" Wil asked Maya.

"What?"

"It's not a research question." Before Maya could say anything, she had removed her hand and was holding it out to Maya, in the form of a gun. "Don't drop it."

Maya clutched it, trying to suppress her disgust. *They may have flesh but they're not alive*, she told herself. Anyway, she'd already done worse fighting for the Frenro.

The room was crowded with bodies and constructs. Wil led the way, pulverizing with one hand as she went, her arm a massive air canon. She had Liam slung over the other shoulder. Auncle swung the mallet xe'd brought from the hangar. Maya took up the rear, firing wildly, and doing her best to avoid damaging anything. A whole stack of boxes toppled down, and she winced. But she didn't stop running. She wanted to live.

They exited out a different door, Wil blowing it open with something that made Maya's ears ring. Several Dr. Huangs came with them, leading the way out.

"Be careful!" Maya shouted.

"You really test me, Hoshimoto!"

Maya looked back once and saw Dr. Huang copied a hundred ways, dying, being born, fighting. One of them caught Maya's gaze and smiled. The floor was scarlet and slippery.

"Come *on*," Wil shouted at her. "Please don't tell me I have to carry you *and* this one up the stairs."

"I may not be an athlete," said Maya. "But I'm an excellent thief. I think I can manage an escape."

Several times, they came to invisible barriers, but Dr. Huang was able to disable them.

They barreled through the hallways past all the things they would never know.

A massive, shrill screech filled Maya's comm—the Mind's final protest—but Maya muted the sound, and then they were just running through a muffled world.

Beyond the clear walls they could see dawn was breaking. They had been inside longer than Maya had figured. The pink predatory dust lingered in the air, but it didn't descend. Here and there, new purple growth budded under the rising sun.

Maya scooped up her backpack from where she'd left it on the floor of the hangar. "I'm sorry for the damage we've done here," she said. "I hope we're making the right choice."

"I'm never sure," said one of the Dr. Huangs.

"You can't live in the universe without leaving footprints," Maya said.

"Right," said Dr. Huang, smiling wryly.

As they moved to the door, Dr. Huang called her back. She handed Maya a crystalline object from one of the worktables.

"I can't take this," Maya said.

"In this one case," said Dr. Huang, "I think it is right—it'll even things out a bit. You may need it."

Maya hesitated, then slipped it into her pack.

"Hurry up!" said Wil.

They crossed through the open door and didn't slow until they reached the forest intersection. Nothing had followed them. The world was full of crystal tones, like water falling on glass, as if nothing bad had ever happened and everything was waking up. It was beautiful.

"How is Liam?" Maya asked.

"I am afraid he needs more than we can provide on the *Wonder*," said Auncle. Maya could only see the bloodless curve of his cheek through his faceplate.

"In that case," said Wil from the front, "it's a good thing my ride is here."

CHAPTER FIFTY-FOUR

They made it back to the shuttle without being attacked or devoured. They were practically sleepwalking, their stimulants having run out long before.

"What horrible things we did," said Auncle, as their shuttle lifted off the ground. Maya wasn't sure if xe meant the last few weeks or all of Frenro history. The dusty plain shrank beneath them. In the distance, Maya saw the barest glint of water.

"I know. But we can only change what we do moving forward." She slumped down in a bucket seat next to Auncle. "I've been wondering what we have in common—humans, Frenro, and everyone else. The thing is, I think it's that question itself. We're all looking for the answer to it. Yes, we want to survive, but we also want to be understood, respected, valued by other people. It's a social thing, I guess. You don't get to space-faring without that.

"Maybe it isn't possible to get along. We make war, even when we want peace. We fail, and we keep trying anyway.

"What I've seen is, life seeks other life. Humanity spent so many years looking skyward, hoping we weren't alone, and look what we were willing to do to keep the door open. It doesn't matter that I don't know what you're thinking, or even, frankly, *how* you're thinking when you don't have a brain. You're my best friend, and even when you get on my nerves, there is no one I'd risk more for."

"I feel the same, Mayyyaa. You are my Whole." Auncle wrapped an arm around her arm.

Wil opened her bag and removed the grail. She considered it a moment, and then she offered it to Auncle. "If what that thing said was true—I guess this has no value for us. The CNE's going to hate it, but they're just going to have to trust you're better with it than without it. If you can ever find where the Frenro ended up."

"I will find them," said Auncle. "They are beyond the Dead Sea. It will be a very long way, and require much preparation, but they are still out there."

Maya knew what this meant. This was the ending, as Auncle had promised. Their last job.

It was always going to be this way once they found the grail. Wasn't this what she wanted? She was looking forward to going back, eating blood orange ice cream from that place in Palmer Square. So why wasn't she happy?

Auncle squeezed Maya's hand, and Maya tried to project joy. It was too hard.

"My sweet child," Auncle said, and there was something different about the way xe said it, the way each word fell heavy in the air. "Life is long, and the way is ever changing. You will always be welcome to fly with me again when you desire."

"I thought you were going to, you know." She gestured at the grail.

"Someday," said Auncle, "does not have to be tomorrow. I would like to see first if one can be made into many. The Mind said it might be possible. Anyway, you know Frenro live much longer than humans."

Maya's spirits lifted. She looked down at Liam, unconscious at her feet. She felt suspended on a wire between two points, but then that was how she lived, wasn't it? "I'm sure my advisers will want me to do additional fieldwork after generals. And we do still owe Wil money."

"You certainly do," said Wil. "And something tells me you're going to need my help to get it." Wil shook her head as if she couldn't begin to make sense of everything that had happened.

"You're not going back to Earth?"

Wil hesitated. "I hope so, eventually." She took out Medix's memory box. "He wanted to travel. Maybe we could do that first."

"As long as you don't ditch us again, you could come with us," said Maya.

"I believe I proved to be very useful," said Wil.

Maya dug out of her side satchel the thing Huang had given her from the vault. Despite the number of things she had stolen in her life, it was the first time she had ever done something she considered theft.

"What's that?" Wil asked.

It was a prism the size of a human skull. It flickered under Maya's hands.

"Mayyyyaaa," said Auncle, who understood. "It is their door maker."

"Huang wanted us to have it. We saw it in that history room. I think she thought maybe we can learn to build our own nodes."

Wil shook her head. "You continue to surprise me, Hoshimoto."

"I don't know if it was right to take this. We are going to mess things up, we always do. But all the same, I was born to parents of different worlds in sunlight that won't even reach the Earth for thousands of years. I guess what I mean is, I believe in roads. But it can't just be for the CNE," said Maya. "It's got to be for everyone."

They broke through clouds, and the land beneath them disappeared entirely. The sky thinned and turned to the clean surface of a quiet world. They were approaching the *Wonder*.

Their ship was already tethered to a CNE battleship.

"We need immediate medical transport," said Wil.

"This is O *Canada*. Nice to see you alive again, *Wonder*. Crew are at the ready."

Maya thought of telling Commander Browning to feel free to fly herself into the local sun, but decided that was probably not to her benefit right now.

Dr. Garcia's voice added: "Find anything interesting down there?"

"I suppose you could say that. But what do I know? I'm just a graduate student."

"I thought we already agreed you were never just that. I can't wait to hear all about it. You know, if you wanted to transfer . . ."

"Hell no," croaked Liam, opening his eyes. "We have serious projects ahead of us. With proper permits and funding, of course."

"Have you been conscious the whole time?" Maya demanded.

He coughed. "No, thank god. You know I don't like flying."

Wil poked Liam in the arm. "You better not have faked it just so I'd carry you all the way back to the ship."

"Take it easy. I almost died."

As they docked with their ship, Auncle tapped the window with an arm. "Look." There, on the planet-facing surface of the largest moon, was the bronze ring they'd seen before. It was rimmed with lights that had not been on the first time they'd come. The inside of the circle was a concave surface that glittered with stars that were somewhere else.

A new interstellar door was open.

Auncle touched the window. "It is a beginning."

ACKNOWLEDGMENTS

This was my first book written under deadline, and I could not have done it without many people holding my hand along the way.

First thanks always go to my agent, Mary Moore, and my editor, Maxine Charles. You get me and root for me and make my books better, and you manage my anxiety on top of all of that: thank you!

Thanks also to the early readers who gave me critical feedback: my twin sister, Hana, and Tessa Yang, who even reread bits; Kylie Lee Baker (who also shared her insight into archives and how they run), Sarah Starr Murphy, Valerie O'Riordan, Alison Fisher, Daniel Bauer, and Rosa Lumagbas; and my older sister Saya, who gave up sleep to plow through the final version in a feverish several days while on deadline for work just because I asked (oops, sorry!). Also Paul Ochoa, who read early chapters and gave me the rah-rah I needed early on.

I'm constantly trying to anticipate and shape how my words might be perceived—I believe that's an essential part of becoming a better writer if your goal is to be read and understood. I make mistakes and say things that don't always land as intended, and I'm keenly aware this novel may still include issues I've missed. But I'm forever grateful to the people who do professional sensitivity reads, and to Emma Mieko Candon, who did so for this one. Emma's thoughtful insights made this a richer book; any fault you find is mine.

I took liberties with the archives and the graduate student experience, but I did endeavor to make them at least a hair based in reality. Thank you to Davina Kuh, Jerry Zee, Emily Hammer, and Sarah MacIntosh for answering all my questions.

I've suffered from migraines since I was young, but many migraines are different (see *Migraine* by Oliver Sacks), and I appreciated Chelsea Davis, James Archer, Ariel Jensine, Sonam Velani, Fiona Cook, and Alice Easton for sharing their experiences.

Thank you to Addison Duffy and Jasmine Lake, my TV/film agents at UTA. If you make movies and want to make this into one, please call them!

I am so appreciative to the Flatiron team for everything you've done and continue to do for me as one of your first (!) science fiction authors: Jonathan Bush, who has now designed two stunning covers for me, and is therefore probably responsible for selling ten times more copies than I am; Maris Tasaka, Cat Kenney, and Bria Strothers, my marketing and publicity team; Emily Walters and Morgan Mitchell; Bob Miller, Megan Lynch, and Zack Wagman; and Keith Hayes and Kelly Gatesman in the art department. Thank you to Jonathan Bennett for the interior design and the map, and to Nicole Hall for copy edits.

Thank you to Carl Weisbrod, Danny Fuchs, and Bret Collazzi, none of whom as I am aware read science fiction, but who were so supportive while I worked on the first half of this; thanks to Sheena Wright and colleagues—especially Meagan Chen—for all the cheerleading!

I'm an extroverted writer, so this book would not have been finished without the company of my friend Julie Shapiro, my roommate Killeen, and new writer friends from the 2023 Debut Slack group—much love and can't wait to write the next ones with you!

Lastly, thank you to each and every friend, family, bookseller, librarian, reviewer, reader, and stranger who bought, borrowed, read, or reviewed my first book, *The Deep Sky*—and to *you*, for taking a chance on this next one. Your support and kind notes keep me going. Thank you.

FRENRO—The original architects of the Interstellar Web. They are primarily aquatic and invertebrate, with an ability to glimpse both past and future. They are vaguely potato shaped, with ten thick arms at their base, which they use for propelling through water or perambulating over ground, and hundreds of finer filaments and tentacles on top, which they use for sensory perception. They lack a central "brain," instead storing their memories and knowledge throughout their bodies. A Frenro can live for hundreds if not thousands of years, and they continue to grow throughout their life. They are nearly extinct, having lost a key part of their ecosystem that allows them to reproduce, and are these days rarely encountered in the Human Nodal Region.

QUIETLING—These communal people are roughly the size of a golf ball. Each belongs to a larger colony that moves as one and operates with a "hive" mind, with different members performing different roles— sensory, movement, etc. Colonies range from thousands to hundreds of thousands, and the oldest are millennia old. This quality enabled the Quietling to travel to and settle other systems outside the Interstellar Web. They lack auditory senses, hence their name. They are technologically very advanced and, unlike other people, share their knowledge relatively freely. Because of this, they're sometimes stereotyped as the "gossips" of the interstellar community.

FARSTARS—The Farstars occupy several worlds in the Quietling region. While they've been in the interstellar community longer than the Belzoar, they're less advanced than most; their First Contact occurred before they had developed language or agriculture. They live farthest from the Human Nodal Region. Because of this, they're rarely seen close to Earth. Their skin is covered in needles several centimeters long.

They are approximately a meter in height and their vocalization tends to be louder than most peoples'.

BELZOAR—The Belzoar are the most prolific advanced people, with diverse cultures across nearly a hundred worlds and stations. The average life span of a Belzoar is only thirty years. They live in family "clans" that can occupy one or more worlds. One of the most militaristic Belzaor clans, the Lithians, are responsible for the deaths of millions of Frenro. Most of their clans are governed by instant referendum and an AI Governance System. They have eight appendages and colorful, hard carapace backs. At the center of their body is a large organ that vibrates constantly in an orchestra of tones far more complex than any human musical instrument. It can make walking with one a little distracting. Despite physical differences, they are culturally the most similar to humans, including their taste in art and music.

OORANI—Once an advanced space-faring people, the Oorani experienced First Contact several hundred years after broad societal collapse. They've recovered somewhat since then but are infrequent travelers, as they used up much of the resources of their planets. Their bodies naturally form gems on their skin during hibernation, which they augment with other precious stones. Invasive species and exploitation by their neighbors have contributed to a decline in the Oorani population.

HUMANS—The most recent addition to the interstellar community. Humans are bipedal and soft fleshed. They are less communal than most of the other advanced peoples. At the time of First Contact, they were at the beginning of establishing settlements on other bodies in their system. Humans are considered one of the more adaptable species and have rapidly expanded to other systems, though some of their Belzoar neighbors believe they are societally too immature for interstellar travel.

Yume Kitasei is the author of *The Deep Sky*. She is Japanese and American and grew up in the space between two cultures—the same space where her stories reside. She lives in Brooklyn with two cats, Boondoggle and Filibuster. Her stories have appeared in publications including *New England Review*, *Catapult*, *SmokeLong Quarterly*, and *Baltimore Review*. *The Stardust Grail* is her second novel.